Simon Louvish's 'archeology' includes a father born in Kimpulung-Bukovina, a mother in Stepney Green. He himself emerged in Glasgow, attended school in Jerusalem, where he was threatened with expulsion for his satirical forays. He and the Jerusalem school system both survived. Louvish served as a military cameraman during the Six Day War. In 1969, under cover of a Cambridge student theatre group presenting *Marat/Sade*, Louvish and a group of black and white South African exiles covertly made the documentary film *End of the Dialogue*. He has since made three other unconventional documentaries. He has been accused of being an agent of Red China, the Kremlin, the CIA, the PLO, and the Zionist Conspiracy, and is, in truth, none of the above. He is married, teaches at the London International Film School, writes, laughs, and writes.

*Critical comment on THE THERAPY OF AVRAM BLOK:*

'His humour is often incandescent and poetic . . . often witty, the book is not about reality but about the hallucinations reality sometimes provokes'
*Publishers Weekly*

'A timeless hotch-potch of memory, fantasy, history, graffiti and parody and black Israeli humour . . . THE THERAPY OF AVRAM BLOK deserves a wide readership – if only for bringing Israeli street humour to England – but read it at your peril'
*Jewish Chronicle*

*Author photograph by Jerry Bauer*

'Cheaply derisive . . . he has set up a gallery of Aunt Sallys that are to be remorselessly and indiscriminately knocked down. No sacred Israeli cow must be ignored . . . indiscriminate, numbing use of scatalogical language'
*The Jerusalem Post*

'Painfully post-modern . . . I haven't seen the word "zap" so many times since I was in short trousers'
*City Limits*

'A kind of fictional equivalent of *Monty Python's Flying Circus*'
*Yorkshire Post*

'Merging fact with fantasy – and the plain fantastic! – Avram Blok's story is in turn funny and sad, but always provocative'
*Review Magazine*

'A well-aimed, funny slap of a novel'
*Time Out*

'Mr Louvish has created his novel with the zest and generosity of a grandmother making stuffed cabbage, and he's also done it with the glint and intensity of a physicist bent on finding a new, fun way to split the atom. Into it he's thrown high and low (mostly low) humour, bouts of fornication and masturbation (mostly masturbation) and coprophilia, a subplot having to do with the exorcism of a wild bear (Satan? Judas Iscariot?) from subterranean Jerusalem and, overriding all, a politically angry peroration of a sort of the Jerusalem Chamber of Commerce won't be excerpting for tourism brochures'
*The New York Times Book Review*

# The Therapy of Avram Blok

*A Phantasm of Israel Among the Nations*

## Simon Louvish

**BLACK SWAN**

to Mairi, of course

## THE THERAPY OF AVRAM BLOK

A BLACK SWAN BOOK  0 552 99236 4

Originally published in Great Britain by
William Heinemann Ltd.

PRINTING HISTORY
William Heinemann edition published 1985
Black Swan edition published 1986

The author and publishers thank Citadel Press, New York,
for their permission to quote from *The Poetry of Heinrich
Heine*, translated by Aaron Kramer, 1969, and Warner
Bros Music Ltd for their kind permission to print lines
from *Gates of Eden* and *Maggie's Farm* by Bob Dylan,
© 1965 M. Witmark & Sons, British publisher Warner
Bros. Music Ltd.

This book is set in 12/13 pt Mallard

Black Swan Books are published by
Transworld Publishers Ltd., 61–63
Uxbridge Road, Ealing, London W5 5SA, in
Australia by Transworld Publishers (Aust.)
Pty. Ltd., 26 Harley Crescent, Condell Park,
NSW 2200, and in New Zealand by
Transworld Publishers (N.Z.) Ltd., Cnr.
Moselle and Waipareira Avenues,
Henderson, Auckland.

Made and printed in Great Britain by the
Guernsey Press Co. Ltd., Guernsey, Channel Islands.

"How often we talk to one another
and only hear hollow ringing."

– Chinese fortune cookie,
   Hunam Taste, Broadway & 81st, New York

"On mount Wu-t'ai the clouds are steaming rice;
Before the ancient Buddha hall, dogs piss at heaven."
                                        – from the Zenrin

"If you are honest, you will go to jail."
                          – Polish exile in London after
                            five pints of bitter

"At that time I was still living in the barracks of the
Second Infantry Regiment in a little room that still very
distinctly bore the traces of the revolution. During the
day I was out, mostly with the Forty-First Rifle Regiment, or at meetings, or lectures in some other army
unit, etc. Only at night did I sleep in my quarters. Since I
regularly woke up before five o'clock in the morning, I
had got in the habit of putting a few left-overs or crusts
of bread on the floor for the mice which amused themselves in my little room, and watching the droll little
beasts chasing around after these choice morsels. I had
known so much poverty in my life that I was well able to
imagine the hunger, and hence also the pleasure, of the
little creatures."
                          – Adolf Hitler, *Mein Kampf*

"MENE MENE TEKEL UPHARSIN!"
                          – Anonymous graffito on the
                            walls of Babylon

I

'The road to hell is paved with good intentions.'
                                                    – Mother

When They arrested Avram Blok for peeping, on
27th November 1967, the Judge of the Jerusalem
District Court, Justice Henrietta Ben-Horin, sent
him to the Moses Klander Institute for twenty-eight
days of psychiatric observation. Seven years later,
to the day, Blok submitted himself voluntarily for
treatment at Klander, presenting a unique com-
plaint: he claimed to be living in an alternative historical epoch, in which Germany had been a wholly
Communist state since 1923, Leon Trotsky had
ruled Soviet Russia for forty-four years, and Adolf
Hitler and colleagues had escaped to the United
States, where Adolf eventually became a Senator
for the State of Illinois and his son later ran for
President on a third party ticket. In this fallacy the
Second World War and the Holocaust had not taken
place, Jews were living in their millions throughout
Eastern Europe, and Palestine remained under
shaky British control until 1973.
    The creation of the State of Israel amid the Civil
War of that year brought Blok partly back into line
with Jerusalem reality, which is not, at the best of

times, concomitant with the rest of the world. However, intercourse (purely verbal, at this stage) with his few remaining friends, showed him, so he said, that no one else seemed to share his hermetically deduced conviction. Doctor Flusser, re-checking Blok's file, and after a futile attempt to persuade him to abandon his childish pretence of insanity, finally allowed him in for the usual one month's observation. Blok, delighted, immediately sought out Nietzsche, Klander's Eminent Inhabitant, and before the afternoon was out they were both engaged in a marathon game of parchesi. Flusser sighed, gathering his notes on 'Neuroses of Our Time: The Immorality of Inhibition'. In the corridors of the asylum, the Forlorn gave voice, and, beneath their feet, the ground was deaf to the cries of those trapped in hidden depths. Outside, Jerusalem's brief evening scarletly faded, the call of the muezzin choked off by a power-cut caused by a terrorist sabotage.

In 1967, when Justice Ben-Horin committed Blok to the nuthouse for observation, she said (*falsetto*):

'The privacy of the individual is a hallowed right, not to be tampered with or profaned. People have the right to expect that Society and the Law should protect them against those for whom their private activities and conduct are an object of prurient and lewd curiosity. The fact that the subjects of the defendant's unwelcome attention are a devout, religiously observant couple, gives all the more cause for anxiety. The charge of indecent conduct is a serious one in a world unhappily beset by moral laxatives (*sic*), disrespect for the rights of others and incipient vice and depravity. The weakening of parental authority must especially be noted in this regard. However, in reviewing the case before us we must take into consideration that the defendant is a young man who has just completed three years of national service in the Israel Defence Forces, including service in the glorious Six Days' War which saved us all from Armageddon. His demobilization card, which we have before us, shows that his commanding officers regard him as a soldier who fulfilled his duties to the best of his abilities. Our national gratitude for the sacrifices and conduct of our soldiers in this great Victory dictates to us caution in saddling this young man with a criminal conviction which would weigh heavily upon him in his path through society. Blah, blah, blah. I am therefore committing you, Avram Blok, for twenty-eight days' observation at the Moses Klander Institute for Psychiatric Care, following which a report will be tendered by the probation officer attached to this court. I would like to make clear to you, Blok, that this leniency in no way signifies the court's indifference to your behaviour, which we hold in the utmost abhorrence, and that any subsequent offence may well meet with the full severity of the Law, including actual imprisonment. 'Next case!'

Blok's defence, which neither the police nor Justice Ben-Horin believed, was that, in gazing through the window of Cordovero Street, Number – ,ground floor, he was not engaged in any voyeuristic, unlawful or prurient act whatsoever, so help me, but was solely and merely attempting to find out, ascertain and make sure that the ex-flame of his heart, Malka Halperin (her neck as the Tower of David, her breasts like two roes, which feed among the lilies . . .) was no longer domiciled there. Perceiving the name Friedman upon the jamb, he was about to retreat when the light in the open window made

13

him step up just to see if the flat had indeed changed hands, a fact which would be indisputably proven by the presence of different furniture, curtains, wall-hangings, bric-à-brac such as lamp-fittings, flowerpots, paperweights, fruitbowls, etc., but, when he did arrive at the window he was riveted by sheer astonishment at the sight of Mr and Mrs Friedman, whom he did not know from Adam, was not in the least acquainted with and had no interest in, prurient or otherwise, making love, so he claimed incessantly, through a hole in the sheet. 'It had been a living room, not a bedroom, before ...' Blok explained, and continued, 'I'd heard that the devout carry on in this way but had assumed these were old wives' tales ... I mean, why should I ... it's obvious ...' He meant, it was not quite a sight for sore eyes: Mr Friedman, his sweaty black beard and the Mrs, with a face like a bunch of garlic cloves, patchy hair and a glass eye. Though they went at it hammer and tongs ... still, it was not a vision conducive to erotic emotion by any stretch of the imagination ... Another second and he would have run, Blok swore blind, putting as great a distance as possible between himself and this dire apparition but, before he could so much as turn, the heavy hand of Patrolman Abutbul, uniformed minion of the Law of Jerusalem City, descended on his shoulder, like the paw of a bear, his guttural voice booming:

'Caught, you vile stinking degenerate! Peeping, hah? We'll soon put a stop to that! Come with me, you pervert, I'll soon have your nuts for breakfast!'

Blok's mother said:

'I knew this would happen. The boy's troubled, he's sunk into himself. He can't make up his mind what to do with his life. And is this surprising? What guidance does he get from his father? Answer me that, Baruch! A fine example you are to a young man, your only son, who must find his way through the trials and temptations of this rotten world. Just look at you! When the boy needs a firm hand where are you? Locked up in your study with your infantile stamp collection. A grown man playing with little coloured bits of paper! You ought to be ashamed of yourself. You're more wrapped up with your crazy pen pals scattered to the four winds of the earth than you are in your own flesh and blood. Africa he writes to, getting messages from deep in the jungle! Tasmania, where blackamoors walk about without even a loincloth to cover their nakedness. Oh, the shame of it! A father who abandons his son to a world that has no elementary decency, no sense of a human being's worth! A people like all the goyim, that's what we've truly become! When there's no moral guidance from the father, what can you expect from the son? How do you expect him to know right from wrong? I've always known this is what lies at the end of a secular culture. Run away from God and what do you get? Everything twisted, people running about like chickens with their heads cut off. All sorts of perversions become normal and the fabric of society rots away. Two thousand years of continuity flushed down the drain, lost completely in the mad rush to be like everyone else . . .'

But Blok's father said:

'Asargelusha, Avremel, why couldn't you at least have peeked into the boudoir of some beauty queen instead of those two frum choleras? This is what really beats me. Why tangle with religious fanatics when we have one home-grown right here?

'Calm down, Shushu, it's not as if the lad has done any harm to anybody. It's just like you to take the word of some dumb police ox against your own son, just because it fits into your own gloomy

Weltanschauung. There's nothing wrong with Avremel, and the suburb of Kiryat Moshe hasn't been struck down like Sodom and Gomorrah, goddamit! What really worries you is what the neighbours will think! What will Gaga the Bulgarian Bloodhound on the floor below have to say? and Mrs Saporta-Yecchs, and the Rebetsen Twilliger-Syphilis-Face and all the other lunatics, perverts and religious maniacs who make this block the Number-One fruit-machine crazy house of the entire Holy City, May She Be Rebuilt in Our Time, amen, et cetera . . . Well, I'll tell you what they can do: they can all come crawling upstairs, right into my backside, which is their Real and Destined Homeland. So help me. Now quit bawling and let me be. I am going to classify the Ruanda-Urundi Anniversary tête-à-bêches if I have to do it with my last dying breath, and even if it takes me all night.'

Doctor Flusser, Director of the Klander institute, would, in principle, have preferred not to be saddled with 'patients' committed for observation by the courts. It imposed an intolerable burden on the voluntary doctor–patient relationship which he considered crucial. The 'patient' often knew a diagnosis of 'no case for treatment' could well lead to criminal sanctions. The doctor would often not know if he were wasting his time with someone who was 'putting on a show'. Denial of facilities, however, would mean all the court assignees would go to the State Hospital of T – t, where the arms of bureaucracy and electro-convulsion would grip them in a vice-like embrace. So Flusser took Avram Blok in and, after three personal interviews, found him articulate and intelligent, curious and concerned with his environment, though prone to serious bouts of depression and in many ways a disturbed young man.* But then, Flusser thought to himself, in our day and age, who isn't? (Disturbed, that is to say, not young . . .) Is it perfectly sane to be gay and happy when wars threaten to devour us, when mankind is poised on the brink of its own destruction? But Justice Ben-Horin, however, must be appeased. Flusser racked his brains and ruminated for some time about this question, a mere fragment of the great cosmic malady and scourge which threatens to destroy us all . . .


## Of the Klander Institute in History:

Moses Klander, a disciple of Freud, practised, like his illustrious mentor, in Vienna. Peter Flusser was Klander's favourite student. All three were victims of a tarnished future. For together the pupils saw off their old teacher at the Nordbanhof, 4th June 1938, when the Great Man, then aged eighty-two, left Vienna to die in England. It was a deceptively bright summer's day, the baroque façade of the station gleaming in its lost imperial splendour. The sun massaged newly familiar uniforms, mud brown and jet black. Three months earlier the National Socialists had marched in, their fifes and drums punctuating the New Order: Austrian-German Anschluss. A plebiscite held two months prior to that had proved 99.75 per cent positive. The People's

* Blok's first responses to the Rorschach Inkblot Test:
Card 1: Three camels trying to pass through the eye of a needle.
Card 2: Bats doing push ups on a mirror.
Card 3: My grandmother being attacked by asparagus from outer space. (*The tester, Psychologist Schotz, began to look a little worried.*)
Card 4: Extreme low angle of headless SS man sitting on a fireplug.
Card 5: Count Dracula with antennae.
Card 6: Two bears climbing up a giant phallus. (*Psychologist Schotz was relieved.*)
Card 7: Rabbits caught out in a nuclear explosion. (*Schotz, worried again.*)
Card 8: A Centaurian flying saucer with deformed testicles.
Card 9: Something very sexually profound and meaningful.
Card 10: A diseased psychoanalyst's doodies.

Choice! Does anyone cavil? Who dares represent these as false hopes?! To the gallows, Jews, Commies and their hybrid, the psycho-analysts . . . So many Aryan faces glowing radiant in the gloom of newsreel theatres. Yet the patriarch of escaped dreams and nightmares, with his snow-white beard and his thick bifocals, was helped aboard the Orient Express, occident-bound, young Flusser grabbing hold of his elbow as he seemed for a moment to totter on the high carriage step. His wife and his maid followed him up, waving their white lace handkerchiefs at the small group of apostles who stood tearfully on the platform as the train chugged off under a fresh awning of swastikas, black, white and blood red.

Again, an era comes to an end.

A seven-year interval, as the lights dim and fail. Holocaust, Donner und Blitzen. Peter Flusser found his way to Palestine, enrolling in the Zionist cause (the Jewish Brigade, Palmah Commando – Medical, psycho department). Klander vanished for the duration into the rotting corpse of Europe. It was rumoured that he fulfilled secret tasks, for the Zionists, the Allies, for the Red Army. The true facts, as usual, remain veiled. Suffice to say, eliding controversy, he emerged in 1945, as night and fog lifted, to rejoin his former pupil in Palestine. In '46 they received a brief from the British Mandate authorities to found in Jerusalem, the Holy City, an Institute of Advanced Psychiatry. It would be dedicated to the Progressive Approach in the treatment of mental affliction, with particular emphasis on those whom the Holocaust had plunged into their own twilight. Their motto would be 'Nil Desperandum' – the heart and the mind *can* be salved. Yes, Klander believed in phoenixes rising from the ashes of Faith . . .

Today the Institute is a complex of three buildings on a hill in the south-east of the City, overlooking the Valley of Kidron and the Jericho Road, just between Abu Tor and the Claire nuns, up away from the Hill of Evil Counsel: 25 Rabbi Nahman Me'Bratslav Street, named after the old mystic story-teller. (In fact the Institute was originally named for Reb Nahman, an institutional parapraxis perhaps, or just a ploy to schnorr some orthodox funds?) It lies on the route of the Seven Aleph bus, which leaves the corner of Strauss Street every hour. From the city centre, it meanders up the dusty Hebron Way, turning left up the brown pine-topped terraced hill to stop right by the gates of the nuthouse. Until 1940, the main building of the Institute had been the well-known Scottish Sisters' Hospital. Till 1948 it remained a central location, but then, for nineteen years, until 1967, the Institute found itself spot on the border between Arab and Jewish Jerusalem. Bare and bold, it looked out over the Kingdom of Jordan, devoid even of the buffer of the wide swathes of No-Man's-Land that divided other parts of the City – pitted with craters, bristling with barbed wire, dotted with the rusting carcasses of old armoured cars and trucks. Indeed, patients would now and again wander off, abroad, down the hill, to be handed back later at the Mandelbaum Gate, drooling and jacking off cheerfully in full sight of the United Nations.

How came this lump to be on the map, this hilltop, sticking like an engorged prick into the arse of the Hashemite Kingdom? This is the alleged tale: Moses Klander, Psychology Officer of the newly formed Israel Defence Forces, was providentially present, in the summer of '49, at the actual drawing of the armistice borders between the State of Israel and Jordan. It is claimed that Major Abdullah, Jordanian in charge, left the room for an extremely brief moment to relieve his bowels in the john. Klander, peeking at the map, noticed, to his chagrin, that the pencil line dividing the City had been drawn just across the lower, Hebron Way end of Reb Nahman Me'Bratslav Street. Seizing the time, and the pencil, he swiftly erased the line and re-drew it round the top of the hill. Moshe Dayan, who was also present, turned his eyepatch to the occasion. Major Abdullah, who had not closed an eye for three days and was still recovering from the sight of the Jewish emissary Mrs Golda Myerson disguised in Arab headdress for her meeting with the Hashemite King, was in no condition to spot this small act of skilful fraud.

Thus the Institute remained in Hebrew hands, and now stands gazing absently over newly conquered vistas: the walled Old City, Bethany, Silwan and all that lies between; a landscape not quite yet lobotomized by the bulldozers of constructive progress. Klander's heritage: the three-storey main building, the staff annexe, Annexe B, of Nachtnebel fame . . . All the buildings were of quarried Jerusalem stone, as decreed by the wise Colonialist Sir Ronald Storrs, overseer of the New City's architectural harmony until the new concrete Israelites, post-'67, began to dethrone his concern . . . The lawns, the curling paths of crazy paving, the old Andronicus sundial . . . not to mention the morgue, connected to the main building by the underground tunnel, of which more, so much more, later. And above, the waving bougainvillaeas, the fair cypresses and the pines. Patients ambling about, counting the pine cones, listening to the tweet of the birds. A well-planned, respected refuge for certain categories of the psychotic. For the Progressive Approach has its limitations. Klander introduced mixed wards, allowed patients and staff to wear their own clothes and abolished, way back, the electro-convulsive machine – though, of course, he embraced chemo-therapy. He was a pioneer of group-therapy, about which he wrote volumes. Flusser, taking over after Klander's sad and abrupt demise, was even more prone to lean with the winds of change agitating the clover fields of shrinkdom, his goal as different as possible to T – t's, the State Mental Hospital, where electro-therapy and psycho-surgery reigned under the gibbous moon. But the open approach meant the Institute could not cater for the Criminally Insane. People who had chopped their grandmother into segments with an exe, or disembowelled their cousins, or tried to burn down the al-Aqsa Mosque hoping to precipitate World War Three, could not be admitted to Klander and had to chance their luck with the eager sawbones and electricians of T – t. Alas, sometimes patients who had not previously exhibited any symptoms of violent aggression fell from grace, and a small locked ward was available for such eventualities. On such rare occasions Male Nurse Elkayam, who had been a strong man in the Egyptian circus in his youth, did the honours, and, as successfully as he had wrestled with orang-utans in Luxor bore the unfortunate malefactors of Klander off to their padded cells.

This, then, was the place to which Justice Ben-Horin consigned Blok for a month after rejecting his plea that, in the matter of his alleged infringement of Mr and Mrs Friedman's legal right to do nookie in peace and privacy, there was really no case to answer.

(Klander said:

'We have stood on the edge of a great and dreadful abyss and looked down, and seen there that multitude of dry bones, heaped high upon each other, many pits filled with the charred remains of

21

once-great forests, decked with green leaves of spring, open to the blue canopy of hope. And we cried out as the stench of the dead invaded every orifice, every pore of our skin, as bulldozers ripped and rent more heaps of broken dry bones on across the muddy ground towards the great mass graves. And we vowed that never again would we come close enough to see that sight, to bear the odour of our own decay. This time, we said, we'll build a true new world, dependent not on the great nations that had let us rot, but on our own devices. And we vowed that we ourselves would never tread upon the slippery path that might lead us, too, to the burial ground as executioners. We would deal with our fellow man, we said, according to hallowed principles of mutual respect, eschewing all forms of coercion, domination, arbitrary compulsion. Ah, we made a powerful mountain of vows, we did, which storm winds of reality have ripped and torn and stripped of many a decaying layer, since then . . . How mightily we huffed and puffed to blow life into the dry bones, and yet, was all the flesh and skin we seemed to conjure up to cover them and fill them with life, just one of those far lost mirages of our might-have-beens?')


## Everything You May Have Wanted to Know About Blok But Didn't Bother to Ask (I)

He was born on the illegal immigrant ship *Irma Klein*, approaching the waters of Palestine. Talk of the birth trauma! There they were: Rosa (Shoshana) Blok, mid the reek of engine grease and three hundred incontinent wretches saved, as the leaflets put it, from the Ovens of Europe; Baruch Blok, out with dysentery, up on deck, miserable; Mendel Plekhanov (no relation), ship's doctor and shoddy raconteur, holding her down on a plank in the galley while cauldrons of thin gruel (specialité de la maison) slopped about beside her, caressing her brow and whispering sweet nothings in Yiddish and the only Hungarian phrase he knew – 'How deep are your blue eyes, maiden of the far flung marches' – in her ear.

Then heave ho! plunk! Blok was born, grabbed and tossed, like a lump of dough, by Maître Plekhanov, who said, 'Voilà, another one with no passport.' Blok screeched in impotent despair.

His first real memory, apart from flashes of Jerusalem sky glimpsed from his pram, was the first day at kindergarten, when Mama Blok deposited him at the gate and then vanished, leaving him clinging to the wrought-iron railings, rattling them and screaming in desperate rage. Resentment at such helplessness was his first true emotion. 'I don't care about the education laws,' he once told Flusser. 'They could have made an exception for me.'

He next remembers standing alone, his back to a wall, holding a rye bread sandwich, while other kids cavorted about, mocking his ignorance of the Hebrew language and chanting in fake Hungarian: 'Egan megan fritz mit shnegan, kick the magyar in his teacan.' He learned the virtues of silence.

During his first year at primary school he did extremely well in algebra, of all things, a subject he later succeeded in forgetting to the last square root and fraction. In his second year he discovered girls, mainly by the agency of the pigtail. This was in another school, for his parents had moved to a quieter suburb after living for a number of years in a small narrow street running from the Jaffa Road towards the border district of Musrara.

They had a ground-floor flat in a large Arab house surrounding a courtyard, with a matsoh-bakery in the back. Pungent smells and loud oaths issued from there as the Passover season approached. There was a hole in the bakery roof through which Blok and the neighbourhood kids would peep at the feverish activity as lanky men with beards and gnarled elbows sweated, coiled twists of dough and thrust them into the ovens. A favourite game was to spit as a man bearing a tray passed directly below and run as the occasional bull's eye brought forth dire threats of revenge. The well in the centre of the courtyard was a great source of mystery, and there were railings on the windows of the apartment, in which Blok tended to trap his head at the most inconvenient moments. One time he was stuck so fast that only the combined efforts of the entire personnel of the Hebrew Broadcasting Service, domiciled one block down the road, procured his release from bondage. Two or three times during their residency firing broke out across the Jerusalem border, about four hundred yards east, bringing the sephardi inhabitants of Musrara streaming up the winding street carrying babies, bundles, cooking pots and light wicker chairs (they were ready for any emergency), to sojourn in the courtyard and the cavernous ground-floor Blok living room. Mama Blok, the spectre of unity banishing all ethnic differences, served up helpings of goulash in the Passover soup plates (Preservation of the Soul defers Sabbath) and Papa Blok tried in vain to pretend all was normal, attempting to read the Hungarian newspaper *Új kelet* by the light of a candle, seated among the multitude in his Haganah – issue tin helmet . . .

Several years pass.

Blok never had the full confidence, in his childhood, to do what everyone else of his age did with glowing panache: riding a bicycle with no hands, falling off the top branches of trees. He never broke an arm or a leg and was looked down on by his contemporaries. He was thin and physically awkward and was totally useless at games. His gym teacher was later to say to him: 'Blok, you are the most dismal example I have ever known of physical decadence.'

Let it not be thought, though, that Blok shunned all youthful activities. As mentioned earlier, he discovered the pigtail and the strange feminine creatures attached to it. He hurled rubber bands and erasers at them, but could not quite understand why. The problem of the hour, in this second grade, was the practice of corporal punishment by the teacher, an elderly gorgon of twenty-eight, administered by means of a ruler upon the palms of disobedient pupils. A clique formed, of which Blok was a member, whose purpose was to steal the tyrant's rulers when her back was turned and hand them over to Kalderon, the class basketball champion, who hurled them far into the fields. This is the first known instance of a Blokkian rebellion, if one discounts, at a far earlier age, the stubborn withholding of faeces.

Soon the family moved again, from the large Arab house in mid-city to a suburban block where Mrs Saporta-Yecchs and Gaga the Bulgarian Bloodhound and the Rebetsen Twilliger-Syphilis-Face were already in evidence. Papa Blok's war with what he termed 'the plague bacilli of 43 Yehezkel Hacohen Street' began almost immediately. Soon he also commenced his philatelic retreat, sealing off the study, subscribing to foreign journals, launching himself on to permanent safari at home. Mama Blok, finding refuge in scripture, particularly in Psalms, kept one eye on her growing stranger. Blok, whenever he could, would traipse westward over the hills rolling from Kiryat Moshe, searching for buried treasure, Arab spies, aliens from outer space. In this phase, like most of his male contemporaries, he became highly misogynous and maintained strict self-discipline in the field of rubber erasers and pigtails.

Before one knew it, it was Bar Mitzvah time! And Blok, in the breathless expectation of gifts such as money orders, cheques or envelopes full of cash, turned to study the portion of the Torah he would have to recite at the synagogue when the great day dawned. He learned text and *te'amim* fairly easily and, when the moment came, stood up to the congregation and belted out the following passage:

> 'Thus ye shall separate the children of Israel from their uncleanness; that they shall not die in their uncleanness, when they defile thy tabernacle which is among them. This is the law of him that hath an issue, and of him whose seed goeth from him, and is defiled therewith. And of her that is sick of her flowers, and of him that hath an issue, of the man, and of the woman, and of him that lieth with her that is unclean.'

With this, Blok officially became a man. In the same year, he finally mastered the art of full-scale masturbation.

On his first day at Klander, Blok was assigned a room with two other occupants. One was short, thick-set and tanned, with the look of a beach-loving clerk. The other was tall and wispy and swayed like a willow in the wind.

The thick-set man offered his hand cheerfully. 'Davidov,' he said, 'hypomaniac. Our friend here is Schwartsbart, hebephrenic first class. You can depend on me, despite my cyclothymic temperament.'

'I am Avram Blok,' said Blok.

'Pleased to meet you,' said Davidov.

'Kiss my arse,' said Schwartsbart, turning to face the wall.

'Don't worry about him,' said Davidov. 'A small libation?' He rummaged and produced from behind his bed a flask of wood-coloured liquid which Blok nervously declined.

'Whisky, Glenfiddich,' Davidov explained, 'all the way from the Highlands. The best. Don't worry about anything,' he added, noticing Blok's despondency. 'You've fallen on your feet here, I can tell you. This is the best room they could have put you. Schwartsi and I have got everything under control. Nothing goes on in this dump that we don't know. We have all the secret passages mapped, not to speak of those no one has been able to find yet. Our network extends into the highest echelons of this Institution. Those who think they have us under their thumb should laugh on the other side of their face. You want a peek at your file? Give me twenty-four hours and it's sitting right in your lap. Captain Davidov, late Ordnance Corps, delivers. In the Sinai Campaign I kept two battalions on roast turkey throughout, and white steak on the Sabbath when they gave the chaplain home leave. Yes sir! When Davidov's around, no one wants for anything. Foreign cigarettes? Pipe tobacco? Liqueurs? Pink gin? J&B? Brandy Napoleon? Vat sixty-nine, eh, sixty-nine, know what I mean ...? Vodka? Slivovitz? Ouzo? Metaxas? Arak? Formosan rice wine? Champagne? Veuve Clicquot, name the year, give me forty-eight hours – à la table! On the table, my friend! On the table! Everything the discerning mental patient needs. Why moan with despair at being cast out by the "normals"? What's wrong with life here, on the crazy side of the fence? Look at Them on the outside – wars, pestilences, blood, lice, plagues of the first born ... what do we care? We're snug as Pharaohs in here, thank you very much. You have to laugh, I tell you. What else can you do? Say yes, and the world is yours. Give up, and you might as well take a trip down the tunnel, to Dr Nachtnebel's basement.'

Indeed. Blok found his fellow inmates, on the whole, no more frightful or repulsive than any other random group of people he had known. In fact the asylum had a distinct advantage over the army – there were no criminal psychopaths. A small number of the patients were obviously quite mad, mumbling nonsense to themselves in the corridors, drooling into their food or masturbating at the top of the stairs. Others were lucid most of the time, but tended to sink into reverie at odd moments, for example, when one asked them a simple question such as 'which way, please, to the toilet?' Still others seemed to him perfectly normal, though generally depressed. (Does one expect joie de vivre here? Anyway, many were slowed down by medication.) As in the army, there were the usual identifiable types: the Fixer, the Scrounger, the Wailer, the Whiner, the Joker, the Liar, the Pervert, the Thief, the Con-Artist, the Arse-Licker, the Stoolie, the Saint, the Philosopher, the Religious Maniac. 'A society like any other,' Davidov said, in a moment of relative calmness, 'madmen and doctors with one common aim – to keep the outside world at bay.' (In this he inadvertently expressed the hidden principle of Klander himself.)

The staff, too, apeared to Blok no more, no less than the average. Often dressed informally, they mingled with the patients and were generally known by their nicknames: Ursus – Male Nurse Elkayam, Maciste – his assistant, Marciano. El Bzaz – Nurse Nitsa, of the giant breasts, Nurse Nili-Honey – of whom, more later. Yama Pasta – Mrs Patchouli, Chief Cook. Big Golem and Little Golem, laundry boys. Then there were the occasionals: Dr Feifinkoklootz-Ear-Nose-and-Throat, Dr Blinder-Eye-Surgeon, Kretshmar-Schuldorff, physiotherapist. Patata, from the social services. And the less famous – clerks, secretaries, temporary nurses, psychologists and the sephardi charwomen cackling gleefully about family business as they scoured the asylum floors with Kleen. At the top of the pyramid, the Director, Flusser, known alternatively as Herr Doktor, Commander, Papa Fluss, and, on good days, Flussie. His Vice, an American immigrant, Dr Veltsch, had no affectionate nickname. He was usually referred to as 'that fucking bastard', and was inclined to the Behaviourist creed. His aim, it was said, was to turn the Institute into a greenhouse of reward and punishment. Awaiting, in Flusser's shadow, the hallowed day when all this would be his . . .

And beyond this hierarchy, the inescapable legend of the invisible patron: Dr Nachtnebel, said to be ensconced in his laboratory, hidden in the locked Annexe B. There were few actual sightings, three reported by Old Leib, who was a Treblinka survivor. He was convinced Nachtnebel was the escaped Commandant of the death camp's Block 27. He had a hold over Flusser, declared Old Leib, a dark secret from the past. Others said, no, he was Flusser's twin brother, struck down in childhood by a disfiguring disease. Paranoids vied with depressives for the best Nachtnebel theory. He was a Christian diabolist, imprisoned in the Annexe by his own occult spells. A Man from the Ministry, working on the Final Solution to the Mental Helath Problem. But Old Leib did not budge from his certitude and spent hours, as he had done for several years, writing aerogrammes exposing the outrage to the leaders of the world's nations. He had a signed photograph in his room of President Eisenhower, who had sent it to him with a mimeograph stating: 'I am with you in your struggle for Justice.'

In short – Jerusalem routine. Blok's month at

Klander was undramatic except for the event, at the end of his stay, to which we shall turn later . . . He filled in questionnaires, performed the TAT, the DPI and the Minnesota Multiphasic Inventory. He blew up balloons and made up silly stories to fit nondescript illustrations. He poured out his troubles to Flusser in three pleasant sessions in the director's office. He had a less pleasant scrape with Veltsch, who pressed him to confess further acts of voyeurism and/or acts of nameless perversion. And Davidov, who was no idle boaster, kept him in Swiss chocolates, imported beer and pornographic 'stalag' paperbacks. Like everyone else, he fell in love with Nurse Nili-Honey and even secured her phone number. He made unusual friends, of who more later. In fact, he enjoyed the asylum: the tall cypresses swaying softly in the hilltop breeze, the odiferous bougainvillaeas, the green lawns, the paved pathways which curved into nooks where one could hide to put one's thoughts in order, the magnificent view of the walled Old City from the northeastern terrace, scudding winter clouds alternately lighting and greying the silver dome of the mosque. His short sojourn with the mad, the obsessive and temporarily round the bend seemed to provide a long-sought haven. This may well be why, in the years to come, he returned there, again and again. Or was it perhaps . . .?

Flusser used to say: 'I don't know about God, but I rather believe in Man.' Klander said: 'Neither God nor Man can be trusted.'

Klander was assassinated in Zion Square in Jerusalem on 10th May 1960, by a 'wild-eyed man' who materialized out of the Friday morning crowd and shot him three times in the chest and face, crying, 'Sic semper tyrannis!' as the great psychotherapist fell. The killer was found to be one Pesach Zilberschvantz, a well-known Jerusalem vagrant, who used to perambulate the streets with a small battered attaché case tied with string round his neck, filled with plastic combs, razor blades, shaving cream and brushes, matchboxes, balls of string, shirt studs and further knick knacks. He was commonly named Groise-Metsiyes, after the loud nasal cry of 'Groise metsiyes, alles für gurnischt!' (Great bargains, all for nothing!) which he uttered wherever he went. Where he had got the Luger pistol, his murder weapon, no one ever found out. Nor was his motive discovered. He claimed that Klander had 'stolen his soul', but, curiously, there was no evidence that he had ever been the victim's patient, nor met him in any capacity. He was yet another of the poor flotsam of Europe washed up on Palestinian shores. His papers dated from 1947, but no relative or acquaintance ever turned up to claim him as their own. The Zilberschvantzes of Bnei-Brak, reputable dealers in dry goods, denied him vehemently. They produced a family tree, going back two centuries, absolute proof of their dis-avowal. The assassin, apart from repeating ad nauseam his strange accusation, provided no fur-ther clue, and he was tried, found guilty but insane and committed for life to the State Mental Hospital, T – t. Moses Klander was buried with full civic honours in the National Cemetery at Mount Herzl. Thousands followed the coffin to its final resting place. The Institute he headed was named after him. Five years later, a stamp was issued in his memory. It was for IL8.50, and was very handy for overseas parcels.

Peter Flusser mourned his mentor deeply, but firmly took up the burden of the great work that Groise-Metsiyes's bullets had bequeathed him.

\*    \*    \*

Meanwhile, as Blok's adolescence progressed, Mama Blok's anxieties and Papa's withdrawal deepened. She suffered from recurring migraines and would take to bed with a cold schmutter pressed at her forehead and the Bible, open at Psalms, or, at times of crisis, Ecclesiastes: 'What profit hath a man of all his labour which he maketh under the sun? One generation passeth away, and another generation cometh, but the earth abideth for ever.' Papa Blok became even more virulent in his atheistic responses and would shut himself up with his new set of Monaco Grace Kellys. 'For all his days are sorrows, and his travail grief, yea, his heart taketh not rest in the night ... This is also vanity and vexation of the spirit.'

And Blok pursued his own mysteries. The sun rose, the sun fell, autumn followed summer, then came winter, et cetera. He did reasonably well in school at some subjects, not so well in others. He was hated by his gym teacher and treated with suspicion by several other teachers. He made a name for himself committing practical jokes, of a sneakily cerebral kind: lampooning hostile teachers by making wall posters out of newspaper headlines carefully revised with scissors and glue. For example: 'Varkin [the tyrannical physics master] Found Bound and Gagged in the Suitcase Discovered at Athens Airport.' 'Varkin, Notorious Rumanian Spy, Jailed for Life. A Menace to Society, Says Judge.' Feeble threats of expulsion followed. Years passed. He grew a straggly moustache which failed to make him look like Clark Gable. Masturbation continued throughout. But yearnings waxed ever stronger ... In 1963 Mama Blok had a hernia operation and Papa Blok triumphantly unveiled a complete set of French Melanesia (1869–). In 1964 Blok graduated from Secondary School with unexpectedly high matriculation marks. He received a

Bible signed by Headmaster Aricha who shook his hand on the conveyor belt.

Five months later he was drafted into the army. Mama Blok was prostrate for three weeks with the worst migraine in living memory. Papa Blok abandoned his stamps for the duration, to sit loyally by her side. (A time to rend, a time to sew, a time to keep silence and a time to speak.) While this touching process was occurring, Blok was crawling through the winter mud of the coastal plain, ripping his kneecaps and being yelled at incessantly by a loutish Corporal Simha: 'You arsehole! You piece of dried shit! You'd bring shame on the Egyptian army! Take your leg out of your arse and move on there, dungface, or you'll soon know what sucking cock means!'

Just as he was about to end his army service, war broke out with three Arab states.

'Existence begins in every instant. The ball There rolls around every Here. The middle is everywhere. The path of eternity is crooked.'

– Friedrich Nietzsche

On the last of his initial twenty-eight days at Klander Blok laid his head down to sleep with his suitcase all packed and ready for his release the following morning. But at eleven thirty, one hour past lights out, Davidov shook his shoulder.

'Wakey wakey!' he said.

'What's the matter?' said Blok.

'Don't you know what night this is, brother?'

'I don't know and I don't care,' said Blok, readjusting his pillow.

' 'Tis Christmas Eve,' declared the lunatic, 'the goyim's most holiest hour! Come on, get your pants on. We'll give you a send off the like of which you wouldn't imagine!'

The man was highly agitated. He was wrapped up in two sweaters, scarf and balaclava, in his gloved hands an immense pocket torch. Blok, scared he would wake the whole ward, dressed hurriedly and followed him out. 'Where are we going?' he whispered groggily. As if he wanted to know.

'Shsh!' said Davidov, touching gloves to wool helmet. 'We are off to the tunnel, of course!' He led the way down the corridor, padding past the room where Elkayam snoozed away his night duty, tip-toeing down the stairs, halting under the staircase, at the lumber room door.

'It's locked,' said Blok.

'Who d'you think you're dealing with,' said Davidov, 'your Aunt Fanchukha?' He held up a colossal ring of keys and deftly released the pad-lock. Inside, he made a beeline through piles of old cartons, broken cabinets, crates, mops, de-wheeled trolleys, straight to a far corner where, beneath filthy rags, he tugged at a large iron ring. 'Davidov promises. Davidov delivers,' he said, pulling a trapdoor.

They made their way breathlessly down neglected, winding stairs. Plop plop, went little drops of cold water on Blok's bedraggled head. 'I forgot to ask you,' said Davidov, as they ran, dou-bled up, along a five-foot-high shaft, 'are you claustrophobic?'

'I don't think so,' said Blok.

'Very good,' said Davidov. 'I once took the Mag-pie down this way and the bum began screaming his head off. I had to abort the mission, pronto. It was absolutely disgraceful.'

'What mission?' called Blok. 'What the hell's going on here? Where the fuck are we going?'

'We are in an auxiliary shaft,' said Davidov, 'which links up soon with the morgue tunnel. Thus we bypass the alarms and booby traps They set to stop people like us getting nosy.'

'But what's it in aid of?' Blok moaned, in frustra-tion. 'I'm cold and it's freezing here, damn it! And I'm due out of this place tomorrow!'

'Nothing will happen to you,' said the other. 'Trust Davidov. You may be about to have an experience you'll remember the rest of your life.'

'That is what I'm afraid of,' said Blok, but they had reached their destination. It was an iron grille at the end of the shaft, which Davidov unlocked with his keys. 'Of course,' he said, 'we may be wasting our time, it's all pot luck, ya habibi.'

'Now he tells me,' said Blok, putting his head in his hands. 'And why might that be the case, prithee?'

'Well, it just might not appear,' said Davidov calmly, 'it doesn't every year, you know. It's due Christmas Eve, midnight, or noon, Good Friday, but the actual year is erratic. It's more off than on, if you get my meaning. The whole thing's a bit of a gamble.'

'What gamble?' said Blok surlily, lost to the world. 'What is it that's supposed to appear?'

'You mean,' said Davidov, eyes wide with incredulity, 'you mean you really don't know? You've been a full month in our Klander Institute and you haven't even had the whiff of an inkling of the Judas Iscariot Pig??'

?   ?   ?

OH WOE IS ME FOR MY ABYSMAL IGNORANCE!

The Judas Pig, Genesis (I):

Father Andronicus (Oswald Hittlemacher Probst) was a rather shadowy figure. A Scheutt Father, he was sent from the Order's headquarters in Ulm to serve in the Holy Land in 1908. For a time he stayed quietly in a chapel at Nazareth, but, in 1913, he set out (no one knows why), clad in a monk's habit, barefoot and wielding a battered ash staff, to travel the length and breadth of the land, living off roots, herbs and whatever he could cadge from Turkish army camps. From Capernaum to Jericho, from Mount Gerizim to the Wilderness of Sin he wandered, a strange pilgrim with a far-off look, perturbing the sheep and bemusing the Ottoman soldiery. In 1916 the Turks, furious and panic-stricken by their reverses in war and the imminent collapse of Empire, vented their spleen on Jews, Moslems and Christians alike and carted everyone off to chokey. Accused of espionage, the Wandering Father was held at the dreaded prison of Jerusalem, fief, in that era, of the fearful sadist, Major Ismet Uscuglu. Some say he was subjected to terrible tortures, others, merely to the bastinado. But by a twist of fate the British general, Allenby, arrived in the Holy City. The Father was freed, in late 1917, and went into isolation in a small chapel off the Via Dolorosa, by the Church of Our Lady of the Spasm. There he stayed, locked in a tiny bare cell for thirteen years, poring over a manuscript that, according to rumour, he had brought with him from the *kishla*. (The story is vague here, the witnesses dead, or zonked out in hashish dens.)

In the summer of 1930 he emerged from the chapel and, as suddenly as he had left Nazareth seventeen years earlier, left the Walls, climbed down through the Valley and up Abu Tor towards the Scottish Hospital on the hill beyond. There he confronted the startled Hibernian Sisters with the outrageous claim that in the grounds of their hospice lay the burial place of the Betrayer, Judas Iscariot.

The Matron, Sister MacTavish of Fife, was a lady of granite visage and temper. She was in no mood at all to pander to the eccentric old hermit's delusions. Brushing aside the proffered parchments, which were yellow with age, covered with minute gothic lettering and somewhat bizarre illustrations, Matron said: 'Awa' wi' ye! Ye're diggin' up nae bones o' Judas in ma ain backyard!' The priest left. Being a pragmatic woman, and immune to the cranks of the City, Sister MacTavish gave no further thought to her curious visitor that day. But in the dead of night he returned, stealing over the perimeter fence with a pick-axe, a shovel, an oil lamp, several iron files and a length of stout rope. He stole through the rhododendrons, lovingly planted to give a whiff of a distant homeland and, crouched low, he carefully perused the runes of an ancient map. Ha! Finding the correct spot, just behind the sundial, he began to break the ground. Sister MacTavish, at the time, was having the most singular dream. She dreamt she was present at Calvary, and the foot of Golgotha was thick with street vendors' stalls, selling endless varieties of coloured boiled sweets enclosed in immense glass jars. One vendor was touting pink sugar apostles, which sold like hot cakes to the Roman centurions. One unshaven brute bit the legs of a Paul, spitting out scrunched-up toenails. The multitude accompanying the saviour were labouring uphill from the town, from whence came a clamour of merry-go-rounds, hurdy-gurdies and the gibbering of chained chimpanzees. Drawn by a compulsion, she walked towards the procession to peer at the man bearing the great wooden cross in its midst. As she expected, it was her father, the Reverend Randall MacTavish, wearing his usual apologetic smile. 'At it agin, I see,' he said ruefully. Two centurions seized her and, holding her upside down, began shaking her vigorously. From the folds of her dress cascaded showers of mint juleps, liquorice allsorts, nougats, Turkish delights, Berwick cockles, soor plooms, sherbet dabs, pan drops, English hum-bugs, togles, brandy-balls, sugarellies, aniseed balls, dainty dinahs, Refreshers, dragées, butter-mills and striped balls, all scattering upon the ground. Taking her firmly by the arms, the Romans dragged her to the summit, where her father laid the great cross beneath her. Two other centurions were digging the hole in which it was to be embedded. They were humming 'Lili Marlene'.

Meanwhile, out on the Jerusalem hillside, a shepherd by the name of Nagib Abd-el-Khalik, known by all as Abu Shawareb on account of the immense and luxurious white moustache he had been cultivating since his days as a muleboy in the Turkish pressgang, was meditating in the sharp nocturnal air. He was considering whether the time had not come to divorce his wife Fatima (the Jackal of Silwan) and go off to join the nascent forces of the National Army of Liberation, forming in the hills of Samaria in preparation for the war to drive the Jews and the British out of the Revered Homeland. The moon was almost full in the sky, casting a ghostly glow. He thought: my children are old enough now to look after the sheep and the goats, but the Jackal will follow me, seething with vengeance, even unto the deepest hide-out. Even after the Jews are thrown into the sea I will not be able to rest . . .

Just as he was about to light another hashish cigarette to clear his mind, he suddenly noticed a figure sliding over the low wall of the Hospice some fifty yards ahead. Seizing hold of his Lee Enfield rifle he stealthily moved up the hill. The Scottish Sisters had always been good to him, they had snatched his son Omar from the jaws of a feverish death, and that steely-eyed Matron – mmm! what a woman! may God overlook one's wet dreams . . . Silently he climbed over the wall, following the intruder.

Unaware that his every move was being watched by Abu-Shawareb, Father Andronicus dug away fiercely in the rhododendron patch, his breath coming in short rasping gasps as his excavation deepened. Soon only his head was visible above ground as shovelfuls of the brown earth of the Holy Land flew through the midnight air. Did he really hope to find the crumbling remains of Judas there, and if so, to what purpose, sacred or profane, would such an exhumation be put? Mysterium. Suddenly, upon a mighty wallop of his pick, the ground gave way beneath him and he fell, throwing his arms in the air and emitting a loud, poignant cry of 'SCHEISSE!'

Sister MacTavish, wakened from her nightmare by the sound of digging, had crept up behind a bush to within ten feet of the trespasser when he uttered his expletive and plunged out of sight. Undaunted, and outraged by the destruction wrought upon the rhododendrons, she rushed forward, tripped in the dark over the priest's cache of ropes and iron files and followed him, head first, down the hole.

Abu Shawareb, rushing up, rifle in hand, saw the two figures which his twenty twenty vision told him were Matron and the stranger, writhing tangled in the deep recess. 'Avast, malefactor!' he cried, or words to that effect, adding a string of Arabic oaths. 'Unhand the woman, Son of Asmodeus!'

Father Andronicus looked up and saw, between himself and the moon, two blazing eyes and a giant white handlebar moustache beneath a white burnoose. 'Judas Uscuglu!' he cried, incomprehensibly, and fled underground into what seemed to be an open tunnel. Crying 'Allahu akbar!' Abu-Shawareb leapt into the hole and, passing by the befuddled Matron, pursued the priest into darkness. 'Stop, Enemy of God!' his voice boomed in the inky depths. Then came one rifle shot and an immense, blinding flash, lighting the entire hill, accompanied by an explosion which threw Matron, who had just managed to rise, flat on her back again.

The other Sisters came running and were stunned at the sight that met their eyes: coughing and choking, caked with what appeared to be white clay, Sister MacTavish reeled towards them in a cloud of dust while, behind her, from a crater hewn out of the rhododendron patch, clambered an Arab with tattered burnoose, his moustaches ablaze and crackling like two giant roman candles.

So much for hyperbole.

The British police arrived with sappers, alsatians, and budgerigars in cages. They dug out of the rubble the charred corpse of Andronicus, his eyes and mouth open wide with astonishment. (Some described it as fear, others as awe, but some, as an immense joy.) The CID cast a veil over the investigation, not a chink of light escaped from their files. (Some say a dossier exists in Whitehall; others: no, it was burnt in the blitz.) They announced that an accident with construction materials had uncovered an underground tunnel. Archaeologists examined it and declared it to date from the Abbassid period. (800 AD, give or take a century . . .) No one mentioned the era of Christ, though, of course, dig deep enough under any piece of the City and who knows how far back you'll go . . .

They cleared out the passage and added it to the map of Jerusalem curios. It did not attract much attention at first, apart from a few trysting couples. Three and a half years later it sprung to prominence, for it was then, on Christmas Eve, 1933 AD, that the Judas Pig made its first grisly appearance . . .

An incident of supreme significance occurred to Blok when he was eleven years old. Together with his friends Fat Avi, Square Gideon and Muki the Squint-Eyed Mutt he was exploring the hinterland about the abandoned building which overlooked the Diskin Orphanage, the Tel Aviv Highway and the ruins of Lifta beyond. The house, sealed off from the world by rusted shutters and bars, surrounded by a sargasso sea of old tin cans and shredded election posters, rotted orange peel and fused gunge, exuded an air of graveyards and fates too fearful to contemplate. No one would dare approach it after dark, except Nachumi the Mouth, who was later to become a Naval Commander and director of a Panamanian shipping line specializing in gun-running to Latin American dictators deserted, in their death rattle, even by the CIA. Occasionally he reported sounds of low moaning, as of lost souls in agony. Surveying the hitherto uncharted area to the lee of the haunted house, Blok, Avi, Gideon and Muki came across the partially blocked entrance to an old bomb shelter, which must have been unused since the Armistice. Squint-Eyed Muki dived in, conveying by vigorous, ululating howls that no marauding Arabs or man-eating spiders appeared to be lurking within. The boys pulled aside the detritus of years and squirmed into the dank interior. As their eyes adjusted to the dark, they saw signs of former inhabitance in the shape of burnt, crumbling circles of stones – remnants of cooking fires, perhaps – but as their pupils expanded further they also made out, thrust in a corner and covered with damp earth and dust, three large red-bound heavy books, each one a foot in height and in width. Excitedly they bore these out into the open air. Muki was designated to stand first watch while they gingerly opened the tomes. The books appeared to be heavy folders enclosing hundreds of pages of yellowing tabloid newspapers, printed mysteriously in gothic Latin type and including the most grotesque illustrations. They involved bent and menacing hook-nosed figures, with features of the most repugnant coarseness, beards matted and straggling like lumps of dried turds, talon-like hands grasping forth out of the page. Some held strange scales, upon which slight figures cowered in abject terror. Others leered over voluptuous blonde women whose torn apparel thinly hid immense breasts. One picture in particular stuck in

Blok's mind: the monstrous beings clustered round a child, who lay prone on a table, wide-eyed with fear. Two of the figures held long thin stakes which were plunged into the child's body. The child's blood ran back from its belly into a chalice or bowl. The eyes of the tormentors were popping out in what could only be described as ecstasy.

Neither Blok nor his friends could bring themselves to reveal this incredible find to their parents. For a year the red books were kept hidden in a niche on the roof of Blok's house, until one day a routine check showed them missing, gone, stolen or spirited away. The boys speculated, shivering, upon the mystery owner who might have tracked down his lost property. Many a silent night was darkened by the thought of his chuckling vengeance. The origin of the volumes and their subsequent fate remained unknown. An impenetrable, occult enigma.


**From the *Palestine Post*, 26th December, 1933:**

Jerusalem's sharp mountain air seems to be doing strange things to one young couple in love! She is Helen Jacobson, a typist from Talpiot. He is Sergeant Fred Willis of the King's own Grenadiers. Smitten with the local beauty but spurned by her Revisionist father, the good Sergeant prevailed on the lady to meet him in secret in the newly excavated tunnel in the grounds of the Scottish Hospital, near Abu Tor. It was Xmas Eve, and perhaps the young lad wished to toast the festive night with Scotch, though he claims absolute sobriety. The romantic midnight rendezvous was not long underway, however, when the couple heard strange sounds in the tunnel. 'An eery snorting and snuffling,' says she. 'A scraping sound, like a bull pawing the ground,' says he. They rose, startled, and were transfixed by the sight–here it comes–of a gigantic pig, some ten feet away, looking straight at them and shining with a 'luminous glow'! The giant porker advanced towards the trysting couple, his eyes 'like two blazing coals' (Miss Jacobson). His Majesty's brave warrior, rather than proclaim a curfew or apply the law of Disorderly Conduct upon the phantasm, grabbed his poor amoureuse by the hand and they made off down the hill, waking everyone with their cries of terror. But lo and behold! the aroused citizenry found no trace of life in the Hospital tunnel. Miss Jacobson denies liquor was imbibed, but love, as we know, is blind ... They also claimed they never heard of the odd circumstances of the tunnel's uncovering, $3\frac{1}{2}$ years ago, and the death of the hermit Andronicus while digging there, so the story goes, for the grave of Judas Iscariot. Was it the mad monk's demon succubus the couple encountered down there? Or even more sinisterly, the ghost of the traitor Iscariot himself??! The Judas Pig! What gaunt vision! At any rate, we can all glory now in a brand new Jerusalem bogey ...

Nietzsche fondled the paperback editions of his works on the shelf, gazing out of the asylum window, through the glass flecked with fly specks and the tiny squares of mosquito netting, towards the Jericho hills. *Beyond Good and Evil, Zarathustra, Ecce Homo, The Antichrist;* scurrilous editions, stolen, dishonestly printed and disseminated by corrupt academics; copyrights breached with an axe and not a penny for their living author. Clouds darkened the horizon. He heard the spatter of rain. Small rivulets flowed, higgledy-piggledy, chasing each other down the wires of the netting, forming into minute bubbles. 'He who rejoices even at the

45

stake,' he thought, 'triumphs not only over pain but over the fact that he feels no pain where he had expected to feel it. Did I not write one hundred years ago: "Profound suffering ennobles and separates"?' Now came another moment of insight: as the rain-waters filled the holes of the netting – one here, one there, meshing into a celestial jigsaw – he suddenly knew how the great work was to be brought forward to its next stage. It had to be done in a manner no robber, thief or plagiarizer could co-opt. The Revaluation, the Final work that Nietzsche Number One barely started. O Will, my essential, my necessity, spare me for this one great victory! . . . Yes, a completely new language was needed. An unbreakable code. A shield no Flusser nor Veltsch could dent.

The rain, hammering as it gathered pace, now spat at the inner window. I greet you, comrade of my youth. He smiled, smoothing with firm, untrembling fingers the sleek reaches of his walrus moustache. Rain, upon the Swiss Engadine. The fog over the mountains lifting, to provide a glimpse, one glimpse – sufficient – of the radiance that was there, ready, waiting for the One who was to come. Was it not there I had cried out first: 'If there were Gods, how could I endure not to be a God? Therefore there are no Gods!'

He did not look up as the Magpie entered the room, thrusting under the bed his latest haul of knick knacks, discarded shoelaces, fag ends, and abandoned pills that the day had garnered, and left softly humming a Spanish Civil War refrain, his voice, 'ho carmela, carmela . . .' trailing off along the corridor. What is Time? Nietzsche held his palm flat against the windowpane, marvelling at the smooth cold. Did I not write: 'I am that which must overcome itself again and again . . .Time is a circle . . . The path to eternity is crooked.'

And the rain, the rain . . .

Liam O'Habash, pornographer extraordinary, crouched below the walls of Klander, adjusting his balaclava in the midwinter moonlight, reshuffling his illicit portfolio. In a long career Liam has learned to satisfy every demand. To each his own. There's no accounting for taste. One man's meat is another's flaccidity. For instance in one pouch of his knapsack is the elegant *Hilde's House of Bondage*. In another, the crasser products of San Francisco – *Cum Flying, Just Jissim, Ass Whole*. In a third, the more mundane *Stalag* paperbacks of native vintage: *Scourged by the Swastika, I Was Goebbels' Hand Maiden, Mengele My Gynaecologist*. Something for everyone. Liam's writ runs wide. He is the one-man messiah of sexual subversion in the entire Fertile Crescent. The one-man canker in the body moral of a dozen zealous nations. Several governments have gone so far as to designate him Public Enemy Number One. Even the fedayeen armies have put a price on his head after incidents at Fatah camps. But he has his protectors in every country, often in the highest echelons: the cabinet minister with a one-breast fixation. The mullah who is a cellophane freak. The field-marshal driven to frenzy by fish. The secret police noodle-fetishist. Thus Liam reigns supreme, prevailing, untouchable, the scarlet pimpernel of erotic crime, the ultimate creeper down forgotten alleyways, the crawler in unnoticed sewers, the seeker in darkness, the peeper in parks, the man round the corner with the goodies shrink-wrapped in the tatters of his under-garments . . .

A rope is slung out of the second-floor window, Liam instantly recognizing the dark ribbon of Davidov tied as a signal to its end. Swiftly he secures the rope round the requisite package, giving it a vigorous tug. The rope rises with its burden, skimming the bricks and waterpipes, disappearing in the dark. Liam, in commando boots and sweater, readjusting his balaclava, retreats noiselessly through the asylum grounds. The night is yet young, comrade punters, there are more deliveries to be made, elsewhere . . .

(Many years after he and his friend had found the three red volumes in the shelter by the abandoned building, Blok found out the significance of the thick gothic word at the masthead of each of the tabloid newspapers within; a portent, perhaps, resonant of genetic nightmares: 'STURMER')

**From the *Palestine Post*, 15th April, 1945:**

### PORCINE GHOUL SIGNALS TWILIGHT OF GODS?
#### by A. Himmeltraub

As the world approaches the end of the most terrible conflict in human history, as Russian troops close in through the rubble of Germany on the madman of Berlin, was a gruesome footnote to History written on this Easter Good Friday on a peaceful Jerusalem hill? Reports have come in of a strange re-occurrence, in a tunnel below the Scottish Hospital near Abu Tor, of an enduring Jerusalem legend. At 12 o'clock, mid-day, witnesses claim, the 'Judas Pig' made its fourth manifestation . . . Who are we, in these days of events too fearful to have been hitherto imagined, to put down such daunting visions to mere chicanery or superstition? Indeed, these years of Gog and Magog have taught us that Man's darker, primeval passions have not been eradicated by an era supposedly of progress and rationality. Who knows, one might say, for whom the pig paws, it paws, perhaps, for us?

(Ed.'s comment: 'How did Himmeltraub get that shit past me? Get that fucking clown off my back! Transfer the schlemiel to Religious Affairs, or even, goddamit, to Sport!')

It was nine thirty p.m. at the Waldorf Astoria Auschwitz-Birkenau Reunion. People who had not seen each other since they had been plucked out by the Allies in that icy January, dressed in striped camp pyjamas, shattered and shrunk to skin and bone, now met and shed tears all over their starched dinner collars. The speeches were almost over, the Vows of Eternal Remembrance vowed. The last speaker was Daniel Manchinsky, who had a two-digit tattoo. This meant he was one of the camp's first arrivals. His survival, through torments of hell, was a triumph of the human spirit. Today he was an armaments consultant with the Call Corporation of Muncie, Indiana. His speech made a lump throb in every throat, and several members in whom fearful memories were awakened slumped in cataleptic stupor. Then, as the peroration approached, a man at the Block Three table, gnarled and strangled by the terrors of his past, stood up, scattering caviar like sheep's turds over the pure white tablecloth and, pointing a quivering finger, exclaimed: 'That waiter! The one over there, with the cocktail tray! That is Heinz Kammler, Chief Wermacht Builder, Constructor of the Crematoria! It is Kammler, I tell you, there can be no mistake, that face is seared into my mind!'

The hall froze catatonically. Five hundred dinner jackets seemed suddenly full of wax figures. A pin was heard to drop. It came from the canister which the accused waiter held in his hand, brandishing it above the throng.

He walked to the podium. 'I have here,' he cried loudly so that everyone could hear, 'a canister of Zyklon B.' A low groan, like a forest of oaks in a gale, rose from the ornate floor. 'You will stay where you are,' the waiter cried, 'or an unfinished job will be finished. Here and now, we will all go together. But first, we will sing a tune to gladden the heart, a lyric to bring back just those memories this occasion is held to indulge. All together now, with me . . .' and he broke into a horrible cracked falsetto:

'Wenn Juden Blut von Messer spritzt, Dann ist nochmals so gut . . .'

An athletic black waiter, one Bad-ass Johnson of Lennox Avenue, Harlem, crept up behind him and walloped him with a baseball bat. The trespassing Nazi's brains flew out in a scarlet and grey parabola, marking the white Axminster carpet with the splodge of a pentagram. From its centre thick black smoke rose up, burnt a hole in the penthouse roof and flowed out against the red Manhattan sunset.

Patrolman O'Hanahan, jingling his handcuffs on Columbus Avenue, looked up at the dark plume and shook his head sadly.

'Bejasus,' he said, 'they've failed to elect His Holiness again.'

An imbecile once accosted Blok in a bar.

'Wars are good,' he said, 'they keep down the population. They unite people who would otherwise be at each other's throats. They create fantastic leaps in technology. Look at the jet plane, magnetic recording, hi-fi, the space age, the bikini, the zipper, atomic power, teas-mades. Wars keep us from getting too soft and pampered and unfit for the struggle to survive. Wars make us brainier, by killing off those who are not quick enough on the ball. Wars are good for business, they make people look out for a bargain. Wars break down class barriers, rich and poor buddy-buddy together in among the muck and bullets. Wars free women and turn them into productive social units. And don't forget, wars bring us in touch with our real, aggressive selves and help rid us of our neuroses. Wars, in short, are what make society tick. They make you test yourself, to check out how strong, how self-reliant you really are. Wars make you a man, so you can look the world in the eye. Wars clean out your soul, purify the blood, wars make you healthy wealthy and wise. Two wars in the hand are worth one in the bush. A war a day keeps the doctor away. Make war not love, eh, what do you think, buddy?'

'Kiss my arse,' said Blok, and went out alone into a cold drizzly street.

From Europe there came to Klander a young visiting analyst, an Englishman with flowing hair and curiously sleepy eyes, who had opened several asylums in Italy and let all the loonies out into the community. 'Fraud, Addler and Junk,' he drawled, 'more chains to hold us down. Madness is a form of permanent revolution that should be encouraged, not suppressed. The social revolution occurs in every mind that capitalism seeks to enslave. There are no personal problems, there are only political problems. Psychiatric imprisonment is the worst form of torture: They say They torment you for your own good! Pardon me while I collapse on the floor . . . But madness is a form of speaking the truth in a context which suppresses every form of the truth. Mind-Imperialism is the highest form of Capitalism. All mental hospitals should self-destruct from within. Every suppression of our full autonomy should be fought to the bitter end!'

Flusser said: 'A charming young man. Perhaps a little extreme.'

Veltsch said: 'A clear case for lobotomy.'

The young man got stuck on Nurse Nili-Honey who, unfortunately, was congenitally incapable, so she said, of making it with a goy. Nurse Nitsa, on the other hand, took him in eagerly, and he spent all the latter part of his stay in her flat, caressing her giant bazooms . . .

They plot, they plot, they plot everywhere, the reds, the blacks, the dark, the fair. They watch around corners. They hide under beds, the ogpu, the cheka, the cia, the feds. The jews, the gypos, the wogs, the coons, the half-castes, the mulattoes, the octaroons. Wherever you look, wherever you tread, a yid, a nigger, a chink, a red. Nowhere's SAFE! There's no safety in numbers! The mass only attracts! *The One, repels*! Divide, disunite, scatter, vamoose! The beast's *ON* the rampage, the night is loose.** Sink, sink deep into your inner iron MAIDEN, spikes turned out, the INNER hedgehog *curled* into a ball. Dig trenches/deep that cannot be expelled, build fortresses high, DEFY! Even that's no use, They can see inside, They have the latest *TECHNOL-OGY*, laser beams, death rays, particle guns, cyclotrons rolling upon massive hippopotami feet. They can reach into your INDIVIDUAL CELLS, (*!) did you *know*? They can do anything They want. I heard a *radio* interview, once, where THEY told about fertilizing *hamster eggs* with our sperm, to check on male *infertility*, They said. Even the interviewer was aghast! But won't we produce terrible monsters?? *he wailed*. They assured him the blastopods were aborted; a likely story. They are moving ahead, advancing, while we tread in one place, munching nuts. Soon none of us will be what we were at the *start*. They are into our genes, you know, where anything *goes*. So watch it! I won't bother to WARN you again. They're after you *too*, so watch it, you fucker, They are after you too, you too . . .

Blok and Davidov spent two hours crouched at the iron railings giving on to the morgue tunnel, but the Judas Pig failed to materialize.

'Well,' said Davidov, 'win some, lose some. I said it was a gamble. Still, I can tell you, sometimes you just gotta laugh.'

'Ha ha,' said Blok, and remained silent the rest of the way back.

'When a city suffered from plague, famine, or other public calamity, an ugly or deformed person was chosen to take upon himself all the evils which afflicted the community. He was brought into a suitable place, where dried figs, a barley loaf, and cheese were put into his hands. These he ate. Then he was beaten seven times upon his genital organs with quills . . . while the flutes played a particular tune. Afterwards he was burned on a pyre . . .'

– J.G. Frazer, *The Golden Bough*

On 5th May, 1968, Blok embarked on the passenger ship *Flaminia* bound for Marseille, France. His father and mother waved a tearful goodbye from the Haifa dock. They were funding his trip out of reparations paid to Baruch Blok by the German Federal Republic for the death of his father and brothers and sisters in the death camp of Sobibor. Blok underwent a twinge of sadness as they receded from view along with Quay 24. But this fleeting emotion was soon replaced by delight at escape.

This trip was Flusser's idea, his proposal to pluck Blok free from the claws of Justice Ben-Horin and also take him out of his doldrums. Blok's parents wished him to apply for the University, but Blok could not make up his mind.

'I will get you released into my custody,' said Flusser, 'then I'll clear you for the travel agent. It broadens the mind, you know. Of course, if you'd rather stay and get stuck into some useful WORK...'

The trip took five days. Blok shared a cabin with three members of the Israel table-tennis team, who were en tour to France and to West Germany. Of the latter they spoke with enormous enthusiasm. Last time, in Hamburg, they had all got laid daily, and only one had caught a social disease. They therefore recommended German whores without a hint of reservation. Blok wandered about deck, trying to avoid their repartee and calisthenics. He saw several girls, with whom he fantasized a shipboard romance. But they all made for the ping-pong team.

The sea was calm most of the way, except for one stormy night. Even the red hot lovers were glued to their bunks, exhibiting shades of green. The food varied, between kibbutz-like fare, and that of Instruction Base Four. In the dining lounge people talked of troubles in France, dislocations and General Strikes. The students were rioting in the streets of Paris. Communist plots were rife. Blok had never met any Communists, discounting his schoolmates, Gad and Benjy, of the Mapam Youth movement. They had scrawled 'Yankees Out!' in the girls' convenience. Blok had written beneath: 'Better Dead Than Red'. There had been no ideological content to his act, it was merely a reflex provocation. Both inscriptions were denounced by the Headmaster at a specially convened school meeting. 'Vandalism,' he cried, 'and in the ladies' toilets!' The assembly was struck dumb by apathy.

Well away from all that, Avram Blok . . . No return! for a while, at any rate . . .

At Marseille, he gave his garrulous cabinmates the slip at Customs and ventured alone into Europe, carrying a maroon tartan suitcase with his name and Blok address pasted firmly on all four sides. As his train north was due to leave two hours later, he took a taxi direct to the station. He was tempted to say 'Vite!' to the driver, but pressed his lips together and abstained. Blok's English was excellent for local standards, but his French n'existait pas. He knew only some phrases from Jean Gabin movies: 'Merde, alors.' 'Tiens!' 'Allez, les flics.' At the station all was confusion. No one knew which train left for where and when, and none of the officials spoke English. Finally he came upon a group of young English people with rucksacks who were looking for the same train to Paris. There were three somewhat pimply boys of around eighteen and a very tall blonde girl, obviously a little older, who said she had just come from Tangier. Her arms were bronzed smooth by the North African sun. Her hair fell in golden waves to her shoulders. Her eyes were light blue. Blue jeans hugged her thighs. Blok fell in love with her instantly.

She spoke French fluently. In consequence, they located the right train and boarded, breathlessly seizing a compartment. The train sped through pastures green and lush the like of which Blok had not seen before. (The parched sparseness of the Homeland, the brown sombre hills, the emptiness of the ochre desert . . .) Little villages nestled in fertile valleys, church spires glinted in the sun, grassy knolls with cows chomping at abundant verdure. Clickety-clack, clickety-clack, clickety-clack. Magic names flashed by on signposts: Roquenare, Vivière, Montelimar, Loriol, St-Peray . . . cows, sheep, valleys, and more green hillsides, spires, grass, the gasworks of Lyon. ... Giant breadrolls from raucous platform vendors. Ham and cheese, for the apostate palate. Blok, munching gingerly, waited for the bolt of lightning.


## The Girl's Name Was Victoria

The girl's name was Victoria. She said she had spent three months travelling from Egypt to Morocco, by hitch-hiking and public transport, with nothing to her name but a rucksack and a male companion who seemed to have dropped out in Casablanca, perhaps in search of the Blue Parrot Café. Previously she had acquired her BA in political science, she revealed, at the London School of Economics. But now the place to be was Paris where the Revolution was nigh. Apropos nothing Blok commented he had once been in Egypt himself. Albeit illegally, he added, along with the entire Israeli army. She asked him what he had thought of the war. He gave her the party line, saying it was forced on Us by Them, was it not, but, he added, he had no intention of participating in another. He had proclaimed his own separate peace. What did you do in the war? she asked. Most of my time in the army, he said, I was a hack for the official army magazine, In The Base. A conscripted correspondent. Rubbish, really. In the war I kept just a smidge behind the front, within the margin of safety. A lot of people couldn't do that, she said, gazing down at him from a cloud.

He could see she was a girl with a strong personality. She had their compartment completely under her thumb. The three youngsters, whom she'd met only minutes before Blok's arrival, jumped at her every whim. They ran errands to the buffet car, bringing her coffee, black, no sugar, cigarettes, sandwiches. Once, when she invitingly held up a butt, they all rushed for the honour of throwing it out of the window. Blok beat them all to it. She smiled at him, but he could not tell if that meant 'You poor schmuck' or something more complimentary. She looked so sexy sitting sprawled, open-legged by the window, her right hand over her crotch, her left resting on the multilingual Do Not Lean Out sign – the cows, the sheep, the valleys, the place signs – her nipples stating their case through T-shirt and bra, her gold locks tossed to this side and that alternately. He had a minor erection, and considered going to the toilet to masturbate. But the risk such an act might entail in a crowded French train cast a damper upon his ardour (the hand, pumping, the sheep, chomping outside, le conducteur, rattling the handle: 'Ouvrez la porte! merde, alors!' Policemen's whistles, disaster, obloquy ...) He sat, sighing inwardly, day-dreaming, of Victoria and he, he and Victoria, as the church spires flew by, and the cows, and the green green fields, and the billboards, clickety-clack-clickety-clack ...

Paris!

The Eiffel Tower! The Bastille! The *Mona Lisa*! Et cetera.

There was little sign of revolutionary fervour at the Gare d'Austerlitz. A number of flics stood around giving youthful embarkées the evil eye. Victoria and Blok parted from the three boys, who were continuing directly to England. Blok had intended to seek out a cheap hotel or youth hostel, but Victoria said: 'I'm staying with some people where there's plenty of room to crash. Why not stick around a couple of days till you can get your bearings?' His heart leapt! Did this mean a desire for his company? Or merely his portering services, as he carried her incredibly heavy rucksack down the platform to the Metro. At the stairs, a young man thrust a stencilled tract in his pocket. Victoria, plucking it out, said: 'Listen to this: "Camarades, étudiants, lycéens, enseignants, travailleurs! Dans l'espace de quelque jours une situation pre-révolutionnaire s'est crée dans le pays et qui evolue maintenant vers une situation révolutionnaire . . ." '

'Fantastic,' said Blok. 'What does it mean?'

'It means we've arrived just in time,' she said, beaming. 'It means the shit will soon hit the fan.'

'Ah,' he said, thinking: four years of English with maître Gidon Cohen have just bitten the dust. He humped her bag, huffing, down the long tiled corridor, past two uniformed persons scrubbing away with long brooms dipped in suds at an immense graffito; what was left proclaiming: ' – 'UN DEBUT, CONTINUONS LE COMBAT!'

'*Formidable!*' cried Victoria. 'Zut, alors! magnifique! vive la France!'

They emerged at the Place Saint-Michel. Lights, noise, bustle. Jerusalem on a Saturday night, only twenty times stronger, and permanent, and on the banks of the Seine! Loud catcalls, stubborn honking of car horns. A riot of jeans, coloured T-shirts, bizarre clownish costumes, djelabiyas. A kaleidoscope battering at his fatigued senses. He seemed to be walking on air, his footing lost in the tide, even the rucksack borne along like a feather in the press. Victoria had to guide him like a blind man, pulling him across the street, through the flowing traffic which thoroughly ignored the flashing beacons of green. Across the road further hallucinations awaited him: three looming grey buses, with opaque wire-meshed windows, drawn up furtively along a side street. In front of them, a dozen or so figures encased in strange overalls, head to toe, face masks, heavy boots, odd metallic bric-à-brac dangling at their waists. They looked like invaders from Mars. 'CRS,' said Victoria, 'police storm-troopers. Very bad vibes indeed.' Propelling him firmly by the arm in the opposite direction.

Back into the throng: young men with beards and hair so long it was a wonder they could keep their balance . . . well-dressed middle-aged stockbroker type blowing soap bubbles through a ring . . . lush girls, each more beautiful than the other . . . Arab men with fierce piercing eyes . . . a tramp, lambasting them with fervent conviction – 'de Gaulle! communiste! cannabis! OAS!' . . . young couples kissing solemnly under lamp-posts . . . the smell of a dozen different countries' cooking . . . the shards of a dozen languages other than French splintering in the warm evening air . . .

Through a tiny open gate in a narrow street, the Rue Danton, into a wide open courtyard, three grey shanks of old buildings leaning towards its centre. Here and there a square of yellow light, a silhouette head and shoulders, hands clasped over a sill. Curt comments passed from window to window. Suddenly a burst of rock music. 'Ah, the crew is in residence,' Victoria announced, leading him up winding stairs. One, two, three floors up. A heavy door with a painted mandala and a defiant beat behind it. Knock, knock went Victoria's knuckles, a tiny sound lost in the blare. She bent to the keyhole, put two fingers in her mouth and emitted an ear-splitting whistle. Blok, filled with a new admiration, perspired around the rucksack. The sounds within faltered, tinkled, stopped. A loud crash and heavy scraping ensued. A bolt was squeakily drawn, the door opened, revealing a blaze of light.

A halo round a coal black face. Black frizzy hair shooting up from each temple, forming an inverted pyramid. In its midst, two clear headlamp eyes, a widening, toothpaste-ad grin.

'Vicky! Shit! Motherfucker!'

The tall blonde and the black man embrace, pummelling each other on the back. Four other black faces with new-moon smiles peer round the door of an inner room and further repartee: 'Shit! Motherfucker! Vicky! Shit, man! Fuck me! Holy shit! Hey, man! Motherfucker!' et cetera.

Victoria, disengaging, introduced Avram Blok: 'This is Avram, we met on the train.' And with a flourish, avoiding another bear hug: 'The one and only Wellington Frog!' 'You better believe it!' said her friend, relieving Blok of the rucksack with one hand and clasping his paw with the other. He introduced the supporting cast as they gathered round, pointing them out anticlockwise: 'Leroy Smith, an' Jonathan Sig-lala, and this dude is Mahmud, Imam of Oakland, retired, an' this here cat with the real mean look is none other than the great Jay-son I-saac . . .'

'Delighted,' said Avram Blok as his hand was crushed again and again. Chortling and snortling the phalanx moved in to a room filled with musical instruments: saxophone, clarinet, bass guitar, set of drums, and with sculptures: totemic, phallic masks, indeterminate shapes made of God knows what, suggestive of who could guess, and with paintings: jagged blobs of exploding colours, manic brushwork with eyes bursting out all over in such unlikely locations as kneecaps, toes, sandwiches, the panels of Metro trains.

And Vicky asks: 'What's the news from the streets? What's going on out there?'

'The streets,' Wellington Frog said, 'the streets, ah, baby . . . the streets, man, you better believe it . . .'

'We saw some CRS, just around the corner . . .'

'The Man is set up to blow his cool . . .' the black man shook his head as if throwing off shower water. 'Those dudes . . . They are mean, sister, and I mean mean. M–E–A–N . . . Those cats leave their house in the morning, they leave their humanity right behind them, man . . . "Hey, chérie, hang up ma humanity in that closet there . . . tough shit in the old town today . . . got to give them subversives that little old boot . . . know what I mean, ma belle?" Shit. CRS . . . They are thick on the ground like flies, like cocksuckingroaches . . . Cat escapes from the old US of A, man, the motherfucking US of A, runs like a rabbit from the pigs of Oakland, an' Watts, an' motherfucking Harlem . . . crosses the sea to Paree, man: "Hey, man, think, I'll take me a stroll in the sun, man, Paree, liberté, egalité, fraternité . . ." Shit! an' whammy! there they are again, cocksuckers, with their motherfucking riot guns an' mace an' shields like some motherfucking Roman Empire epic: "Gone to keep the Scythians under control, Ma; while I'm at it, kill you a few motherfucking Greeks for good measure . . ." Shit! These kids here think they have the streets, but a skirmish or two don't win wars. I've seen it all before . . .'

'Well, this time . . .' began Leroy.

'Shit!' said Wellington, 'let's leave it for now. Our friend is back from her travels so we're goin' to have us a celebration.'

'Right on,' said Leroy.

'Motherfucker,' said I-saac.

'Shit,' agreed J. Sig-lala.

There was an air of communion about them as they sat down on cushions and tattered stools among the litter of the room. Like a family of tigers. Two bottles of wine, a half flask of Scotch and a depleted vodka bottle appeared. Leroy Smith vanished to forage for more food while the contents of the fridge were expropriated. Bread, cheese, ham, olives, materialized on large plates covered with curious mosaic designs. Victoria squatted cross-legged with a naturalness Blok envied. He sprawled, legs thrown straight ahead, on a tatty red bean bag. He noticed the glances that were darting between Victoria and Wellington Frog. Even while they were talking about matters of state, they seemed to be carrying on another, more personal, subterranean discourse. How strange this all is, Blok thought. I came innocently to France to see Paris and here I am sitting with a beautiful English blonde and four huge American negroes gabbling away in a language that certainly Gidon Cohen, who wished to acquaint us with Life through his English classes, utterly failed to prepare us for. And yet, here I am, scoffing bread, cheese, olives, downing vodka and wine (the Scotch being his thin red line), accepted among these weirdoes. No one asks: who are you? where the fuck have you sprung from? what the fuck are you doing here? He felt a gush of maudlin emotion at the thought, but did not know how to express it. So he downed more wine. Then the great Frog produced from a shelf in a cupboard a great glass jar filled with what appeared to be an odd genus of light-green tea leaves. Deftly he rolled them into cigarette papers, lit the consequent concoction, fiercely sucking in smoke, coughed, passed it on and commenced to roll another. Blok, a non-smoker, gingerly took a puff, expelling the smoke hurriedly.

'You ain't never smoked joints before,' observed Wellington Frog amicably.

'Um . . .' said Blok, admitting his shame.

'Draw it into your lungs and hold the mother-fucker down as long as you can.' Blok did so and his face went purple. 'Let it out! Let it out!' cried the others, thumping him on the back. Collapse of Blok, in coughing fit. 'My grandmother always said,' offered Wellington Frog, 'if at first you don't

succeed, try, try again.' Leroy Smith fell over, dis-
solved in the giggles. Blok became aware they must
have been smoking the stuff all day. He raised the
paper tube again to his lips. 'Right on,' said Sig-lala.
'Have more vodka,' said I-saac, 'it gives the motherfucker that little extra *jay-nay-say-quoi* . . .'

They laid him to bed somewhere, in a room
cluttered with further eyes. Eyes in doors, eyes on
doorknobs, eyes in ship's riggings, on the backsides
of parakeets. Eyes bloodshot, ferocious, or just
melancholy, watching him through the night. In the
next room he could hear Vicky and Wellington,
whispering softly, the tinkle of her muffled laugh.
Then the creak of movement, a mattress shuffle, the
low moans and murmurs of fucking. He turned over,
pulling a cushion over his ears. Then turned again,
and put the cushion away.

Yes, and his memories take shape, cholera!

    'What was thy pitys recompense?
    A silent suffering, and intense,
    The rock, the vulture and the chain,
    All that the proud can feel of pain,
    The agony they do not show,
    The suffocating sense of woe . . .'

Malka Halperin! you, that were never mine, and
spurned me, as I lay, hands clasped in prayer,
seared with the pain I could not bear, hoping hope
was still alive, hoping against hope that hope could
survive . . .

Aaargh! What, Blok, that useless fellow, that
quivering adolescent blancmange, casts his eyes on
this Guinevere of the Fourth, Fifth and Sixth Grade,
following from bus windows, down school corridors, round corners, through peepholes and what
not with his absurd secret pash? Glowing embers
fanatically nursed in solitary alchemies . . .

Wherefrom this utter lunacy, comrades?

Imagine: once upon a time – wee Blok, Fat Avi, Square Gideon and Muki the Squint-Eyed Mutt, short-trousered over the terraced hills, thrusting planks of wood with rusty nails for masts and old torn knickers for sails into battle in the hillside cesspool; each side throwing stones to sink the other's fleets, or propel them upon jagged rocks or the sargasso sea of the rubbish tip nor'-nor'-east from which no ship returns (leviathans, masquerading as frogs, lure invisible matelots to fates worse than death in the depths) ... Ah, innocence! Blok, in prepubertal restlessness, turns his energies to churning out comic strips, space adventures, detective stories and strange plays no one can make head or tail of, on oodles of 'jora' or 'Scheisse-papier' Papa Blok brings home from the office, light blue or billious yellow sheets stencilled on one side only with the effulgence of the Jerusalem Municipality Department of Sewer Surveys ... halcyon days in the rapport department with Papa: Aye, hear, O my son, and receive my sayings, and the years of thy life shall be many ... I have taught thee in the way of wisdom, I have led thee in right paths ...

But Mama Blok says: 'Avremel! Don't stand with your hands in your pockets like that! You shouldn't be touching down there!'

Touching?? Forsooth, pretty soon *rubbing* is in full swing. Our hero's pantaloons become often stained. Mama Blok cries silent tears into the weekly laundry. Who can weigh a mother's burden? I cried unto the Lord with my voice ... I shewed before Him my trouble ... but behold refuge failed me, no man cared for my soul ...

He is mortified by his Secret Sin. Why me, from the one and a half billion males on earth? It makes you go blind, they say. He begins examining his eyes in the mirror, doing eye exercises, rolling them about as Square Gideon, who is the son of a doctor and Knows, advises. Mama Blok says to Papa: 'The boy's acting terribly strange lately. You really must have a word.' But Papa says: 'It's just growing-up pains. Leave him be, Shushu. You don't want to stunt him and end up with a midget or dwarf?' She begins measuring his height, setting up a scale in the kitchen. Blok tells his friends: 'My mother's acting terribly strange lately. I'm afraid she may be going bonkers.' 'Don't worry,' says Square Gideon, 'it's the menopause without a doubt.' Still, he cannot get rid of the feeling that Fate has dealt him, Blok, a particularly dud hand.

A girl, Daniella, is seated in front of him in class. During lessons he surreptitiously unties, from behind, the belt of her dress. Discovering this, she turns and takes a swipe at his nose. He is put out of class. His ears, his face burn.

What's this?

Blok, in the gilded cage of learning, undergoing the silent phase (unlike Fat Avi, who is always on his feet in class, currying favour, drivelling about this that and the other), suffering intensely, yearning for the saving bell, the droning of his Educators – Varkin the Physics tyrant: 'If you're a numskull d'you think I'm a numskull too?' Bar-Yotam the kibbutznik Maths master: 'Who needs the matriculation certificate? My brother's a cobbler in the kibbutz and he's perfectly content.' Vissotski, one-time English teacher, who used to sing 'There's a hole in the bottom of the sea' at end-of-year parties. Bikel, aged Biology teacher, who said: 'My genotype is blonde. Your genotype is brunette. If we made a child what colour would its hair be?' While notes of a more urgent nature pass from hand to hand under desks: 'Gidi, what's the truth about Sarah and Michah in the park?' What is Bella's secret name? Acknowledge and eat this note.' 'Why not pass a note to Gila from Gidi requesting Friendship; suggested text: "I love you madly. Will you be mine?" Over.' Halcyon days. And Kalman, thick-lipped master of Talmud and Mishna studies, breaks the chain, bellowing: 'Sodomy and rape go to a court of twenty-three judges. Blok! I am amazed you can go to sleep at this moment.'

Asleep? Not at all. He is daydreaming, as usual. Sodomy and rape? Why not? But not with Malka Halperin. For she is Holy, Divine, unbesmirched by the prurient thoughts of mere Sex. At most a chaste kiss. An electric embrace. A Marriage Has Been Arranged. Somehow – children. Grandchildren. A common grave on a hillside. The epitaph: 'In Life and In Death Were Not Parted.' Fall of curtain. Applause. But no. She is not even aware of Blok's existence, except perhaps as that awkward looney who is no good at games and goes around with the fat kid, the dumbo nature freak and that flea-bitten mongrel dog.

Let us take an objective view:

Blok – fourteen and callow as a callow youth can be. Gideon, Fat Avi, Muki the Mutt, et al., the sole companions to his soul. His hand, the sole companion to his prick. Papa Blok – philatelicus. Mama– migraines. A normal tale of Jerusalem, hotbed of sexual repression. Religion and paranoia hang in the air like a permanent hamsin. The City – surrounded on three sides by the Enemy. The streets buzzing with rumours that the infamous Nazi, Adolf Eichmann (May His Name Forever Be Erased), has been snatched by our spies in Argentina and is to be brought here to Justice. Fat Avi and Blok put a makeshift doll in a shoebox and pump it with DDT. An instant comeuppance for the butcher. (A throwback, perhaps, to earlier years when they hanged a teddy bear named Pedro upon the Blok balcony, for what crimes no one can remember: Mama Blok, taking out the washing, almost swooning at the sight of the woollen marsupial twisting slowly in the wind, its glass eyes horribly aglaze.) And from violence to Sex: Fat Avi has acquired on the sly the Hebrew translation of *Lady Chatterley's Lover*. In secret rendezvous, he reads out selected passages. (Separately, since none wants to be thought common, each has also discovered the standard salacious paperbacks that grace the lower-class kiosks, the *Stalag* series: *I Was Colonel Schultz's Bitch*, or *Stalag of Sex-Starved Women*.) Heads together, like yeshiva students bent over a passage of the Gmara, they pondered: what does it all mean? How does one get girls to do it? Why should anyone want to, anyway?

Yes, they are now in transit, from the misogynist phase. Ripe for Malka Halperin – tall, blonde, her curves beginning to fill out like a slow-motion pneumatic tyre. One day the clique is visiting See-Through, a friend who is a peripheral member. As Fate would have it, Malka Halperin lives on the ground floor of the same block of flats. As Blok and Avi stand in the stairway, pushing See-Through's doorbell, she emerges from her own door, brushes past them to open the letterbox and, letters in hand, returns homewards, nodding politely at them.

Says Fat Avi to Blok: 'You're in love with her, aren't you?'

Blok is outraged. '*Moi*? In love? You must be out of your mind!'

' 'Tis obvious,' observes Fat Avi, 'the way you followed her with your eyes. Damning evidence. Guilty as charged.'

How could this vile allegation be countered? Treason to the clique, no less. Although his friends understand. Man must Fall. Did not Adam? And he was the original model. What chance the imitations running off the production line? It will come to us too, says Fat Avi, wisely, but one must fight it to the end. Blok laughs bitterly. Not me, he says, I am immune.

To prove this to himself he begins taking notice of her. After all, they travel to school on the same bus. He sits behind her, fixing his eyes on her golden flowing hair, her brown neck and arms, the curve of her spine under the T-shirt. His eyes are private detectives, glued on her trail. He watches her in class, his head twisted leftwards as Zussman drones about stoning adulterers. Pretty soon, of course, he is smitten, enraptured, head over heels, bananas, launched on the long voyage of his private woe, the agony that does not show (and blame Gidon Cohen for topping his lessons with snips of Shelley, bursts of Byron) –

'Which speaks but in its loneliness,
And then is jealous lest the sky
Should have a listener, nor will sigh
Until its voice is echoless . . .'

Hic, haec, hoc.


**Further Adventures of Blok in Revolutionary Paris:**

He smokes his second, third and fourth joint.

He visits the Eiffel Tower.

He grooves in the outdoor cafés of the Boul-Mich.

He encounters more clochards.

He begins reading a Penguin book, *Karl Marx, Selected Writings in Sociology and Social Philosophy.*

He listens rapt to the tales of Wellington Frog,

Leroy and Co. about Oakland, Elijah Muhammad, Malcolm X, the Panthers.

He throws a stone at a flic.

He is trapped for forty-eight hours in the besieged AGF offices.

He gives blood to wounded comrades.

He is shown by Wellington Frog the five places in the body where a man can be killed by one blow. He tries none of them.

He smokes his fifth, sixth and seventh joint.

He joins in an assault on the Hôtel de Ville.

He barely escapes arrest and terrible torture in the police cells with 'toasters' and electrodes on the balls.

He runs through the sewers of Paris, with Victor Hugo and Charles Laughton in hot pursuit.

He smokes his eighth, ninth, tenth joint et cetera.

His love for Victoria is not requited.

In 1962 Blok launched a major operation to make contact with Malka Halperin. It was planned and organized to the smallest detail, like a military campaign. The mission: to create a common interest between them. Blok amazed himself with the single-mindedness with which he embarked on this task.

The first phase of the project was simple. During a period of six months a series of letters was sent, two at a time, one to her address, one to his own. The letters were anonymous, the handwriting was disguised. Their effect was to depend on feminine curiosity, a trait he had read about in books, and which Fat Avi assured him was indubitable. The letters to her contained cryptic hints of a romance between two unidentified persons, and suggested a meeting at a certain hour by the old abandoned house on the hill. The letters Blok sent himself were similar, but culminated in one in which Malka Halperin was named.

On the day of the first proposed meeting Blok

prepared himself well (it was a Sabbath) with cucumber sandwiches and a pair of binoculars borrowed from the Rebetsen Twilliger-Syphilis-Face, who said: 'Good poy. For the birds watching, yes? Day is beautiful. Exquisite, no?' So it is, he said, so it is. He was at the site early, hid securely in the bunker where the *Sturmer* volumes had been found. Through the binoculars he examined minutely every stone, every rusted shutter of the empty house, every tin can and orange peel at its foot. By sunset she had still not come. Blok made his way glumly home. ('Is good, the birds, no?' said the Rebetsen. 'Exquisite, exquisite,' said Blok.)

This recurred three times. Papa Blok, relieved that his son had a hobby that meant he would not covet the stamps, bought him a manual of ornithology, with two hundred coloured plates. Too much contact, however, with the widow downstairs was threatening to unhinge Blok's mind. He advanced the plan to Phase Two.

He sent out an even more cryptic note guaranteed to raise feminine curiosity to fever pitch. It ran: 'The truth about your trousers is known. Fly at once.'

This could not fail to lay the grounds for an approach. So Blok, plucking up courage, made his way on rubbery legs towards the back of her block. There was a bell on the jamb of the wire-net back door with 'Halperin' inscribed upon it. He stood, afflicted for a moment with knee failure. Then he pressed the bell. Nothing. He thought, good, I'm reprieved for the day. I can go home and forget the whole ridiculous plan. Then he heard the sound of the toilet flush from within, and the sound of soft, floppy footsteps.

She came to the door, dressed in white pyjamas with blue stripes, the golden hair crowning her perfect shoulders. Her divine feet clad in tatty old kitchen slippers. Here I am, take me, I'm yours . . . loyalty you could not dream of is at hand, worship Olympian Gods could not hope for, sacrifices beyond reason for one touch of your fingertips, one echo of the music of the spheres that is your voice . . .

'What's up?' she said.

'I have to talk to you urgently,' he said.

'What was wrong with the main entrance?' she said.

'I couldn't find your door.'

She threw him an odd glance. 'I don't have much time,' she said. 'Come in, but just for a minute. I have to go somewhere soon.'

He entered the hallowed portal, knocking over the rubbish bin. Clumsily he helped her sweep the trash back in the can. She offered him an orange squash, which he took with trembling hands.

'So what's it all about?'

He took a deep breath. 'I've been receiving weird letters,' he said. 'I don't know from whom. They mention your name, and set up meetings in sort of weird places. You know . . . do you know anything about it?'

'I got some stupid letters too. I didn't take any notice.'

'You didn't try to find out who wrote them?'

'I'm really not interested.' So much for feminine curiosity. Fat Avi, I shall have your hide . . .

'Don't you think you should try to turn up for one meeting? This whoever's annoying me . . . I want to know who it is . . .'

'I don't care. It doesn't bother me at all.'

'Well, maybe let me know then, if you get any more.'

'If you want. They don't bother me. I just throw them in the can.'

Blok retreated, strangely elated. She has spoken to me! Her fingers brushed mine over a glass of squash! Contact is established! She knows I exist! The locked door has opened a crack – the dialogue has begun! Courage, Blok, all may bot be lost . . .

He despatched a letter, which could not fail. It said: 'The archbishop will never agree to the status quo. Where have you put his galoshes? Saturday, 3 a.m., usual place.'

He waited there three hours, but in vain. Not a footstep, a groan or a sigh. Not a breath of her mouth, not a hair of her head to brighten the darkening sky. He remained in the bunker, alone, with the ashes of old secret fires, the droppings of lizards, the rotted bones of a starling, the flattened dry skin of a toad, the Rebetsen Twilliger-Syphilis-Face's binoculars tied round his neck with a strap from an old school satchel, till far revving roars were heard, and the headlights of the Sabbath-end buses toiled up the main road beyond. A dark mantle falls on the Judaean hills further on, concealing the tall aerials of Ramallah across the border. The city's populace stirs, ready for the night on the town; ice cream and falafel at the corners of King George and Jaffa streets, couples necking in the back of cavernous cinemas as the lumbering air-conditioning fans creek and whir above them. The madding crowd, from which Blok, sunk in gloom, is far, far away.

A month later, they executed Adolf Eichmann in a cell in Ramleh prison. The scaffold was specially built for the occasion. Carpentry firms fought for the order. They put a noose round his neck, and an anonymous guard pulled a switch, plunging him through a trap door. They cremated his body and scattered the ashes from a helicopter over the Mediterranean, beyond the Nation's territorial waters.

Papa Blok said: 'Good riddance, pascudniak!'

But Mama Blok only groaned for the victims whose ghosts had paraded during the many months of the trial.

A light earth tremor hit Safad that year. Some mystics claimed it was the first pulse of the Messiah.

Oddly enough, the Judas Pig did not put in its guest appearance until the following year.

Blok's secret passion did not wane.

LE PAVE; PARIS, MAI 1968; TRACT No. 1:

... Il est évident que le socialisme, de par sa nature, ne peut être octroyé, ne peut être établi par ukase. Il a pour condition préalable une série de mesures violentes contre la propriété, etc. Ce qui est négatif, la destruction, on peut le décréter; ce qui est positif, la construction, NON. Terre vierge. Problèmes par milliers. Seule, l'expérience est capable de faire les corrections et d'ouvrir des chemins nouveaux. Seule, une vie fermentant sans etraves s'engage dans mille formes nouvelles. Improvise, reçoit une force créatrice, corrige elle-même ses faux-pas.

ROSA LUXEMBURG

La société capitaliste crée, par la répression et le chômage, un état de violence générale. C'est contre cette violence permanente d'un régime de concurrence et de pénurie qui s'appuie sur l'autoritarisme du gouvernement, de l'enterprise, et de l'Université que les étudiants et les travailleurs se soulèvent ...

Ouvriers, employés, professeurs, étudiants, paysans, nous appartenons tous à ce que le gouvernement ose appeler la pègre. Nous occupons les usines, les bureaux, les universités, la rue ...

NOTRE FORCE EST IRRESISTIBLE!

TOUT EST POSSIBLE A LA CLASSE OUVRIERE EN ACTION!

VIVE L'UNIFICATION DE NOS LUTTES!

ETUDIANTS, TRAVAILLEURS, UNE CHANCE UNIQUE S'OFFRE A NOUS: NE LA LAISSONS PAS PASSER!

VIVE LE GREVE SAUVAGE!

MARCHE COMMUNE OU L'INTERNATIONALISME!

La Révolution est un moment d'inspiration exalté dans l'histoire.

TROTSKY

**Report from the Parisian front:**
Yeah! Motherfuckers! Pretty soon things began to get hot for Wellington Frog and Co. Shit! Les flics got the word from the Man to flush foreign agitators out of the national bloodstream. Yeah. Ain't it enough that our own long-haired intellectuals have run riot for nigh on two months now, bellowing slogans, blocking traffic, disrupting normal commerce and annoying the decent citizenry, making bizarre and impossible demands such as control of their own education, liquidation of the State, promulgation of anarchy in every sphere of activity and in general a life of excitement, 'growth' and neo-poetic 'meaning' tinged, to those in the know, with the obscurely abhorrent ideas of the ageing commie pinko Sartre? Not enough that they disseminate leaflets inciting the armed forces to mutiny, scrawl lewd and coprophagous remarks about the Président de la République on every wall and quai, and throw paving stones, rotten fruit, eggs, bottles, trash-can lids, bricks, iron bars, hub caps, tyres,

manhole covers, grilles, pigeon carcasses, flower-pots, tiles, cellophane bags filled with piss and excreta, inkpots, paint, sulphur bombs and even Molotov cocktails at the representatives of Law and Ordure? Shit! On top of all this, do we have to tolerate, mollycoddle and nurse outsiders who, under the cloak of our Gallic hospitality, and at the behest of foreign and hostile powers, engage in the stoking of fires, the pouring of benzine on blazing battlefields? And not just any foreigners, mind you, but COMMIE NIGGERS, BLACK PANTHERS who have infiltrated into our bosom, COP-KILLERS from the American ghettos with French visas stamped in their passports by Communist Party moles (prob-ably Jews too) in Our Immigration Service, or even without, come to think of it, snuck in under orders from MOSCOW and PEKING with the sole, express and declared intention of spreading the poisonous gospel of the Jew MARX, the spick GUEVARA, the slant-eyes HO and MAO and the coons MALCOLM X and AMILCAR CABRAL and, as a treacherous and bestial means to this end, have, no doubt, pawed, slobbered over and put their huge vile black penises into our innocent jeune filles, thus cutting them off from THE RACE – do we have to accept all this quietly?

A thousand times–*NON!!*

Remembering Tonkin and the Casbah, Dien Bien Phu and the Rif, the Avengers – in thick booties, armoured shields and mace à la mode, armed with warrants in the shape of large sledgehammers and full clips of 9mm bullets – come crashing in one fine morning (the sun bright in blue blue sky over the Tuileries, the birdies in the trees a-twitter) at the door of 13 Rue Danton (Apt 19), ready to blast the damn kaffirs into total oblivion at the merest hint of resistance. But, merde, alors! les oiseaux have departed, leaving the apartment empty of all but softly swirling dust and a portrait in oil of the Head of State disappearing nose first into his own arsehole. Rat-tat-tat-tat! Patrolman Fouchet, with his Uzzi, riddles the atrocity right between the eyes, a row of holes dissecting the bum cheeks, before Sergeant Babouche, with his trusty flame-thrower, zaps it to a smoky ruin.

Meanwhile, the scene is this: Frog and Co., tooling up the motorway towards Belgium – five men, one woman, packed in an orange Fiat. Wellington Frog at the wheel, Isaac beside him, noisily consuming jambon. Mahmud, crushed in the left back corner, glumly silent and brooding. Victoria and Blok, pressed together between him and Leroy Smith, zonked on terminal fatigue. Blok can feel her left breast up against his right arm. Happiness. Wellington waves his hand out of the window at the bright landscape passing (the cows, the sheep, the grassy valleys, hills, church spires et cetera):

'Ah, la belle France, motherfucker!'

Blok, the Innocent, escaping from the fiery furnace –

This is How it Happened: 24th May, after two weeks of riots, General de Gaulle spoke out. O, la France, la France . . . This cannot go on, mes amis . . . He dangled a referendum, a red rag to the bulls. The CGT union held two restrained demonstrations, with the motto Provoke Not the Cops. Elsewhere, however –

– Out of the Latin Quarter, everybody who was anybody swarmed . . . A hundred thousand gathered at the Gare de Lyon. The atmosphere was electric. One's hair stood on end. They would have stormed the Bastille, a hundred yards down the road, but it had already been done over, one and three-quarter centuries previously. They would have pulled down the Vendôme Column, but that

too had been accomplished, on 16th May 1871. No
stone head of Bonaparte to roll in the dust, hélas.
Nevertheless, suggestions swirled in the maelstrom
of youthful discontent: the Champs-Elysées? String
the bastard up by his vile proboscis? Too fortified,
too extreme . . . the Hôtel de Ville, which no self-
respecting French Revolution could pass up? But it,
too, was surrounded by CRS, army, armoured cars,
machine guns, poison gas; the hedgehog state with
all bristles erect . . . the Ministries likewise. But
what the heck! Après moi la deluge! A moaning,
undulating leviathan, the great insurrection flows,
eddies, surges over the Pont Neuf. Nearby, the
Tuileries loom dark against a stark red sunset. A
Kodacolor dream. Hee haw, hee haw, the evening
traffic blares, the brazen ass of the bourgeoisie
gives tongue. In vain. Like a papier-mâché beast in
a Japanese epic the cataclysm swallows all in its
path. Gobble, gobble, gobble! The CRS guarding the
Louvre quake and quiver. Is it here they are heading, the new Visigoths, to sack Our Glorious Heritage (sarcophagi from Egypt, marbles from Greece,
masks from Senegal)? No, the sons and daughters
of the bourgeoisie pass by, sparing the Palaces of
Culture. Onwards they press across the Rue de
Rivoli, thousands of fists shaking, thousands of
voices raised, hundreds of banners rippling in the
swell – 'CE N'EST QU'UN DEBUT, CONTINUONS
LE COMBAT!!'

There is Blok: you can identify him in the mass by
the same knot of surrounding black faces, the aureole of blonde by his side. True, he does look a little
lost. After all, people are chanting slogans he does
not understand, and their faces are contorted with
enthusiasms he does not really share. He is, after
all, a tourist. Only the other day he popped a postcard of the Eiffel Tower in the letter box to Mama:

\*     \*     \*

Having a great time. Paris is wonderful. Meeting new friends from different cultures. Atmosphere a bit hectic. Will write longer letter soon.

Indeed. Victoria is holding a placard which reads: 'VIVE L'UNITE DES SOLDATS AVEC LES OUVRIERS, LES PAYSANS, ET LES ETUDIANTS', though no one knows how she came by it. Wellington and comrades are uniformed in black leather jackets, berets with red stars (which Victoria sewed on overnight) and sunglasses. Everyone is impressed with their ferocious look, which is in fact so militant that there is a recognizable space between them and the surrounding throng, as if people fear if they crowded them they might be seized and garrotted en passant. Leroy had prepared a placard, which got lost on the way: 'OAKLAND PANTHERS FOR WORLD REVOLUTION'.

'La Bourse!!' The cry rises from every direction. The crowd has hit at last on a target. The dragon shakes itself, thrusts on into the Rue Etienne Marcel, pausing reflexively by Notre Dame des Victoires – a soupçon of desecration perhaps? Clergy hung by their bellropes, peals sounding for the throttled Quasimodos? Mitres, croziers, pews, pulpit, devoured in a counter auto-da-fé? No, the horde surges on to the steps of the Stock Exchange, where it ebbs, changes shape, coalesces around the forbidding structure. Up the steps, like the proles of *Metropolis*, swarm the front ranks. Three uniformed guards at the main doors take one look and scarper. Cohn-Bendit, at the top of the stairs, gobbles into a microphone. Red banners wave at the very gates of Capital, shades of 'eighty-nine, 'forty-eight, 'seventy-one . . . The crowd pours in at the entrance, Blok, Wellington, Victoria and Co., borne along like corks upon rapids. Mon dieu! The night watchmen vanish into the walls, under staircases, into out trays. In and out of offices the students scurry, carrying off mounds of papers. Situationist comrades orchestrate the sacking. Heave ho! The documents, lockers and files are flung over the balustrades into the trading hall. Blok pulls back, wheezing heavily, his back to a wall, under a portrait of Clemenceau. Someone shoves a Molotov cocktail into his hand, its petrol-soaked rag aflame, claps him merrily on the back, cries 'Bonne chance!' and melts away into the crowd. He looks at it stupidly. 'Wake up, Avram!' shouts Victoria. 'That fucking thing is real!' He comes to with a start, turns, looks about and, with all the strength he can muster, hurls it into the empty trading hall. Desks, papers and cabinets burst into flames. 'Out! Out! Out!' cries Wellington Frog. Grabbing Blok by the arm and Victoria round the waist, he bowls them back down the stairs to the entrance, Leroy, I-saac, Sig-lala and Mahmud covering their retreat with brass candlesticks.

Yes, children, that's how it was. (Crackle crackle, the flames, me-oh-my, the police cars, Urrah! the crowd, Merde, alors! the Head of State in his bunker. Shit, man! Motherfucker! the Panthers, licking their lips.)

*Le Figaro*, the next day, carried the following description of the 'petrolleur' of the Bourse:

> . . . a tall, thin figure in an old grey sports jacket, bespectacled, with a fringe of boyish beard and moustache. Dark, with, some say, a 'semitic' nose. Perhaps Algerian or Lebanese. He was said to be highly excitable, bent clearly on an orgy of savage destruction . . .

The police issued an identikit picture, but it did not look much like Blok. Apart from the spectacles, it bore a distant resemblance to Abu Jilda, the notorious Palestinian bandit. Nevertheless, given the presence of police spies in the throng, and the proximity of black faces around him, the company could take no chances. The flat in Rue Danton was cleared, the artworks and instruments whisked to a safe house, and the gang decamped en masse to stay in the apartments of friends. Blok – on the run. The portrait of Abu Jilda – on the wall of every police station in France. Fernandel-like cops quaffed their vin rouge, devoured their *pain*, beneath 'wanted' posters. Plain-clothed men who had spent their whole lives trying to look like Jean Gabin studied the features closely. A psychologist analysed them in *Paris Match*:

> The nose [he wrote], which some have superficially described as 'semitic', or 'jewish', is in fact at an angle due to the contortion of the facial muscles, brought about by a lifetime of mistrust, fear and suspicion. The twisted mouth and 'hangdog expression' bear witness to the numbing effects of unceasing pathological impulses. This face gives the lie to the canard, so beloved of 'liberal' sociologists, that crime is produced by the environment, by the pressures of poverty, the vicissitudes of a difficult childhood or a broken home. This man, at any rate, is clearly a hereditary criminal, a degenerate personality.

Blok sent another postcard to Mama:

> Things are still a bit hectic, so only a short note. Still having a good time. Lots of Paris night life. Will probably be going to London soon, some friends have offered a lift. Hope you are both well. Love to the Rebetsen and Gaga-the-Bulgarian-Bloodhound!'
>
> Servus, Avremel.

On receiving this note, Mama Blok went into a spasm. 'He's going with shiksas!' she cried. 'Paris

night life! I knew it would happen! 'chob gesagt –
it's just as I always feared . . . !'

'Good luck to him,' said Papa, looking up only
briefly from a rare Patagonian Air Mail. 'A good
screw's what the doctor ordered. All holes are the
same in the dark.'

'Your mind is a cesspool, Baruch Blok,' said
Mama. 'I should have listened to my father. He said
you would turn out a scoundrel.'

'Late thoughts, like late fruits, are sour,' said
Papa, screwing in his viewing glass. 'Time the boy
sowed some wild oats,' he mumbled, but Mama had
retired to her couch.

Ah, qu'elle est belle, La France! The orange Fiat
rattles through Artois, approaching the minor
border post of Condé sur l'Escaut.

'Any trouble, you just ram her through, man,' says
Mahmud, 'just ram her right through the pigs . . .'

'Don't worry,' says Wellington, 'our papiers are
in order. As long as we ain't running nothing
through the lines. We gotta be prepared to be
searched. Even if we make it here we could be in
trouble at Dover. Those British pigs are thorough.'

'Better smoke up the rest of the dope then,' says
I-saac.

'Man, you crazy? I told you to leave that behind!'

'Hey, man, just a toke or two for the road . . .'

'Shit!'

'Don't worry, man, it'll be all gone by Condé . . .'

'!!*!**!!!'

'. . . motherfucker . . .'

Putta-putta-putta, the orange Fiat skims on,
enveloped in Lebanese haze . . . Blok, high as an
escaped kite, glimpses the nirvana of chaos. He
floats, gracefully, above the fray.

There let us leave him a while . . .

'You can't make an omelette without breaking eggs.'

'I can see the broken eggs; where's the omelette?'
– from Victor Serge, *Memories of a Revolutionary*

**Truth or Consequences: a Tale of Nurse Nili-Honey:** Nurse Nili-Honey first joined the staff of the Klander Institute in 1966. Her full name is Nili Grunbaum-Yakir. Her date of birth was 12th January 1946. Like Blok, she was a child of the post-war hope. Her place of birth was Poznan, Poland, or what was left of it. Her father had been an officer in the Polish communist underground, and had spent the entire war in freezing dug-outs in the depths of the Zamosc forest. For years he could recognize no one unless their features were caked with snow. The partisans would hide in their holes by day and emerge by night, at the howling of wolves, to walk, crawl or sled their way towards the heartbeat of German blood. His name was Janek Grunbaum, his code name was Fox, but his comrades called him 'Granit' since throughout the war he was never once seen smiling. His face cracked for the first time since 1939 when he met a girl, with whom he had been at school, pottering about in the ruins of their Poznan neighbourhood upon his return from battle. She was his only link with his past, he was her only link with hers, since both their families had died in the camps. They were married by a civilian clerk who demanded fifty cigarettes for his services. Then they buried their mutual past in a field of rubble – a black battered box, filled with faded torn photographs garnered between the two of them. Nili often thought of that box – the sole evidence of her roots – lying under the foundations of some ill-attended youthclub, tavern or council monolith in the rebuilt city.

Janek Grunbaum's Dilemma:
So They decorated him with the Order of Valour (First Class) and gave him a top job in the Party hierarchy. But in 1950 he wrote a report criticizing inefficiencies and corruption in Party circles. Naive schmuck. They denounced him as a Nationalist, Zionist and petit-bourgeois deviationist. But he was lucky. He spent only four years in jail. This was because he signed no confession, not even of his own name. All who signed any paper whatever were lost. A salutary lesson to us all. On release, Janek Grunbaum, reunited with Marta, his beloved, eked out his life as a cypher. But then, far to the east, the tyrant Djugashvili died. The ice began to thaw. Doggie leashes were loosened. Janek Grunbaum, however, saw no future in the land which had betrayed his ideals. He and Marta had a daughter who was being taunted at school with anti-semitic jibes. He remembered the years in the freezing holes, frostbite, Germans and death. He recalled the jibe about 'Zionism'. He thought, what the heck. In 1956, when emigration restrictions were eased, the nuclear family took train and ship to Irael.

*    *    *

But Lo and Behold!
They settled in a kibbutz, on the coastal plain,
which had been named Mas'at-Nefesh. That meant
'soul's desire', or perhaps 'wish-fulfilment'. It was
a place of green lawns, puttering water sprinklers,
fertile fields of wheat, barley, sugarbeet, with
peach trees and cherry orchards. Most of the members were from Eastern Europe, though there was a
small clique of Tunisians. Janek became a tractor
driver, and Marta, his wife, the head nurse of the
commune. But two years later, in 1958, he suddenly
died of a heart attack. What?! Four years in the
snow, twenty-five below zero, subsisting on kasha
and roots, walking fifteen, twenty miles a night,
four more years in a cell, with mould and inter-
rogators, then to kick the bucket at the prime of life,
forty-seven years of age, in the haven of his salvation? Granit, smashed by happiness? Everyone was
astonished, including himself, for as they wrapped
the shroud round him his face was still fixed in the
rigor of total amazement.

Life Goes On:
The little girl and her mother mourned, but the community helped to soften the blow. The girl went to
school. The mother met and moved in with a genial
farmer named Sasha, a large fellow of graceful
ungainliness or ungainly grace, with a shock of
brown curly hair, a snub nose and a great pot belly
which protruded under his vest as he sat for hours
on the verandah. They never married, but Nili, at
eighteen, added his family name, Yakir, to her own.
He was an easy man to like, but he was not Granit.
Despite her love for Sasha, Nili sought Granit ever
after.
    One day, on her way to secondary school in
Hadera, Nili, now sixteen, met a soldier on the service bus. The seat beside her was the only one left

unoccupied. 'May I sit here?' he said. She nodded, with a fleeting smile. He was a large, ruddy man of about twenty-five, broad-shouldered, red-haired and sporting a flaming red moustache. He was a captain in the regular army. They chatted as the bus rattled manically down narrow roads, the fragrance of the citrus groves like a brightening drug in the dry heat of spring. When they got off at Hadera he asked if he might see her again. She invited him to her home in the kibbutz. He came on Friday afternoon, Eve of Sabbath. Marta Grunbaum baked her speciality chocolate cake. Sasha snoozed in the deckchair on the verandah, curly hairs sticking out of every gap in his outsize net vest. The water sprinklers, putta-putta-putta, on the lawns. Utopia beckoning in the soft silence, tempered only by the dissonant digging in a private allotment, the sharp yap of a dog, the wind in the bougainvillaeas.

He went by a strange nickname, of which he was perversely fond – Eisav. The name on his identity card was Ilan – 'Sapling' – but it was never used. His original name was his unrevealed secret, for he was a Holocaust orphan, brought at the age of nine to the shores of Palestine, to the children's farm of Ben Shemen. Before that he had been a number, a blurred pinpoint in the refugee mass. He had no family and no close friends, and was a Sub-Operations Officer of a Northern Command battalion. He had taken part in retaliation raids, and had parachuted at the Mitleh Pass with Arik Sharon and with the legendary Colonel Zetz. Marta Grunbaum viewed him somewhat coolly from the first, but Nili saw the ghost of Granit. Yes, and his voice was the Voice of Jacob, soft, low and mellow. He slept that night on the guest room couch, had supper and breakfast with the family in the communal dining room, and left for his base in the morning. A week after, Nili and he met secretly in an empty shack on the farm to which she had secured the key, and made passionate love till dawn. Years later, to Blok, she related:

'It was something I couldn't describe, and wouldn't even want to try . . . an Olympus, a ride in the clouds . . . It was everything that sounds corny and trite, but was very real for me.'

Indeed, thought Blok. And he might have added: Amor fati, like Nietzsche's . . .

Now Eisav was a man of few words, and them mostly of immediate, pragmatic use. Affirmative. Negative. All in order, sir. Proceeding forthwith. Mission accomplished. All forces returned safely to base. His life was the army, the army his life. But Nili liberated in him a capacity for communication he had not hitherto imagined. Torrents, tides, fountains, floods, hidden geysers of undiscovered thoughts, virgin emotions. He gushed, flowed, bubbled, steamed, spilled over in their dead-of-night debates, discussions, marathon discourses, marathons; exchanging longings, aspirations, dreams, visions, apocalyptic fears. Swept away, the Polish girl was swept away in the tornado of his needs, Granit, melted by the power of her love, possessed by, possessing, wholly, without question, doubt or hesitation. Amor fati, grand amour, olympus of the soul . . .

Marta Grunbaum caught him alone one afternoon when the girl had been sent on an errand. 'I'll marry her,' the soldier said. 'Over my dead body!' said mother. 'Marriage at sixteen? Cholera! The girl's a free agent, and she will stay that way for a while yet. You will take care of her, you will take proper precautions, and if you get her pregnant, or hurt her in any way I will personally come after you, big soldier boy, hero or no hero, Mitleh Pass or no Mitleh Pass, and break every bone in your body. I want that understood, without ifs or buts, just like that, punkt, over and out.'

Ah, so much certainty in the air. The Sixties, an optimistic era. He gave her his word and, we have to say, he kept it. As far as he could, and within reason, and for a serious length of time. Despite the pain of the passing of years, and the dance that she led him, and the terrors of his nights, cataclysms of his days, he did, plod-plod, keep his promise. He had staying power. One thing one could not say of Eisav: that the furrow he ploughed was a shallow one.

Nili, following her mother's profession, enrolled in a nursing college. Eager for the best, she applied and was accepted for a course at the Hadassah Hospital. She passed her army service as a nurse, in a time of calm before the storm. There she became involved in psychiatric nursing, in ego combat with reluctant soldiers. Eventually demobilized, she was accepted for a job at Klander and entered the fold. She took a flat with another student nurse, in the same Jerusalem suburb where Avram Blok had his unfortunate encounter with the Friedmans and Patrolman Abutbul. 'Your bad luck,' she said to Blok in a moment of brusqueness. 'If you'd toddled a bit further down the road for your peek you might have seen something more juicy.'

Thus was born Nurse Nili-Honey, wonder of Klander: the eighth marvel of the world. Like a knife through butter she moved in her milieu, charming doctors, ensnaring patients, weaving a tight web of total control about every heterosexual male. Let it be said, she was no raving beauty. But tall, well-built, auburn-haired, with a smile in the eyes that spelled mischief and trouble and, apparently, ready for anything. If the madness got under her skin she showed little outward sign of it. She would comment approvingly at the throw of Old Leib who, fly open, hands hard at work, would climax in her direction. She was adept at avoiding more tactile advances and only once had to resort to defensive action, uppercutting a somewhat lissom Croatian who leapt on her from the stairs. She performed miracles in getting patients to take their pills, go to the bathroom, attend therapy and group meetings; dealing with the incontinent, calming fits and deliria and foiling assaults on the Nachtnebel Annexe. She received dozens of offers of marriage each year, and was once left an estate of forty-five trillion dollars by a Litvak who had swept streets all his life, from Memel to Koenigsberg, from Gdansk to Trieste, from Bnei Brak to the Jaffa Road (yes, off to the morgue he went, wheeled along the tunnel, clutching his broom in rigor).

Since Eisav had pierced her virginity, fulfilling the mission to the best of his abilities, there had been, give or take, some eight lovers. First, a young intern from Hadassah, who was gentle but nondescript. Second, a footballer of Moroccan extraction who was good at the sideways dribble. Third, a married eye surgeon of international repute. Fourth, a tattooed merchant seaman. Fifth, a starving bisexual writer. Sixth, a student of Spinoza. Seventh, Male Nurse Elkayam, the strong man. Eighth, a handsome young drifter from Haifa. And others, lost in the mists of time . . .? She also had as well the numerous platonic relationships with various waifs and strays encountered at railway stations, grocery stores, park benches, cafés or in midnight gutters. There was a pimply soldier of eighteen who had tried to cut his wrists, in an alley behind Hamashbir. A politician of the National Religious Party, who was terrified by the loss of his faith. 'Have I lost God or has he lost me?' he agonized in the Ta'ami café at three o'clock in the morning. There was a young sephardi girl escaping a violent husband, found collapsed at the Haifa bus station. And a Polish old clothes man, perched on a fence, reading a Stefan Zweig novel.

These and others of similar ilk were likely to be marched up to the flat in Onkelos Street, Number –, undressed, washed, fed and put to bed in the lounge at any hour of the day or night, Hava, her flatmate, having long become accustomed to this curious compulsion.

You see, Nili had a special talent for listening, which was so rare in a culture of criers, sooth-sayers, false prophets and preachers of doom. She would sit, chin on hand, head cocked just a bit to one side, her blue eyes, blinking not very often, fixated on the person before her, pouring out his or her woes, over an Eshel yoghurt or an omelette. Sufferings, anxieties, anguish, afflictions, angst, miseries, despair – the slings and arrows of outrageous fortune, Nili deftly fielded them all. She was a walking Klander Institute, and no one but she could know how much was cathected and discharged without and how much remained within. Outwardly she pranced, swore, blew kisses, back-slapped, yelled coarsely, brayed like a hyena. Eisav would appear periodically, only to be introduced to current lovers as her cousin from the wilds of Galilee. Sometimes he would stand outside her flat in the rain, looking morosely at the drawn curtains. Sometimes he would be inside, in her bed. Nobody quite understood this. Flusser said to her: 'Nili, you are a force of nature. But because of this, beware earthquakes.' And yet the lava continued to gather, sloshing about inside her. Slosh slosh, as Avram Blok joined the cast list, bearing his own burden . . .

In his second week at Klander, Blok attended a group therapy meeting chaired by Flusser in person. It was held in the ground-floor session room, overlooking the eastern garden. Outside, the December rain whipped cypress-tops and lashed against the windows. Inside, both central heating and electric fires were full on, giving the cream-tiled room the air of a Turkish bath lobby. Flusser sat on an ordinary wooden folding chair, leaning forward on an old oak cane. Tufts of white hair, horn-rimmed glasses, red cheeks in a nexus of wrinkles. Daddy. Twelve patients, in a semi-circle, pensively faced him.

Blok was introduced as 'our young friend here, who is with us for a short while'. The only other newcomer was Charlie, a sullen youth of seventeen, also a court assignee for pouring a bucket of piss, as a regular pastime, over his own mother. The rest were long-term patients, though only four were regular group-attenders: Paradjanov, who believed the football Toto held a code for the meaning of life. Scriabina, who saw every person about her as two, three or four people. Davidov, who seldom passed up a chance to shoot his mouth off about everything. Bertha Bloom, who was pregnant with the Atomic Bomb. The remaining six were foul weather fans: Benesch, the Magpie, who hid useless things all over the place, and whose detritus could be found clogging holes and drainpipes months after he'd left on remission. Margarita Conforti, who was a machine controlled by the Bulgarian OGPU. Almozlino, an ancient Iraqi reliving his youth in Baghdad. Old Leib, who – on and off – still believed he was back in Block Twenty-seven, singled out for Experimentation. Shrik, who heard Arabs tunnelling under the earth. Srul, who was an Elder of Zion.

'At our last meeting,' said Flusser, 'Almozlino was beginning to tell us about Baghdad, and the sense of loss he felt having left there. Perhaps it would be a good idea to start off by going on with your story.'

'It was a sunny day,' said the old man, 'on the riverbank, opposite the Isle of Pigs. I was lounging

93

about, sick of hauling sacks for Hawadja Johnson for three piastres a day. I see her, under a palm tree. Her sleeves are up to her elbow. Her blouse allows me a glimpse of the white tower of her neck. Her hair is raven, her eyes blackcurrants. Her teeth are ivory . . .'

'Sounds like the Supersol . . .' mumbled Davidov, but Flusser raised his cane.

'. . . my heart leaps. Perhaps she is one of the "modern" students at the conservatoire. Such girls are not like the traditional Jewish shrews who open their legs to no one without cash or 'ktuba' . . . I examine my hands. They are clean, I have even shaved in the morning. The signs are provident. I approach her. She looks up, curious but unafraid . . .'

'I thought of a number in the night,' said Paradjanov, 'six-seven-nine-five, seven-eight-two B. At dawn there were floods in Indo-China. Many people and cattle were drowned.'

'The river is the mirror of the Gods,' I say to her, 'do you come here often?' She looks into the distance and smiles. 'Observe the sun,' I say, 'sparkling off the ripples like a hundred thousand gems. I often marvel how the waters flowed past this spot, for a thousand, ten thousand years, past high priests, kings, wazirs, sorcerers, common people, lovers . . .' She turns her head, showing me the full radiance of her smile. 'My name is Mardukh,' I tell her, 'Mordekhai, the Jew.' She says nothing, but shrugs in a manner that makes my heart heave. 'I come here every day,' I say, 'at exactly the same hour.' She does not answer, but strides off towards the town. The next day Hawadja Johnson, the swine, catches me by the collar. You shirker, he cries, I will dock you a full week's pay! I tell him where to put it, I do not have to live by licking the backside of a rabid dog. He foams at the mouth,

94

trying to strike me down with his cane. I strike him, like this, with my fist. He falls, eating dust, spitting bile, calling for the gendarmerie. I run, twisting through the labyrinth of the souk, shaking the bastards off my trail. By the time I arrive at the river the sun is high in the sky. It is noon, and the girl is not there . . .'

'Why are we listening to this rubbish?' asked Davidov, who was in a depressive phase. 'We heard the same story the last time!'

'And the time before that!' cried the Magpie, hiding someone's scarf in his pants. 'And before! Since the days of the Deluge, the same old fucking romance!'

'Yes, I fucked her!' Almozlino shouted suddenly, stabbing his forefinger in the air, 'I fucked her good and proper in the end! On the rug in the conservatoire study! I stuck it to her! I balled her like crazy! She never had it so good in her life!' He stood up, hurling a rain of spittle from which people took shelter with headscarves, bandannas and handkerchieves, yelling 'I fucked! I fucked! I fucked! I fucked!', an endless insistent litany. Flusser, watching inert, owlishly blinking. Male Nurse Marciano, hands folded, wary, keeping an eye on the door. The rain, spattering against closed windows. Almozlino sits back and cries. It wells out of his eyes, running down his grizzled cheeks like thawing mountain streams. Old Leib toddles over, takes his head in his arms, croons softly: 'There there, don't take any notice . . . all of them Nazis, you know . . .'

'I did fuck her!' Almozlino sobs. 'I fucked them all! Tall ones, short ones, fat ones, thin ones, three, four, five a day . . . sisters, mothers, aunts, granddaughters, virgins, convent nuns . . .'

'Great days . . .' soothes Old Leib, 'before the

Nazis came. Stand straight, look them in the eye. We don't cry in front of them. We don't go like sheep to the slaughter. We hold our heads high and spit in their faces. What's death to us? We've died a thousand times. We just spit in their faces.'

Almozlino: I'm a dead man . . . I'm the corpse of a dog . . . I'll never fuck again . . .

Old Leib: You'll show them. You'll spit on their graves.

Almozlino: Never again . . . (*he takes out his limp pecker in full sight of the congregation*)

Davidov: Oh shit!

Scriabina: Ach! he has three of them!

Almozlino: Dead as a dog.

Margarita Conforti . . . Dead souls . . . snow, damn you, snow! Well, you wanted it that way. Bitch! you hated them all! all the bloody lot of them. Dripping piss and shit. To their ears! Move a hand on your own then . . . *They* wouldn't let you. *They* want an ocean of tears. Every breath, on the elec-trocombobulator. Dictators of the Bulgariat! Hell, milestones . . . who gives a shit! molten lava, okianos of dung . . .

Srul . . . those were the times, in the shop, when messages were passed to and fro . . . A box of matches – the torch of freedom! By the Orient Express! always the last carriage – men, women, dogs, chickens. Keys to the pedigrees. Zorastrian coats of arms. Oh yes! burnt offerings . . . Frozen intestines – three fifty a kilo. And the poison pens. Voltaire – we got *him* that way. And Yossi Goebbels too! Method? Results! didn't we? volcanoes? didn't we see it all, Leibeh, before?

And on, and on . . .

Davidov: It's a madhouse. You can't hear yourself think.

Almozlino: Then in 1941 they burned down the synagogue. They slit throats over the ark of the law.

I was fucking the wife of a notable in the Ezrat Nashim. They doused the building with petrol. Get out! Save yourself! She lay there, smiling ... I leaped, gazelle-like, over balconies ... burned to the ground ... every last candlestick, every menorah, goblet ... ark, book, woman, flesh burns so easy ... how I laughed ...

Margarita: ... or move a leg! an arm! switch off on your own! over to Commitaj Flusser! the dis-colectrodifer ... Shit, not a chance! God, these people are disgusting ...

Srul: We did it to ourselves, hey Leibeh? We showed them all! They thought we were suckers! we fooled them all! Well ... bide our time again. Two thousand years, wagonwheels ... I saw it all, didn't I, Leibeh? Mose, Ike, Abie, They took the Book! Oh yes, no flies on them. Ach! Ach! what a waste! what a fucking waste. Eh, Leibeh? Eh? Eh? Eh?

Old Leib began humming the litany for the dead: 'El Maleh rahamim ...' God, full of mercy.

Davidov (*shaking his head*): 'A lost case, every one of them. They'll stay here till their bones crumble. And you know the best joke of all?' he turned to Blok, beside him, 'my insurance is paying for this! God almighty! I can't take any more of it.' He stood up. 'I'm off. You coming?'

'Not yet,' said Blok for no reason, 'I think I'll stay to the end.'

'Your funeral,' said Davidov, pouting glumly, and walked directly out of the room. Blok turned back to face the blinking gaze of Flusser in the fallen lull.

'I remember,' Blok suddenly said, surprised at the sound of his own voice, 'years ago, when the Eichmann trial was on, I collected newspaper cuttings of every day of the trial. I didn't really know why I was doing it, or what it all meant to me. Holocaust, and Six Million Dead, those were phrases I couldn't connect with. Witnesses came, witnesses went, I cut out their photographs. I remember feeling at the time, that . . . they seemed unsympathetic to me . . . I mean many of them . . . the more they described their sufferings the less able I was to . . . empathize with them . . . Why did they want to re-live all that? Was it a sort of masochism? Revenge, retribution, for the man in the glass cage? A small, weaselly clerk, squinting through thick-rimmed spectacles . . . I found I could neither hate nor fear him. Nor even pity him, the whole stage-play appeared absolutely meaningless. The men and women of the past, naked on the brink of mass graves, were they really the same people who put on white shirts and ties and gave their evidence at the great Eichmann show? I felt totally confused. What were these witnesses to me? Many had faces very like my relations', the ones I had never liked. The ones who always mumbled rubbish about the Old Days, and why we should Never Forget . . . and how in the name of that we should ourselves become brutes, in the war they bequeathed to us . . . What I wanted to say was . . . well . . . as I see it . . . we can't be obsessed with the past. We can only live each moment as it comes along. That's all we can actually deal with . . . or just . . . just give up, I suppose. Well, anyway . . . that's all I had to say . . .'

There was silence, except for the stentorian snoring of Bertha Bloom who was fast asleep. Margarita Conforti gazed at the ceiling. Srul smacked his lips absently. Old Leib in the corner; Charlie bewildered, fidgeting, twirling his thumbs; Almozlino down in the dumps, head sunk low, carefully perusing his crotch; Shrik as wrapped up in himself as he had been when the session started; Paradjanov flaked out. Benesch, the Magpie, sending Blok a shrewd look from the corner of his eye.

Flusser beaming widely, hands loose on his cane. Spatter spatter, the rain outside.

'Well,' said Flusser, 'food for thought from our young friend. Does anyone wish to chew the cud?'

No one did. Flusser wrapped up the meeting, nominating the next wank for Thursday. Exeunt all, luno intacto. The Magpie, on the way out, was stopped by Marciano and, casually but firmly, divested of two scarves, three handkerchieves, a watch, two keyrings and a number of kitchen spoons. 'Frankista!' hissed the felon, shaking his fist at authority. 'At Guadalajara, icho de puta, we shot fifty like you before breakfast!' Blok, strangely depressed, tried to bother Nili, but she was sunk in her own troubles.

Now Eisav's problem was simple, if inexorable. Since the army was and remained his only true family, he could only accomplish a full sense of social engagement within its apotheosis: war. War provided the extended clan of civilians in uniform a veritable orgasm of belonging. Not that Eisav enjoyed the killing. He was no butcher, ghoul, SS guard. It was just that he was at his best when killing was the job at hand. In uniform, in full combat gear – with belt and sidepockets and Uzzi nuzzling his thigh and the weight of the netted steel helmet on his head – squatting low on the flank of the foremost half track as it bucked and roared through desert dust towards the final, inexorable gamble with death, he felt fully and completely alive. The only other occasions he felt anything similar were the first four times in Nili's bed. There was nothing he could do about this odd fact, for it was the very core of his being. The killing itself he justified thus: I am taking the same chance as the poor fucking bastard whom I am shooting at. We each place the revolver of Russian roulette to our sweat-encrusted temples.

The parachute jump over the Mitleh Pass, 29th October '56. Eisav, nineteen years old, an expendable corporal, dropped in the second wave. Poised at the hatch, the burning wind tugging at his shirt and face, the black stars of anti-aircraft fire erupting like overdone popcorn over the ochre range below, the strap flapping above him, the next man breathing down his neck, the red light and the roar of the old Dakota, it first struck him – *kerwang!* – through the blood vessels: His vision cleared, the plane seemed light as a glider, the thrum of the engine seemed to be in his head, the very pulse of his brain cells. It was definitely what Colonel (later General) Zetz called 'Reincarnation Blues'. 'You *know*,' said Zetz, 'you *know* you have been here before. Like Patton in Tunis, you *know* you've been out there, thousands of years ago, with a mule-hide shield and an anvil-forged sword, with the High Priest laying God's blessing upon you. The Lord God of Hosts, sonny. Believe me, when it hits you, mother's cunt, you'll *know*.'

He dropped, and floated, rising in the blast of desert heat. Sun, be still in Gibeon, and the Moon in the valley of Ayalon . . . there is nothing new under the sky. Below, he could see the scurrying forms of the first wave running for rocky cover. Some dots, black on desert yellow, were not moving. He landed, and there was Zetz at his side, his brawny arm helping him unharness the chute. The chatter of machinegun fire echoing across the Pass. Zetz pointed. He looked up ahead. The closest racket was coming from a niche in the rock two hundred yards on. There was a glint of sun on steel. Dust flowing from the crack. Zetz pulled him down, grinding his face in the ground. He could hear the bullets pass, like the angriest wasps in the world. Then Zetz was up and away, zigzagging up the hill, followed almost immediately by the clapping thunder of exploding grenades. 'Zetz!' He threw himself in his commander's wake. Zetz was at the cavern's mouth, pressed to the rock, emptying his clip inside, plastering the niche without aiming. Eisav ran, pressed flat to the rock beside him. 'There's still life in there!' Zetz bellowed. Eisav opened fire at a blur. An Egyptian soldier twitched and exploded in a red and black splodge. He could just glimpse the flash of two rolling eyes before they too were sunk in the smudge. Two more grenades went in, throwing splinters of rock to gash his forehead and cheek. He leapt into the dust cloud, emptying his entire clip, releasing, thrusting in a second. Zetz said: 'That's enough, it's over.' Eisav stood, choked in swirling particles. His knees were trembling. Sweat glued his clothes to his body. And he had one hell of an erection, stiff and solid, throbbing against his thigh.

Zetz always said: 'Yes, there's nothing to match the first kill. Man's a carnivore, a hunting animal. You can't take it wholly away from him. Civilization? Morality? Cobblers. Let a man loose, he goes back all the way. I know, because I have been there. You may not know where you're going, but you sure can find out just where you started from. Self-knowledge, good as gold, brother. Beatniks try to get there by drugs. But there's no high like that Truth, my son, that knowledge of your inner core.'

Did Eisav believe that? He once told Nili he did, in the dead of night of confession. But that might have been sheer embroidery, a light frill of Sturm und Drang. Still, there was without doubt that hard on, that lingering, thrilling rigor . . .

*Apropos*
**Blok's Own Six-Day-War Experience as a Phantasm by Dali:**
(à la Fried Egg on a Dish Without the Dish. Phantom Wagon. Paranoiac Critical Solitude. Le Visage de la

Guerre. Atmospheric Head of Death Sodomizing a Grand Piano.)

On the left, under a russet sky, a garbage pile: old opened tin cans, mangled tanks blackened by fire, roast torsos, glistening, flakes of skin floating, like so many cigarette papers, above; a napalm-melted comb, a keyring with twelve keys, over a sepia portrait (framed) of a dark-faced woman, raven-haired, with two dark black-eyed children. On the desert floor, foreground, a finger, torn off at the root, and the skull of a second lieutenant. Flies, not ants, crawl out of the dead man's eyes, the tin cans, from tears in the portraits, dunging over the keys, riding the skin flakes like banshees.

On the right, on a ladder, Blok, straining to paint a golden city on the sky from a paintpot marked 'Glory of Effluence'. At the foot of the ladder the war issue of the army rag *In The Base* – *BABASIS*, with the one-eyed general on its cover; the legend 'From Our Correspondent, A. Blok, at the Front' dribbling off the page on to the sand, the letters light brown straggly turds. By the ladder, the khaki camouflaged magazine jeep, with the driver, PFC Sa'id T – , dreaming a three-strip technicolor dream: the Jaffa seafront, with dancing whores, their luscious brown skins a-glint in the Mediterranean sunset, cotton shirts tied in bows at their midriffs and their skirts rift open, revealing muscular thighs. In the eyes of each glows a star. A tongue, out of the sky, drips saliva, which turns into golden bullets. From the sea, a candelabra-limbed octopus spouts blood, sprays of which fleck Blok's golden city (it is the blood of menstruation).

Across the top of the frame spiders, cockroaches, maggots, earwigs, fly through the air, raining bars of chocolate and tinned beef marked 'Property of the Israel Defence Forces'. In the centre of the phantasm, dwarfing everything else, an enormous transistor radio, melting black into the sand like pus from a giant abscess, its station settings an elaborate collage of images strung on two lines of barbed wire: a mini Wailing Wall, a garrotted Spanish grandee, an auto-da-fé of *Das Kapital* and Sigmund Freud (*The Interpretation of Dreams*), a long unattached beard, a camel wearing longjohns, a watchtower and fence, a bloodied Brit judge's peruke, the dome of the rock, a nuclear mushroom, a tiny girl in bikini, the Warsaw ghetto kid surrendering, a concrete palm tree, Charlton Heston lurking behind a stone with ancient Hebrew lettering, a grape cluster of sheep's turds, a tuxedo crucified, a kefiya with no face, seven bare women's breasts, Hitler, as played by Alec Guinness, a cigar curling smoke into limbo, a blood-red tomato, an orange, a clementine, a hundred-dollar bill. The transistor is loudly blaring the song 'O Sharm a-Sheikh/We Have Returned to You Once Again/You Are in Our Hearts/In Our Hearts Forever.'

In the lower left corner, in a minute scrawl, the graffito:

'DO AS YOU ARE TOLD, WHEN YOU FIGHT THE ROTTEN WOGS, WALK LIGHT AS IF ON FEATHERS, AND NOT ON FUCKING CLOGS.'

Flusser said to Blok:

'That was your parents you were talking about in group the other day, wasn't it, when you spoke of the Eichmann trial witnesses being like your despised relations? You saw *them* stripped naked on the edge of the grave, in front of the firing squad. It was them, was it not, whom you despised as victims?'

'Not at all,' said Blok blithely, 'the thought never entered my head.'

'There is no need to be either afraid or ashamed,' said Flusser. 'After all, on that syndrome we have built us a nation.'

'He thought he saw an argument
That proved he was the Pope,
He looked again and saw it was
A bar of mottled soap.
A fact so dread, he softly said,
Extinguishes all hope.'

　　　　　　　　　– Lewis Carroll, 'Sylvie & Bruno'

In the tents of the archaeological dig at Masada:
the red, cragged mountains rearing out of ochre
desert over the deep sulphurous blue of the Dead
Sea; where, eighteen centuries ago, the desperate
remaining Hebrew rebels slaughtered themselves
rather than be slaughtered by others. A trenchant
symbol, it is said. Of what? The glory of a Jewish
hara-kiri? 'Masada Shall Not Fall Again', goes the
cry. It's a wonder the Romans bothered. What stubborn craziness brought those ancient Italians to
broil in the burning sun of this celestial microwave
oven, mounting siege in this godforsaken wilderness which only poisonous creepie-crawlies call
Home? . . . Yet at Masada, one thousand eight hundred years later, the Yigael Yadin expedition
burrows for the zealots' remains. Professionals,
soldiers, foreign lunatics, 'volunteers', under the

auspices of the Gadna Youth Corps, from the penultimate year of high school. Blok, among the unfortunate. Yea. By day, nudging at the hard-baked ground with a trowel to the pace of the Chopin funeral march, dunking soil on fan netting, bouching it about to separate mother earth from her hidden treasures – old coins, bones of ancient suicides, potsherds, Roman condoms, whatever. Running the sediment in wheelbarrows to the edge of the cliff and thrusting it eight hundred feet down the abyss, hoping barrow and barrowman manage to stay behind. Ah, the Glory of Our Heritage! By night, the pimply adolescents of Jerusalem's 'Beit Hakerem' School ('House of the Vineyard'; sweet wine from sour grapes) gather in their communal tents to discuss the Facts of Life. Square Gideon (sans Muki the Squint-Eyed Mutt, at home, now senile, moulted and incontinent) recites the Hebrew Encyclopedia's official definition of Love:

One of the Spiritual Virtues, which appears as a strong attraction towards someone who gives one pleasure and is able by his or her actions and presence to continue to do so. Sexual Love is a Tremendous Force which motivates and guides Man's actions. QED

Rafi, class boaster, explains the female monthly period: 'Well, you know that, for instance, whores don't give all the time ... there are days in the month when there's nothing doing ...'

Yosef, who professes serious experience: 'When you first see the woman's you know ... well, it's a bit disgusting, isn't it? But when you're in the Ecstasy you find yourself kissing it. My girl friend didn't let me have it, at first, because she thought the sight of It would turn me away. But after a while you think nothing of it.'

Indeed. Away with all that. Blok dreams chastely

of Malka Halperin. She too, of course, is on the
Rock, enjoying it, more's the pity. She is always
working at the edge of the cliff, amid the little signs
squeaking 'Attention! Danger of Collapse!'. Malka
Halperin, gold hair, firm features, her prominent
nose, grey eyes, against a backdrop of mountains
rising in a blue-red haze ... Caked with desert
dust, she attacks the primeval rocks with her little
pick, keeping up a pattern of shaggy dog stories to
tease and bemuse her admirers (of which Blok, alas
for him, is but one) –

'I was born in Egypt, you know. My father was
born in China. Believe it or not, as you like. I'd like to
have five sons. No daughters. I won't marry anyone
who can't guarantee me that.'

– Take me, I am here! what care I for random
biology? Five, ten, twenty sons, your wish is my ten
commandments! Head first down the gorge, if you
wish it, a modern zealot's amorous sepuku! But perhaps she might slip, on the crumbling edge, hang by
one hand from an outcrop as Blok, the Devoted,
springs instantly to the rescue. She kisses him in
mortal gratitude. He invites her out to a movie (the
Masada Odeon: Showing Tonight: Maciste Versus
Bar-Kokhba, zut, alors!). They clasp. Marriage,
ever after, etc., their souls entwined in paradise,
double halos ...

Now and again, at school, Blok made further
attempts at contact, although, since the secret
notes fiasco, he had abandoned the grand strategic
design. He tried the tactical approach: trying to get
her involved in the school plays he wrote and produced with Fat Avi. They wrote a satire, entitled
'Jowliest Shyster', which only just passed the censor (class tutor Mishael, wielding the blue pencil,
bowdlerizing hints of obscenity). But she refused to
play the part of California, Shyster's wife, because
she said the lines were still too lewd. Anyway, she

had no thespian abilities. Prose and politics were her forte. She had joined the leftist Mapam Young Guardians, who were busy at the time painting indelible red slogans on the walls of Jerusalem, castigating the official visit of Franz Joseph Strauss, the right-wing German politician. 'STRAUSS – RAUS', Kameraden, on every bare piece of stone. Blok briefly considered joining the movement, in her wake, but was distressed by the prospect of blue uniforms, campfire singsongs, baked potatoes and lengthy confessional debates. He had already spent one week, aged sixteen, in the Scouts, but left due to obligatory swimming lessons. The only result of his experiment in the communal endeavour was the unforgettable memory of the following imbecile chant:

'I-leh, I-leh chu,
Chubaleh chubaleh chubaleh chu,
Imkam kimkam vala-val-vatsa,
Imkam kimkam vats-vats-vats
I-leh, achrileh brileh, I-leh, achrileh brileh,
Miki-rak-rak-rak, miki-rik-rik-rak,
Miki-rak miki-tusi miki-dai . . .'

And so the last year of school passed, and the matriculation exams, and before he could re-gather his wits from that frazzle he was seated in the school's General Hall, in a pressed white shirt, waiting his turn for Headmaster Aricha's signed Bible and listening to Malka Helperin, no less, deliver the official student oration: 'How truly I enjoyed all my years in this shithole', or babble to that effect . . . Yes, this was the moment to end it all, to cut out the cancer of four years' puling puppy-love and stamp it with one's shiny shoe into the waxed school floor, there and then with everyone's parents present, beaming as their polished tsatskes tottered down the aisle to receive their bound benediction ('and thou shalt meditate within day and night'). But instead, such is the Tremendous Force That Motivates and Guides Man's Actions that he just went home meekly and that evening lifted the telephone, dialled her number with trembling fingers and said: 'Malka, there's something I really need to discuss with you. Would some time tomorrow afternoon be all right?' And she hesitated a moment and then said, 'Well, okay then, make it three o'clock, if you like.'

So at three o'clock, on the nail, he stood again outside the back entrance of her ground-floor home, the grimy netting of the kitchen door staring him in the face when she came, in blue slacks and a maroon short-sleeved shirt, to open it with: 'Always the back door, I don't understand you at all; what is it this time?'

And finally, after four years of silent yearning, anguished days and nights, wringing of hands and furtive self-abuse, sweating in his secret limbo of corrosive longing and infatuation, finally he screwed up several kilos of courage, took himself securely in hand and, taking a deep breath, declared . . .

Blok, in London, June 1968. Moderate sun on Victorian and Edwardian façades. Green green the trees, the garden lawns, the parks. Flick flack, the lights of Piccadilly. The stone grey City mansions of money. The black statues of death and Remembrance. The joy of being a pin in the metropolitan haystack, flowery, the hopes of the Free . . . *A Space Odyssey* at the Cinerama, the freaks sitting zonked in the front row gazing back at the bemused Starchild. It's all happening out there, by Jupiter's moons, in the studios of Boreham Wood. The Medium is the Massage. The Global Village is

Within Us. Extras in monkey skins, led to Technology by the beam of Metro Goldwyn-Monolith.

Nineteen-sixty-eight. Holy shit, man! Saigon, the Tet Offensive. Zapping the city of Hue in order to save it, just a foretaste of what's coming. Generals see light at the end of tunnels. (Could one say that about the tunnel of Klander?) Martin Luther King's body lies amouldrin' in the grave but the soles of the National Guard march on. American ghettos burn in America. Mayor Daley says, 'Shoot to kill.' In Biafra children starve to the whir of Western newsreel cameras. Harold Wilson sends guns to their assassins La social-demokratia. Viva! Bang bang, the Society for Cutting Up Men almost cuts down Andy Warhol. Bang bang, Robert Kennedy is shot in Los Angeles by an incensed Jordanian. Just like home, while in Prague the sun shines briefly on Alexander Dubcek, everybody's favourite Party Chairman . . .

Lest we forget, lest we forget:

Of war and peace the truth just twists,
its curfew gull just glides . . .

The nasal whine of the tousled prophet echoes, at 33 rpm, through the barely furnished rooms of Victoria Happenstance's apartment. Stamford Hill, comrades! The working class lives! Not quite within Bow bells, but ample. Scruffy cats drowse in abandoned flowerpots. Motorcycles, down the road, rev fanatically. On the two balconies of the second-floor flat, to the unease of the native proletariat peeking through chinks in net curtains, four large black men lie prostrate, stripped to their underpants in the summer mid-day sun. No mad dogs and Englishmen here, just Victoria, catching the rays en bikini, and, on a deckchair, a pinkish Blok, purusing a Trotsky anthology:

'. . . why does Moscow so fear the voice of a single man? Only because I know the truth, the whole truth. Only because I have nothing to hide. Only because I am ready to appear before a public and impartial commission of inquiry with documents, facts and testimonies in my hands . . . I declare: if this commission decides I am guilty in the slightest degree of the crimes which Stalin imputes to me, I pledge in advance to place myself voluntarily in the hands of the executioners of the GPU . . .'

♩ '. . . upon four-legged forest clouds
the cowboy angel rides . . .      ♫
. . . all except when 'neath the trees of Eden . . .'

'. . . I try my best to be jest like I am,
but everybody wants me to be jest like them . . .'

'You know something, man,' says Leroy Smith, 'that white boy sure got rhythm.' Dissolve, in a fit of giggles, whoops, snorts, wheezes, smokers' coughs. 'Shit, man, where did that motherfucking roach go . . .'

Dreams, myths, fata morganas. Blok appears trapped in the flypaper of other people's fantasies. Tambourine men, in jingle jangle mornings that someone else remembers. 'Getting his head together' he stayed behind one day when Victoria and the blacks zoomed off in her Morris Minor to a political meeting in Oxford (Solidarity with Vietnam, NLF, the Black Panthers, and Everything You May Care to Name, to debate Socialism or Barbarism while the punters glide under the arches). Aimlessly he roamed the deserted rooms, ogling the wall posters: a Vietnamese woman in tears under a great straw hat, wrinkled arms stretched in supplication; Mao Tse Tung, full face, composed of red hammers and sickles; Che Guevara in Kodacolor (hair brilliantined, cut neat and short, great big cigar in kisser); an African guerrilla, festooned with bandoliers – 'FRELIMO – BUST THE CABORRA BASSA DAM'; a black woman, ditto, with child attached – 'ZANU – FORWARD TO VICTORY': President Johnson, above swastika'd stars and stripes, raining bombs from his arsehole. A pig in police uniform – 'FREE ELDRIDGE CLEAVER'. An unidentified black man in dark glasses. A souvenir from Paris – de Gaulle, nude, clutching his balls, with a quotation from R.D. Laing.

He mooched along the bookshelves, climbing on chairs, absently leafing through the volumes: *The Works of Spinoza. The South African Reich. The Message of Krishnamurti. Steppenwolf* by Herman Hesse. Trotsky: *The Prophet Unarmed. To The Finland Station,* by Edmund Wilson. Marx-Engels: *The German Ideology.* Guevara: *Guerrilla War.* Hobbes: *Leviathan.* Machiavelli. Locke. Kaunda: *Zambia Shall Be Free. The British Cabinet.* Nkrumah: *Consciencism. Speeches* by Rosa Luxemburg. Maxim Gorky. Babel. Kafka. George Orwell: *Homage to Catalonia. Fathers and Sons,* Turgenev. *The Possessed,* Dostoyevsky. Malcolm X: *My Story.* Bertrand Russell. Emma Goldman. Virginia Woolf. Doris Lessing. Sartre. Genet.

Kulture. The curiosity of another breed. Blok thought of the bookcases back home. For Papa: *Sewer Reconstruction and Drain Design* by Y. Efrati; *Philately* by Bartlett; *Tales of Panfilov,* Agnon, Shalom Aleikhem, *Collected Works;* Hebrew Encyclopedia, Volumes 1 thru 12, when the money for the subscription ran out, leaving everything from the letter 'Het' onwards a mystery. For Mama: Stephan Zweig; Dostoyevsky: *Crime and Punishment; Karamazov;* the complete Tolstoy;

Shalom Aleikhem in the original Yiddish. Ahad Ha'am: *This is Not the Way*. In Blok's corner: the juvenile Hasamba adventures, Baron Munchausen, Agatha Christie. Mickey Spillane, *Zhivago* (unread), Henry Miller, a discovery of Fat Avi who had not slackened, since the days of *Lady Chatterley*, his search for literate erotica. Throughout his army service Blok devoured the Tropics, then the Rosy Crucifiction trilogy. A hard job in a foreign language but rewarding, conjuring vistas of sweet liberation which pronounced: Life, my boy, is not what Papa and Mama insinuate – stout abstention followed by monogamy; the Glorious World of Fuck is out there, waiting to be explored.

Not, alas, with Malka Halperin . . . nor with golden Victoria neither. Oddly tucked away on a top shelf Blok finds the elusive clues to her roots: *The Collected Works of Virginia Happenstance*, The Bodley Head, 1950: *The Severed Rose, Red Marsala, The Virgin of Samothrace*. Beside this, dog-eared and well-thumbed, Max Happenstance: *The Measure of Man's Wealth*. 'That's the tale, Jack,' Wellington informed him, 'the Happenstance tug o'war. Max, Professor Emeritus, runner up for the Nobel Prize. Mama, the aspiring pulp liberationist. They called her the last bloom of Bloomsbury.' 'Is that the street with all the luggage and umbrella shops?' asked Blok. Wellington nodded sagely. 'She died, two years after Vicky was born. Max raised her, in his Oxford hideaway. Bookcases and pipe smoke and a hundred atlases, no wonder the kid itched to move . . .' Thus she jumped ship, Frog told Blok, and criss-crossed the world, with poor schmucks like you carrying her rucksack. One day, he said, I'll tell you the full story. Sometimes you just gotta laugh.

And the days passed, and strange guests arrived one morning, two black men with African accents.

One was thick-set, dour and bearded and wore coal-black spectacles even inside shuttered rooms. He never seemed to walk across the centre of a room, but moved slowly around the walls, keeping within sensuous reach of the central heating radiators. The other was tall, thin and nattily dressed, with a flash gold ring on his finger. She embraced them like long-lost cousins and they babbled for hours in what seemed incomprehensible code about people such as Brickbat, and Jayjay, and Ahmed K., and mysterious events and entities like the Rivonia Trial, the Litvaks, the Spear of the Nation, Robben Island and the Caprivi Strip, and shebeens and AK-thirty-sevens and Mama Ngina and Umkimvoto Beer and boervurst and kaffir-boeties and Sophiatown and Soweto. Peepholes for Blok into places he could not imagine, lives he could not fathom. All this added to the avalanche dumped on him by Wellington Frog and Co., blithe babble of the Muslims, and Brother Elijah, and the White Devil Syndrome, the Oakland Bust, Rap, Stokely and Eldridge and the Imamu Baraka Balewa, acid-heads, Berkeley, the Hashbury, SDS and Burn Baby Burn et cetera. And, add the blazing Paris Bourse and the plug mug of Blok/Abu Jilda in the pissoirs of gendarmeries – and one ends up with one very fucked-up Hungarian Israeli Jew from the flotsam of saved oven fodder. Yes, indeed!

But Wellington Frog diagnosed him unerringly, telling him, one night, having dragged him out walkies – after two or three joints and a libation of Bell's whisky (neat), just to get the right twist on things – west towards the Seven Sisters Road: 'Man, what we really need is to get you laid. You are getting hung up on me and Victoria, but it is a false trail, my friend. Let me tell you, the girl likes excitement, the whiff of grapeshot, that touch of jay-nay-say-quoi. She has travelled the world, chasing the atlases in old Max Happenstance's study. First time I met her was in Mexico City, on the Paseo de la Reforma. The rucksack carrier then was a cat called Miguel, an exile from the Dominican Republic. His country had just been zapped by the CIA and he was in a pretty pickle. The next time I saw them they were living in Mission, San Francisco, revelling in real hard times. They were so broke they made the roaches in their apartment pay rent. It was a true happenstance meeting. I had just stashed myself nearby with some dudes, far from Oakland as I could reach. Those days you couldn't walk the streets among the brothers without some crazy cat laying some weird ritual handshake on you ... Hey, brother, how y'doin'? And wham, you are tangled as a boa constrictor. It was all show, Jack, the hot times were over. The West Coast had died on us, the white kids had blown their brains with acid, and were flirting with Hell's Angels, man, bikers, Nazis, all manner of deep insanity. Malcolm X was shot. The Muslims had split. Oh, we made the headlines, sure, we had Mister and Missus America pissing their pants at the sight of a black face but we were on the decline, man, we had passed our peak. The white kids had their pills but we were soaring on rhetoric, Jack, way up above the clouds. Some of us were burning up so fast you'd be charred just passing by our wind. So me and some other cats opted out for a quiet time, man, got ourselves into creative shit, stuff I'd never given mind to, sculpture, painting, music. Some were even into ba-llay! Man, Brother Elijah would have had their ass as FAGS! But we were happy, doing our thing. And there was Vicky from Mexico, with Miguel, and the roaches, them that paid the rent.'

By this time they had reached the Seven Sisters Road, and were both suddenly assailed by ravenous hunger. A sign flashed 'Wimpy Bar – Open 24 Hours'. Within, a few people appeared to be frozen in a bleak, melancholy landscape. A young couple, hunched over the remains of a shanty-burger and chips. An old man talking to himself in sign language. An old woman with wispy white hair staring at a retrieved teabag. A bored hard blonde waitress and a slick-haired Greek dude at the cashbox. Muzak laying doom over all. 'Motherfucker!' breathed Wellington. 'It is the Greyhound Station of Kalamazoo, Michigan!' They entered, seizing a vacant table. Ordering, after a brief flurry of indecision, two large Wimpy King Burger Specials and a double helping each of fries. Wellington, launching into a recitation of a poem he had written about his native land:

'AMERICA – first canto, man:

If I could tell the honky world just what I think of it
Then I would fart and out would come a huge hunk o'shit . . .'

Then he seemed to forget the rest, and sank into reverie: 'America! Man, people talked about Hitler, but they ain't seen nothin' yet . . . when the Washington Man sets to rip off the world, things will really get moving, brother . . . those poor Veetnamese peasants . . . the Great Society! Savin' the poor gooks from Communism, the godless creed o' Karl Marx . . . "Here, Mama San, take down this spoonful of napalm . . . jus' lemme light this match here . . . ooops! well, plenty more where she came from . . ." America, shit! One big lump of pure hate. An' the only way to fight them is to become just as goddamned mean, ornery, ruthless and blindshittingmad with hate as they are. And once you're there, man, it is *over*, bastards lie down on the ground shitting themselves laughing because they

116

have got you, boy, right there by the nuts. They have made you in their image, man, in the motherfucking Man's image. . .'

The wispy-haired old woman began singing softly: 'Land of Hope and Glory'. Wellington Frog snorted, shook his head as if in search of something he'd just lost . . .

'Ah, Vicky!' he regained his thread, 'out there in Mission, with Miguel, chased from home by the CIA, man. Then one day he upped and left. Nobody knew why. Maybe he thought the spooks were after him. Or the roaches got to him. Or he just got homesick and took his guitar. He was one truly loopy dude. She was real cut up about it, they had had two good years. Enter W. Frog. C'est la vie, Avram, my boy,' he suddenly lapsed into a maudlin phase. 'They don't come any better than Vicky, I can tell you . . . Whatever she does, she don't go about it half-assed, brother. Maybe that's what she got from Daddy. The Ee-conomics wizard, Jack . . . He started out a so-shal democrat but got stuck on the Free Market Forces . . . He wanted to stomp Keynes into the ground, and strew salt on the cat's grave . . . You should see them two fight, the father and daughter, but they are the same clay . . . Not like my Pa . . . shit, he was a real shade and fade man . . . Don't stand out in the crowd, nigger . . . you can't beat The Man, boy. Jesus.'

Ah, yes. Fathers and sons. Blok, through a fog of grease fumes, sees Baruch Blok, trapped in the Jerusalem Sewage Department and in the affections of Mama. And she . . .? Even in the false glow of Marijuana Truth he cannot view them with anything but perplexity. Who were they? What did they want from life? What was the bloody world in their eyes? Far, far from home, now, from Fat Avi, Gideon and Muki the Mutt, Flusser, Davidov, Nietzsche, and Nili, Nili-Honey too . . . oh my God!

. . . and Headmaster Aricha and Malka Halperin and Dali as the Six-Day War, Sinai and the gaseous stench of the dead, Jerusalem the Golden and Sharm-a-Sheikh We Have Returned to You Once Again, You Are In Our Hearts Forever . . .

gaaah! Bubbling bullshit under the bridge . . .!

– walking back up the Seven Sisters Road, the old woman from the Wimpy Bar preceding them with 'Onward Christian Soldiers' . . .

'Ay-bra-ham, my friend,' says Wellington, 'I am going to fix you with your heart's desire. Man, we are going to get you *laid*. This is the first item on the central committee's agenda, an' all the comrades had better get their shit together and lay this on us or heads will ROLL, man, the Moscow Trials will have nothing on the shit that will fly that day . . . Now what we will do is have one hell of a party – a slambamkalamazam affair! A So-shal Oh-kayzhun! Everybody who is anybody will be there, an' the chicks will be dripping with honey. All you have to do is stretch out your hand, man, an' say – Hey baby! this is your big night tonight!'

'Hey man,' says Blok, highly infected, 'I can take care of myself . . .' Lying. 'I'm quite capable you know . . .'

'That's cool, man,' says Wellington, 'that's cool. We will lay on this Big Do, and everything will be cool. Everybody will do their own thing, just like the old days . . .'

Not the old days, friend Frog, not the old days! Bring Out Your Dead: deep Hebrew blues – Remembrance Days and white shirts on Independence Eve, getting pissed on one paper cup of Carmel wine . . . fireworks on the grass, alas . . . and an empty ache in the heart . . . Bury 'em! Malka Halperin, I'll piss on your grave! Here We'll Live and Here Create, Freedom's Life and Freedom's Fate . . . saw away at them umbilical cords, Avram

118

Blok! whup whup, whup whup, the jagged teeth cut through – Mama, Papa, Malka Halperin, the Nation – sayonara! I piss on your grave! Bring Out your Six Million Dead too – Ash from the Chimneys – whoosh! with Blok's pee down the gutter – Uncle Shmil, Tantie Anna, Grandpa Yankel Blok – goddamn it – kersplash! down the plughole . . . I repudiate you all! Free, Free at last!

. . . and he said:

'Malka, you'll probably think what I'm going to tell you is absurd, as I've never said it before . . . I mean, I'm not saying it to you because I think anything will come of it, but because now that school is over we'll be going our separate ways and –

'Well: I don't know why I fell in love with you . . . I've known a lot of girls, girls that were . . . well, maybe more beautiful than you, but . . . it did happen, some years ago, and didn't go out of my mind . . . It's funny, I suppose, that I loved you for such a long time and didn't say anything to you . . . four years . . . I was just a kid then . . . I know this . . . confession is probably a pain in the neck for you and you just want me to get the hell out of here. That's the truth. I loved you from far away for a long time and I still feel the same way.'

She looked at Blok. He looked at her. She said: 'Didn't you ever try to get rid of this feeling?'

'I tried . . . a lot, but at first . . . I saw you as someone . . . I don't know, pure, sacred . . . then I tried to see you as someone wicked, unworthy of being loved, and so on . . . But that didn't work. It wouldn't matter to me if you were an axe-murderess, I would still feel the same . . . you don't fall in love with the character of a girl, but with her beauty . . . for me you were always the most beautiful girl in the world. I've gone out with other girls, but I could never . . . really feel anything for them . . . Whoever

I was with, you were always between us . . . I think that even if I'd fall in love with another girl I'd still be in love with you. I don't expect you to say anything, just let me have my say. I want you to know all this, before we go separate ways, and don't see each other again . . . Just tell me one thing – during all these years, did you never suspect or realize what I was feeling towards you?'

'No, I never thought of it.'

'Never?'

'It never even crossed my mind.'

'Well, that's the story, anyway. I don't want to bore you any more. That's the whole mess, brief and to the point.'

'No, you're not boring me, I don't mind you telling me all this.'

'Do you think . . . there was ever a chance, the smallest, bitsiest chance . . . if I'd spoken to you before . . . that, that I would have had a chance with you . . .?'

'No, I don't really think so. I've had a life of my own. I don't think that would ever have happened.'

Blok thought, at least that's a relief, I haven't missed out on what I wouldn't have had anyway. Spared, at least, that final, crashing irony . . .

They shook hands politely over their official farewell. It was the only time he had firmly touched her. They agreed to regard each other as friends.

The day of the slambamkalamazam party dawned gustily, with August showers. Then the rain gave way to a bright sun in a blue and grey dappled sky. The cats in the flowerpots stretched and gazed wistfully into tweeting branches.

Blok arrived in the afternoon. He had been staying for some weeks in a bed-sitting room in Stoke Newington, proclaiming his independence from the nest . . .

He found Victoria alone with an ex-schoolmate, Davina, watching an arts programme on the TV. A rapt audience watched as an artist, in simulated slow motion, climbed out of a bathful of shit. 'Very tame,' said Davina who had just returned from a summer in San Francisco. She had an upper-class accent so sharp it could have been used to drill through a concrete slab. It was soon countered by other argots, dialects and brogues of the guests who began arriving, drowning Victoria in a smother of curly beards, beads, amulets, shark's teeth on leather thongs, braying, chattering, whooping, ululating fit to burst.

From a psychedelic coloured van a black South African band emerged, unloading vast amplifiers the very sight of which made the neighbours' net curtains shudder visibly. Like a string of native bearers, they carried their drums, bass guitars, saxes and clarinets into the house, filling it, as sunset shot its gold-red shafts through the windows, with tweaks, scrapes, twangs, clangs, jangles and clashing chords, the wail of Kwela music, lonesome, defiant, steeped in the woes of far-off places . . .

Shit! those memories again! of what, Blok could not say, but they were certainly wafting about the house. The two South African friends arrived, bringing with them a third, hypomanic comrade, a small plump jelly-like man with quick yellow-flecked eyes and a loud braying laugh that shook the cupboards and shelves. Blok found Zeph, J.D. and Walter and Vicky huddled in a corner. They gave him the clenched fist salute as they proceeded to uncork the wine.

Rapping on old times. This party may have begun in Wellington Frog's head as a means to get Avram Blok laid, but it had obviously mutated into an opportunity for everybody to meet everybody else whom they hadn't run across in years. Cool cats summering away from the heat. Student radicals who had poured acid on college files, and defended their malfaisance later in court by reading out the Communist Manifesto. A burly unshaven Irish lout from a proletarian phase of Vicky's. Several Davina-like young ladies, ex-schoolmates, with accents that blew Blok's head off. A fat, bedraggled long-haired Jewish fellow, with skullcap and protruding tsitsis who, it turned out, had founded the Marxist Torah School of Manhattan, with an enrolment of one. He had a loud, maniacal laugh, and a fund of dirty jokes, which kept him, if no one else, in stitches. In fact, a great deal of maniacal, downright fiendish laughter was going on, infecting Blok, causing him to lose touch with his goal. He sat catatonically, against the wall, smoking joints and pouring down vodka while the exiles howled and guffawed before him to the trembling wail of the kwela –

'Har Har Har!'

'. . . ach man, remember Joe Mareka? How he prowled in the Marlborough, telling the white girls dreadful tales of Pretoria jail? – how they nailed his penis to the table – '

'Har Har Har! That story never failed to deliver. . .'

'Ya man! that mournful face!'

The music got louder. It's Wellington himself, giving a blow job to a saxophone. See the sweat gather and run down his face, contorted in to-tal concentration.

'– and Mrs Conch the French teacher, remember we put the toad in her bed – '

'– the IRA? that's a dead duck. Don't give me that now – '

'– either you're for Imperialism or against it – '

'– she married an Albanian fishmonger – '

'– wasn't Marx the greatest talmudist of all – '

'– so I told them, man, I've no truck with this non-violence shit.'

'– and had an audience with Mao Tse Tung – '

Crash, bam, kazam, the drums . . . wail o' wail, the sax . . . tinkle tonkle the glasses and cups, glug glug glug madly downed the booze . . . Blok pissed as a newt . . . dancing has commenced adjacently . . . hypomanic Walter hooked on a statuesque blonde . . . Leroy Smith and I-saac entwined round two stunning black girls in African gowns . . . dour Mahmud tentatively swaying with Davina . . . the militant Irishman doggedly on their heels . . . Vicky vanished . . . a rather plain girl is beaming at Blok through the mist, and he leers back, unable, unwilling to move, the room glowing with the beat of the music, each drum, thwack, nailing him to the wall, self-fenced in his reservation with the Smirnoff shrewdly in reach. The girl sits down beside him, letting out a whoosh of relief.

'God, it's pretty hectic in there!'

He pours her a shot.

'You ought to down this stuff in one gulp,' she says, 'the way the Russians do.'

He waves her on. After five or six such attempts they are both absolutely stinko. They lie groaning, backs to the wall, watching the frenzied tangle of arms and legs in the next room. Joints have been passing in there like nobody's business and the band is full streak into the beyond with marijuana smoke coming out of their ears. Everyone seems to be groping everyone else. Blok and the girl's fingers are entwined, and pretty soon they are exchanging sixty-five proof kisses. Somehow he has become informed that her name is Dianne, she came with someone and a friend who appeared to have vanished into the nepenthean haze –

'Why don't we split somewhere?' sighs Dianne. 'I

123

don't think I can breathe in here . . .'

A brilliant thought, but can one make it to the door . . .? Blok: I know this place like the back of my hand . . . What? in here? cubicle number two, the extra extra desperate guest room. Nothing but a foam mat on the floor. Twill suffice. Holy shit! They have undressed somehow, Blok and Dianne . . . or are these her pants coiled round his ankles, his trousers round her ears . . .

No. Yes! naked they lie. He caresses her quite large breasts . . . he passes his hands through her thick tawny hair . . . don't blow it now, Blok, asargelusha! First fuck of freedom, and no furtive grapple under the frozen eyes of Bloks senior (a tale yet to be told) . . . The door opens and Wellington Frog peeps in, beaming, with a bottle of red wine and two glasses on a tray. 'Hey man, how'y'doin'?' he sets down the tray and exits, closing the door on the clash of the band. Blok gets back to work, reaching down gently towards the lush bush of her mons. Yes, his cock, a friend in need, is reliably stiff. She hooks her legs about him, hungrily pulling him down. Ah, he guides it in there, good boy, presto! and away they go, he huffing, she sighing heartfully . . . (What was thy pity's recompense? A silent suffering, and intense . . .?)

Blok, fate accompli: as the girl sleeps soundly, her bum cheeks turned sweetly towards him, he is seized with what Freud calls the need to micturate and pads unsteadily out to the corridor. The band has ceased. On the stairs leading down to the front door the South African exiles are tottering, flourishing clenched fists and singing what are later revealed to be Boer patriotic songs. Plump Walter still is enclamped upon the big blonde girl, she is giggling into his hair. Victoria and Wellington are kissing them all goodbye, they are slowly but surely being shooed down the stairs, hushing each other amid bursts and snuffles of laughter as they stagger out to the street. Blok locks himself in the toilet, resting his back against the white plastic cover, letting the Smirnoff drain away. He hears the last 'Byeeee!' and the snib of the door and Walter's raucous bellow in the street of 'Hey kaffir! where's your dombook? Gotverdommen, this is a white area!' He stays rooted paralytically to the bowl for a timeless time, till the rattling door handle and a hoarse cry of 'Mayday! Mayday!' remind him he is not alone. It is Leroy, poised, doubled over and clearly in need of a puke. 'Ooh, that bootleg liquor . . .' Blok closes the bathroom door upon the unfortunate, staggers along the corridor and without thinking turns in at the door of Victoria's bedroom.

'Hey man, how's it goin'?' Wellington whispers from the dark.

Eek. He can make out those glinting black eyes in a shaft of moonlight, which also shines softly on the aureole of Vicky's golden hair. 'Hi, Avram,' says she.

'Oh, sorry,' he says, 'wrong room . . .'

'Take a seat man,' Blok sits on the edge of the double bed. 'Wanna toke, Brother Ay-braham?'

'Uh . . . no thanks . . . had enough tonight I think . . .'

'Yeah man, some blow out, huh? How'y'getting on with that nice Jewish chick, what's her name now. Dianne?'

'Oh. Is she Jewish?' Fuck me, the journey stretches on . . .

'Just like mama makes, huh? I like her. She's real nice.'

Cholera. A dozen questions well up in Blok – no matter. 'Yah,' he says, 'real nice.' He can make out now the black man's powerful shoulder just inches above the sheets. Victoria has them drawn up modestly to her neck. He remembers a game he used to play with Mama Blok, as a kid of three or four, pulling the blankets up to his chin. My head's cut off! Where's the rest of me? She would pull down the blankets and show him. Bloody hell. Well, no lay with a shiksa after all. Blok, hoist with his racist petard. Serves you right, bigoted pascudniak. Who cares?

'Yah,' he repeats, 'she is a real nice girl, she is.'

'I want to sleep now,' says Victoria, turning away from him.

'I'm going . . .' he gets up from the bed.

'Take care,' says Wellington, 'fuck 'em an' feed 'em beans.'

'Sure,' says Blok, 'I'll do that.' He edges away, leaves the room, closing the door behind him.

'Fuck 'em an' feed 'em beans . . .' he mutters as he scuffs along the corridor. Where the hell is that dinky room? I am doomed to wander along endless corridors, searching for a door I cannot find . . . He finds it, tiptoeing in, crawling in beside the soft, warm, cuddly flesh of slumbering Dianne. He squeezes her thighs. 'Ah, good yiddishe pulkes,' he breathes, seized with a fit of the giggles. He lies with her. On the closed insides of his eyelids he sees Wellington Frog and Victoria, twined together, he snuffling, she moaning with consummate passion. His hand fondles his cock. Oh, shit, he says to himself, shit oh shit; what the hell, fuck 'em an' feed 'em beans . . .

In mid-September Blok returned to the Holy Land. He had to catch up with the *Flaminia*'s return voyage at Naples, circumventing dangerous France (au secours! Abu Jilda!) by means of a rail trip through Germany. (Nazis! Auschwitz! Zyklon B! Bokwurst at Mainz station, midnight – no, the mind refuses recall . . .) The sea trip back was uneventful. No table-tennis players. No shade of romance. Merely shellshock, a little vomiting, and bad sunburn on the shins. Papa Blok met him at Haifa port.

'Did you have a really good time?' he asked, meaning 'I hope you made love to the shiksas every which way, but don't breathe a word to your mother.'

'Sure,' said Blok, 'a really good time, really.'

Papa offered him a cigarette, which he refused. They were silent, in the service taxi the rest of the way home.

SPECIALIZED TRAINING AVAILABLE to responsible groups in the arts of 'catastrophe survival' – nuclear, chemical, bacteriological warfare, economic collapse, riot, revolution, ecodisaster, etc. Intensive, tailored instruction. Will travel. Box 1334, 3000 Center Avenue, Berkeley CA 94704.

UNINHABITED ISLANDS. Need a hideout? Or a quiet staging area for a clandestine operation? Exciting new book contains detailed descriptions of more than eighty uninhabited islands, with maps showing exact locations! $5.00. Loompanic, Box 456, Mason, MICH.

– Classifieds, Soldier of Fortune magazine

**Tales of Olde Jerusalem:**
Judas Iscariot sat a long time below the tree before deciding to hang himself on it. From the rock on which he sat he could clearly see the crosses across the Valley. The crowds had melted away. The only person at the foot of the mount was Sister MacTavish, laboriously picking off the ground her fallen rum truffles, dainty dinahs, dragées, soor plooms and other scattered delights. The man on the central cross was haranguing the sole Roman

soldier who remained, nonchalantly smoking a Marlboro. A lone cloud scudded past the spring sun. Judas put his head in his hands.

'They'll blame me for this,' he groaned. Uncoiling the length of rope he'd been handed with the money by wily old Caiaphas ('this might come in handy about the house, especially if you're on an upper floor . . .'), he strung it over the strongest branch of the tree and secured its end to the bole. Laying the largest stones he could lift one on top of the other he raised himself far enough from the ground to stick his head through the noose. Then he drew the noose tight round his neck.

'Goodbye cruel world,' he said, waving his hand towards the City, where merchants plied their trade as usual, Temple guards took baksheesh from the pockets of serfs as on any Friday afternoon and the shitkickers shuffled along the alleyways, bemoaning their fate. Then a thought struck him: fuck it! After all, with thirty pieces of silver I can buy a berth on an ocean-going vessel, break free and show all this dullness and misery a bloody clean pair of heels! But as he scrabbled to free his neck from the noose the precarious cairn of stones he had laid collapsed, leaving him swinging in the wind, kicking wildly, frothing at the mouth and cursing himself for a schlemazl.

'ASARGELUSHA!'

Far away in the belly of the barren hills, the braying laughter of the gadarene swine could be heard, over the market hubbub of the pre-Shabbes closing-time rush.

. . . from the *Index of Dreams* analysed by Freud:
'Oedipus dream, disguised;
Operation on penis;
Orvieto wine;
Pains in jaw;
Piano – a disgusting old box;

Pilgrimage to Jerusalem;
Police Inspector;
Pornic, lady from;
Pulling woman from behind bed;
Revolution of 1848 (Experimental dream, Maury);
Roman Emperor assassinated;
Running downstairs and copulating with little girl (Alexander the Great – Artemidorous);
Sappho (Lovely Dream) (Up and down);
Schoolboy exposed in bed;
Seal-like creature coming through trapdoor;
Seven kine (Pharaoh, Bible);
Syphilitic primary affection (Physician, A. Starcke)'

When Blok was three or four years old there was a man, feared by all the neighbourhood children, who went about in very raggedy clothes, pushing before him a small wooden cart with terribly squeaky wheels. This was the Child-Snatcher who was an Arab, of course, on the look-out for Jewish children whom he'd grab, snatch and stick in the cart and make off with when no one was looking. On the other hand, he may not have been an Arab at all, but merely that bum Groise Metsiyes, who had not yet, at that early date, acquired his little case of pekelech.

A recurring dream, related by Blok to Flusser:

I am on the top of an extremely high building, an immense warren of numberless rooms and corridors. I am trying to make my way out of the building, in which I have spent my whole life, to escape to an outside world I have never seen, whose nature I can't imagine. I proceed, sometimes with a friend – who it is I can't make out – down endless liftshafts and, when these are blocked or watched by those whose job it is to block or watch them, down

131

immensely wide and long curving stairways. The ground floor, reached after an eternity, or never reached at all (which, Flusser pointed out, amounts to the same thing), is like a vast enclosed city, with crowds of people going about their indeterminate business. There seems to be no way of knowing in which direction the exits may lie. Nevertheless we make our way through ever contracting passage-ways into tiny claustrophobic storerooms, kitchen-ettes, broom cupboards, till we find the single opening – a minute window or hatchway, through which we squeeze, with immense difficulty, to be greeted by a blinding grey, a brilliant light of abso-lute vagueness ... (Ah well, said Flusser, Ah well . . .)


**Tales of Olde Jerusalem (cont'd):**
Inspector Tarablus, of the Jerusalem Homicide Divi-sion, investigated the murder of Moses Klander for over fifteen years. He first became dissatisfied with the court's verdict of Guilty but Bananas on the itinerant Groise Metsiyes in the autumn of 1962. The seeds of doubt were sown in the course of an investigation of a fire in the United States Con-sular Annexe in Shivtei Yisrael Street, just behind the Russian Compound. The blaze sent documents flying in the air and steel-eyed crew-cut WASP per-sonnel in black suits and ties were seen climbing trees and rushing down alleys to retrieve them. Some papers wafted over the Jordanian border. One, however, was picked up by a Constable Yehoshua, who showed it to Tarablus in the back of the crisis police van. The Inspector took one look at it, folded it, stuffed it in his pocket and swore Yehoshua by Scouts' honour, mama's grave and the mingling of blood at their elbows to silence. Later that night, when the fire was out and the CIA men

had come down from the trees, he made a telephone call to his only acquaintance in the Mossad Secret Service and arranged for a secret meeting. They met at the Ta'ami Café on King George Street, haunt of taxi drivers, weirdos, whores and their pimps, who spent hours over their eggplant salad telling the tallest tales you could imagine, so that no word that was uttered on the premises was ever considered veracious. Tarablus's acquaintance was called Agent XBZThree, and he read the document carefully, as if to record every letter and comma on the dictaphone of his mind. Then he burnt it in an ashtray inscribed Copacabana Hotel, São Paolo, and scattered the ashes in the grate of the old-fashioned fireplace that was keeping the chill October night from their bones.

'You must mention this to no one,' he said.

'I will keep it to myself but I cannot let it by. I cannot let a pawn languish in the asylum when others, behind the scenes, are free.'

'You are a man of honour,' said XBZThree, 'let me say this: if you can nail the perpetrator without revealing this evidence, then the State has no reason to stop you. But you will have to act alone.'

'Thank you,' said Inspector Tarablus, digging into his eggplant salad.

After Patrolman Abutbul had had a brief word with Nehemia Friedman of Cordovero Street, Number –, and hauled the peeping malefactor, Blok, off to the copshop, that devout worthy, whose privacy Blok had outraged, placed a person to person telephone call to a Mr Hersch Leib Kalisher, of Division Avenue, Williamsburg, NY, and said:

'Listen: you don't say anything, let me speak. Just now the police took away a young man who was watching the house. He was looking in the window. Didn't I say don't say anything? They'll charge him with indecent exposure or something, that side of it is all right. What d'you mean what did he see? Are you my Rabbi? The important thing is somebody's watching. Can we afford to take a chance? I ask you. Blok is his name, apparently. Avram Blok. Yes, tell your friends to run a check on him. Let me know the results. Don't say anything more, riboino shel oilem . . . this is a telephone call, not a private conversation! Yes, with the help of the Lord, Reb Herschl, just with the help of the Lord . . .'

The document Constable Yehoshua had retrieved from the fire at the US Annexe, and which Agent XBZThree burnt at the Ta'ami Café, was a carbon copy of a Central Intelligence Memo to HQ in Langley, Virginia. It concerned the surveillance, by all methods known to modern man, of Jerusalem's most well-known beggars, Babelech-und-Farfel.

Babelech-und-Farfel had roamed the streets of the City since the early Thirties, carrying all their worldly goods about with them in two enormous grimy sacks. They were of indeterminate age, and though they were assumed to be a couple, no one could tell which of them was the woman and which the man, which Babelech and which Farfel, contrariwise. They were always dressed in the same filthy, decaying rags which seemed to stick to their bodies, since they were too torn to be attached any other way. They communicated between themselves in a weird babbling patois that some took to be petrified yiddish, others bastard Ladino, yet others, Esperanto, and real wise guys claimed was Montenegran. They collected coins in an ancient chipped wooden begging bowl and their method of soliciting alms was to thrust their unbelievable putrescence right in the face of the subject, emitting, amid the general pong, shrill cackles pitched dangerously high upon the decibel scale. If the victim failed to respond immediately a terrible claw-like hand, sometimes two, would clamp upon the unfortunate, who would not leave the spot undivested of copper or brass. No one knew where they lived. In the early Fifties the municipality, glowing with Socialism, tried to tempt them with a small council flat, but they just guffawed oafishly at the poor bureaucrat who approached them and stained his nice new trousers with drool. Their abode was generally assumed to be one of the small caves dotting the Jerusalem hills, but which side of the border it might be, no one knew. It is not known if they were seen in the Jordanian sector of the City proper, where they might have been trespassing on the turf of the King of the Old City beggars, the notorious clochard, Bin-Zabl . . .

Now the United States Central Intelligence Agency had determined, apparently, that Babelech-und-Farfel were not really Babelech-und-Farfel, but dangerous Russian spies, whose true names were Boris Kolyakov and Lizbeta Stefanovna, Heroes of the Soviet Union. No further information about them was contained in the document that had fallen into Inspector Tarablus's hands except the date when the surveillance upon them commenced: It was 10th May, 1960, the very day the famous Moses Klander was shot and the infamous Groise Metsiyes arrested, in Zion Square. And Zion Square, everyone knew, was one of Babelech-und-Farfel's favourite pitches. They would sit there for days, shrieking raucously and harassing the passers-by. But if they had been there that day, obviously no one had considered taking them in for questioning.

Inspector Tarablus of Jerusalem Homicide was a Good Cop. His motto was : The Arm of Justice Is Long. So, respecting the limits of Agent XBZThree's demarcation he began, on his own and in his spare

135

time, evenings, nights, off-shifts, holidays, the long quest for his unholy grail . . .

Meanwhile, Father Andronicus hammered on the iron door of his cell in the Jerusalem kishla. He knew Major Uscuglu was on home leave in wartime Constantinople, attending patriotic rallies or maybe watching his kiddiwinks play bat and ball on the beach, beaming, no doubt, at their cries of merriment, and so was not around to indulge in his favourite penal pastime, i.e., kicking prisoners in the balls with his big Ottoman army boots, leaping up and down on their spinal columns or just hanging them by the thumbs and flaying the soles of their feet with a huge knobbed club. Deputy Chief Jailor Merkedes was a modernist, of a relatively benign mien, who used to say, twirling his moustaches: 'The twentieth century has arrived.' 'Cut the cackle!' whined the bored warder, Private Pusht, who came running to see what was up. 'I protest!' cried the Priest, 'there is no latrine paper!' 'All right,' said Pusht, 'simmer down. I'll bring you something. I don't want to live in your stink.' He went away and reappeared a mere three minutes later, throwing through the bars of the cell a very old bindingless volume of crinkling yellowy pages. It was only after Father Andronicus had wiped his arse wite the title page that he noticed it was a copy of the lost alchemical keywork *Cabalologus Sephiroticum* of the Gnostic martyr Iphictitus, busted in 343 AD for Valentinianism and Heresy One. Excitedly he wiped the last of his shit with his fingers and, keeping one furtive eye on the rusty doorhatch, began to peruse the script . . .

**Further tales of Olde Jerusalem: More encounters with the Judas Pig:**

Round One: The Klander Institute, Easter 1946, Good Friday:

A hebephrenic patient named Jan Inkandinsky, troubled by visions of God, who had, it appears, taken up lodgings in his left testicle, was trundling laundry down the tunnel, which had only recently been refurbished and linked up to the morgue, when, suddenly, he abandoned his load, rushed into the main building, wrestled several staff to the ground, leaped out of a window, vaulted over the perimeter fence and did not stop running until he had reached the roof of the Jerusalem railway station, from where he had to be removed by firemen with ladders, the riot squad and beefy Salonikan porters.

'Face of Satan!' he said later to Klander, '. . . belly of Asmodeus . . . Pubic hairs of Beelzebub . . . Eyes of Sheol . . . Snout dribbling the semen of Samael . . .'

'What did it say to you?' asked Klander. 'Did it speak?'

'Of course not!' scoffed the lunatic. 'Pigs don't speak, you schlemiel!' (In 1948 he was released as cured, and joined the Rabbinate's Kosher Certification Department.)


Round Two: Christmas Eve, 1951:

The whole Institute shaken to a ghastly nocturnal groaning. As if, someone said, a leviathan was being strangled, deep in the bowels of the earth. As the building was punkt on the Armistice border the Security Services scrambled. They brought drills, shovels, mine detectors, Geiger counters and a blind, Polish water diviner. They never released their findings, and told the press a cock-and-bull story concerning defective cisterns. But one day, when the files are dug up ... And yet there are some who say ...

Twelve years later, 1963:

Klander pushing up the daisies at Mount Herzl. Flusser his inheritor. Easter Friday, in the corridor of Ward Three. A full face, full blown, slambam-kalamazam sighting. Present: Dr Feifinkoklootz-Ear-Nose-and-Throat, Nurse Bella (now in Australia), Male Nurse Elkayam, and five patients, unnamed. At noon, the Pig, unannounced, and without being formally introduced, confronts them, rounding the corridor corner. Bloated, white-stomached, black-eared, snot-nosed, bloodshot, with red-smudged bandages unwinding from each of its four uncloven trotters. (Description noted by Davidov, years later, after several weeks spent under Elkayam's bed, noting psychic regurgitations.) Elkayam, who had after all faced King Farouk, grabbed a broom and advanced, crying authoritatively: 'Yallah, imshi min hun!' But the creature opened its mouth, outflowing the fetid stench of neglected graveyards and organic decay which bowled them all over like nine-pins. As they all scattered, climbing up walls and behind cupboards, the beast confounded them further by standing up on its hind legs ('eight feet off the floor!' – Davidov) and, giving a positively ladylike piqued toss of its head, exited around the corner. Despite posses and tumults, alarms and excursions, it was not seen again from that day.

A grim silence descended upon all the witnesses (in a mental home, who wants to push it?) ... They put it down to mass hypnosis, hallucinations, delirium tremens and incipient coprophagia (there was no trace at all on the floors of the blood or drool that had been seen). Reb Drek (Rabbi Druk), however, Staff Chaplain (a post later abolished), demanded an exorcism. He had found, he said, that seven of the Institute's mezuzahs were counterfeit, i.e. not produced under Rabbinate seal. Who knew how many of these vicious fakes, he fulminated, which deprived the Faithful of genuine divine protection, were infesting the jambs of Israel? It was a wonder ghost swine were not busily chomping at half the doors in the land. The Pig, he declared, was a collective dybbuk of the poor lunatics of Klander, brought to manifestation by the signing, only weeks previously, of a Pact of Ishmaelite Unity, between Egypt, Iraq and Syria, dedicated to the 'liberation' of the 'usurped Homeland' which the heathen scoundrels called 'Palestine'. Flusser could not afford to antagonize the Orthodox charities which donated some funds to the Institute, so he receded, mumbling, into the background as Reb Drek gathered a quorum of sages from the depths of Mea Shearim, the crème-de-la-crème of religious authorities on phenomena of the Other World.

The exorcism took place on 13th May. In charge was the Reb Zvi Kook Zweischaften, alias the Monk, who had performed similar ceremonies in New Jersey, Przemysl, Aden and Costa Rica, to name but a few, but spent most of his life in a small room in Hevrat Shas Street, eating nothing but eggs and honey and bread baked in Levinger's Bakery. (Nietzsche, it can be noted, lived just around the corner, and they shopped at the same grocer, Fassbinder, in whose queue they sometimes lingered, chatting about the Nebenmenschen.) Second in command was the Ilui of Tshernovitz who, though only fourteen-years-old, was already a Gadol Ba'Torah. Then Reb Drek, and seven Rabbis from the Seven Courts of learning originating Within the Pale. They were accompanied by Flusser, nightwatchman self-designate, wriggling unaccustomedly in the swathes of prayer shawl and phylacteries.

At the appointed hour, 4.45 a.m., they proceeded down the liftshaft and into the tunnel, led by the wild vision of the Monk, his shoulder-length hair swinging under his battered black Homburg, the bulbous nose sprung from sunken cheeks, his gleaming emerald eyes gazing out of unknown depths. They set up their paraphernalia on a cleared laundry trolley: the embers, the purification board, the censers and incense, the silver candelabra, the black wax candles and an ark of the Torah rescued from the sack of Bialystok.

4.55. The Ilui lights the candles. The Monk casts incense on the embers, takes the ram's horn in hand. Two Rabbis open the scroll of the Book at Leviticus (Chapter 10). Curls of red and black smoke. Creak creak, in background. It is Flusser fidgeting on a wooden folding chair. Incense, faintly mingled with lysol. Ugh. Monk puts the horn to his lips: an intermittent blast –

TOOT!TOOT-TOOT-TOOT-TOOT! TOOT!

'BEGONE!' he bellows, like a street vendor in Mahane Yehuda at a bargain stall. 'VILE SPIRIT! OUTER ONE! RETURN FROM WHENCE YOU CAME, INA'AL DINAK! DOWN, BOY, DOWN INTO THE GREAT ABYSS!'

Not a sausage. Candles guttering. Flusser breathing through a stopped-up nose. The Ilui's new shoes, birthday present from his mama, squeaking as he shuffles in place.

TOOT!

TOOT-TOOT-TOOT-TOOT!

TOOT-TOOT!TOOT-TOOT!TOOT-TOOT-TOOT!

A shape, materializing from the musky, miasmic air? The monster from the id, as in *Forbidden Planet*? A guffawing demon, sliding down the tiles with a bathtowel? The mournful voice of a lost soul, crying Let Me Out! Let Me Out!?

Absolutely nada.

So Reb Drek read out 10–12 Leviticus, Deutero-nomy 1–3 and several pasages of Ezekiel. The seven Rabbis accompanied him with a subsonic hum, while Ilui read out a special version of Genesis, using only every fifty-third letter. The Monk, as a coup de grace, released into the air the pubic hairs of a virgin plucked out personally by the Enemy of Mankind, Torquemada, in 1492.

It was a complete failure.

At 5.30 they picked up the purification board, the embers, the incense, candelabra and candles, and ark of the scroll from Bialystok and sadly, dispiritedly, shuffled back to the lift, harassed by the Ilui's squeaky shoes.

'I enjoyed that,' Flusser soothingly said to Reb Drek, 'despite the anticlimax.'

'Never mind,' said the Monk with a philosophical shrug, 'some you win, some you lose. That's show business.'


**Coda: From ' "Nietzsche" – A Case History of Pos-session', by Dr Peter Ze'ev Flusser.**

'. . . we tend to recognize as "mad" behaviour which appears chronically inconsistent and irra-tional in the context of the society in which such behaviour occurs. We accept as sane beliefs which we totally reject, as long as they appear to have their own inner consistency, their own rationality as it were. The famous Judge Schreber, of whom Freud wrote his *Notes on a Case of Paranoia* (1911, of 1884-5), insisted he was totally sane, despite his conviction that God had launched a conspiracy to turn him into a woman so that the new female Schreber could, by intercourse with God, give birth to a new world after the old had been brought to an end. While not renouncing this somewhat unusual belief, the Judge won an appeal in the German courts of his era for his discharge from the asylum in which he had been placed and for the restoration of his civil rights. (Food for thought in a supposedly more enlightened age . . .) The court evidently bowed to the unshakable consistency of the plaintiff's self-created universe . . .

'Is our "Nietzsche" then another Schreber? On what grounds do we categorize him as "mentally ill", even "insane"? One need only accept one basic fantastic premise – his being a "reincarnation" of the great philosopher who proclaimed the death of God (and himself died insane after many years of illness and decline) to accept his entire behaviour as absolutely logical. His central presumption has been steadfastly maintained over a period of many years. His "delusion", if such it is, is systemic and rational. He is able to discuss it "objectively" and assimilate the accusations of madness with a wry, gentlemanly humour. Were it not for his bouts of depression, migraines and recurrences of the dysmnestic syndrome he might never have come to our notice. (And do his successive voluntary commitments to the Institute indicate a desire for a "cure" or are they just another stage in his obsessive "plan"?)

' "Nietzsche", like many chronic, but consistent psychotics, (our labelling once again) severely challenges long-cherished assumptions about the nature of "madness" and "sanity". His case again poses the question: is not every "delusion" in some sense true? And if so – on what grounds do we adopt our own particular "truth", our own axiomatic belief system?

'These, and other questions I shall attempt to examine in the following disquisition . . .'

FOR SALE: Inflatable rubber dinghy, domestic utensils, football, fur coat, samovar, ladder. Margolis, tel. 436865.

PSYCHOANALYTICAL LIBRARY – Complete Freud, father & daughter, Rank, Binswanger, Reich, Jung. All offers – A. Peretz, 643221.

GRAVE WARNING to desecrators of the Sabbath: For he who desecrateth the Sabbath is liable to stoning, and for (desecration of) Yom Kippur, to excommunication . . . Any Jew who calleth himself non-religious is wicked or a perpetrator of wicked deeds . . . It is forbidden to switch on the radio (on the Sabbath) or to switcheth it off, and it is forbidden to speak on the telephone or to drive an automobile. He who transgresseth against any one of these prohibitions his judgement shall be stoning, and if he transgresseth in public or before ten of Israel he shall be considered a Stranger, and he shall not be joined to a quorum for any matter of Holiness until that time when he shall make full repentance, with all his heart.

GIBSON ELECTRIC GUITAR, a bargain, call Arieh, tel. 413208.

DUSHKA, PLEASE RETURN! Father forgives everything. Mother.

> – from Jerusalem notice boards, 197–

JERUSALEM, AGED WHORE OF A THOUSAND
PANTING SUITORS, IRON KEY CLANGING
RUSTILY AT HER CORRODED CHASTITY BELT.
OPEN SEZ ME! THEY CRY IN TWO HUNDRED
AND FORTY TONGUES. CLOSED FOR BUSINESS,
THE OLD BAG CROAKS, COME BACK IN THE
SUMMER, SCHMUCKS! DOUR AND FROWNING,
SHE LOOKS OUT, OVER THE RAIN SWEPT HILLS.

January, '69, the Old City. The Christmas pilgrims,
even the Russians who stick perversely to the Julian
calendar, have drawn in their net of piety till April.
The religious fakers' stalls are trundled away.
Total collapse of the price index for true nails from
the cross. The seven sects in the Holy Sepulchre
have opted for hibernation. A single bored Israeli
policeman, his blue sweater a dab of colour against
the grey of the compound, guards the Sepulchre
gate. He is chatting to a grey-bearded Greek priest
about Saloniki, where coincidentally they both
spent their youth. The priest is scratching his left
ear bemusedly. 'Kostas Iorgos' Sweet Shop? Was
that in Papasiou or Themistokleous Street?' Ah,
nebesch, they both gaze wistfully into the lost past.
   Round the corner, not a stone's throw from the
very spot upon which the Saviour was nailed up by
the Roman fuzz, Blok, Nietzsche and Nili were on
this day perusing the smörgåsbord menu at the Old
City's Swedish Tea Shoppe.
   'I shall try the Swedish pancakes,' said Blok.
   'Nothing but a tea for me,' said Nili.
   'As it is Thursday,' said Nietzsche, 'I shall have
the Swedish Pea Soup with Pork.' The waiter, a
sullen youth named Farouk who seemed to spend
the entire day listening, his head cocked to one
side, for a trumpet call that did not come, nodded
absently and padded off.
   It was a cold day, eleven thirty in the morning,

and they were the only customers. They sat outside on the patio, protected only by a low stone fence against the ravages of the wind. This was a Nietzsche affectation, since it was perfectly snug and cosy inside, where a fireside heater was on. 'It reminds me of Sils Maria,' he said cryptically. 'Low temperatures toughen the mind. Heat turns the brain to sludge.'

'Pneumonia kills you dead,' countered Nili. 'What would Flussie say if I lost him his prize patient?'

'Buki-sriki,' said Nietzsche, 'don't worry, I've already contracted to accompany his Nobel acceptance speech. Wait till you see me at Uppsala, knocking their eyes out with my psychiatric presti-digitation. Who else can unravel his own Oedipus Complex while doing a De Lubbock handstand and twirling three hoops on his feet?'

Blok shot him an askance look. One could never be sure when Nietzsche was joking and sane, or in deadly earnest and quite off his chump. Such was the man. Ecce Homo, cholera.

The muezzin in the mosquetops began the second call to prayer. By the aegis of Messrs Grundig, his amplified voice wailed over the cupolas, echoed in the alleyways, reminding the just of their obligations and the heretical of their perfidy. It joined with the lilt of Amman Radio, jingling inside the Tea Shoppe. All the way from Enemy Territory, an ethereal Trojan Horse.

'Who knows what that song's about,' ventured Nili, 'for all we know it's Aleihum – Up and At 'em, Kill all the Jews and be done . . .'

'It's a love song,' said Nietzsche. ' "Come my Beloved, Let Us Cuddle Under the Lemon Tree and Perfume Ourselves With its Fragrance".'

Her turn to shoot him a glance. Since when did you know Arabic, magister? Or is he just ragging again? Their order arrived. Nietzsche enthused over the Swedish Pea Soup with Pork. Nili made a sour face. 'Pig meat!' she said. 'Yecchh!'

'You Jews don't know what you're missing,' he said disingenuously, tucking in with a will. He nudged Blok in the ribs. 'She thinks I've gone nutty again.'

'Nuttier than you they don't make 'em,' she said, in her best bedside manner. 'Let's eat up and get out of here. It's freezing cold and I don't like this place at all.'

Nili, though a patriot, had not yet adjusted to Empire. Lo, the Old City is Ours these nineteen months now, taken by storm in the war of June '67, annexed by decree soon after. Within weeks the Israeli tourists, bedazzled by this new 'abroad' only ten minutes' walk from home, had divested the bazaars of their original stock of gew-gaws, old porcelain bric-à-brac, antiques fake and real, bedouin saddles, Hebron glass, carpets, schmutters galore, et cetera, but the workshops and merchants had pretty soon caught up with the new indiscriminate demand. If Jerusalem is the Methuselah whore, the bazaar is her ancient vagina, dank with the odour of the millions of suckers who have had their quick jollies there, leaving their lucre tinkling in her vast sweaty bodice. Come and Get It, is the cackle of a thousand streetwise vendors, with eyes that are taloned hooks. Nili, daughter of Europe, still very much a stranger here . . .

'Pazienza,' said Nietzsche, raising a wet green walrus moustache from the soup. 'I am waiting for someone, who is due here at any minute.'

'Sometimes at Klander,' said Nili, 'I can't make out patients from staff.'

'I often felt that way myself,' said Blok.

'It's easy,' said Nietzsche, slurping. 'The staff are the earnest, neurotic ones. The patients are the ones having a whale of a time, putting the lot of you on.'

'Do you really think so?' Nili, charmante, talons in.

'Ah,' he said, pointing a heavy finger, 'you think that you can trap me into an admission now, don't you, that, following what I've just said, I'm not who I am, but just some potz with delusions of grandeur, who knows all along the full truth of his insignificance, but doesn't have the pisspoor gumption to stand up and be himself, face the world as he is and not through his fruitcake fantasies. Looking for the miracle cure, Nilikins? Succeed where twenty-five psychoanalysts with degrees de-la-zig-zig-line fell flat on their miserable faces? Don't give me that innocent look, Honeybunch, it wasn't yesterday I was hatched from the egg. I am who I am, and that's all there is to it.'

Nietzsche and Nili . . . What strange chemistry? No deadbeat nebesch he, to be hauled half drowned from the gutter. Perhaps she is drawn to the touch of Granit in him, that iron self-confidence that makes the old scoundrel Klander's abiding star . . .

Blok first met him the day after the group therapy meeting at which Almozlino broke down, spilling his woes, like the flow of the Tigris, upon the tiled floor. Blok, walking in the maze with Davidov, spotting a figure rapt in thought by the sundial.

'Hey, Philosopher!' Davidov cries (he was now in his manic phase). 'How are things? What's the Meaning of Life today?'

'Ah, Fixer – ' the man turned, 'I was looking for you. I need a new German original. Schopenhauer, *On the Indestructibility of Our Essential Being by Death*. Somebody stole my copy.'

'Probably the Magpie,' said Davidov, 'but don't worry, consider it done. Out of print, or burned in bulk by the censor, nothing escapes Davidov. We missed you at Group, yesterday, I can tell you. Fun and games, a scream from start to finish.'

'Group shtoup,' the man waved a disparaging hand. 'Nothing but a childish derivation from inferior minds. Adler, Jung, Sullivan, Bion. Psschtt! I have better things to do with my time.'

'You bet!' Davidov pummelled Blok's shoulder. 'The Philosopher is reshaping the world. Meet Avram Blok, a new lamb to the slaughter.'

'Pleased to meet you,' said Blok, warily.

'My card,' said the other. It read:

FRIEDRICH NIETZSCHE
Privatdozent – Philologus;
Institut Klander, 25 Reb Nahman Me'Bratslav;
also:- Harav Salant St, Jerusalem 90564.

He was not a large man, but unlike most of the shuffling, depressed patients of Klander he exuded an aura of power, holding himself ramrod straight and thrusting his great moustache forward under challenging, steady, brown eyes set below jutting eyebrows. He was neatly dressed in a grey light jacket and a pale blue rolltop sweater.

'You have read the Herr Professor's books, have you not?' said Davidov, punching Blok again on the shoulder.

'Not really,' said Blok, 'I have not yet had the honour.'

'Boys' stuff,' said the man, 'compared with what's coming. We'll show them yet, eh, Fixer?'

'Sure,' said Davidov, 'ace in the old asshole. The Professor,' he explained to Blok, 'is now writing in a code language known only to himself.'

'Let Veltsch rave, let Flusser wriggle,' the Philosopher gave Blok a wide wink, 'let them call in their ciphernauts and idiot savants, not one iota will they unravel. You won't forget that title now?'

'Schopenhauer,' said Davidov, '*Essential Being,*

148

by *Death, Indestructibility of.* In the oven. Forty-eight hours maximum. We'd better be going now.'
And they walked on, as if they had a particular place to go. The next time Blok met Nietzsche was in the ward corridor, the day before his discharge. The Philosopher dauntingly came straight up to him and said, 'You are Hungarian, aren't you?'

Blok nodded.

'Budapest?'

'My parents came from there.'

'They left then, that's good, that's good.' Nietzsche's eyes glazed over, as if his thoughts had just winged into a distant field. 'Ah, Magyars . . . what an idiot race. We're well shot of them, you and I. We must talk of this, sometime. But not today . . .' and he walked on absently, as if placed suddenly under remote control.

Then, after his trip abroad, Blok returned to Klander, for the life of him he knew not why. Just about one year after his first admission (discount for beginners) he found himself winding up Reb Nahman Me'Bratslav Street on the Seven Aleph bus to the gates with the fair cypress trees; to the front office, with its framed portraits of Klander, Freud and Ben Gurion on the walls, together with the carefully screened milder patients' paintings which the staff thought the public could bear . . .

Flusser poked his head round a door and invited him into his office: 'Avram, good to see you. You're looking well. How's the big world out there? Stirring times, no? Paris in May . . . You must have had some experiences . . .'

Well, not really, nothing much, quite a mundane time, really . . . some skirmishes, which one watched on television, nothing to do with me . . . what conclusions did I draw? Well, Europe . . . doesn't seem to be going anywhere . . . young people there don't see much of a future . . . cogs in machines, really . . . a lack of vision . . . whereas here, in this country . . .

'Well?' said Flusser.

'There is a vision. But is it a dream or a nightmare?'

'What do you think?' asked Flusser.

'I haven't made up my mind.'

He walked around the asylum, saying Hi to Elkayam and Big Golem and staff and patients he knew and trying to figure out what he was doing there, voluntarily in the nuthouse. Mrs Patchouli gave him an unwelcome bearhug and the ageing charlady Matilda asked him about her two emigré sons, whom she was sure he had met in Marseille.

'It's a big country,' he said, 'I was too far north, Paris, you know, most of the time . . .'

'Ah, Paris!' she understood immediately his distractions, 'Moulin Rouge! Folies Bergères!'

He moved on. Both Davidov and Nietzsche, he found out, were out on remission, though both were expected back as usual. The Magpie passed by him and pressed into his hand a perfectly nondescript pebble. 'Guard it with your life!' he hissed, urgently. 'None of the old hidey-holes, mind!'

Finally he found Nili (of course, journey's end here) in the north-eastern garden. Together with petite Nurse Pitsi she was walking a reluctant Old Leib. 'I'm not going to the showers!' the old nut mumbled. 'You're not sweet talking me in there . . .'

'Suit yourself,' said Nili, 'when your brother comes you'll be ponging like an old boot.'

'What brother?' rasped Leib. 'More Gestapo fiddlesticks. you know you shot him in '42 . . .'

'I'll take him back to the ward,' offered Nurse Pitsi, who while tiny, was in total control. She took hold of Leib's arm and propelled him, still protesting, by the force of her personality.

Blok walked with Nili to the outer fence, where

they stood, leaning their forearms on the weathered stones and gazing over the Valley. 'It still gets me here,' she said, thumping her lower ribcage. 'How often before '67 I used to stand here and stare at the Old City walls, just about within reach but at the same time a whole world away . . . Don't you think? Like a part of our collective unconscious that was split off and now has been joined up again . . .'

Oi, she had been reading Jung.

Blok just grunted non-committally. They looked out over the crumbling stone terraces, the brown arid earth, the cypresses swaying in the wind down along the main road, the higgledy-piggledy Arab houses of Silwan nestling in the crook of the hill, the few scattered dwellings curving towards them, among them, if but they knew, the ancestral home of Abu Shawareb . . . gazing, into the dark grey rain cloud which sat upon the Jericho hills, hiding the Dead Sea from view, trailing its misty tendrils up the Valley and the hill to caress them . . .

'God, I love this country,' she said, greedily breathing in the wind.

'It could be pretty nice,' he said.

'Avram,' she said, 'what are you going to do with your life?'

Why do they all ask that? Papa, Mama, Aunt Pashtida, Fat Avi who had enrolled for political science at the U., the court social worker, Flusser ('Well, well, what now, Avram, eh?') . . . He gave Nili the answer he really wanted to give the lot of them:

'Why should my life have meaning when everyone else's is meaningless?'

Pause. 'Avram,' she said, 'what can I say? Meaning is what we make for ourselves. We each have to decide who we are. Nobody can do that for us. The most other people can do for us is to kick us towards independence.' She gestured towards the asylum

151

building. 'That's all we do here, really. Other places have their miracle cures, their electrodes, their surgeon's knives, superdrugs. But here people do come back to us more often of their own accord. We try not to make patients into zombies, but to help them fall back on their own resources, to build up that shattered confidence . . .'

'Confidence treatment . . .' he said, 'that's what I need. Can you book me a room and bath?'

She unexpectedly ruffled his hair. 'Hey, sorry about the trumpet and drums. I didn't mean to lecture you, schmendrick. Forget the nuthouse. Listen, come and see me, any evening this week, except Thursday. I want to hear a full report of your doings, especially in Swinging London . . .' She brushed his cheek with her lips and turned off down the path. 'That's a prescription!' she called out to him, and was lost behind the hedgerows. He stood there, the feel of her fingers prickling his scalp, the moist of her lips still cold. Then drops of rain began spattering on him from the cloud moved up from Jericho. Rumbling, grumbling above him. Blok, gathering his jacket tight around him as he trotted back towards the main building . . .

. . . Nietzsche finished his Swedish Pea Soup and dried his moustache with his hankie. 'There's nothing like a proper piece of pork,' he said smugly. 'The conquest of the Old City is a godsend to all true Jerusalem atheists.' He leaned back and sipped a tall glass of tea. 'Why the Jews are turned off by pork is beyond me. I agree, pigs are ugly beasts. But so are some fish. Have you ever caressed a bakala? Not to speak of cows, with that stupid look, as if they're stoned on Bazooka bubble gum . . .'

'You don't have to make love to them,' said Nili, 'only eat them.'

'QED,' said Nietzsche, 'my point about pigs is

proven. I must have a dessert,' he added, lifting a finger. 'I have a sudden craving for, ladies and gentlemen – King Haakon's cakes. A Norwegian dish, this, but what's the difference. Farouk! The owners of this maison,' he explained, 'were a Maronite couple who had spent fifteen years in Stockholm. But the present owner of the joint is an Austro-Sudanese transvestite. He is still somewhat confused as to Scandinavian nuance . . .'

The sullen garçon, his head still cocked for the elusive ping of salvation, sauntered up and whispered in his ear.

'Ah!' exclaimed Nietzsche. 'Forget King Haakon! The man I am to meet has arrived.' Blok and Nili looked round but apart from the four of them and a mangy black cat, there was no whiff of a newcomer.

'He won't come out,' said Nietzsche, 'we'll have to go inside.'

'So why couldn't we have been indoors in the first place?!' Nili, ready to strangle her charge.

Voilà! inside the Tea Shoppe: ersatz wood panelling painted on the walls. Little vases of plastic flowers. Chintz figurines in the niches of small arched windows. Round tables, dinky chairs, red chequered tablecloths. To the right: the bar and smörgåsbord, Farouk, lounging thereabout, pretending to attend to business. Above him, the framed oval sepia portrait of Stockholm in winter, and a vignette of a blonde King and Queen. The whole melange lit by dim orange-tinted bulbs set in heavy flowery lampshades, arranged in all the wrong parts of the room. Bits of floor were illuminated, tables remained in darkness. In the back, in a recess which might have been carved out especially for him, an immensely obese man sat. A dim glow upon his vast scarlet waistcoat, stretched tight as a drum, doughy hands fingerclasped upon it. His head, in shadow, appeared to be a fearfully pyramidal shape, until one made out in the gloom he was wearing an old-fashioned fez. He was like Sidney Greenstreet in *Casablanca*, pumped up to three times the size.

But Nietzsche ignored this apparition, crossing over to the opposite, left side of the room, where a diminutive figure was hunched over a corner table, nervously twiddling its thumbs. The man was dressed in a light tattered leather jacket. He had receding hair and a smudgy moustache and five o'clock shadow and weak shifty eyes darting about like mice behind exceedingly thin-rimmed spectacles.

'Hello, George!' said Nietzsche, tipping an imaginary hat, 'chi fache? bine? This is George,' he announced, beaming, to Nili and Blok as they came over and drew up chairs, glancing uneasily at the phenomenon in the niche across the floor. 'Nurse Nili and Avram Blok,' he presented them in turn, 'colleagues in the fruitcake racket.'

'I thought you were coming alone,' said George.

'Friends of mine you can trust,' said Nietzsche, expansively. 'Farouk, cognac all round, s'il vous plaît.'

'I trust you a piece, Madman,' said George, his mice running over Blok and Nili, 'but don't push it.' From the recess, came the soft wheezy breathing of the fat man, with metronome regularity.

Nietzsche laughed, taking out a comb, and began grooming his moustache. George's mice, having completed their examination, retreated behind the cage of his eyelids. Farouk brought four glasses, and the tattered man waited until he was out of earshot.

'I have what you wanted,' he said to Nietzsche, 'but you wouldn't believe the trouble . . . typhoons, anticyclones, Pathan marauders, bandits, customs officials . . .' he spoke in an eastern-accented

154

Hebrew, in a hoarse low tone impressed with a sadness befitting his lugubrious features.

'George deals in various rare goods and services,' explained Nietzsche, deflecting the guests' curiosity. 'I happen to have a corner on his antiques division, a very special arrangement.'

'If I hadn't given you my word, Madman,' George said mournfully, 'I could get a price for this elsewhere that would make your hair stand on end.' Carefully eyeing the bar he pulled from under his seat a worn khaki US Army surplus knapsack, out of which he tenderly produced a thin quarto-sized tome with a crumbling spine, rebound in peeling cardboard. Nietzsche whipped from his coat a pair of white cloth gloves and a spectacle case with his reading glasses. Hands professionally thrust in the gloves he took the volume and laid it on the table. Blok and Nili leaned forward to peek as he opened it. Blok saw yellowing parchment-like pages crammed with black gothic lettering interspersed here and there with passages of red and green. In the margins were strange symbols, bizarre diagrams and fierce illustrations that jogged his childhood memories.

'I once had something like this . . .' he began, hesitantly, 'but it got mislaid, forget it . . .' George and Nietzsche briefly looked up, then returned to their rapt perusal.

'It is the cat's sleeping garments, without a doubt,' said Nietzsche, peeling off his reading spectacles. 'You have done well, Igor. The gods are pleased. You have earned your purse of gold kreutzers.'

'Dollars, cash, will do nicely,' said George, picking his nose, 'as agreed, not a cent less or more.'

'God, I should get out of here,' said Nili, 'this is too much like work.' As Nietzsche took out his wallet and began laying crisp notes upon the table, 'You'd better not let the Health Authority see that wad,' she added, 'I thought you were skint, Philosopher.'

'Easy come, easy go,' he said breezily, 'the Bourse is a fickle mistress . . .' George swept up the notes, flipping through them expertly, tucking them away in an inside flap of his jacket right over his heart. Business done, his face miraculously filled with colour, and took on a catlike beam. 'A pleasure to do pleasure with you, Madman,' he purred, 'and now I shall be on my way.'

'Just another round of cognac,' declared Nietzsche. 'Why risk the freezing steppes unarmed? Farouk, the bottle!' he cried, staying, with open palm, the faint protests of his vendor.

Pretty soon they were all glowing with robust conviviality. They forgot fatso, wheezing away in his niche, and Farouk, and the smörgåsbord. Nietzsche, telling tall tales of his first life in Prussia, and of his spartan schooldays at Pforta. George, loosening up, recounting odd tales of bondage and domination in the Caucasian mountains. They finished one carafe, began another and rapidly became utterly plastered. Several loutish youths wearing old army greatcoats, poked their heads in the Tea Shoppe but withdrew hurriedly, clip-clopping away down the alley. Nietzsche, rising to his feet, climbed on the table and began reciting sections of Goethe's *Faust*. Mephistopheles meets the Witches:

'I'll shriek with glee, I'll lose my brain,
My Squire Satan has come back again!
Such appellation, hag, is out of place . . .
It's now a name for fairy tales and fables;
the people are as miserable as ever –
the Evil One is gone, evil remains.
Call me Baron, and we'll have no more of this.
I am a cavalier, a gentleman like others . . .'

'Bravo, maestro!' cried Blok, 'Think what the stage has missed!'

'The stage??' quoth Nietzsche. 'The fucking stage??'

'Hail, Mephisto!' gurgled George, and fell backwards off his chair.

While this was going on, in the recess, just below the obese man in shadows, a trap-door, unseen by anyone, slowly lifted in the red lino floor. A dark head rose with hydraulic smoothness, eyes glinting in the Tea Shoppe's dim glow. The head slid up into the fat man's anus, but he did not give so much as a quiver. A small peephole opened in the folds of his waistcoat, and the lens of a miniature camera peeked through. Click-click, click-click, its shutter flipped imperceptibly, as the foursome at the far table frolicked, Nietzsche pouring cognac at the supine George and bellowing, basso profundo:

'– What is the drift of this performance?
Why all this junk and mumbo jumbo?
I detest such cheap and obvious trickery,
with which we are all so familiar!'

Click-click-whirr, the camera in the fat man's abdomen synchronized with his snores. Its exposures completed, the peephole closed. the dark head withdrawing, the fat man's sphincter muscles recontracting, the red lino trap-door re-closed. Wheeze-wheeze, wheeze-wheeze, the leviathan breathing, the continuing metronome . . .

Ding-dong, ding-dong . . . Without, the tolling of the old Sepulchre bells. Quasimodos in the belfry stirred fitfully, then turned over and resumed their slumbers.

The man Nietzsche introduced to Blok and Nili as George was not really George at all. He was Liam O'Habash, notorious chief pornographer to the entire Fertile Crescent. His running of rare books to Nietzsche was merely a sideline, a subterfuge to gain his confidence and draw closer to the Klander Institute, upon which he was keeping a close eye. This surveillance was in the nature of an obligation he owed one Constantine Zorza, the Levantine Scopophile, head of the Beirut KGB Office. Zorza had, in the intervals between his other duties (which consisted mainly of attempted exegesis of the Lebanese TV's skiing news), developed an interest in the strange events surrounding the assassination of Klander and the legend of the elusive Nachtnebel. Thus O'Habash would receive sporadic instructions to expedite his investigations, which he reluctantly pursued under threat of the revelation of his eroto-commercial exploits to his mother, one Annie O'Halloran, who, having spent her mid-years in the Levant evading British justice, had now returned to the old sod and, still hale and hearty at the age of seventy-eight, was now stockpiling gelignite in County Monahan for the resurgent Nationalist offensive. Thus Liam pursued his half-hearted connections while Constantine Zorza tore out his hair in the Corniche Mazraa, trying to interpret the coded meaning of bulletins such as 'Set fair at Laqlouq; moderate precipitation at Bazaaoun.'

By this time, of course, Blok was head over heels in love with Nili. He had taken a job as a sound recordist with Holyland Films of Ein Karem. Now he could afford to move out of his parents' apartment and take a room of his own, close to the centre of town, in Takhkemoni Street. This was off the Jaffa Road, where the bus to work passed, and the Mahane Yehuda market: the packed street stalls in tight narrow alleyways, vendors raucously battling for the attention of the masses, crying the virtues of plucked chickens, choice cuts, vegetables just a moment ago wrenched from the ground, peaches and plums the like the world has not seen, tomatoes that could put your eyes out, oranges that would change your life. Blok never tired of plunging into this whirlpool, this splodged palette bright even in the dullest weather: loud yellows and reds of the vendors' shirts, heavy blacks of the ultra-orthodox, speckled, chequered, print dresses stretched round middle-aged sephardi housewives, lumpy balloons, poised for lift off . . . and the hundred and one intermingling smells of crabapples, oranges, lemons, wet fish, slaughtered poultry, sumsum, halva and roast nuts and good solid down-to-earth donkey's turds, dog poo and chicken shit of the live specimens crammed in cages, waiting for the ritual knife. Grand guignol, larger than life, *ya'ani*, an Italian epic in Ferraniacolour.

His room was with the family of a small and friendly Iraqi grocer, Nissim, whom Nili, in some unexplained way, had taken under her widespread wing. He had a collection of children, small, medium and large, uncles, aunts, two or three grandmothers and a number of undefinables, clan raggle-taggle, who rarely impinged on Blok whose room was self-contained in the back of the old stone house, with its own kitchenette and shower. And a yeshiva adjacent, where wild silhouettes bobbed across yellow-lit barred windows. And nobody in the vicinity collected stamps! Mama mia! A godsend! Nili visited him there, playing with the kids, charming the uncles and cackling with the aunts over the shortcomings of men. She took Blok for walks in the adjoining streets, the twisting alleys of semi-orthodox Jerusalem, the beards! Merde, alors! The fur hats! And betimes to the nearby Biblical Zoo, a magic tour linking both their childhoods – the enchanted, encaged, garden of Eden: giraffes, lions, tigers and bears, pangolins,

wilde-beestes, zebras, gibbons, baboons, hippopotami, seals ... crocodiles, elephants, jackals and
wolves ... Purchasing their little yellow tickets,
their Artik ices and a large bag of peanuts, Blok and
Nili ambled clippety-clop down the neat paved
trails and terraces, through the dark green pines.
Past the vultures and buzzards gazing aspiringly at
them, past the famous masturbating chimpanzee
which delighted the children and scandalized the
devout, past the big cats that Nili refused to watch
in their misery, to stand by the warthogs' pen. The
ugly beasties hunkered there in the mud, their
black eyes bulging over their horrid pimples and
knife-sharp, filthy tusks. Through the trees one
could see the hills across the valley, pre-'67 Enemy
Land, from where a berserk Jordanian sniper had
once opened fire, mortally wounding the aardvark.

'I feel for the animals,' said Blok, tossing some
peanuts to the apathetic monsters. 'There they are,
just like us, stuck with the roles that other people
want them to play.'

'You have to be true to yourself,' said Nili.

Blok quoted himself: 'That's fine, but I haven't yet
found me a self worth being true to.'

'You're a worrier,' she said, 'that's your problem. You're like a dog that wants to discover the
last ounce of mystery in a bone, instead of just
quietly sucking it. Everybody has hard knocks in his
life. You just have to float with the tide and grab
those little moments that can be enjoyed.'

'But don't you see,' he said loudly, with a vehe-
mence that even alarmed the warthogs, 'there has
to be more! There has to be something there that
can be grasped! Some nugget among the trash!
Something to redeem the soggy bloated wasteland!
Shit! All those stinking swamps one's bogged down
in! Philatelic jungles, curare-tipped silences ...
wasted years of school, the fucking army, for what?

Rubbish and half-witted wet dreams of "Home-land" and "People" . . . always what *they* expect of you, never what *you* may need – caged as tightly as these silly animals, with imbeciles who like it so much they don't even see the bars!'

'Ah, so Avram Blok is something special!'

'For myself I'm as special as I'm ever going to be . . . Shit! At least they taught us how to lie in the army, one useful piece in the garbage . . . maybe I should rejoin Klander and sink into easy melancholy with the other nuts . . .'

'You don't need that crutch. And I'm not going to carry your bedpans. You seemed to cope all right with France and England. What's so different here?'

Ha, if only you knew! 'It's all different here. A fucking straitjacket. Any direction I move I'll be fulfilling someone else's expectations.'

'Is that so bad?'

'It's murder. It's . . . complete castration of the soul.'

'Bullshit!'

'Yes, it's that too.'

Quel angst. They walked on, leaving the warthogs behind. Silent, down the stone steps, by the jackals' sunken artificial den, up to the perimeter wire fence.

'I'll tell you, Avram,' she said, 'I often feel that way myself. But we can't all be extra special, Albert Einsteins, Sigmund Freuds, Lenins. Most of us just have to make do with the shit.'

'But it's still shit.'

'That's true.'

They joined hands and, enclasped together, proceeded towards the grey wolf's cage. Now Nili, as we have mentioned, lived in an apartment in Onkelos Street, Number – , to which the exiled of society were oft-times ingathered, and this street

161

was but a stone's throw from the scene of Blok's primal shame and misfortune, or the commencement of his anabasis, depending on how you may wish to view it. She shared this apartment with a plain, rather dowdy young woman called Hava, who often resembled nothing so much as a piece of the tattered flotsam, rumpled bedlinen and scattered clothing that was her habitat. The other permanent tenant of the flat was Papishik – 'Little Pope' in Polish, Nili's fat, furry, supercilious cat with its mean and calculating eye. Hava lived on various foods out of cans, but Papishik would dine only on the choicest fish fillet, which Nili acquired at ridiculous cost from the grocer across the way. ('Intestines? Cow's kishkes,' Franz the Grocer would offer, 'a beanfeast for the Queen of the Moggies?' But Nili, in proxy for Papishik, would turn up her nose and demand the regular, spurning all counterfeit dainties.)

The first time Blok visited her there, in her dishevelled nest, was an evening of alarums and confusions: first the drifter from Haifa telephoned, from somewhere up north, brusquely demanding her presence. 'I'm not at your beck and call,' she said, 'cut a hole in a melon. I'm not a wanking machine.' She plonked the receiver down. 'Nili, everyone's a sucker,' she said to Blok. 'Hungry? I'll fix you a Spanish omelette.' Blok did not like Spanish omelettes but said Yes, he would love one. She had hardly brought out the frying pan when the telephone rang again. This time it was the religious politician, plaintively transmitting his angst. 'I don't know how I can help you there,' she said, after he had rapped for ten minutes. 'You know I don't believe in God, but I'm afraid I can't disprove His existence for you.' She took the phone into the kitchen and, cradling the receiver, began cracking eggs into a bowl. 'For all I know, He's out there

162

watching, and we'll both get a drubbing when the final day comes round ...' Onions and tomatoes were chopped and diced as the lost soul droned on. 'No, I don't think suicide will solve your problem. They'll bury you outside the fence, won't they, and then you may never know ...' The vegetables sizzled in the pan. 'No, I don't mind you phoning one bit. What are friends for if not to drive each other bananas?'

Next, just as Nili and Blok were tucking in to their omelette, a neighbour rang the doorbell and Nili stood for half an hour at the door fending off a harangue about Papishik having eaten the said neighbour's new pot plants. 'But she eats only fillet ... Ask Franz the Grocer ...' nothing was of any avail. The plaintiff left, dropping dark allusions about man-sightings at all hours ... It's the 'dosses', Nili explained to Blok, the ultra-religious. Now the Yeshiva's down the road they've encircled us. This was the Seminary of the great Rabbi Yehuda Zweitlin Nerya, a brown barracks-like block a little way down the hillside built in the past couple of years. The counter-revolution! Nili had evidently become an issue in the neighbourhood politic. She tended to pass by the Seminary on her way to the bus stop dressed in summer in the meagrest fashion. The resident youth were delighted but the old fogeys in charge were outraged. (Return of the masturbating chimp.) 'Bloody hypocrites!' scoffed Nili. 'How many times you see them filling the sherut taxis from Tel Aviv late at night, coming back from the brothels ... isn't it sanctioned somewhere? "If the urge overtakes you, go to another town?" ' An old Rabbi, it was rumoured, had a heart attack and died on seeing her traipse up the hill in hot pants. 'Well, if bare thighs can kill 'em off,' said Nili unbendingly, 'they're not much use down on earth, are they? Better pastures up there, along with the Righteous, the Wise Men and all the Saints.'

Of course, it meant war. Meat coated with rat poison had been left in the garden, and a neighbour's dog found dead. Only Papishik's indescribable snootiness saved her from a similar fate. Slogans had been daubed on the outer walls of the house: 'Prostitutes Out!' 'Death to Sabbath Profaners!' 'Down with the Powers of Darkness!' But Papishik fought back, lying in wait at night behind bushes and, lithely pouncing, sinking her little sharp fillet white teeth in the calves of Yeshiva students.

Hardly had they scoffed the lukewarm omelettes when the telephone rang again. This time it was Eisav, stuck in the pouring rain in a telephone booth at the Jerusalem Central Bus Station. He had fifty-five minutes between buses from one base camp to another and was urgently, desperately, existentially in need of a brief encounter.

'I can't come,' she said, 'I'm with a friend.' Pause. 'You'll just have to sort it out yourself,' she said . . . 'What's that? . . . No, nobody that's any business of yours . . .??? . . . And that's the second time tonight someone thought I belonged to him . . . My, you're waxing lyrical . . . What? Come off it. If the Egyptian army hasn't done you in you'll survive one fucked-up night. Lord knows you've had plenty . . . What did I mean by that? Nothing except what's in your own fucked-up head . . . All right, listen, I don't want your blood on my hands. I'll be there if I can make it in time. But don't expect anything from this . . . You too, Big Schmuck . . . Well,' she said to Blok as she put down the phone, 'care for a walk in the rain?'

'Listen, I don't want to stick my nose in your affairs . . .'

'No affair, stupid. That was just my fucked-up

cousin. Come on, I want you to be there. A walkies will do you good.'

So there the man stood, just under the platform overhang, looking like a becalmed walrus. His thin hair was wetly plastered over his head and his red moustache drooped as if it were about to deposit twin rainwater pools on the ground. His flying jacket was gathered about him like a tent. Immense red mittens were on his hands. On his shoulders the single pips of the rank of Major glistened. All around him a multitude of would-be passengers pressed and crowded to be out of the rain, under which the big Leyland buses growled and snorted, kicking out their exhaust.

'When does your bus leave?' asked Nili, looking up into his moist ruddy face.

'Fifteen minutes,' he said. 'Who's this?'

'Avram Blok,' she said. 'A friend.'

'I want us to speak alone,' he said.

'I'll go get myself a coffee or something,' said Blok. 'I'll be near the ticket counters.'

He went off, leaving them to face each other like two gunslingers in Tombstone at dusk. Belatedly he bought the evening newspaper:

JARRING MISSION DOOMED TO FAILURE
AMERICAN ASTRONAUTS APPROACH THE MOON
CHINA EXPLODES NUCLEAR WEAPON

What a fucking mess, he thought, irrationally: I can't leave the world aside for a moment and it goes to rack and ruin. Guilt again, the stranglehold of solipsism . . . place an ad in the Classifieds: Would-Be Superman Seeks Appropriate Phone Booth; Aims: To Save the World From Itself. Where art thou, Vicky Happenstance and Wellington Frog? Quixotes of the World Unite, your yiddische Sancho awaits your call . . . Blok, fatigued, bewitched,

165

bamboozled, while the rain in Jerusalem falls . . . as down the platform, under the yellow sign proclaiming Bus 435 – Ramat Raziel, Eshtaol, Tel Shahar, Gedera, milestones of the Zionistic redemption, Nili and her 'cousin' hammer into the concrete the wreckage of their amor fati (which, like all amor fatis, is destined to rise, Phoenix-like, from its own ashes) . . . What they actually said to each other, out of Blok's earshot, was this:

'It can't go on.' (he) 'We have to make a decision now.'

'Why now?'

'I'm off to the Canal tomorrow. There's going to be an escalation along the lines. The casualty rates are mounting.'

'We've had this sort of blackmail before, my honey, and you know it doesn't work with me.'

'I may be dead in a month.'

'You've been dead in a month before.'

'It was different before. When you're in combat, in movement, you have some control. But when you're just stuck in a trench for four months you're in the hands of Up There. Any shell that comes down the line can be the one that has your name written on it.'

'I'll pray for you, Eisav. Your luck will hold. We've been through all this before. What you're doing, your life, is important to you, I know. I've never asked you to live any other way. But I won't let your iron fates rule me. What we had is over. Each of us is the oldest friend of the other and that's something we'll always have. I never abandon a friend, and you know that. But I also have my own life to lead. So go with whatever God you believe in and come back to me, if you want to, when it's over.'

And the rain poured down, poured down . . . They were drenched where they stood by the flank of the bus, away from the overhang's shelter. The irascible driver called out: 'Hey, soldier! Are you boarding or not?'

He gave Nili a deep sorrowful Russian look, with all the weight that a lost Pale of Settlement past and an early reading of Tolstoy and Dostoyevsky could muster. 'I adore you more than life,' he said, and kissed her as she turned her lips to him, and swung aboard the bus. 'About time,' said a stout kibbutz woman in the front window seat. 'With all this down-pour and shitty deluge you'd have thought it would dampen their passion.'

Blok walked alone that night in the torrent to the cold comfort of the family home: Mama, deep in migraine, clucking over the state of his clothing, his health, his mind, his soul . . . He wants to kill his poor mother, the epikoros, by dying of double-pneumonia . . . and Papa: Don't provoke her my son, times are hard, the years rolling . . . au secours, these crashing discords . . . life as a Stockhausen symphony . . . But later, the flat in Takhkemoni afforded some peace, some long-yearned-for moments of silence . . . And he could walk the long road there from Nili's apartment, late at night, through the empty back ways of Romema in the slush of the day's sleet, his old army boots breaking patches of isolated frost, insulated by the warmth of Nili's welcome and by Eisav's spare army winter socks . . . And when, on the seventh of January, in her flat, he was holding her hand and wondering whether it would be wise to open his mouth and gush and risk repeating past painful fiascos, she suddenly upped and said to him: 'I know you want to sleep with me, Avram, but do you think you can compete with me physically?'

He was thrown into confusion, but for once, recovered swiftly, saying: 'Why not? It's not the all-in wrestling, is it?'

'You'd be surprised!' she said, and led him into the bedroom, neatly peeling back the covers and beginning to undress, pulling her sweater over her head, whipping off her trousers and underpants and then, unclipping her bra, standing before him in the full pride of her magnificence . . . and, oh, did he swiftly clamber over . . . glory, glory, glory . . .

And the days that followed were the best of his life, so far – no less than a fulfilment of dreams (and a fulfilment must come, at some stage, must it not, despite terrors and despite aftermaths . . .). As it was freezing without they remained within, over an extended weekend. It was not unlike the old Sabra joke: 'I can see they're living on the fruits of love, but why do they have to throw the peels out of the window?' But, we know, paradise does not last: late one night, in the midst of a fervent encoilment, Eisav telephoned from the front. All the way from the Suez Canal, to enforce coitus interruptus. She put the phone down on him, once, then he rang again, and she listened to him droning on about Death for forty-five minutes. Then Avram and Nili resumed their passion, but the measure of enchantment had vanished. From that moment on, the pumpkin of Eisav was ever present, somewhere behind a curtain . . .

*II*

'Adolf Hitler was right. He would have won the War, but he had stomach trouble.'

— Ignorant British youth, 198 —

Snow, snow, snow in Jerusalem. Cupolas capped, icing on a celestial cake. The celebration, some religio-poetic nut has babbled in the daily press (was it Himmeltraub?), of the nuptials of the City with God (Jehovah, he means, not Allah). When can we expect the consummation? Will the union be blessed, inshallah?(Remember the scandal the last time . . .) Prime Minister Eshkol has died. No more *The Thoughts of Chairman Eshkol*, that slim book of blank pages. His successor, they say, will be Golda Meir, the Only Man in the Cabinet. Q.: Why doesn't Golda wear a miniskirt? A.: So you shouldn't see her balls. Mute applause. So much for the affairs of the nation. Blok, awake late at night in bed, gently tracing the curve of Nili's back with his fingers, harkening to the rise and fall of her breath, listening with trepidation for the tell-tale tinkle of the telephone from Suez . . . Who would choose the army, merde, alors, for a living?! A terminal career. An experience to be buried, deep in the Unconscious, not to manifest on a payslip. Zut! Zut!

171

Zut! What deep insanity . . . Commanding his mind to forget, he remembers, ragged snippets . . .

Blok, a sliver of raw meat, on the day of his draft in the Absorption and Classification Camp: white-washing trees, cleaning the loos, scrubbing out the great cooking pots. Standing outside the messhall, directing the victims of the day's luncheon towards the washing-up troughs: 'Messtins This Way Only.' From humble beginnings . . . and later, as each recruit is called in to the Classification Officer and presented with his choice of unit: 'Golani Infantry, Golani Infantry or Golani Infantry. Armoured, Armoured or Armoured. Blok: Communications, Communications or Communications.'

Communications? What? Running about on the hilltops with half a ton of tin on your back babbling 'Fishtank to Base, Fishtank to Base, do you read me, cholera, over?' or hunched on a bench, signalmen in a row, having one's brains mashed to powder by Morse? On home leave, Blok exhibits signs of terminal panic. Papa Blok, for once, is in a position to help. Does not Mama have a second cousin, one Colonel N., in the GHQ, Education Branch? A phone call. Eureka, there is actually a post in the official army rag, its weekly magazine, *BABASIS – In The Base*. Papa sends Blok off with some of his Scheiss-papier, and school essays, and his best three-bags-full face. He does the tests. Asargelusha, accepted! No bleeps in the ear for our hero! Yanked out, after basic training (six weeks in the winter frost, mama mia! Stalactites on the mouth, the eyelids, the neanderthal NCOs and their verbal abuse – 'We're making a man of you, shithole!' Words fail me). Apprentice Journalist! 'Army Correspondent' on coveted blue shoulder tags. Dashing about the length and breadth of the land, covering army ceremonials, current affairs, the aftermath of a

Fatah raid on a cowshed up north, Paratroop manoeuvres in the south:

> Close to midnight the doors of the great Nord Altas planes opened and they parachuted into the desert sands ... beginning their long trek through the moonlit night towards their simulated objective ... the red shafts of the dawn sun lit the advancing columns ... Private Emil Farajula said: 'Was it right to volunteer? So many hardships ... but then you feel the comradeship of the corps, the experience of testing one's physical stamina and one's spiritual resources ...'

(Aaargh!! He thought later, Was that really me? – as he burned the old copies of *BABASIS* with his articles in the *Sturmer* bunker by the abandoned house ... ash of past follies, God, what rubbish! how shall I ever be cleansed??)

Blok, military correspondent. But his frustration remains. Slavering for the secretaries of the army magazine (Reserved for Officers only), in the shadow, also, of the great Sa'id T –, rag driver and man-about-town, the drivers being the lynchpin of efficient unit functioning, their co-operation being vital to arrive anywhere on time, keep a deadline and avoid general disaster, snafu, court-martial, or at times of crisis, Death. The Big D. When you are out there in the saltpans west of Hatserim, or later, in the Sinai wastes or the enemy hills of Hebron, boy, you know you need Sa'id T –, his eternal goodwill, his brain spry enough to have filled up with petrol ... The wild sephardi youth from the slums of the nation, with his gold tooth shining in subversive nonchalance and his lazy grin as he reminisced of Prison Six, where he had often done time for Indiscipline. He flaunted a non-existent symbiotic companion, some might say, a Jungian shadow:

'Yehoshua', as in 'Yehoshua's not in today.' 'How's Yehoshua?' or 'I'm out. Tell it to Yehoshua.' As the tight-lipped Prison Six commandant would say to him, when he was reported again, regular as clock-work, for being caught hatless or brawling: 'This is one place Yehoshua can't help you.' And Sa'id flashed him his gold molar.

But Sa'id was making it all the bloody time, albeit with women of the lower classes . . . Taking risks, but what the hell! He was always turning up, shame-faced, at the medical officer's with a new event on his dingus. But he was not deterred. In this. if nothing else, he was the ideal IDF soldier, always fulfilling the mission to the best of his abilities. One time he and Anton, the Number-Two driver, were caught in delecto flagrante by a sergeant major in the GHQ offi-cers' showers ('The Officers' showers!' cried Lieu-tenant Colonel Tswingli, rag second-in-command. 'I take off my beret to them!') doing what is known as a sandwich with a young lady from the seafront of Jaffa. Nabbed, as luck would have it, by some bastard they'd once swindled in a matter of pornographic postcards. In vain did Tswingli try to subvert Justice, claiming, 'I can't lose two drivers, damn it!' But the duo went down for twenty-eight days each, to the joy of the prison commandant: 'My oh my. Just can't keep away. Yehoshua's a real glutton for punishment.' The stubborn sergeant major, who would not cancel his charge, went down in the *BABASIS* black book. A year later he fell in an exposé of GHQ cigarette smuggling, and tasted chokey in person.

One evening Blok said to Sa'id: 'I feel like getting laid tonight. Take me to your hunting ground.'

'Trust Yehoshua,' Sa'id replied. He collected Blok at eleven o'clock that night in the rag's civilian Wyllis and they sped south from the GHQ gates, the car radio blaring, courtesy of the Enemy, a Farid Al-Atrash refrain.

Blok, unconfessed virgin, in Jaffa, the Lower Depths, in search of fuck – 'manousch' in the words of Sa'id, 'which as Yehoshua knows, makes the world go round'. From a crowded dancehall whose entrance is littered with empty Cola bottles, orange peel, torn Artik wrappings, rubber detritus, where, alas, there was nothing doing tonight, to a gloomy apartment block in Bat Yam, windows slammed in one's face by stout mothers . . . somehow, they end up with two girls in the van, one plump and dark skinned, the other fair and skinny. They bought them some Goldstar beer in an effort to get them tipsy, but the only result was the girls fell asleep. 'A strike out,' said Sa'id, as he propelled them somnambulantly through the dancehall door; from humid shadows to light, to an uncertain fate. 'It's a dry night,' he said to Blok, 'I feel it in my bones.' They drove back north, to the Esplanade. 'I know a couple of pieces there,' he explained, 'professionals, but they may have friends. Themselves, you don't want your meat in there, you don't know who's been in before you, leaving a calling card.' Knowing whereof he speaks, he pressed the accelerator, thundering past Manshiya . . .

. . . Dark, one a.m.; the gravelled sand; the inky water smelling of tar; luminous suds whispering in towards the beach; the flotsam of night and day: used condoms, sweetie papers, tin cans, soggy fag packs, matchboxes bobbing on waves; out at sea, the lights of a merchant ship bound for Ashdod. The roving headlamps of cars upon the highway; beyond, the hotels, Plazahiltonsheraton, glittering tourist preserves. Sa'id and Blok, bucking over the sands as if in the depths of the Negev. On to the asphalted Esplanade, sea to left, clipjoints to the right, where watered-down gut rot and the false promise of fuck linger to lure the naive. Two girls and a man amble towards the Wyllis, emberous cigarette ends glowing. A cryptic exchange ensues between Sa'id and the ladies: 'How's it going?' 'A hard night.' 'Life,' he comments. A long pause. 'Matilda out tonight?' he asks. 'In,' they say. 'Life,' he comments again. Blok has never seen him before in such a full-blown philosophical mood. 'Time is money,' say the girls, as their pimp slides past. 'Money is money,' he says, 'that's for sure.' The whores pass on muskily, glow-worms in the night, against the hiss of the black sea . . . Sa'id guns the motor, the Wyllis shoots off, towards the safety of Tel Aviv north. Thus endeth Blok's first descent . . .

But there is a balm in Gilead! (no?) In the winter of 1966–67 Blok met the girl he first slept with. Her name was Georgina and she was an English new immigrant studying Sociology at the Hebrew University. She was plain, but sweet-tempered, with fine flowing brown hair framing a pear-shaped face, and brown eyes that were sad and plaintive. He met her through Fat Avi, who was dating her room mate, and was about to strike paydirt one evening. Do a buddy a favour, take the girlfriend out tonight . . . Blok obliged, and was soon entangled in her quiet susceptibility, her matching loneliness, her (eventual) willingness to take him to bed.

Bed! Asargelusha! the consummation – as first nights go, pretty lacklustre. In, in, damned spot, he pants aspiringly, lacking the lubrication. Patiently she led him along the path, until he was there – huffing, puffing, shooting his load, so what's all the fuss about, comrades? Not that it happened instantly, as for weeks in fact she hummed and hawed and stalled and stopped him short at crucial moments with his hand in her bra and his knickers about to come down . . . 'It's not that I don't want to . . . but I can't decide now . . .', 'Not tonight, it's my period . . .' Ye Gods! Must we all re-live history, each personally crawl out of the sea before we can run and gambol . . .? Join, schmuck, join the human race . . .

So she became the first audience for his suppressed fantasies, Scheisspapier tales re-embellished, icky fairy tales told in the small hours, whispering between sheets amid much licking and petting and the gentle caress. Their imaginations soared together, speculating on a shared life of crime, piracy, high life in Acapulco. Under her silent veneer she was impishly passionate, sometimes at embarrassing moments. She would take hold of his banana in the dark of the cinema, or pull him into side alleys in broad daylight and feel about for his jumblies. The joy of another person's hand on one's prick, not to speak of the softness of tongue . . . But, alas, it could not last. Shared fantasies are not sufficient. The Reality Principle, cholera! The jungle rules, ya'hribaitak!

One night, when Fat Avi and room mate Dalia were in occupation at the U., the lovers bedded at the Blok household. Ma and Pa supposedly away in Ein Pippin (a kibbutz in the Lower Jezreel), consoling Blok's Aunt Pashtida on the imminent visit of West German ex-Chancellor Adenauer, the prospect of which threw her into epileptoid convulsions. However, her condition must have improved miraculously, for Mama and Papa arrived back the same night, at midnight, just as their son was threshing about in coitus.

'Avremel, are you all right?' called Mama, alarmed at the desperate sounds.

'Oh my God,' whispered Blok, 'the warden's returned!' But Georgina only pressed him more strongly to her and dug a finger into his arse.

'Avremel?' Mama called again, 'is that Avremel in there?'

'It's not the burglar,' said Papa wryly. 'Don't worry the boy, let him be.'

'Is there somebody else in there with you?' she cried, all a-twit.

'Come on, Shushu,' pleaded Papa, 'let him be. He's nineteen years old, dammit!'

Unperturbed she banged on the door. 'Avremel, come out this instant!'

'Aaaargsh . . .!' said Blok, caught between the flood and Pharaoh's forces.

'Really, Shushu,' Papa pleaded, 'the neighbours will hear. Gaga the Bulgarian Bloodhound has her ears permanently to the ceiling . . .'

'I don't care!' cried Mama, 'if improper things are going on in my house I want to know all about it!'

Bad, bad vibes. The mother and father of all rows as Blok emerges in his pyjama trousers with something not quite flaccid behind them. He, yelling blue murder at the invasion of privacy. She, accusing him of corrupting an innocent young girl. Papa, locking himself in his stamp study with a transferred migraine. Georgina, acutely embarrassed, buried for two hours in a pillow. Gaga the Bloodhound, downstairs, banging on the ceiling with a broomstick. Join, schmuck, join the human race . . .

But it was only one symptom of their waning affair that faded, for lack of interest perhaps, like a Polaroid snap in reverse. She abandoned him for a kibbutz boy from the plain, someone who smelled of apples and clean white shirts on Saturday and ethnic dancing round the campfire. Someone in harmony with her newly adopted land instead of an internal exile. While Blok resumed his army routine, his khaki anabasis towards a different consummation, devoutly to be unwished, which was about to engulf his generation:

Commenting on the build-up of Egyptian forces in Sinai, General H. of the Southern Command said the Israel Defence Forces were ready for every

178

eventuality. The mobilization of Reserve units was proceeding efficiently and according to plan. War was far from inevitable, he told an Artillery Battalion somewhere in the Western Negev, but we, entrenched in our defensive positions, cannot afford to lower our guard . . .

War??? What the fuck . . .? It was not for this we joined up . . . not that they gave us a choice . . . War, in our term of recruitment?? Fate dealing dud hands again . . . In the corridors of *BABASIS* magazine, tumult and terrified exultation. Rumours breed like rabbits: the Egyptians will attack, punkt on midnight of the 30th May . . . The Russians have threatened to use the bomb on us if we try a preemptive strike . . . The Enemy will deploy long-range missiles, developed by German scientists . . . Prime Minister Eshkol has succumbed to panic, he is flat on his back with the lurgi . . . one-eyed Dayan, Musa D. of legend, is about to take charge . . . there he is, sitting deep in the bunker, studying the maps and warplans . . .

War?? Into the desert roll Blok, Sa'id and a photographer, jauntily at first bucking the magazine Wyllis over the Negev sands, roaring along with the columns of ordnance rumbling endlessly towards the border: tanks, half tracks, command cars, trucks, mobile artillery, trailers, inducted Egged buses and fleets of civilian vehicles, Opels, Chevrolets, Susitas, Macks, Fiats, Mercedes, Toyotas, Desotos, splattered with camouflage mud that would drive their owners spare were they not themselves too splattered with mud and sand and fatigue somewhere in a hasty foxhole . . .

Yes, WAR!!! From the movies, straight into Life – the inevitable, that no one believed in. Our Avremel, whose Mama was only yesterday trying to pry his schmock loose from the groin of a woman, is rattling over the midsummer sands with five days' growth of beard and a dusty rifle and Nagra and eyes that are like orange sunsets, clambering over immense cast steel weapons of death, poking microphones in the faces of people who might be about to die, or who have just survived by the skin of their kismet, recording the hack phrases of clichéd patriotism, dry bones that have suddenly come alive, conjured out of the great ecstasy of common cause and shared danger, tying man to man – and woman – in all the foxholes of the land, so that no voice is raised crying: Is this what has to be? But no one wants to be cut off from this great chain of solidarity, this great group coitus that soon reaches its full, thunderous orgasm of blood, fire and steel, and then subsides, as people pick their way silently among the corpses, trying in vain to cough up the gaseous reek of Death and decomposition, to shut away the living Dali phantasmagorism behind the brightly painted doors of –

VICTORY!!! CHIME BELLS, BEAT GONGS, CHEER, DELIVERED POPULACE! THY KINGDOM'S COME, THY GENERAL WILL IS DONE . . . throw sweeties and flowers into the jeeps and Wyllises of the returning sandcaked conquering heroes, fresh from the battlefield or from as close behind it as one could get without actually having to remain there, yet one more heap of filleted human bones, with the flies munching one's eyes . . . Yes, even Blok, Avremel – with Papa so proud, and Mama hugging him close, shedding ghetto tears on his uniformed breast, to mingle with the desert detritus. And Oh My God! The Victory Ceremonies, and Celebrations, and Thanksgivings and Remembrances – the scribe always following the host, scribbling, scribbling scribbling on the malleable slates of History (magnetic ordnung, jawohl!) – Donner und Blitzen! Join, Blok, join the human race.

When the Lord turned again the captivity of Zion,
We were like them that dream;
Then was our mouth filled with laughter
and our tongue with singing;
Then they said among the heathen: The Lord hath
    done great things for them;
The Lord hath done great things for us,
Whereof we are glad.
Turn again our captivity, O Lord, as the streams
    in the south;
They that sow in tears shall reap in joy;
He that goeth forth and weepeth, bearing pre-
    cious seed,
shall doubtless come again with rejoicing,
bringing his sheaves with him.

                                        Psalm 126

'Nietzsche's' true name was Yerachmiel Farkash-
Fenschechter. The date of his rebirth, as he termed
it, was 13th October, 1918. A time of vast, incalcul-
able change. Four years of war had ground Europe
into a phantasmagoria of blood, mud and shattered
braggadocio. In November 1916 the old Emperor,
Franz Joseph I, had died, aged eighty-six, the last
surviving afterimage of the hallucinations of
Metternich. On the Eastern Front, the Good Soldier
Svejk was approaching the grand apotheosis of his
capture by his own troops. So he, at least, was out
of it. But the Central Powers, lulled by Brest Litovsk,
were not. Bled in the East, broken and zapped in the
West. Bye-bye, Austro-Hungarian Empire.

In Kecskemét, a medium-sized Hungarian town,
an old merchant named Nathan Farkash took a
bride of twenty summers, Alicia. She came from a
family of Jewish patriots whose able-bodied
menfolk were all wiped out on various fronts,
leaving her mother to die of heart failure. Thus she
was an orphan and poor, he was a widower and

rich. Nevertheless, oddly enough, it was a marriage of love. Nathan, though past his bloom, appeared a sturdy and vigorous man. All the more surprise among neighbours, friends, well wishers and customers that he popped off suddenly, in the midst of the night, punkt upon the consummation. (Tempestuous passion on the old four poster, above the warehouse stacked with all the pischifkes you could hope to salvage from the wreck of a civilization – old rugs, third-hand army coats, army utensils, battered sewing machines, Imperial pots and pans . . .) Is it significant, Doctor Flusser was to write fifty years later, that our 'Nietzsche's papa died at the very moment of his conception, leaving a life for a death?' He could find no answer to this question, and ended up deleting the entire paragraph from his prospective opus . . . At any rate, nine months later, a son was born to the widow Alicia and she named him Yerachmiel – the Lord Have Mercy On Me.

By the time the Kecskemét mohel was cutting into the poor babe's ding-dong the old order in Europe had crumbled. On the very day of his *briss* Czechoslovakia declared Independence. When he was thirty-four days old the Magyar Republic, too, opened for business, under the liberal Count Károlyi. But soon chaos intervened. The victorious allies ceded Transylvania, with three million ethnic Hungarians, to their Eastern crony, Rumania. The Socialist–Communist alliance of Garbai and Béla Kun replaced the easy-going Count. What with Bolshevik Russia consolidating in the East, the Allies didn't like this at all, and gave the Rumanian army the task of recapturing Hungary for Freedom. By the summer of '19 they had reached Budapest, shooting Communists, hanging Jews. Béla Kun scarpered south to Vienna. All Hungary became a battleground of Revolution and Counter-Insurgency.

In Kecskemét, too, Bolsheviks and Jews were red meat for the White chopping block. The mohel was impaled by outraged monarchists. Blood ran freely in the streets. A Communist major named Josef Fenschechter swept up the young widow Farkash and her infant and bore them away to a temporary safety, far in the plains of the marshland.

(On Circumcision, its history:
It was widespread in Pharaonic Egypt, they say. The Lord said to Abraham: 'And ye shall circumcise the flesh of your foreskin, and it shall be a token of the covenant between me and you.' 'Sure, sure, Boss,' said Abe, who had been promised a profusion of goodies. Siggy Freud, on the other hand, laid the blame on Moses, and blew the gaffe on the whole damn schmeer: 'Circumcision,' said he, 'is the symbolic substitute for the castration which the primal father once inflicted upon his sons in the plenitude of his absolute power, and whoever accepted that symbol was showing by it that he was prepared to submit to the father's will, even if it imposed the most painful sacrifice on him.' But some anthropologists said it derived from the clipping of the vine, without which it would bear no fruit. A wag in Jerusalem's Ta'amon Café, though, had the last word on the issue, claiming Jewish boys were circumcised so that their foreskins should not get caught in their zips.)

Ah! Suckled by Socialism! Luckily it was summer, or the poor mite might have died of the deep clammy marshy cold. On the other hand, they were on the losing side. Betrayed by the peasants, picked off by the forces of the counter-revolution, cadre after cadre, in the depths of the swamp and the bog, the Communist partisans starved. And as they starved, huddled round their peat fires in the miasmic nights, they sang sad, patriotic songs of the soil, of the working class and of lovers who might never turn to face the red dawn of their hopes. Did that melancholy seep into the small babe's psyche? asked Flusser five decades later. And he reflected: isn't that true for us all, the ageing remnants of that age of endless mourning . . .? and what of our descendants, nebesch?

(Blok once, in a creative depression lingering in the diaspora, thought of writing a story one day about the little clerk who must have counted the eye-glasses, false teeth and clumpets of hair at Auschwitz. Weekdays he meticulously does his job, weekends perhaps he goes home, to blink owlishly in the bosom of his family. Oddly enough, this idea was inspired by a man Blok used to observe on the London Underground Central Line, who always boarded the same train every evening at twenty past nine. He wore a Post Office jacket and a face it would be difficult to love – piggy eyes and a weak blubbery chin and thin lips and a flat closely shaven head – but emitting a look of such weari-ness, loss and oblivion that one could not help feel-ing compassion. The man Blok was thinking of was really a nice man at heart. It was just that everyone else around him, from the lowest to the highest rung of his hierarchy, was such an irredeemable shit.)

In the autumn of '20 Fenschechter sent his new wife and stepson to the city, hidden in a manure cart. He stayed behind to die anonymously in the marshes, but whether this came about by bullet, noose or starvation, nobody ever knew. For no one in his unit lived to tell the tale, and the executioners were silent.

In Szeged, an aunt and uncle of Fenschechter took the fugitives in, hid and fed them. Outside, the counter-revolutionaries of Horthy raged, singing patriotic songs (some the same the partisans had sung, but with different lyrics) while they shot Reds and hanged Christ killers from any available lamppost. But as resistance died down, their fury was soon assuaged, for your average Magyar is a reasonable and peace-loving person. The Allies, as the threat of Bolshevism receded, leashed their Rumanians, who withdrew from truncated Hungary, taking with them everything that was not nailed down (and much that was). Admiral Horthy took power as Regent – the Admiral without a fleet for the kingdom without a king. He signed the Treaty of Trianon, ceding further chunks of the Fatherland, while denouncing it to all and sundry. 'Nem, nem, soha!' they chanted in all the schools of the realm. 'No, no, never!' cried little Yeri-Yerachmiel, in unison with the rest. As the little boy was fair like his mother, and his name could be suitably christianized, Alicia Farkash-Fenschechter enrolled him in a general, rather than a Jewish, school. So the boy grew up as a good Hungarian, reciting such official bilge as this:

'Our glorious ruling Lord, the Regent His Serene Highness the Great Hero Miklós Horthy of Nagybánya, who came hurrying into our midst from the ranks of the heroes galloping eternally with Prince Csaba on the path of the Warriors in the sky to lead his forlorn race in its most terrible hour.'

No wonder his sense of reality was addled.

Flusser wrote:

'From an early age the little boy became imbued with the need to conceal, to dissimulate and, if found out, to react with the utmost guile and cunning . . . his quick intelligence soon told him that power over the fantasies of others comes to him who can control his own . . .'

Meanwhile, further north in Budapest, Blok's papa to be, Baruch, was trying again unsuccessfully for a place at the University. An unofficial numerus clausus prevailed, keeping the Yids in their place. Baruch Blok failed his entrance exam for the Faculty of Engineering, though he knew he had answered most of the questions correctly. In 1930 he was eighteen years old and adrift in a small world of middle-class Jewish youth, cleft between the torpid life of the cafés and the tug of internal politics. He joined the local Revisionist Zionist group, Jabotinsky Youth. Their idol, Vladimir Jabotinsky, urged the reconquest of the Biblical Homeland with fire and sword. It was a prudent choice over the rival Socialist Zionist groups, Socialism of any kind being dodgy (hard times, hard times, thank God it can't happen again . . .). They drew maps of Palestine including Transjordan and put pins in the exotic locations of glorious battles to come. Of course neither Baruch nor most of his cronies had any intention of setting foot in Palestine, let alone fighting bitter wars of possession in the barren swathes of the Levant. It was a congenial club, and a sop for his father, Ephrayim, who was becoming religious in his old age and spoke of dying upon holy soil. He did not however die in Holy Palestine, beneath his own vine and fig tree, but in Gas Chamber Number Three in Sobibor, gasping for breath and scrabbling for a life that was gone as the German guards played skat for their wages in the backyard outside.

(Blok once reflected uselessly that the world had lost something when sadness departed from it, when the oppressed no longer bore their oppression but fought back, often with the utmost ferocity, with atrocities, bombs, massacres, maimings . . . could it be or should it be otherwise? His grandfather, tearing his fingernails on the gas chamber door . . . the Jewish Zionist revenge, against the wrong people . . . a black South African, gazing at white citadels through gunsights . . . an Arab, pissing in the gutter of a refugee camp, planning his own bloody return . . .)

In 1932 a new Prime Minister took office in Budapest, the rabid nationalist and supposedly reformed anti-semite, Gömbös. He was a pompous and vain fart and an admirer of Mussolini, aping his manner (as did another leader of the victims several decades later, one Menachem Begin). He said: 'Our path will be rocky and steep and thorny . . . but I feel, I know it will lead us to our goal. Hungarians! Brothers! Ignite the candle of trust at the life fire of my soul which burns for you, my Nation! Spread this illumination!'

This latter-day Diogenes was a front for a whole parcel of nationalist and fascistic groups such as the Awakening Hungarians, the Etelkoz Association, the Scythe Cross, the Turanian Club, etc. They believed, so they said, that the Turkoid and Uraltic races were the founders of civilization, that Jesus was Hungarian and that they were destined to once again rule the globe as they had in the mystic past. Once in power Gömbös tried to disown them, but their babbling did not diminish and was strengthened in January 1933, when Adolf Hitler's National Socialist German Workers' Party came to power in Germany.

Adolf Hitler did not agree that Jesus Christ was Hungarian, nor did he care much for the Turko-Uraltic race. He had written:

'If we were to divide mankind into three groups, the founders of culture, the bearers of culture, the destroyers of culture, only the Aryan could be

187

considered as the representative of the first group. From him originate the foundations and walls of all human creation . . . If he dies out or declines, the dark veils of an age without culture will again descend on the globe.'

He added, for good measure: 'All who are not of good race in this world are chaff.' He blamed the Jews, in particular, for racial decline, and for the syphilitic nature of German women. 'By defending myself against the Jews,' he said, 'I am fighting for the work of the Lord.' Here is another example of his prose style: 'With satanic joy in his face, the black-haired Jewish youth lurks in wait for the unsuspecting girl whom he defiles with his blood, thus stealing her from her people.' The German electorate, in two successive democratic ballots, elected him to be their Chancellor.

'The burnt child shuns the fire.' Adults never do.

So why, thought Blok, do we have to live on the inside of our 'Leaders' ' fantasies, why should *we* suffer from the presumed infant traumas of Genghis Khan, Napoleon, Adolf Hitler, Lyndon Johnson, Golda Meir? Don't we have enough trouble with the time bombs of our own childhood? Oral, anal, narcissistic fixations, to name but a few? Oh Siggy, where are you now that we need you?
    The first Nietzsche expressed this sort of feeling more forcefully, a hundred years ahead of time:

'Who gave us a sponge to wipe away the horizon? Why did we unchain the earth from its sun? Where is it moving now? Where are we moving? Away from all suns? Are we plunging down-wards? backwards? sideways? forward? in all directions? Is there still an up and a down? Are we not drifting through an infinite nothing? Do we not feel empty space breathing in on us? Has it not become colder? Is not night after night closing in on us? Do we not need lanterns in the morning? Are we still deaf to the sound of the gravediggers digging God's grave? Can we not yet sense the smell of divine putrefaction?'

In Budapest, Baruch Blok worked as a clerk for a firm which made industrial pipes. In Szeged, Yeri Farkash-Fenschechter was up against tough opposition. A cell of the pro-Nazi National Will Party of one Ferencz Szálási was active in the upper school forms. The watchwords of the day were Patriotism, Religion, Discipline and the religion was the Catholic Church. The aim was to restore the Carpatho-Danubian Fatherland. Talk abounded of the 'Hungarist Idea', but no one could quite make out what it was. One thing was clear: Jews were out. As were Slavs, Galicians, Ruthenians, Poles, Czechs and others who happened simply to live in the country. Even some of Yeri's friends began joining the movement, whispering to him in corners – with that typical Magyar combination: warm heart, addled head – that when the going got really heavy, they would be glad to hide him in their homes . . .

Is not night after night closing in on us?

Blok once said to Nietzsche and Nili (she had long since revealed to him snippets of the Farkash-Fen. past): 'All very well for you two. You had fathers you could look up to. They may have croaked early, but at least they gave hell before going. Mine hid in a cupboard, as far as I can gather, for just about seven years.'

This was grossly unfair to Baruch Blok, who had merely kept a low profile while the world went to sheol in a handbasket. By 1938 he'd lost touch with his Revisionist pals, some of whom had gone into business or become too shrill for comfort; one or two had actually emigrated to Palestine. His motto had become: 'I shall be neither a hero nor a scoundrel. I shall be kind to my friends, polite to my family and indifferent towards mine enemies.' And as for the Great Leaders out there – may the ground open and swallow them up, greedy schmendricks the fucking lot of them. Meanwhile, at some community do the previous year, he had met a diminutive young lady, the daughter of a grocer in Törökvész on the other side of the river. She had lived a protected life influenced by Borokhovian ideals. Palestine was a romantic place for her in which a proletarian Jewry could rise, like yeast, from the fungi of exile. The kolkhozes of Soviet Russia were her example. But when Hitler and Stalin signed their pact two years later she found solace in religion. They met again in 1940, with the war one year old, both merely desiring to burrow away and hide, like desperate moles, from the gathering fireball. Others ran, squeezing past guarded borders, to Palestine, Switzerland, Sweden. Blok never found out why his parents made no use of these conduits, spending most of the war in Budapest being inconspicuous, and then, for its latter part, locked in separate apartments, hidden by courageous gentile neighbours. But by the time he was old enough to ask any such questions, Rosa Blok was in no shape to be challenged about anything, and Baruch was hunched, eyeglass screwed into his eye, over his Hyderabad commemorials . . .

Yeri's mother died in May '37 of an infection of the lungs. He had graduated from college with excellent grades, despite Turano-Uraltic harassment. But there was nowhere to go from there . . . The young man had developed an academic bent, and it was about then he discovered Nietzsche. 'One can imagine the impact,' Flusser wrote decades later, 'at that particular moment of European history.

The towering prophecies of the coming age of nihilism, the fall of morality, the dethronement of God, the new era of barbarism, the twilight of compassion . . . Many thought, or deceived themselves into thinking, it might all blow over. But for someone as shrewd and alert as Yerachmiel Farkash-Fenschechter, the writing was on the wall . . .'

Austrian Anschluss. Freud at the Nordhahnhof. Klander's farewell. New government in Budapest, of Béla Imrédy. New restrictions on Jews. Attempts to protect the Magyar State from the full Nazi cyclone by adopting its outer shell . . . a strategy ebbing and flowing until its final collapse, the hurricane breaking in 1943, and from then on Baruch and Rosa, from within their sealed capsules, could only pray to be spared the deluge . . .

Yeri packed his bags in his Pest lodging house. He sent a message by hand with his last trusted friend to Aunt and Uncle Fenschechter and at half past ten on 20th May, 1939, he boarded the night train to Zagreb. There, at the Café Alexander he rendezvoused with a Zionist underground agent smuggling Jews illegally into Palestine. He boarded a ship at Trieste, with a forged certificate, and set sail on 26th May, for the Syrian port of Latakia. It docked on the 30th, disgorging the youth in a welter of sweat, dung and baksheesh, contorted brown faces yelling in a language he had not imagined existed, dust rising from a sun-baked ramshackle waterfront, thirty-four degrees celsius, in the shade – Zapadoom! – into the Orient! Who would believe it? Two days later he was driven, with his false papers, lickety-split in the cabin of a patched-up jalopy, tossing over the potholes in the boiling hot road, across the Lebanon border at Rosh Hanikra and into the Promised Land.

Rosa Blok might have said:

'I will lift up mine eyes unto the hills, from whence
cometh my help?
My help cometh from the Lord, which made heaven
  and earth.
He will not suffer thy foot to be moved; he that
  keepeth thee will not slumber;
Behold, he that keepeth Israel shall neither slumber
  nor sleep.
The Lord is thy keeper,
The Lord is the shade upon thy right hand;
The sun shall not smite thee by day, nor the moon by
  night.
The Lord shall preserve thee from all evil; he shall
  preserve thy soul.
The Lord shall preserve thy going out and thy going
  in, from this time forth, and even for evermore.'

But are we still deaf to the sound of the gravediggers
busily digging God's grave?


**But lo! Suckered too by our own bootstraps!**
Have you seen the old beggarwoman, swathed in
schmuttes, who drags her game leg from corner to
corner of the City, from Beit Yoel to the Municipality, from the Jaffa Road pillars to Zion Square, from
the Rabbinate to the Mahane Yehuda market?
Pushing before her a ramshackle, rusty old pram, in
which an infant of indeterminate gender and age
caterwauls loud enough to shatter plate glass or
melt the heart of a tax collector? Her face, sunk
behind hooded rags, seems a mess of carbuncles
and warts, and hairs like the bristles of a hog issue
from her nostrils. She sits, with her horrible leg
thrust out on the pavement before her, accompanying the shrieks of the brat with the rattling of a
corroded tin can. You must have noticed her, coming to the fore, pushing even Babelech-und-Farfel

down into the also rans . . . She is in fact Inspector Tarablus, who has initiated a phase of Deep Cover. Tenaciously he squats in doorways, behind fences, by strategic bus stops, beneath market stalls, at the central bus and railway stations, outside concert halls, cinemas, night clubs, pizza and ice cream parlours, falafel kiosks, synagogues, nests of the Mapam Youth, taxi stands, late-night cafés, whorehouses, billiard dens, police stations, army barracks, yeshivas. Alone, and with no hope of succour in sight, he communes with the night of the City. His ears pricked constantly, poised for the one hint, the one inadvertent clue that will lead him on to the next phase of his quest. Yes, doggedly, courageously, with infinite detective patience, he is still stalking the killer of Klander . . .

Eisav and Zetz, on the Suez Canal. Flush in their bunker, looking out through knife-narrow slits across oodles of sandbags and barbed wire behind which, behind his own knife-narrow slits, sits the Enemy, Ahmed the Gypo. Bang, Bang, Bang! Between them, shot and shell pierce the bright blue sky, steel splinters, the confetti of a warped devil's wedding arrested in time.

'This is what really makes you a man!' said Zetz. 'This tests your mettle! Standing firm in the trenches! That takes guts! Verdun! There was glory! If you came through that you could truthfully say: Gentlemen, I have lived!'

'And if you didn't come through you were hamburger,' said General Palanka, wry C-in-C, Southern Command, who, because he was fucking a gorgeous blonde Women's Corps sergeant back in Beersheba, was more than usually pissed off at being trapped in the bunker, especially with General Asael Mahatz, alias Zetz, whom he considered a raving fanatic. 'God, this fucking war is boring

. . .' Palanka fell into reverie. Eisav, too, day-dreamed as far as possible amid the din of exploding shells . . . oh, for Nili, waiting, candle in window, diaphragm in chest-of-drawers, for the return of the hero . . .

On the other side of the water General Mahmud Abu-Ali, C-in-C Kantara Sector, had retired mean-while to his private bunker with the latest consign-ment of British pornography delivered just the other day, by submarine, by an agent of Liam O'Habash. Fondly perusing the advertisements: the Clitoral Stimulator, the Bunny Rabbit, the Strap-On Cocky, Duo Balls, the Vibrating Dick, Electric Orgasmo Vagina, Angel's Delight: 'After centuries of use in the Far East by girls who like to tickle their fancy, the Sex Egg has at last been switched on . . .' he looked up as an aide rapped on the door for instructions, and shouted out: 'Keep those shells in the air, ya manayeg! Don't give 'em a moment's rest! Let the infidels eat dust, by Allah!' and he relaxed on his Bauertrim mattress, idly, fondly flicking the pages.

'How did "Nietzsche" become the way he is?' Blok asked Nili one day. (Domestic bliss, she ironing her skirts and blouses, he leafing through *Beyond Good and Evil*, a well-thumbed copy from her shelf. ' "One is punished most for one's virtues," ' he read, 'that's very true. But what's this? "In revenge and in love, woman is more barbarous than man . . ." – that just sounds silly.' 'It's also very true,' said Nili, bearing down on a shirtsleeve.)

'Oh, some say it started twenty years ago,' she answered vaguely, 'but Flusser thinks it began in 1960, when he took a heavy blow on the head from a policeman's truncheon at an anti-Wagner demon-stration.'

'Nineteen sixty?' said Blok. 'But my Aunt

Pashtida was at that demo too! Why, it was a famous occasion! She got arrested, for beating up a cop, and my Dad had to bail her out of jail!'

'Wonders never cease,' said Nili, sprinkling water, 'it certainly is a small world.'

## What Actually Happened at the Great Anti-Wagner Demo of May 1960:

Imagine! The bulk of Jerusalem's new prestige hall, Binyanei Ha'Uma, rearing alone from the apex of the hill to the starry sky of a brisk clear Judean night. Discreet posters announce a single, experimental performance of parts of *Tristan and Isolde*, unperformed heretofore in the Jewish State due to the composer's general vileness, extreme anti-semitism and deification by Adolf. 'Progressive' forces are softly pressing for the lifting of such moral censorship on things artistic and cultural. But down by the entrance, the 'Ban Wagner For All Time Society' are going completely bananas. Yelling, screaming, pushing against two lines of bewildered police, brandishing slogans which read: 'The Voice of Thy Brother's Blood Cries Out From the Ground!' 'Insult to the Dead!' 'Used Jewish Blood For Sale!' Hitler = Wagner = Jerusalem Municipality,' and even, impractically: 'Richard Wagner – To the Gallows!' To look below the placards is to court insanity: gnarled survivors, wrinkled faces, darkened by the Mid-East sun, con-torted with anguish and rage, tattooed arms raised in fury, cripples battering the cops with their crutches, maddened women grasping at police-men's ears, small children biting policemen's legs . . . bad, bad vibes indeed.

Yerachmiel Farkash-Fenschechter, contributor, at that time, to the literary column of the Hungarian journal *Uj kelet*, to which Blok's papa regularly subscribes, and Blok's Aunt Pashtida, red with hatred of Germany, are both in the forefront of the struggle, albeit unbeknownst to each other, and on different flanks of the action. Aunt Pashtida, in the name of all Blok's dead relatives, is spitting into the face of an officer with two silver pips on each shoulder, shouting: 'Pimp! Kapo! Traitor! Shame on you! What sort of a Jew are you? You shit on the grave of your father! Go back where you came from, Schweinhund!' The cop, who was born in Marrakesh, is a miracle of sang froid: 'Lady, I am just trying to uphold the Law . . .' Meanwhile, down the line, Farkash-Fen., his upper lip already presciently disguised by the heavy Nietzschean shawara, berserkly wields a placard inscribed 'The Smoke of the Ovens still Rises Skywards', cutting a swathe through the serried constabulary and yelling something in Hungarian that no one can make out, his moustache flecked with foam, his eyes frighteningly abulge. A fellow protestor in a wheelchair is knocked back by his threshing and careens down Yehuda Halevi towards the Tel Aviv Highway, yelling and waving his arms. 'Watch out! Mother's cunt! That guy's dangerous!' cry the cops, trying to encircle the maniac. Finally one brave soul dashes in and lays him low with his nightstick, a good solid wallop, too, and no mistake. The reader will have great difficulty in believing the following fact, but it was Patrolman Abutbul, the same who seven years later clamped his paw upon Blok for peeping, who dealt Farkash-Fen. that decisive zetz. He went down, needless to say, as if poleaxed. Yes. At about the same moment, though one cannot pinpoint it scientifically, Blok's Aunt Pashtida, enraged at the Moroccan officer's serenity, delivered him a kick with her pointed left shoe punkt in the poor fellow's balls. He fell, with the curious look of one who has just realized the full extent of his expected commitment to duty. His colleagues grabbed Blok's aunt and, flailing to no further avail, she was dragged away and thrown into the pick-up. The prone figure of Farkash-Fenschechter was rushed into a Red Star of David ambulance which, sirens wailing, light revolving, sped off towards Sha'arei Tsedek Hospital. In the police van Aunt Pashtida led the other aged arrestees in a rendition of the National Anthem:

'As long as deep within our hearts,
The soul of the Jew yearns,
And towards forward Eastern parts,
An eye to Zion turns . . .'

Thus endeth the Great Anti-Wagner Demo of 1960.

**Nevertheless, Further Tales of The Struggle:**
Have you not heard the legends of General Zetz? The gossip, sparked from campfire to campfire, whispered in the cold night of tents pegged into hard hillsides, across bottles of Tempo and chocolate waffles in the Shekem army canteens, or in guardposts at three in the morning (a sly cigarette in the dark, freezing fingers in mittens, the dead weight of rifle on shoulder): How Zetz, back in the War of Independence, avenged the mutilation and murder of a young kibbutz girl (whom some say he loved) by reducing a house in the Arab village where the atrocity occurred to cinders with a flame-thrower, roasting an entire family? How Zetz, separated from his unit on a retaliation raid deep in enemy territory, survived for twelve days on dry roots, small lizards and the meagre juice squeezed from cacti, bringing back, in his knapsack, the head of a fedayeen leader? The tale of the forty Arab ears? The Mitleh Pass action? The full

frontal charge at Abu Agheila, in the June Six Days' War? Not for nothing did he declare, at the Victory Rally for the fallen:

'Soldiers! You have spread blood and fire upon the battlefield, and you have prevailed. You looked Death in the eyes, and He lowered His gaze. As Gideon smote the Midianites, as Samson gave battle to the Philistines with the jawbone of an ass, so have you, warriors of the Israel Defence Forces, the Few against the Many, defeated the Forces of Darkness . . .'

Och aye, the Lord is a man of War, the Lord is His name . . .

To Eisav, Zetz appeared to be driven by a virulent desire for pure Justice. He was totting up the figures on a private graph of revenge hidden inside his skull. So many slaughtered by the king of the Chaldees. So many by the Villain Haman. So many by Antiochus. So many by Vespasian, Titus, Tiberius. So many by Torquemada. So many by Martin Luther. So many by Bogdan Chmielnicki. So many by Count Plehve. So many by Heinrich Himmler, Eichmann and all the rest. The scale on that side was so weighted that it would take the entire Arab world to appease the hot thirst for a balance. (Not to speak of the Russian muzhiks, raring for a second chance . . .) Like Genghis Khan, Zetz might, in his wet dreams, Eisav imagined, envisage a pyramid of skulls, higher than the tower of Babel, of written-off anti-semites. PAX?? would be inscribed upon it in letters of blazing crimson.

Zetz had said: 'I have two bullets for every Arab, in case one isn't enough.'

Also, on the eve of the Six Days' War: 'They think they'll repeat the six million? No, gentlemen! It'll be the other way around!'

And: 'Why should only we suffer a Holocaust?

Shouldn't other peoples have their turn?'

He had provided Eisav, the young Holocaust orphan, with the only home he had known, before Nili . . . a stern kibbutz berth with that pioneer patriarch of eighty winters, that oaklike man of the soil, Zetz's father. 'Cedars of the Lebanon you can grow on this earth,' he growled, 'and real men also.' He had grown three of them, one in Tanks, one in Ordnance and Asa'el, the eldest, in Paratroops-Infantry. No airy-fairy air force or navy stuff, cut off from the tug of the land: 'Technology, blah! We need all we can get, but the only guarantee of a Homeland is a warrior who fights with his feet on the soil, who can rip out his Enemy's guts at close quarters, sick with the smell of intestines.' With this code he had imbued his two daughters, too, one of whom had disembowelled an Arab guerrilla who was dumb enough to attack their farm, and the other was a judo instructress at a Nahal agricultural outpost. Their mother, a straight-backed Russian babushka whose hands had cracked tilling the soil, had been killed in an accident, crushed by the kibbutz tractor. 'Old age wouldn't have done her in!' snarled the old man. 'Technology, tshorta-mati!'

They held family evenings which frankly terrified Eisav out of his skull. Fridays especially, they'd gather in a bunch to sing the old songs and read out the most blood-curdling bits of the Bible:

'And they brought forth those five Kings unto him out of the cave, the King of Jerusalem, and the King of Eglon . . . and afterwards Joshua smote them, and slew them, and hanged them on five trees, and they were hanging on the trees till the evening . . .'

And the Mahatz offspring would chorus 'Amen!' . . .

'And from Lachish Joshua passed on to Eglon . . . and they took it on that day, and smote it with the edge of the sword, and all the souls that were therein he utterly destroyed that day . . . so Joshua smote all the country of the hills, and of the south, and of the vale, and of the springs, and all their kings; he left none remaining, but utterly destroyed all that breathed, as the Lord God of Israel commanded.'

'Amen!' (Joshua always obeyed orders. He gave Zetz his motto: Never Hesitate.)

'There was not a city that made peace with the children of Israel save the Hivites the inhabitants of Gibeon; all the other they took in battle. *For it was of the Lord to harden their hearts, that they should come against Israel in battle, that he might destroy them utterly, and that they might have no favour, but that he might destroy them, as the Lord commanded Moses.*'

And the old patriarch's eyes would really gleam as he read out this butcher's charter, and Zetz would be seen nodding sagely. The Lord is one mean motherfucker, he hardened their hearts, so that we shouldn't have some easy boy scout pansy time of it – *that's* how you build you a Nation.

Now this was tough meat even for Eisav, who believed in the virtue of hardness and strength for a people besieged by massed enemies, but still saw at the end of the day a rosy dawn hopefully breaking: Each man tending his vine and fig tree, with his wife of valour by his side and his children like the seedlings of olive trees planted about him. The destined woman of valour, potential seedling soil, was always, for Eisav, Nili. This conviction was so strong in Eisav that it abrogated the laws of causation, invalidated the dictates of logic and banished any lingering spasm of doubt. (Amor fati,

200

remember?) The only fly in the ointment of this total certainty was the ever-present spectre of Death. No twist of the threads of Nili's own desires and affections, Major Eisav knew, could tear her from her manifest destiny, but a bullet or a sliver of a 105 shell in his carcase could, despite all, swindle fate ... Between Zetz and Nili, between the rock and the ocean, between Death and Life, the Suez Canal dealt the cards, two hundred-odd items per minute of steel, phosphorus, lead and gunpowder, blitzing the desert bunkers ...

The closest Blok himself came to Death in that era was in that sulphurous June when the *BABASIS* jeep, driven by Sa'id, with the magazine's photographer by him, belted after the troops heading Canalwards out of Bir Gafgafa. As it entered a minor gorge, fire came suddenly from both sides as an Egyptian rearguard and an Israeli mopping-up unit opened up on each other. Blok and colleagues hurriedly decamped into shellholes in the side of the road, while hundreds of bullets flew through the air above them. Although Blok and his colleagues were spared, there were, in the fusillade, eighteen bullets with names and addresses upon them. These were, in order of delivery:

Al-Hawarat, Lutfi Mohamed, 13 Salah-e-din St, Cairo.
Feinbaum, Benny, kibbutz Ma'ayan Hashiloah.
Riad, Sa'ad Mohamed, Abnoud, Upper Nile.
Hilmi, Ahmed Abbas, 45 Kavafi St, Alexandria.
Ovadia, Doron, 2 Harav Kook St, Petah Tikva.
Abd-el-Wahab, Tewfik, 72 Naguib Avenue, Luxor.
Levi, David, 29 November St, Tiberias.
Hafez, Abd-el-Rahman, El-Faiyum.
Hussein, Farid Abdallah, 163 Suleiman Pasha, Alex.

Youssef, Salah Hussein, Abnoud.
Permanente, Pinhas, Shikun H, Block 3, flat 4,
Tsfat.
Waxman, Mordechai, 31 Lord Byron, Tel Aviv.
Darwish, Faud Abdallah, 43 Zaghloul, Beni-Suef.
Butrus, Kokhavi, 38 Hagalil, Zarnuga.
Lutfi, Ahmed Hilmi, Jarout, Upper Nile.
Aziz, Mohamed el-Masri, 12 Naghib, Siwa.
Jedid, Ali Hussein, Abnoud.
Antonius, Edward, 65 Esplanade, Alexandria.

Sic transit, sic transit, sic transit.

'Why, for this existence
There's no man who's meek and mild enough,
All his high endeavour
Is just one more bluff.'

— Bertolt Brecht

And Blok toiled for two years in the vineyards of Holyland Films.

Two years! Consider what went on in the world out there: Chairman Dubcek was dismissed in Prague, Comrade Lin Piao was named Mao Tse Tung's successor, two million Biafrans were killed, General de Gaulle resigned, the Egyptian Chief of Staff poked his head too high over the Suez Canal parapet and got zapped, a Soviet spaceship landed on Venus, an American stepped on the Moon, Moise Tshombe died in an Algerian jail far from his promised land, one Colonel Gaddafi overthrew the geriatric King Idris of Libya, Ho Chi Minh died, Vietnam still burned, four American students were shot dead at Kent State University, the Irish troubles re-started, Brazil won the World Cup, Palestinian guerrillas hijacked four airliners to Jordan and blew them up, King Hussein massacred Palestinians, a Marxist government was elected in Chile, General de Gaulle died, Gomulka lost power in Poland after workers' riots in Gdansk, divorce became legal in Italy, Blok's parents purchased a television set to receive the new Israel TV broadcasts.

Pulses of a new disorder?

Or does Time heal all ills?

In the autumn of 1969, the Zweitlin Yeshiva students finally managed to poison Nili's cat Papishik. By this time a split had occurred between Blok and Nili, over the question of Patriotism. He said it was fake, a trap set to lure the gullible into dying for obscene Causes. She said, That does it, she could not share her bed with a man who did not love his country. Fuck me, fuck my nation, also. Signs of change had been noted for some time. More than once he had caught her, punkt in midsummer, knitting a sweater for Eisav. 'The nights are cold on the Canal,' she said. And in bed too, hélas. With the man telephoning at the crucial hours to transmit his terminal angst.

The Great Love over, or merely interrupted? Was it ever anything special? – Left stuck between Takhkemoni Street and the ancestral home (still the stolid inertia of Gaga the Bloodhound and the Rebetsen and the dead weight of childhood), moping alone or communing with the warthogs in the Biblical Zoo. He throws himself into his work, his sound recording, sounds of the Holyland, under the supervision of Shpilkman, Wilkman and Brodie, the three bald New York dwarves.* Just do the job, Avram Blok, deliver the technical goods. Read. See movies. And on weekends, perambulate about the City. Let your mind, as it were, seek new pastures . . .

(But the kibbutz, Nili's Ma baking the Saturday chocolate cake while Sasha sprawls like a good-natured hippo under the weekend Ha'aretz, and the wind in the cypresses sighs, and the bed in the spare shed creaks as the lovers go at it, Blok proud of his staying power, Nili faking total delight, oohing, aahing, caressing his balls and scratching his shoulder blades, drawing blood with her finger-nails while outside they can hear two old-timers just back from a political potlatch in the city bemoaning the passing of Time: 'what do you expect from Shechterman? the man is a Galicianer.' 'There's no motivation anymore, no honour. The yishuv has gone to blazes.')

When Papishik was killed, smit with an arsenic-smeared lump of fillet, Nili went off alone with the corpse in a plastic bag in a rucksack to perform the last feline rights on a hillside by Giv'at Shaul. Blok called on her when she returned, but when he offered condolences she just said, 'Leave off, it's only a bloody animal.' Eisav's spare uniform was draped over the living room armchair, the shoulder pips newly gleaming.

('Why, for this existence
There's no man who's smart enough,
Life's too short for learning
Every trick and bluff.')

And so he went out, now and then, with girls whom he met in the course of his labours. (Although all in all it was quite a dry period, leavened by mastur-bation.) A nameless lady gave him the clap, which she had got from an itinerant juggler.** Rush to the doctor, plead for mercy, be introduced to the oblong pilules, the balm of penicillin – join, schmuck, join the human race . . . (But the wind, in the bougain-villaeas, hand in hand in the warm kibbutz night, the citrus odour from the coastal plain orchards, one might almost have believed, at such moments, in the Truth of the whole damn schmeer [Ho, The Land, My Trusty Plough in Hand . . .] – 'I love you, you know that for a fact, don't you?' 'You think you do, Avram, you think you do. Love me, if that's what

205

you need, but please, my love, don't expect anything from me. I don't really know where I am, who I am, where I came from, where I'm going. I know about the love I read of in books, or see at the movies, but in my own life – I just don't know; I navigate by friendships, that I can understand.')

Friendship?! Au secours! The first shovelful of sand on the coffin . . . remember the friendships of yore? Fat Avi, now at the University, Gideon, on a foreign scholarship, Muki the Mutt dead in her grave. Requiescat in pacem. Letters from Victoria Happenstance, missives from Another World: Hi, Blokkie, I have done with Political Science, I am reading Anthropology now. The origins of man, man, where our whole troubles came from, digging ever deeper, brother! Wellington Frog – yok, all blacks seemed to have vanished; she was, she revealed, now living with an activist of the International Socialist Party, a card-carrying proletarian who could recite the thirteen theses on Feuerbach while standing on his head in the bath. (Presumably he had other attributes too, mused Blok, or he would soon have been out on his Engels.) Merde alors, she still seethed with political yearnings: the need, don't you think, Avram, to *do* something about the lousy state of the world . . . to *act*, to move one's ass, to put one's neck where one's mouth is . . . He wrote back saying: No, I don't think so. (One burning of the Bourse is enough.) I like sitting on the fence. What on earth could we do, at our best? Martyr ourselves? *Die for a better life?* Is that where our compassion leads us? How's that for negation of the negation? She wrote back saying: You're such a schmuck, Avram Blok, you're staying too long in that goddamn weird country, sticking your head in the sand. Come out again, ostrich! Open your fucking eyes! Pull your finger out of your arsehole! Maybe, maybe sometime, he answered, when I make a bit more money . . .

But till then, there are local escape routes: visiting Nietzsche at Klander, his spates of memory loss and migraines having driven him back into the arms of science. Playing poker one rainy afternoon with the Philosopher, the Magpie, Paradjanov and Scriabina, who was playing two hands. Flusser was away at a Los Angeles conference. Veltsch in charge, whom Blok avoided. Nili delivering him a chaste kiss in the corridors to the applause of kibitzers. First light of a new dawn, last ray of sunset? Who the hell can figure. The patients charged him with the carrying of messages to Davidov, who was on the outside. (He was at his desk, at the Bank B – , Jaffa Road branch, as ebullient as ever: 'I have evolved a plan, better than Paradjanov's system, for winning the Payis lottery . . . Stick with Davidov, kiddo, you won't put a foot wrong . . .' Mama mia. In or out, what's the bloody difference?) Requests for mixed goodies, booze, chocolates, obscene books and magazines. Blok was proud to be trusted with these secret missions, why one cannot quite fathom. Perhaps he'd fallen prey to the belief that psychotics see clearer than others, and their trust's therefore the greater prize . . . (Still apparent, however, the balance of peace and chaos at Klander, as Scriabina, smit by a sudden terror, upturned the poker table, accusing her invisible alter ego of cheating and Nietzsche of bringing his twin brother to spy on her game. Nitsa and Nili, firm on either side, bundled her off to her room. 'The woman's mad,' observed Nietzsche, 'shall we just up the ante?' They were playing for orange peels, which the Magpie had stockpiled over a three-month period.)***

In the summer of '70, Blok found a new paranoia: in the mirror – a receding hairline. In panic he telephoned Nili, who was no consolation. 'Fear of

Baldness,' she said, 'is the castration complex. Elementary Freud, my honey.' Blok replaced the receiver, all a tremble, hit by a flash of a daydream vision: Old Father Time, approaching, wielding, in place of a scythe, a small barber's clipping shears . . .

Yes, the iceman cometh! In January '71 he left Holyland Films. Enough of its air of purposeless yearning and knowitall folderol . . . Whither now, Blok? Hibernate at Takhkemoni provendered with his earnings and a shelf of novels whose time had come: Dostoyevsky, Charles Dickens, Thomas Mann perhaps, *Don Quixote*? But, while in transition, he received simultaneously two missives in the post. One from Victoria, announcing the eviction of Feuerbach and bemoaning a lonely winter. The other, a form from *BABASIS* magazine, prior warning of a March Reserves call-up. Mon dieu, not the battered Wyllis again, Sa'id and Yehoshua, the tantrums of Major Tswingli! Impossible, gentlemen. Blok went, upon impulse, the very same day, to the travel agent, and booked the earliest flight to England.

* The studios of Holyland Films were set among the rolling hills of Ein Karem, just beyond the bounds of the City. Wasps buzzed about brown terraces at the birthplace of John the Baptist, old Russian monks with cotton-wool beards peered over fine stone monastery walls at the 28 bus chuffing by below. The films the studios produced were almost all for external use, soliciting the rustle of hundred dollar bills, or even crisper music, cheques or bankers' orders for the Zionist Cause. The employees, film crews and editors, cared little about all this. They performed their jobs and pursued, on the side, secret lives which they related to Blok at incongruous moments, such as the peroration of a keynote speech at the Hadassah Conference, or in a brief raid into Golda Meir's kitchen, to steal a can of anchovies. One bred hamsters in the dark of the night. Another had a passion for anal insertion, which was illegal in Jewish law. However, the only person around whom Blok considered a friend was one Yissachar ('Juancito') Pri-On (né Peron, like the Argentine dictator), a brash young assistant editor with curly hair and a dark friendly moon face, who had no secret but a burning desire to decamp to the United States, where, he said, lucrative employment could be easily found in the field of pornographic films. Blok and he often fantasized about this halcyon future, lounging at Yissachar's mother's airy San Simon home, a little piece of Buenos Aires in the dusty Levant, with the portrait on the wall of the

family namesakes, the ex-tyrant and his Evita, together with a framed reply to a letter mama had sent him in his Madrid exile, saying: 'My return is certain. Do not despair, I shall never forsake my people.'

** The itinerant juggler was called Flash Yehezkel (the quick wrist deceives the eye . . .). He toured up and down the country, his progress carefully charted by urologists of the Kupat Holim and of the World Health Organization. In 1975 he shot himself on the Tel Aviv Esplanade, over his unrequited love for the Rubber Woman of Beersheba (who will figure further on in our story).

*** Once, a few weeks after he and Nili had parted, Blok met Nietzsche by chance in the street. It was the winding road, named Harav Salant, leading down from the exotic Abyssinian Church to the ultra-orthodox Jewish quarter of Mea Shearim. The Philosopher was toiling up past solemn figures in kapotas and streimels with millennial angst etched upon their foreheads, carrying in each of his hands a bulging plastic bag of groceries. 'Hello, there!' he cried jovially. 'Why, it's Blok the Onlooker, Blok the Peeper in Keyholes! Come on in, I live right in this building here.' What could one do with Nietzsche? One either accepted him as he was or gave him the widest possible berth. Blok preceded him up the stone steps to the third floor of Salant Number-. Nietzsche's apartment consisted of a kitchen and two spare but neat rooms, a hard wooden bed with a thin mattress in one, in the other a wooden table with a small table lamp, shelves with books arranged according to height and files upon files of papers, documents, manuscripts. In neither room was there any picture or ornament on the white walls, but in the kitchen, over an old gas stove there was one portrait, hung on a nail, a sepia print of a very dour old man with two tufts of white hair and rather heavy, grumpy jowls.

'Schopenhauer,' said Nietzsche. 'I need to be reminded of the prime enemy who was once my mentor.' He began to unload his groceries. 'He perceived the age was lifeless but made the error of throwing away his own great discovery, the primacy of the Will. Lemon or orangeade?'

'Orangeade will be fine.'

'What's this they whisper to me, Nili-Honey and you are estranged?'

'We had a row,' said Blok.

'A woman is like an umbrella,' said Nietzsche, 'sooner or later one takes a cab.'

'I don't understand that,' said Blok. 'Is it one of your own aphorisms?'

'Sigmund Freud,' said Nietzsche, 'an inheritor of sorts. A little strange though, the Viennese humour. Still, you must admit what we both wrote of women was true. We gave them Emancipation and look where that leaves us: running around like mice.'

'I don't think so,' said Blok, 'women should be equal. Women are equal to men.'

'That's what I always said: The equal of a slave is a slave. One is either above or beneath. I'll bet you have not read one single word of my voluminous oeuvre.'

'I browsed,' said Blok, 'but a lot of it seemed quite obscure.'

'Buki sriki!' said Nietzsche, 'I am known for my crystal clarity. Consult any of my interpreters, parasitical worms that they are. Obscure? Asargelusha! You should try that fart Hegel, or Kant.'

Blok sipped the cool orange drink. With Nietzsche, one simply had to let the storm spend itself.

'Equality,' the Philosopher snorted, emptying a packet of Hadar biscuits into a chipped clay bowl, 'the mirage of the age! They've been screaming that slogan since they stormed the Bastille: Liberté! Egalité! Fraternité! And the outcome? The same words, engraved on the portals of mass slaughterhouses! I love you, brother! they shout as they thrust with their bayonets into the living flesh! I tell you, if it wasn't so disgustingly common it would be just one hearty belly laugh.'

'What would you have instead of those words?' asked Blok, his liberal instincts stung. 'What's your solution then?'

'There speaks the age again! Oh mama, give me the teat! Feed me, daddy, the nectar of my salvation! Slaves without masters, that's our modern world, with some slaves just brutish enough to temporarily subdue others. Mussolini, Stalin, Hitler, ersatz Napoleons dunking their snouts in the trough. Well, I told them it would happen, but did anyone listen? No, sir! Glazed-eyed they were, all of them, watching the clock for feeding time, ears pricked, like Pavlov's dogs, for the bell of a vanished din-dins . . .'

'I heard somewhere,' said Blok with some malice, 'that in Germany the Nazis adopted the main thrust of your works.'

Nietzsche ceased unpacking and turned to Blok, solemnly waving a beetroot. 'Young man,' he said, 'you will not succeed in getting my goat. The slings and arrows, as the Englishman Bacon wrote . . . That has all been pawed over, milacku. It was a woman, once again, who stuck in the knife. Ah, you will learn, young Blok, especially if you get to live twice over, like me. Cherchez la femme, toujours! You should have such a sister, who dances on your grave and sells out your soul to the devil. I could tell you . . . but what's the use? I foresaw the whole betrayal. For if there were no betrayal, where then would be Tragedy? Where would there be Eternity? If the Christian hadn't been sold by his Judas, where would he be today? Dry as dust, I can tell you, not a dachshund would know his name. He had woman trouble too, anyway . . . that whore Magdalene, I shouldn't wonder . . . like Salome, with the Baptist, or my Lou, with our photograph . . .' He seemed to lose himself in his own wanderings for a moment, then resumed to unpack a lettuce. 'It's all the same, mark my words,' he said sagely, 'just wait till you come full circle, my friend, then you'll find out the weary truth: there is nothing new under the sun. Everything just repeats itself, over and over. The wheel of man's fortune turns, over and over, turning, ad infinitum.'

'Not to have a correct political point of view is like having no soul.'

– Mao Tse Tung

February, London. Sludge, frost underfoot. Nights of black chill to the bone. Days of monochrome grey drizzle, paralysing the brain, seizing up the heart. The flowerpots at the apartment house are empty. Perhaps the pussycats have croaked from the cold. Inside, on the TV screen, a fat pink-faced fart warbles, fixing the frozen millions with the fishy ice of his stare. Gone, the pipe-smoking Wilsonian smirk. Arriba, Britannia of Heath.

Nevertheless, a sense of homecoming for Blok, his re-encampment at Stamford Hill. The wall posters, of the supplicating Vietnamese woman, Mao of hammers and sickles, bandoliered FRELIMO, de Gaulle clutching his balls, the packed bookcases – with a sprinkling of new titles: *Kwakiutl Ethnography, Structures of Kinship, The Family and Death*, indeed ... Victoria, sprawled on her bed in a bright yellow dressing gown, slurping down a bowl of late afternoon cornflakes, *Report on Malnutrition in the Transkei*, Emma Goldman's *Living My Life* and a Chinua Achebe novel scattered about her, the central heating turned up to its highest level in every room, inhabited or not. No sign of Wellington Frog or Panthers, faded in the fog of rumour (to Tangier, Yugoslavia, Belgium? their tracks had filled out long ago) . . . Apart from Blok the only resident at the time was J.D., the black South African exile, temporarily homeless after the friend he had lodged with in North Clapham had been evicted for throwing the landlord's furniture out of a third-floor window. In Stamford Hill J.D. lived like Mole in *The Wind In The Willows*, spending most of his day on a single bed tucked in the room's furthest corner, reading by a bare sixty-watt bulb the latest paperback spy thrillers; his three bags, with his few earthly goods, toothbrush, towel, broken comb, spare tie, shirts and a copy of an unfinished copy of an unfinished manuscript on the Poll Tax Rebellion of 1906 piled tight around him, as if he were ready at the first heavy knock on the door to light out for the Sierra Maestra. At times, in the evenings, he came out of his shell to concoct in the kitchen some bizarre Boer dish which was sheer death to the taste buds, or to regale Vicky and Blok, over a bottle or two of vino rosso or a wee dram of something stronger, with melancholy tales of realpolitik and corruption in far-off climes, among those who clung fast to the trappings of power or others, who lived off the table scraps of Europe's white liberal conscience. Removing and replacing his dark glasses, running the broken comb through the tight curls of his hair and his beard, emitting occasionally a low chortle or a morose moan between words, he would talk of Kwame Nkrumah, buried by his sycophants in the shit of their fawning, of the financial peccadillos of Jomo (Mzee), of the Congo, and the mysterious death of Dag Hammarskjold, of Jean Bolikango, and Uriah Simango, and how he had once met a drunken Belgian named Huyghes in a speak-easy in Marrakesh, who had told him the full gory details of the murder of Patrice Lumumba, revealing a shrivelled ear hung round his neck, which he claimed was the last remnant of the late Prime Minister of the Congolese Republic. Sometimes willowy Zeph would appear, sliding through the door flashing his gold ring to join them at the kitchen table and thrust the discussion into even more rarefied orbits of international scandal: 'You know the whole Czechoslovakia affair was a set up. Dubcek was a Soviet agent provocateur. Matlebane met him in the winter of '63 at the espionage school in Katyn. The aim of that operation was to show Eastern Europe the futility of reform.' Or: 'You know Hitler is still alive and living in the Orange Free State. He has a small farm by the Swinkpan. His name is Johannes Ventner.' Zeph's tales could not be lightly dismissed, for he had stayed at the same hotel in Harlem as the Cuban delegation to the UN General Assembly of '60, and had not only shared late-night cigars with Ernesto Che Guevara but had been lectured incessantly by Fidel himself while the latter was taking his bath. Blok never again in his life met anyone who had seen Fidel Castro nude. 'Is it very large?' Vicky asked, wickedly. 'Sufficient for the job,' Zeph affirmed.

Thus Blok in the new diaspora, the cosmopolitan eye of the cyclone. Occasionally he accompanied Victoria to her place of study, a sedate building opposite the Euston station, and sat around in the cafeteria. Luscious ladies, and appreciably less luscious men, of a dozen different ethnic vintages, floated by, bearing upon trays dollops of quick fried eggs or somewhat dried scones, settling at nearby tables to discuss what Blok first thought was a brand of jeans but soon found out was the intellectual scream of the hour. Alien babble, of Malinowski and mother-rights in Melanesia (and in Kiryat Moshe, nebesch?), the odd religion of the Ndembu and the odder sexual rites of certain senior staff. A loud voice said: 'But isn't the volcanic symbolism of Easter Island obviously orgasmic?' By the entrance, two fair-haired English youths in shabby grey sweaters hawked the ubiquitous works of Mao. *Against Liberalism? On People's Democratic Dictatorship? On Correcting Mistaken Ideas In The Party? The Present Situation And Our Tasks?* Not today, thank you. Ah! already the first glimmers of the twilight of l'age d'or . . .

Now and again, when J.D. decided to chance the air, Blok travelled with him far south to Brixton to ebullient Walter's apartment. A cluttered private storeroom, a time machine of his mind, with shelves and shelves of old pamphlets and leaflets pleading causes and campaigns long drowned in blood or stifled in prison cells . . . faded posters of Durban and Table Mountain, a map of Africa South and all her sea routes . . . pock-marked cork notice boards littered with cuttings which over the years had taken his fancy: 'I DIDN'T KNOW HOW TO GIVE A HICKEY', 'ONE MILLION PEOPLE EAT PET FOOD', 'PUBS TOLD: WATCH FOR ADDICTS', 'HOW A BABY'S RACE IS DECIDED' and

'SSHH . . . YOU'LL DISTURB THE ANIMALS
Whistling in the zoo is now out, as is strumming on your old banjo or listening to your portable . . . such activities are banned forthwith by Johannesburg's new zoological bylaws. It is also unlawful to "blow or imitate the sound of a whistle, except in cases of emergency . . ." '

Here for hours they would sit, on mouldy old cinema seats Walter had rescued from a demolished Odeon, continuing the roster of tall tales, or sighing as Walter answered frantic telephone calls from

214

countrymen in deep trouble. Small voices crying desperately out for aid from the detention centre at Heathrow Airport, or the Hôtel Emmerdeur in Paris, or a shebeen in Margate, or a battered phone booth on the outskirts of Tooting Common. In response, lawyers might be alerted, friendly clergymen implored for the awakening of MPs, or, at times, instant advice dispensed, in the spirit of Self Help and Positive Thinking which Walter seemed to have imbibed into his very bloodstream: 'It's no use, comrade, waiting for your Uncle Zack to turn up and solve your problems. You have to use your own kop. You have to decide what you want of your life, and then grab it, and not smoodge around.' J.D.'s eyes would glaze, his comb scrape through his greying beard. 'There's this kaffir,' Walter would tell them, 'who sold home-made knishes from a street stall in Cape Town. Some enterprising Yidlah, one of your lot, Avram, took him up and you know what – this poor ignorant blackman now sits in a skyscraper, retailing food to Africa!'

'Neither of us can make knishes,' said J.D., referring to Blok and himself.

'You see!' crowed Walter, 'it's just what I said – you defeat yourself from the start!'

'South Africa, my friend!' J.D. to Blok, late night, Stamford Hill, after several libations. 'You would hardly believe it. The sheer pressure of the dilemma ... To remain human although you are labelled as trash from your birth to the grave. There was one incident that crystallized it all for me: I was nineteen, working as a delivery boy for a big Johannesburg store. Riding those infernal trains, every day, back and forth, from Orlando, two hours morning and evening ... I had a package to deliver on my bicycle to an address in Parktown. I had delivered the package and was walking back to the spot I had parked my bike. An old white woman was passing on the pavement, carrying a few small parcels. She was very shaky on her pins and, as she passed me, I don't know exactly how, she tripped and fell on the pavement, scattering her parcels on the ground. Without thinking, I stepped forward and took her arm, to help her up on her feet. Suddenly, without warning, I was grabbed, my arms pinned behind me. I turned, to see two of those really bulky Afrikaaner farmer boys, policemen on the beat . . . Boy, one of them says, with that cold inhuman tone they use . . . Boy, what do you think you're doing? The old lady fell down, I said, I was just trying to help her up. Help, he says. Help?? Who told you you can touch a white woman, kaffir? And they laid into me . . . I can't tell you. It was no mild chastisement, no casual beating that they doled out that day. They went over me thoroughly, there was no part of my body they didn't hit: my head, my stomach, my kidneys, my groin, my ribs . . . nothing was left to chance. The last thing I remember before life became just a blur of the police van, the station steps, the cells, was that massive policeman's boot – one image I will not forget – that huge Boer foot coming down, with the full force of that ox's body – crash, into my face. That is my South Africa, my friend, the South Africa that I have to deal with . . .'

'And the cold,' said J.D., 'the cold of exile! Of that London that is neither yours nor mine – the prickles of gooseflesh on a morning of ice before the shilling drops into the meter . . . the dull grey, through leafless trees, the dull grey that will not lighten. The landlady, downstairs, may have wakened to the cheerleading of Radio Two . . . upstairs, the thumps and shudders of the unknown neighbours you pass on your way, on their way, with a nod and a muffled "morning . . ." The mail, on a table in the lobby, grey with dust, for it is for tenants who have long since vanished with names even stranger than yours: Stassinopoulos, Ostraszewski, Fourouzesh ... Outside – the rat-race, the multitudes going by, heads in their collars, no gaze meeting another – entire days can go by without your exchanging a word with another person. The really desperate talk to themselves; on the top deck of the bus a drunk vilifies his absent wife: "Oi'll t'row her in de river, b' Jasus ..." Men, sunk in their evening newspapers, listen to the lash of the rain. You can go through the heart of the City, my friend, great buildings rising all about you ... tall ghosts of the empire, each stone the pressed blood of a black, brown or yellow person. National Westminster ... Barclays, Lloyds, Kaiser Ullman ... Solid, boy, solid stability ... The Rolls Royces purr down the Strand but on the Embankment a man still lies in his own vomit, wrapped in the *Daily Telegraph*! This is the Motherland, then, my friend, whose passport is supposed to mean so much to me. England's green and pleasant land ... I have been here too long, I can tell you, I have let their cold bite into my bones. If you still have a home in the sun, don't lose it, while you still have a chance ...'

But Blok is full pelt. He had not been nailed down yet; there are still heights in his eyes to scale: Victoria, Victoria, golden Victoria, the shiksa of everyone's dreams ... How do I gain entrance to her heart, to the hallowed zones of her body? He began reading Marxist literature again: shards of Lenin, fireballs of Trotsky, dollops of Marx, lumps of Engels. The philosophers have only interpreted the world in different ways; the point is to change it. The history of all hitherto existing society is the history of class struggles. The proletarian revolution is impossible without the forcible destruction of the bourgeois state machine. (Debooting the Boers, gottevrdommen!) Communist man will be immeasurably stronger, wiser and subtler, asargelusha! The average human type will rise to the heights of an Aristotle, a Goethe, a Marx. And above these heights, new peaks will rise.

Indeed. From each according to his abilities, to each according to his needs. But still she stayed locked away from his yearnings, often poring over papers for days in her room, or with J.D. over the kitchen table, planning some grand main event, something she was not yet prepared to divulge to Blok, the good friend left politely dangling . . .

He ventured without, taking long walks, criss-crossing the A to Z of London. Addressing the old codger, the maestro of *Kapital*, while trudging up the Archway Road: Herr Marx, he called silently, in the pall of a March day still very far off from spring – you say environment makes the man, why is *my* environment, invariably, the mirror image of my mood? Who wants such an environment, any-way, when it includes such horrors as a world bent on suicide, Boer boots and gas chambers, a father who escapes from it in Guadaloupe florials, a Malka Halperin who'll bear in her mind for ever Blok as a frustrated lunatic, a Victoria Happen-stance who would give me all but that that I truly desire? Change the world, you say? You must have been joking! I, Blok, against the universe? Well, Blok, Marx said to him sadly, You seem to have missed the whole point. You have only yourself to blame if you cannot escape from petit-bourgeois manifestations.

The stern voice of paternalism. Fuck it all. Wher-ever you go, you take yourself with you. Cliché of the month. He immersed himself further, despair-ingly, in books and the movies. The balm of the silver screen, yea! nepenthe, the drug of forget-fulness . . . At one such screening, a cinema club showing an uncensored film about a man in a New

218

York meat-packing plant who turned his best friends into sausages, he met Dianne, his one-night bedmate of the slambamkalamazam party. Is this the mark of kismet, comrades? The first cuckoo of the season? There she was, grown just a little chubbier, a living memory of the past. She pecked him on the cheek, then they had a coffee, and she invited him to her flat. A rather neat pied-à-terre behind West Hampstead tube where her flatmate, a petite blonde who strummed the banjo, read his fortune in tarot cards. He had to shuffle and deal out the major arcana, one by one, anti-clockwise. Then the blonde read their meaning to him in turn, while Dianne, remembering, brought out the vodka . . .

Nom de dieu! L'Etoile, the Star, signifying hope, trustfulness and promise. The Hermit – discretion (the better part of valour?), solicitude and self-denial. The Lovers, ah! suggestive of romance – but the Chariot – uncertain ordeals. The Hanged Man, reversed, the blonde looks a little worried. A whole satchel of problems here: ego worship, failure to make sacrifices, warnings of a false prophecy . . .

Soft music from an old hi-fi. Blok, cross-legged on the carpet clutching Dianne's hand which lay loosely across his shoulders. Eyes riveted on the petite blonde, her delicate features, her soft grey eyes, her fine hair falling, caressing her back. He downed a third glass of vodka. 'It's strange,' the blonde girl said, 'your combination of violence and gentleness. I can't make it out at all.' He felt so proud to have a personality that this beautiful, sensitive girl could not fathom. He continued therefore to spread the pack: Le Soleil, the Sun: success and well-being. Achievement, unselfish love. He was warming to the occasion. So far so good, perhaps carnal delights are twinkling at the end of the tunnel . . .

But these are Blok's iron fates, remember? La Maison de Dieu, merde, alors! The Tower Struck by Lightning. Luck running out. Unexpected events. Danger. Chaos. Adversity. Possible ruin – the dissolution of existing forms to make way for new, unforeseen ones. Death, or even worse, perhaps . . . shall we pronounce a misdeal? The vodka having reached his brain, he let his head fall back upon Dianne's bosom, eyelids drooping, loins tense with desire. 'Closing time!' she chose this moment to call cheerfully, 'I have to have an early night. Art gallery duties, eight a.m. sharp! Everyone out! All change!' He opened his eyes. The tarot girl had vanished, pack of cards, banjo, hair, all.

'But I want to stay!' he pleaded plaintively. 'My brain has frozen, I have lost my *A to Z* and my feet are kaput, totally.'

'We'll soon put that right,' she said, smoothly, proceeding to massage his toes.

'Oh, that's so good . . .' he breathed, 'if you stop I shall surely die.'

'The acid test,' she proclaimed, withdrawing. He lay back, alas alive. She pottered about the room, putting things in their place, disconnecting the gramophone. Any moment now, he thought, she will wind up the clock. 'Phone me, Avram, please,' she pleaded, 'I'm really dead beat tonight.' Laboriously he put on his shoes, donned his thick navy blue winter coat which made him look like Admiral Kolchak after his defeat at Irkutsk, as she manoeuvred him to the door. 'Phone me, huh? Ciao, bambino.' And never darken my towels again . . . Erection unabated, he slowly walked down the landing, out, banging the heavy main door behind him, into the frosty darkness. A long, icy, teeth-chattering walk to Stamford Hill and the Happenstance glacier . . .

He did phone her again, and they went out to a

movie, and she revealed to him her fearful secret: she had become engaged to a Jewish accountant, from Hendon, a Litvak no less. An ACCOUNTANT?? FROM HENDON?? Blok's mind was in turmoil throughout the following fortnight. A Litvak! You think you know something about someone and they turn out completely bananas. Herr Marx! He called the old boy desperately, staggering down the Holloway Road, 'How do you possibly account for this? An accountant from Hendon!' But Marx did not answer, his celestial vibrations engaged in weightier matters, no doubt. Fuck you, Big Daddy, Blok cried silently. (Are Oedipal entanglements stirring?) On he trudged, his humour plummeting, the screwdriver of despair . . . It was a perfect day for his mood, drizzly and overcast, damp, dank and chilly. As he passed under the railway bridge a pigeon shat from a rusted girder, hitting him, SPLAT, an absolute bull's-eye, right on his balding forehead. OK, he said to himself, that's it. Message received loud and clear. La Maison de Dieu, the Tower Struck by Lightning, a pictureque demonstration. Dead end, Blok draw your conclusions, time to put paid to it all. A sudden plunge off the Charing Cross bridge to the Thames. A leap, in front of the tube at rush hour. The gas, with all exits blocked, and an ample supply of shillings. Thousands of aspirins, washed down with Cadbury's Drinking Chocolate. He thought: I shall leave notes, and everyone will feel sorry. But then, as he emerged from the bridge's shadow, a series of terrible images struck him: Mama: Avremel! how can you do this to me?! Papa, submerged in the tide . . . His body flown back courtesy of the Embassy . . . (in the diplomatic shroud). Mama's relative Lieutenant Colonel N – might make a speech at the funeral . . . Aunt Pashtida might throw herself into the grave . . . No one would understand so rational a decision, everyone would assume unsound mind . . . Viper's whispers, Klander tales making the rounds: tst, tst, tst, such a sad case, a young man, consumed by vice. The court sent him to the nuthouse, Feigeh . . . you know who's to blame? Liberal psychiatrists – they threw him back into the world. If they'd kept him inside this wouldn't have happened. The temptations of foreign lands. Alone, with no guidance. The fleshpots. Soho. Shiksas. The permissive society. I tell you, Feigeh, we were better off in the ghetto, where we knew who we were. Mon dieu! With such certain prospects death is just out of the question! My environment again condemns me, Herr Marx, to the random oscillations of Life . . . He entered the Holloway Underground station, buying an *Evening Standard* from the newsvendor. In the train he sat back in the brown scuffed seat, idly scanning the headlines: 'SOLDIER SHOOTS HIS MOTHER BY MISTAKE: A part-time Ulster Defence Regiment soldier accidentally shot his mother last night after mistaking her for a terrorist.' In Salt Lake City, a youth had climbed to the top of the Mormon Tabernacle and shot dead thirty-five people. A woman in Cheam was electrocuted while grooming her dog with clipping shears. Civil war in Pakistan. In Cape Town, Dr Christiaan Barnard wants to transplant the heart of a Zambian into a white South African, just to show there's no difference he says. In the United States a Lieutenant Calley is on trial for the massacre of Vietnamese villagers at a hamlet named My Lai. His lawyers claim he is expected to say: I was only following orders.

I Shall Not Die But Live: Blok's indecision. Grey March into muggy April.

Finally, Victoria revealed her secret to him. The locale: Hampstead Heath, open spaces. A sunny day at last, the sky deep blue, here and there, in the underbrush, the jellywhite tum of a native, worshipping a pale northern sun. Blok, beside Vicky, throwing pebbles into the pond.

'I am going to South Africa, on an anthropological study tour. A comparative study of Bantu languages. Remember Davina? She's coming with me. It's a mission, in fact, for the Movement. We are taking a tape recorder with us. Why don't you join us, Avram, and help us record some interviews in the homelands and townships?'

Gevaldt. In the pond wavelets ripple. Mallards squawk as Blok's pebble bounces. Englishmen's dogs leap into the water to retrieve twigs for their masters. So this is what has been cooking in the late nights with J.D. in the kitchen. The slambamkalamazam of commitment, the leap into shark-ridden deeps . . .

But I am not a student, cried Blok, let alone of languages, I am slow of speech and of a slow tongue. No Nagra-carrying Moses, to unscramble Babel and be the voice for another lost people, ground in tyranny's jaws. Bad enough Mama Blok's Ecclesiastes. And anyway I'm a bloody foreigner.

'That's no problem,' she said. 'A group of twelve is going, splitting into twos and threes. We have a German, a Greek, two Swedes and a French girl. They are from different colleges. I can get you put on the list. Everything can be arranged.'

A long pause ensued so she launched into her What I Believe, her Credo:

'I know what you think, mon Blok: see the safe English bitch with delusions of Revolution. A political voyeur, a sad case, thinking she can change the world. But I haven't plucked this move out of a hat, Blokkie, it's been part of me for years. It's not an abstract matter for me but very very personal. Something between me and J.D., me and Zeph, me and others you haven't met yet. Little corners of me like Wellington Frog, like Miguel whom you never knew ... We don't know, in our lilywhite society, what the world is like out there. I know the risks and they scare me to shit, believe me, I'm no Mata Hari of the veldt, my Avram. Sometimes you just have to do something for someone else ... fuck it, this is getting really pompous. You're right, I shouldn't drag you into it. It's my obsession, my fucking hang-up, no need for you to be part of it. I only thought – you've been in tight spots, down there, in your war ... and you're bloody careful.'

'Moi, careful?'

'Si, compañero. Like me, you're not the heroic type. You wouldn't take stupid chances.'

Oh God ... the double bind, the syrupy cobweb of praise ... Listen Vicky, he wished to say, I have had my quota of wars. The bodies, rotting in sand. Their reek, like a burst gas balloon. Velly solly, lady, no cannon fodder I, for idealist pie in the sky. No Blokkian precedent for commitment. On the contrary – remember Baruch Blok, keeping his head down through the firestorm? Surviving to breathe the air of another day, another era, for which countless millions had died ... and what was its face, this new dawn? What phoenix of the human spirit? More like a chicken, starved and wretched, yearning for the chopping block ...

'I don't know,' he said. 'I don't know what to tell you.'

'Forget it,' she said, 'it's nothing. I haven't been fair to you. You shouldn't feel pressured. I don't want you to feel you owe me. What we have we have, we'll be friends whatever happens. That's not a promise, just a fact, milacku. Whatever you do, you shouldn't commit yourself unless you believe strongly.'

'That's good advice,' agreed Blok, 'I shall not commit myself unless I believe strongly.'

But meanwhile, back at the ranch, an earth-shaking event occurred:

*April 1971:*
*Kibbutz Mas'at Nefesh announces*

## The Marriage

*of our daughter*                    *to our adopted son*

*Nili Grunbaum-Yakir*        *Ilan (Eisav) Ben-Gever*

*The ceremony will take place*
*at the kibbutz Cultural Centre*
*18 April, 17:00 hours*

*": Many waters cannot quench love, neither can*
*the floods drown it" – Song of Songs. 8,7.*

What on earth possessed her?

Consider: His iron patience; how he stood outside her flat in the rain, a bedraggled red scarecrow fit to terrorize would-be burglars or cat poisoners, rain streaming down from his head, off his shoulders, from the ends of his drooping moustache. The mountain, waiting in the storm for Mohammed. And the phone calls: Suez Canal angst in the static of field telephones routed via the Beersheba exchange. The threat of the death wish: I pray, he said, for the Arab bullet that will put an end to my torment. Almost wishing for the next war (Let My Soul Die With the Philistines . . .), piling on the guilt – was her blunt rejection to be a cause of more slaughter in the House of Israel? More bodies in the sands, more torn tatters of youths to be wheeled before her to be stitched up, bones stapled together? All due to your stubborn denial, Nili, fuelling visions of Apocalypse? Eisav, like the slow drip of Chinese water torture, steadily reducing resistance.

And her own desires – fatigued by the mêlée of so many male expectations: Nili, rock of ages, save me from my shattered self! No rock am I, comrades, more of a quicksand in which you embed yourselves, in which I absorb all your fears and nightmares into my own, from which I can't spew you out: internee Yitzhak, Eddie the Moroccan footballer, Dr H – ,eye surgeon of international fame, seaman Pinto, Elkayam, Maciste of Klander, poor Avram Blok . . . am I not Woman – yearning, as tradition has it, for peace and security, a strong reliable mate to warm up the bed, a child or two, or three, to put down unbreakable roots . . .? Time to stop farting about, Nili-Honey, time to close down the funfair. And Eisav in the trenches, waiting . . .

So – finally – dawn breaks over the kibbutz: tweet-tweet, the birds in the trees; moo, the cows in the shed; gobble, gobble, the fattening turkeys; rumble, rumble, the day's first tractor, puttering out to the fields. Deep deep blue, the sky of a perfect spring day to be.

Out of the spare bungalow Nili and Eisav creep, he to bachelor quarters over beyond the swimming pool, she to Marta and Sasha's house, where the frosty eye of Mama meets her over the breakfast frying pan. 'Now that you've sampled the merchandise,' said Marta, 'you're still so hot to buy?' Disingenuous, for who but Marta knows just how far back the sampling started.

'It's my wedding day,' said Nili, 'you're supposed to be radiant with joy, dabbing your tear-stained cheeks with Kleenex.'

'Don't worry,' riposted Mama, 'I shall do my best not to laugh.'

Sasha, bleary-eyed, staggered out of the bedroom: 'Good morning, good morning, has anyone seen the weekend *Ha'aretz*?'

'It's your daughter's wedding day,' Marta waved a ladle at him, 'and all you think of is your shitty newspaper?'

'I'll believe it when I see it,' said Sasha, poking about in the porch. 'At the critical moment she'll kick him right in the balls, and that'll be the end of that.' Having located the paper, he padded back in, heaving his vest-clad bulk into the easy chair. 'Anyway,' he aired his real grievance, 'I'm not wearing that hired monkey suit. I will not put a noose round my neck to pander to Polish hang-ups.'

'Sasha Yakir,' said Marta, 'you'll wear that suit and like it, or you'll find yourself out on your arse before sundown, with an itchy blanket around your ears. Come on, eat your breakfast, Sasha, we've a lot of work to do. I told them we'd be down at the kitchens at quarter past eight punkt.'

'You haven't put the child on the roster today?' Sasha was shaken. 'After all, it's her wedding day!'

Marta said: 'You're in charge of the booze, blockhead! Don't think *you* can *shlump* here all day.'

Thus far the Grunbaum-Yakir household. Eisav, meanwhile, roamed the fields, striding eastwards through the waving wheat. On the watertank hill, overlooking the settlement, he sat down, rustling an ear of corn between his fingers, taking in the morning view. Over the higgledly-piggledy slanting roofs, the corrugated iron sheds, set in a sea of green of differing, dappled hues. And the sprinklers, just starting up, putta-putta-putta on the lawns. Songs of his childhood welled up to envelop him. Play, Play Upon the Dreams . . . The kibbutz of his adolescence, in the basalt north, had been an altogether sterner place. The dour countenance of the patriarch Azriel Mahatz, Zetz's father, matching the looming threat of the Golan hills, over the border in Syria. A rocky chain of hidden fortresses from which latter-day Beelzebubs cast their dark nets of menace . . . (Now tourists picked their way through the blasted fortifications, clicking Canons at the burned one-o-fives . . .) How proudly the orphan boy had gazed at the tall soldiers who with their fierce, tender presence protected the Good from the Evil. And how proud he had been finally to join their ranks, to don the khaki uniform. A pride he had never lost, that still rippled through him as he sat above Mas'at Nefesh. Still protecting these green oases planted in a battlefield. A man, alone, is nothing. His willingness to sacrifice, to die for the group, is what makes his existence real. And now Eisav approached his culmination: the group, via Nili, taking him in, accepting him as one of their own in a way the unbending Mahatz clan had never quite made him feel. Mahatz was the rock, which never yielded, but did not bear fruit. Nili was fertile soil.

Play, Play Upon the Dreams . . .

At three in the afternoon the delegation from Klander arrived in a minibus, all the way from Jerusalem. It consisted of Flusser, beaming like an expectant grandfather, nurses Nitsa, Renata and Pitsi and three patients, Paradjanov the football Tote freak, the Magpie and Nietzsche, under the eagle-eye of Elkayam. They brought with them Nili's ex-flatmate Hava, who had done a deal of work on her face and clothing and looked a perfect mensch for the occasion. They clustered around Nili in the dining hall kitchen, kissing, embracing, fluttering and attempting to sample the tshoolent.* They were eventually hustled out, Elkayam, with discretion, removing several knives, forks, spoons and a Swiss army penknife from the Magpie's inside jacket pocket. With Flusser's help, he corralled them round a table in the empty dining hall, where Sasha joined them with a case of beer.

It soon transpired that Sasha, like the Magpie, had fought, in his day, in Spain. In fact they had both taken part in the great and bloody battles of Guadalajara of March 1937. Sasha, who now revealed in public his dreaded past private name – Erwin – had been in the German 11th International Brigade under Enrique Lister, while the Magpie said his unit was the Italian Garibaldi Battalion, under Luigi Longo. In fact they might even have glimpsed each other in the flesh, at the battle of Brihuega, though in the grime and mud and smoke of slaughter that intriguing option was marginal. An argument arose over the snapping of beer-bottle caps, as to whether it was the Thaelman or the Garibaldi which finally took the Ibarra.

'Don't give me this buki-sriki!' scoffed the Magpie. 'Your lot had your heads stuck in the mud like ostriches, while we cut up Mussolini's butchers!'

'Not at all,' Sasha countered, flicking open another Goldstar, 'Longo's mob got lost in the fog,

---

* Tshoolent: popular, traditional Jewish Polish dish, a stew of meat, potatoes, beans and intestines, cooked for over eighteen hours.

– A Jew, on the run from Nazi thugs after the Kristalnacht, is lost in the alien, gentile part of town. As the sounds of pursuit draw nearer he is drawn inexorably to the doorway of a particular house. Desperately he knocks on the door: 'Let me in, I am a brother Jew!' The man of the house, who is a complete stranger, quickly unlocks the door. 'How did you know this was a Jewish household?' he asks as the exhausted man falls into an easy chair. The fugitive lifts his head and, flaring his nostrils and sniffing, says: 'tshoolent'.

229

and ended up half way to Madrid before the schlemiel consulted his compass . . .'

'Vanity, all is vanity,' said Nietzsche, grinning smugly beneath his shawara. 'The main thing is the battle, never mind which side you're on. As a medic, at Karlsruhe, I was most impressed by our French enemies, who had fought so well for their stupid Emperor, dumb prick that he was. Dying with sang froid, that's what it's all about.'

'What battle was that?' asked Sasha, momentarily all at sea.

'Worth, August 1870,' said Nietzsche, 'a mere skirmish in the Franco–Prussian. Ah, but how vividly I still remember the piles of corpses, the blood on the surgeon's table . . .'

'Hmmm, yes,' said Sasha warily. 'Shall we forage for a few more beers?' Mercifully Marta glided up at that instant, pointing an accusing finger: 'Sasha, time to get into your uniform, there's barely an hour to go!'

'Coming!' he said, and followed her hurriedly out of the hall, confiding in her ear: 'Do you know, those loonies of Nili's are genuinely crazy!'

'What do you expect?' she said. 'There must be a dividing line, Sasha, or all of us would be inside.'

Five o'clock at last, and on the lawn outside the Centre, everyone is milling around. The descending sun touches the tops of the cypresses, preparing to bathe the assembly in  strong golden glow. The bridegroom, suitably pio-faced and solemn, his dress uniform over-starched, the shoulder pips gleaming with Brasso, sharp crease in his trousers, moustache carefully combed, the red hair cut and shampooed by Azaria & Bros, Hadera. Each freckle on his face shines proudly. Sasha, beside him, horribly suffering in bourgeois garb, the tie virtually garrotting his thick, ruddy farmer's neck. Marta and the bride still absent, attending to mysterious final touches in the Centre's small dressing room, where Los Trios Costaguanos had once been found, overdosed on heroin, just before a gala performance of The Spirit of Latin America. The Rabbi, one Elisha Eisenschatz from Pardess Hana, is late, but finally turns up at half past the hour with two pimpled, wispy-bearded young minions who unload the blue embroidered canopy and poles from the back of a Ford station wagon. And, briskly, without further ado, the ceremony is on the road: Zetz, Elkayam, the kibbutz treasurer, Caspi, and a local youth who had courted Nili in vain, are charged with holding up the four canopy poles. Eisav, ushered away and then marched down the daisy-lined pathway by Sasha on one side and old Azriel Mahatz on the other, both holding fast to his elbows. Then Nili, in her Ata issue nuptials special, snipped a little here and there, led by Marta and Mrs Caspi the traditional seven times round the hupa, Marta hissing in her ear: 'This is your last chance, maidaleh, are you really sure you know what you're doing?'

Itsho and Rina, artistes de kibbutz, render old Homeland tunes on accordions: I Once Had a Love Like Her, a Love Who Was So Fair . . . pausing as the Rabbi, sombre under his goatee, begins reading the marriage contract. Marta, despite all, has lost her cool, a handkerchief over her face. Sasha, red as a beetroot, wheezing desperately. Flusser also dabbing discreetly at his eyes, while still trying to keep watch on his flock. Despite Elkayam's rigour, how one cannot conceive, the Magpie already has a slice of Marta's après-ceremony chocolate cake and is wolfing it down in great rapture.

'So art thou sanctified to me, in the religion of Moses and Israel.'

Smash! with martial precision, Eisav shatters the glass . . .

Mazel tov!!

The deed is done! Blessings, kissings, sobbings, clappings, Itsho and Rina, in melodic paroxysm –

♪ We'll Build Our Country, Land of Our Homeland/For Ours For Ours This Country Is . . . ♫

Sasha cries: 'Food and drink inside!' and, tearing tie and top shirt button with a surge of his Adam's apple, leads the stampede within.

Bacchanal, Mas'at-Nefesh style:

In the Cultural Centre's hall, walls graced with the works of Moishe Yankel Ish-Sela, the kibbutz's favourite son, who had a painting hung for one day, by mistake, in the New York Museum of Modern Art. At the far end of the hall, above the tables piled with chicken and tshoolent and Marta's famous cakes and more, hang framed portraits of Prime Minister Golda Meir, President Shazar, Chief of Staff Dado, David Ben Gurion and punkt in the centre, Av-Kerem, the settlement's granite-jawed founder who, as 'Jacque' Krakowiak, had wrested first fruits from the soil. Beneath beetled brows he watches haughtily as Zetz, traditionally in the front line, piles a paper plate high with prime pulkes with the aid of a plastic fork.

'Eat! Eat!' says Marta. 'Don't starve yourself, commandante!'

'Excellent poultry,' says Zetz, stuffing his cakehole.

'So what's wrong with the tshoolent?' argues Sasha, shouldering through the throng.

'Hey, Mahatz!' cries General Palanka. 'You know looting's forbidden by General Headquarters' Orders!'

'Now, now, boys!' says Marta. 'Didn't you see the notice – leave your guns at the door?'

'A fine operation, Mrs Grunbaum,' Palanka comments from out of a mouthful of tshoolent. 'The bride, beautiful and blushing, the bridegroom, strong and silent. A sight for sore eyes.'

'Eisav is a brilliant officer,' say Zetz, 'a man with a serious future.'

'When the groom is prettier than the bride,' says Palanka, 'that's when you have to start worrying.'

Downaways in the crowd, someone breaks into tearful hysterics. It is Hava, undergoing a separation trauma. (Papishik dead, no more Nili to bring home a steady stream of [un] desirables to dispel the miasma of loneliness . . .) Elkayam, with more than professional interest, consoles her with a plate of fried aubergines. She clings to his burly arm . . . Elsewhere, Nietzsche has engaged Mrs Caspi, a burly lady with the thighs of a bull elephant, in an argument over Voltaire.

'Morality, psscht!' he says, waving a chicken wing. 'True morality is the will to power, nothing else has any value.'

'But that's Nietzsche!' protests Mrs Caspi. 'No one takes that seriously nowadays!'

'I *am* Nietzsche,' says Nietzsche, 'and I take myself very seriously.'

'Ah,' she nods, 'I thought I recognized you from somewhere . . .'

Yes. Mr Caspi has meanwhile bagged Flusser, and is pumping him about Sigmund Freud. 'What was he really like?' 'Very ratty,' says Flusser, 'but then, he was extremely old . . .'

'Have you seen the Magpie?' Paradjanov, doleful, approaches him with a plastic knife.

'Ask Elkayam,' says Flusser, handing him a plate of cheese.

'He's gone, too,' complains Paradjanov. 'I think he's fallen in love.'

'It's too early for love,' says Caspi, 'look, even the bride and groom are still here.'

So they are, at the further end of the room, looking positively smashed. He is sitting bolt upright behind the top table, grinning sheepishly as if someone at a promotion ceremony had stuck a bangalore up his arse. She with a wry, dreamlike gaze, her eyes resting hither and yon, darkly amused, stashing the scene away among other bizarrities, high spots such as Judas Pig sightings and the Day the Psychodrama Went Wrong. Nili Grunbaum, This is Your Life.

'Nitsa,' Flusser calls, 'have you seen Elkayam or the Magpie?' Negative response, her hand spilling red from a refilled paper cup. 'They must be somewhere around ...' Flusser assures Paradjanov, 'probably chasing each other up ...'

But no! In fact Nili's ex-flatmate Hava has led Elkayam to the spare bungalow, and already they have divested themselves of their garments and are deep into coital pleasure. He thrusts with the full force of his masculine reputation. She scratches his broad back, mewling softly 'More! More!' and rubbing his behind with her ankles. The Magpie, on the other hand, is engaged on a completely different mission. Carrying over his shoulder a purloined rucksack, filled with doggybags of chicken breasts and pulkes, half-eaten sandwiches, cold fried aubergines, meatballs, hard-boiled eggs, selected fromages, jars of pickled cucumbers, three bottles of wine, ten of beer, a bottlecap opener, spoons, forks and knives, the portrait of Golda Meir, a miniature Ish-Sela worth a few herzls on the open market, a fair number of guests' keyrings, handkerchiefs and coins, one of Eisav's shoulder pips, a lock of Nili's auburn hair snipped off with nail clippers, Sasha's ripped tie, folded paper napkins, a bracelet engraved 'Stronger Than Death is Love, Dudik 1968', a phial of fingernail lacquer, some electric plugs, several dozen bottlecaps, needles, trouser buttons, shoelaces, earrings, toenail clippings off sandalled feet, and other bits and bobs; and with all these in his knapsack he creeps stealthily, silent as a cat, past houses, fences, sheds, into the evening fields. It is pitch dark now and no one sees his passing. Ah, the scent of newmown hay, of chicken droppings, sugar beet and barley, fragrance of the orange groves wafted along the threads of spring under the canopy of stars . . . In a hollow by a hillock behind the beet plantation the Magpie halts, sets down the rucksack and with the aid of a spade he has picked up on the way, begins digging in the soft, yielding ground. Way behind him the sounds of revelry fade as the party begins breaking up. Flusser begins belatedly to search for his charges. Nili and Eisav pad off towards the bungalow. The noise of their slurred approach alerts Elkayam and Hava in the midst of their passion. Gathering their clothes rapidly they sneak out of the back door, like the principals of a French farce, leaving socks, pantyhose and Ministry of Health knickers all over the fresh falha.

Too fuddled to ask Who's Been Sleeping in My Bed? the newlyweds shut themselves in, Eisav's bearish form slumped over the four-foot frame, Nili dunking a hankie in cold water to lay tenderly across her husband's brow. 'Oooooohh . . .' he sighs in unexpected bliss. She settles down in the old rocking chair beside the bed, gazing down at the big red giant, unfathomable twirls of emotion twinkling behind her eyes. Her mother looms, stretching a warning finger. Too late now, smiles Nili-Honey. Waste not want not. That's how it crumbles. Might as well make the best of it.

An hour later the Magpie saunters nonchalantly into the Cultural Centre. Elkayam, who was just about to set the whole kibbutz beating the bushes and hedgerows, seizes him in a half nelson.

Flusser: 'Where have you been?' his white hair afrazzle, scalp sweating.

'I was looking for a toilet,' the Magpie lied, 'I

235

locked myself in a shed by mistake and it took me all this time to get out.' Rapidly Elkayam frisks him, ending up empty handed, puzzled.

'All right! Let's go!' Flusser snappily bundles them all in the minibus. The driver, a patient young man from the 'Ayit' hire firm, happily guns the motor. Out from the gravelled path, on to the asphalt approach road ... (Hava and Elkayam sheepishly sharing a seat; Nietzsche and Parad-janov, cradling their canteens, filled secretly with Vat 69; Flusser quietly snoring, the nurses Nitsa, Renata and Pitsi keeping cautious eyes on the Magpie; he, with a far-off look, perhaps floating above private sierras ...)

In the empty, sacked Cultural Centre, an electric clock goes ping. It is midnight, but no one turns into a pumpkin. Paper cups, plates, tshoolent stains disfigure the tiled floor. Amongst used serviettes, a fieldmouse rustles softly. Av-Kerem, alias 'Jacque' Krakowiak, hums in a low bass an obscene Byelo-russian ditty. ('Hoy, maiden of the steppes, with your cunt untouched o ...') Other than that, and the crickets, silence. The wedding day is over.


... And so they settled down to live happily ever after: Eisav, on attachment to the Central Command, receiving from the army an apartment at Nayot, overlooking the Valley of the Cross. (On rare days off walking over to the Museum on the hill to commune with the Dead Sea Scrolls. 'Tell me this land isn't mine,' he'd scoff, with nationalistic fervour, 'when I can read here, as if it were the morning paper, these bits from two thousand fucking years ago.') There were three small but cosy rooms, one of which Nili set aside for guests and for the horde of kiddiwinks that would, as sure as eggs are eggs, come bounding out of her loins. In the corners of the living room Eisav placed his four empty 105 shells, two as ashtrays and two for flowers or plants. His complete Heinrich Heine went on a shelf in the bedroom, together with Nili's Agnon, Tschernichovsky, Bialik, Alterman, Dostoyevsky, Tolstoy, Pasternak's *Zhivago*, Henryk Sienkiewicz, S. Yizhar and other present-day Hebrew writers and the latest intellectual hoot, Gabriel Garcia Marquez.

It was an idyllic summer, that year in Jerusalem. The hamsin had not even arrived by August to deposit its choking canopy of sand particles over the City; the sun shone pin-sharp bright, throwing harsh black shadows on the contours of Jerusalem stone. Now and then light feathery clouds varied the blue monotony. No one ceased to remark, as they passed each other on their Sabbath afternoon walk, with their prams, their white shirts and pressed trousers and well-scrubbed infantry, on the singular climatic clemency ... The political and military front, too, was cool: by spring the Canal 'War of Attrition' was wound up by mutual consent, and the Arab states were once again fighting among themselves (Syria breaking relations with Jordan, or vice versa, Nili could never quite make it out). Eisav was assigned to a surveillance task in the Jordan River Valley. After Sinai it was a doddle. All he had to do was put his feet up and let the multiple warning devices, automatic tripwires, booby traps, infra-red sensors and machine guns triggered by body heat take care of infiltrating guerrillas. In the morning he would collect the corpses. Occasionally a small group would still break through the lines and a manhunt would ensue with jeeps and armed helicopters scouring the barren gullies and canyons. At some points the Valley was a mere thirty to forty kilometres from the capital city, so now and again it was possible to make contact in the morning and have lunch in the

Jerusalem Brigade canteen an hour and a half later, amid the hubbub of everyday traffic and commerce. Once, when Nili was on evening shifts, he even came home to lunch.

'I killed an Arab this morning,' he said, thoughtfully; he had entered a pensive phase.

'I'm sorry to hear that,' she said, 'do you want your eggs scrambled or fried?' This was the only way to deal with Eisav in his periodic bouts of bad conscience and melancholy. Somehow an early injection of humanist socialism by a teacher at the Ben Shemen school had merged with an obscure but threatening image of 'Justice', as the Angel of Death, sitting way up above the earth, noting every life taken with a meticulous impartiality, so that even homicidal armed Arabs, in sufficient quantity, would eventually tip the scales of doom against their morose dispatcher. With professional training, Nili knew the right moment to kick him, with feigned flippancy, off his bed of nails, before he sank deeper into that depression in which death stalked him everywhere – in the field, in the office, on the toilet seat and in bed.

'If the killing bothers you,' she said to him once, on an evening leave of domestic calm, he abandoning Heine for the afternoon newspaper, she fingering *Cinema* magazine, 'why not give up the whole thing? You're not an idiot, there are lots of jobs you could do well.'

'Like what?' he said. 'Pushing papers in an office to send toothpaste around the world? Crawling under a stinking engine to join nuts and bolts together?'

'You could take an engineering degree, for instance. Build bridges, dams, aqueducts.'

'Spanning the Jordan!' he scoffed, 'that would take up a good five hours of one's life. Where d'you think we are, in China? This is a country of twenty thousand square kilometres, damn it! You can't build pyramids in a closet.'

'Conquer some more then,' she said with sarcasm, 'if an empire is what you're after. Delusions of grandeur, that's your trouble, honey. This state is just too small for you.'

'It's the Age,' he said, 'the Age is too small. There's precious little by which a man can prove himself.'

'Just prove yourself in bed and stay alive and in one piece,' she countered, 'that's all I want of you, Big Schmuck.'

They were clearly deeply in love.

She continued her work at Klander. In the balm of the moderate summer the asylum followed its own divergent, private clock. Braced against the mountain breeze between the Mount of Offence and the Hill of Evil Counsel it basked in the sunlight, masking its fears and anxieties, its mourning and melancholia. Patients entered, patients left. The Regulars, like faulty automobiles, passed in and out for their service. Nietzsche, for example, was discharged that July. For the umpteenth time he walked jauntily down the path to the Seven Aleph bus stop, carrying in each hand a battered suitcase full of the books and manuscripts he humped from home to the nuthouse and back. ('They let you out again!' said the jolly bus driver, Nahum, jingling change in his coin machine. 'Tell me, sir, what's your secret?' 'Oh it's nothing,' said Nietzsche, 'I just stopped peeing over the staircase.') Another veteran, Old Leib, had a miraculous cure and staggered out in mid-August, free of the ghosts of Treblinka. ('I don't know how that happened,' said Flusser cheerfully, 'I didn't do anything special.') On the other hand, new sad faces registered: one Barlev, who thought he was certifying his wife and

239

found she had certified him; Schechtella, whose entire extended family had shrunk to microscopic size one day before her terrified eyes – she became catatonic and would not move lest she trod on them all and killed them. And there were deaths: the 'Absconder' poisoned himself with wood varnish. Almozlino, prostrate at the loss of his potency, willed himself to death in his sleep. Both were solemnly wheeled down the morgue tunnel, to 'Dr Nachtnebel's Icebox' (some said the Doctor at this stage took the bodies for research, substituting dead organic robots ... others said warning systems had been installed, to prevent the Judas Pig – long dormant but far from absent – from purloining the corpses for munchies).

And there were internal wrangles – Veltsch versus Flusser, the revolt of Behaviourism ... proposals to turn the wards into 'token economy units', patients to be rewarded for improved social conduct and docked points for anti-social behaviour. 'We are running a therapeutic institution here,' said Flusser, 'not a concentration camp.' Nevertheless, an ideological schism, with some defections of young technocratic staff. Nili allied with Flusser, on geological grounds – no touch of Granit in Veltsch. No, nothing but the synthetic non-ambience of IBM computers ...

In early September, Davidov returned, having spent all his money buying Payis lottery tickets in pursuit of his foolproof system. His wife gave him a choice: therapy or divorce. Pretty soon the joint was jumping again. Illicit goodies flowed free once more, as Veltsch fumed in futile ambushes. Porn from O'Habash, who once more renewed his acquaintance with the asylum, crouched in bushes, masked in balaclava, hooking deliveries on to knotted bedsheets (summer madness and further instructions perhaps from Constantine Zorza –

messages from Moscow Centre: What the fuck are you on about? What's this Klander–Nachtnebel guff? Get on with the job, tschorta mati!) . . . not to speak of poor Rumanian Shrul's mounting obsession with the Elders of Zion, his conversion of Davidov to belief thereof, about which, more anon . . . but the smuggled goods flowed on in the Institute's bloodstream – hashish, naughty magazines, booze, savon 'Je Reviens' – packages flying through the air above Veltsch's dumbkopf, wrapped in celluloid inside Mrs Patchouli's cooking pots, taped round central heating ducts, stashed in mattresses – a bonanza, there, for the Magpie . . . Not for nothing would Nietzsche nod and reiterate sagely: Ah, yes, the old buki-sriki, there is nothing new under the sun . . .

Blok, having decided not to go to South Africa with Victoria Happenstance, was stricken with acute remorse and panic. She embarked with the twelve members of the anthropology study group, on a bright London July morning. Neither J.D. nor Blok saw her off at the airport; J.D., for security reasons, Blok, out of shame, mortification and anguish.

He had said to her: 'I'm sorry, Vicky, but I would just be a millstone round your neck. I'm just not a true believer. I sympathize, but I don't even want to fight my own so-called battles, the ones They ordained me for at birth, those in which we schmendricks out there are supposed to martyr ourselves. If I did come, just because of what I feel for you, that would be ridiculous, wouldn't it?'

'Sure,' she said. 'You're absolutely right. What you're looking for isn't with me, here or halfway across the world. It's something you have to fish out of your own insides. Whatever happens we'll always be friends.'

Friends again, aargh! Another nail in the coffin. Sayonara, Blok. What the fuck is wrong with you? Can't you do something useful for once, for the Good of Mankind?! Blok the hero, jingling medallions, or just the private satisfaction. But no, cholera! I am not the type, not the stuff James Bonds are made of. I could never make a spy, my threshold of pain is low, I would gibber, roll my eyes furtively and sweat, police dogs would track me down by the very odour of fear. Confess, kaffir-lover! they would cry, wielding the heavy sjamboks. Or with hammer and nails, poised over the privates. Hey, Loitnant! the assistant torturer calls. This yidla here has no foreskin! What procedure do you advise? Never mind, says the head dungeon mackamuck, waving a nonchalant hand, just do your duty, Sergeant . . .

Too much imagination, Blok, just keep to the old routine – paddle like hell for the shore . . . Realize the Truth, man: she won't let you fuck her, even if you do jump aboard the revolutionary bandwagon. So forget it, move, pick up the pieces, get along with your life. (But what about her? Vicky, mon amour – as she traipses down the gangway at Jan Smuts airport, squadrons of Boer police, tipped off somehow, waiting, with handcuffs and clinking leg irons . . .)

His mind in turmoil long before her departure, he left the cosiness of Stamford Hill. (Although she said to him: 'Don't be an idiot, Blokkie, stay on as long as you like.') He took a bed-sitting room just off the Finchley Road. It had a creaking single bed, a kitchenette with a rusty one-ring stove and a defective gas heater which shot vengeful flames out to blacken the peeling cream walls. Under the bed, in the dust, the previous occupant had left a stash of German pornography. Thus, he entered into seclusion and cut himself off from society. On the midnight of the day of her departure he fortified himself with a half bottle of vodka and tremblingly telephoned J.D. in Stamford Hill.

'I won't know anything till tomorrow evening,' he was told, 'there should be a telegram then.'

And a long day ensued. Blok drifting, drifting, down the winding Fortune Green Road. The red buses, old men with red noses click-clicking their canes, kiddie voices in the park. Drifting, with the lethal Ascot heater, the creaking bedsprings, the Deutsche farfel . . . Wellington Frog, where are you now that I need you? Fuck 'em and feed 'em beans . . . But there is nothing but the nirvana of solipsism, a receding view down the wrong end of the telescope. In the evening he telephoned J.D. again, to be told:

'Don't worry. The merchandise has arrived safely. Everything is under control.'

'Avram Blok, you say? Yes, I did hear the name somewhere . . . Didn't he almost go to South Africa, to investigate the native habits? Or did he become some sort of revolutionary nebesch . . . Blok . . .? Oh, yes, now I remember – he fell in love, didn't he, with an English shiksa, who was fraternizing with reds and nig-nogs . . . But he had no choice – she went off to Nogland, he was left holding his banana . . . You remember Blok, don't you? He used to moon around that beautiful blonde girl, what was her name – Malka Halperin . . . Then there was that sad business with the police. He spent a year in the loonie bin, didn't he? What was it about? Exposing himself or something, in the Independence Park . . . or was it for molesting children? Anyway, the girl ditched him and he took off to New York, America, mind you, with reparations, bloodmoney the Germans sent his father for an Uncle they had all absolutely forgotten who it turned out got burned in the ovens. It is amazing, yes, isn't it? Papa offered him his cut, he took the money and ran, now there's real gratitude for you! The parents left childless, their past and their future, so to speak, up in smoke. But what d'you expect, Griselda? A generation of vipers we've brought up in this country. We die for their right to remain here, they piss off to Yankeeland! Sometimes I think, God forgive my blasphemy, that the anti-semites are right: We're not a real people, proper, Griselda, just a conglomeration of schmuttes!'

# III

'What you think might happen –
might not.'

– Chinese fortune cookie,
'Hunam Taste' Restaurant

'As a reliable compass for orienting yourself in life nothing is more useful than to accustom yourself to regarding this world as a place of atonement, a sort of penal colony. When you have done this you will order your expectations of life according to the nature of things and no longer regard the calamities, sufferings, torments and miseries of life as something irregular ... but will find them entirely in order, well knowing that each of us here is being punished for his existence in his own particular way.'

– Arthur Schopenhauer


## The KGB in Jerusalem, as a detail from Hieronymus Bosch.

Boris Kolyakov and Lizbeta Stefanovna, Heroes of the Soviet Union, arrived in Palestine in January 1948, hidden in a false cavity of a drum in the hold of a cargo vessel. The ship was the *Jean-Jacques Rousseau*, carrying a consignment of toilet rolls for the bums of a besieged nation. A van from the Soviet legation, which had put in an early bid for a part of this long-yearned-for merchandise, picked up the wrong drum by mistake, and the two spies were delivered to the premises of one Mendel Leib Ibsen,

Dry Goods and Domestic Provisioning, of Petah Tikva. When the unlucky tradesman prised open the lid of the drum they emerged, like the Creatures From Another World, killed Ibsen with ta-ke-do blows, set the store on fire and took the afternoon bus to the Capital.

Eventually they reported to their control, tovarish Ivan Perlmutter, official consular liaison with the Jewish Pig Marketing Board, which, as it did not exist, left his hands free for other duties. He briefed and examined them thoroughly, checking that Boris's circumcision, performed by ace Moscow Centre quack Pilits – who won the Lenin Prize ten years later for grafting cow's udders on an aardvark – would pass a close Enemy inspection. They were then entertained and informed by a moving picture show featuring clandestine footage of the two persons they had come to replace: the putridinous Babelech-und-Farfel, drooling and retching their oblivious way through the streets of embattled Jerusalem.

Behind this minor move of four pawns was a vast anti-imperialist strategy in a chess game of global proportions. The Great Leader, Joe Stalin, himself, had planned the whole thing, with his usual genius, during a parchesi session. 'See here,' the little Georgian prick had said, jabbing a stubby finger at the illuminated wall display of the tangled web of his intrigue (he used to switch it on and off at night: his big toe, pushing a toggle, summoned ninety-five political prisoners at the Lublyanka to pedal furiously on wheelless bicycles, generating the current, until they dropped from exhaustion), 'the smallest details, the merest twistlets of the Grand Design are worked out to the last nut, to the last shade of colour on the palette of Socialist Victory.' 'Sure, sure, boss,' said the lackeys, pressing to the back of the queue. At the top right of this mandalic blueprint the crowning achievement so far glowed a satisfying red: MI6, in London, now staffed totally by upper-class pederasts, agents of Moscow Centre. To the left, the Washington Zone flickered with dim incompletion. But, tucked away at the sou'-sou'-west of the ferris wheel, one spoke end pulsed deep orange. 'See,' the Peerless declared, without fear of contradiction, 'even in that kakky, worthless piece of the Levant, where the Yids and the Wogs are slogging it out for a couple of hundred versts like dogs fighting over a dry bone, even there we have our people, even there our brave operatives are working, night and day, for the triumph of the Working Class.'

Nazdrovya!

Ten days later, Boris and Lizbeta lured Babelech-und-Farfel, with the glint of a Louis d'Or, to a cave in the hills of Giv'at Shaul, not a dagger's throw from the Arab village of Dir Yassin where, three months later, dreadful massacres were to be held to differing local reviews. They killed the two beggars by strangulation in the three-handed Beria mode and stripped them of their clothes, keeping carefully every flea, louse, maggot and roach of the hordes that had made their home in them. To destroy every trace of the bodies they cooked the flesh over a low campfire and ate it, à la russe, with plenty of paprika and sour cream. With the bones they made a beef consommé and, sawing what was left into minute particles, ground them, turning the stone themselves (sans blinkers) in a mill abandoned between the two warring semitic factions. The resulting powder they sold as flour to Mandel's bakery nearby, faking the kashrut certificate. The bread in Jerusalem did taste odd for a while, but then the town was cut off and besieged by the A-rabs, you had to take what you got, no complaints accepted, what d'you think this is, comrades, the fleshpots?

('I'm glad of the change,' said one roach to another in the filthy folds of Farfel/Lizbeta's attire. [It was her armpit, some say. Others – her décolletage.] 'Those two old tsigoiners were getting quite expert at rooting one out with their fingernails. Me, I'm putting my feet up for a spell.'

'Nachtiger tug,' said the other roach, 'these two new ones will learn just as fast. One's still got to be careful. I tell you, Menashe, there's no peace for the just in this world.')

## Isn't night after night closing in on us? (Another Apocryphal Tale):

Gruppenführer Heinz Kammler was an engineer of genius. He designed the great underground silos of the V-1 and V-2 rockets which bombarded England in the latter part of the war. He also designed the crematoria and gas chambers at Auschwitz. His employers, in gratitude, made him Chief Construction Engineer for the Waffen SS and Wehrmacht in January 1945. But by that time the jig was up. The Russians had broken the front at Baranov and were about to advance across Poland towards the heart of the Reich. On the 18th of the month his beloved Auschwitz was evacuated and the miracle edifice to efficiency he had offered the world fell into abandonment and disuse. Nevertheless, in Berlin, Kammler, wiping his tears, presented his new plans for an underground bunker no man, tank or high explosive yet known could breach. It would delve far beneath the earth, a mineshaft reinforced with concrete and steel, hollowed out by the still secret V-3 technology, proceeding deeper and deeper as the Enemy drew nearer and nearer, sealing off section after section as it went, carrying the Führer to the safety of natural caverns hewn in the earth's crust by forgotten civilizations aeons ago, in preparation for the great day when, like the Creature from the Black Lagoon, He would break forth anew, a spearhead glinting in the sun of new eras of Sturm und Drang. Goering, Bormann and Himmler, who were already planning to do a bunk and make a deal with the Allies, poohpoohed the entire scheme, but Goebbels and Streicher, editor of *Der Sturmer,* waxed ecstatic over its vision, enthusing over the thought of the Führer and Eva Braun, together, burrowing evermore into the bowels of the planet while producing, like transcendent rabbits, the new superbreed which was destined to rule the globe. But the Führer himself was neither amused nor impressed, and went into one of his rages. Only traitors could doubt the Reich's imminent triumph and exaggerate minor setbacks, he waxed wroth, kicking the three of them out of the room. Kammler, downcast, was comforted by Julius Streicher: 'Never mind, it is the most beautiful idea I have ever come across.' In fact, so overcome with emotion was he that he came the next day straight to Kammler's office and gave him, gratis and out of the pure kindness of his heart, his own private complete set of *Sturmer* copies, three heavy volumes bound in red leather. 'You are a poet,' he told Kammler sincerely, 'a lyricist of concrete and steel, copper and electronic circuitry, the elements of the future. You are ahead of your time, but mark my words,' he said, 'it will come. What we have lived through is merely a trifling prologue.'

A year later Julius Streicher was hanged, despite the evidence of his wife that he was a fine fellow. Heinz Kammler, all the sources tell us, went missing in the sack of Berlin and his body was never found. His true end is missing, so far, from the written annals of History.

Klander had said:
'Now, those of us who saw it coming were not surprised when it burst in full fury upon the world in 1939 . . . The Old Man had spoken of it as the death-wish, the instinct that strove to do away with life and return to inorganic matter. To him it was inevitable, but to many that was merely the projection of his own desire to die, racked as he was then by cancer of the jaw . . . It was Reich who took the bull by the horns and was excommunicated for his pains: the core of the neurosis is somatic, he said, a crippling of the libido that occurs in early childhood. To Reich we are all incurably maimed. He called the disease the Sexual Staang or stasis, the social neurosis, Modju, the Emotional Plague. Yes, we argued about it for years, shooting venom from obscure publications that no layman ever heard of. Reich set up clinics for the working classes, to teach them to fuck without fear or guilt. It was an impossible task. Long before the liberal bourgeois state could get round to kicking him out on his arse, the Real Thing arrived, goosestepping down the Unter den Linden and into the Chancellery. Out of our sad twisted psyches we had finally fashioned a monster of genuine terror that would consume us all. Yes, we were not surprised. But, after the storm had raged and abated, and some of us survived to climb out of the Valley of the Shadow of Death, we were filled not only with hope, but foreboding: for we feared we were being spared only for a little while, till the Plague, gathering strength again, broke out afresh, this time with instruments of total destruction that would do the job good and proper. All we could try to do was create, here and there, oases of reasoned reflection, monasteries of a sort,

laboratories where we could, in microcosm, work on the virus itself, attempt somehow to achieve its isolation, the Modju germ, under a microscope . . . or perhaps just to achieve, for individuals, what we failed to achieve for societies . . .'

But the mad Pesach Zilberschvantz, alias Groise Metsiyes, soon put a stop to all that. As he emptied his Luger – Bang! Bang! Bang! – into the great man's corpus. In Zion Square, women and children ran screaming, and three burly men from out of the crowd wrestled the assassin to the ground. From the corner of Lunz, just by the Ariel Taxi stand, ersatz Babelech-und-Farfel, while pretending to scratch within their verminous clothing, recorded it all for their Kremlin masters with miniature Ikoda cameras . . .

(An argument was developing between two roaches who were keeping house in different parts of Babelech's, né Boris's, rags. Mandibles clicked in fury over the naming of the pre-shabbes pie. One roach said: 'It's pronounced *koogel*.' The other said: 'It's pronounced *kigel*.' So they scampered off into a trouser leg to consult a third, who simply shrugged and said:

'Sorry, in mein haase ve don't spik Yiddish.')

**Davidov's Basic Assertion Concerning the 'Elders of Zion':**
According to the anti-semites, the Elders of Zion were a secret cabal of Jews whose aim was to rule the world, manipulating, by control of both Capital and Labour, the masses into mutual destruction. On the basis of this belief Adolf Hitler decided that all the Jews should be killed and launched a world war to ensure this outcome. But the real elders, Davidov said, were a select group of scholars whose task

253

was solely to compute the exact year, day and hour of the Coming of the Messiah. At their foundation, in 1762, this had been a matter of urgency. Twice in the preceding century a false Messiah had been declared, precipitating the Jewish people into dreadful schisms, heresies and apostasies. The first had been Shabetai Zvi, who announced 15 Sivan 1666 as the End of Days, and had thousands of Jews waiting, with packed suitcases, for their immediate transportation to Palestine. At the last moment, under threat of death from the Porte, he converted to Islam, taking entire communities with him. The second had been Jacob Frank, who named himself 'Big Brother', and preached salvation through the abolition of all laws, teachings and accepted morality. His followers, like those of Shabetai Zvi, indulged in secret rituals which included, more often than not, the fruitiest of sexual orgies. The Frankists accepted baptism into the Catholic Church, during 1759–60, while continuing in secret to maintain their separate identity.

It was to forestall such upheavals, said Davidov, according to his researches (qua Srul, who had since been discharged as cured), that the Cabbalists of Lodz set up a Committee of Ten – to the number of the sephirot – to examine, meditate and spiritually train themselves for the Ultimate Computation. No more futzing about, they said, let's get down to the nitty-gritty. But the task dragged on, way past the lifetime of the original members, who appointed successors to carry the work on. Decades passed. It became the ultimate committee of inquiry, empowered to follow up evidence from whatever quarter and in the remotest corners of the globe. To subpoena persons natural and supra-natural, up to and including the Scribe Gabriel himself, though this was only done once, Davidov asserted, on Shmini Atseret, 1852.

In 1840, claimed Davidov, the Committee moved to a remote Transylvanian stetl whose name even Srul had forgotten. Then, in 1911, to Budapest, where it weathered the Great War, the extremely brief Béla Kun Revolution and the long White Terror of Horthy. In 1938, however, the inevitability of European cataclysm forced a drastic change of venue. West, old men, across the Atlantic, and there they have stayed, since 1939. Meeting, twice a year, on dates gimatrically computed, in a small pickle bar on the corner of Canal and Elisabeth Street, in what was then the Jewish East Side of Manhattan: Mottel's Delicatessen. Later on the area turned Chinese, but Mottel's survived, weathering the ethnic tides and meticulously serving the Quest. Everyone knew the Elders of Zion met there, but it was only true fans who would know, by the grin that would spread unbidden over Heimie, Son of Mottel's noodle, when the bi-annual binge was due. Anyone else had to take pot luck. It might take place in secret, at four in the morning, or you might just saunter in at seven thirty a.m. for a bialy with a schmeer and a coffee, and find them seated round the big table in the back, all the loud raucous ten of them, singing hassidic ditties, telling bobe maysehs, examining the entrails of a herring for mystic significance, or throwing bagels over the hat stand.

But who are they, everyone asked Davidov, name names, cholera! put up or shut up. Ah! that will take more time, exclaimed Davidov, Rome wasn't built with a finger! They are loath to expose themselves, to be prey of the media, breakfast television and all that razzmatazz . . . But trust Davidov, all will be dug out, even if it takes ten years! Pressed further he would clam up, and lock himself in the bathroom, pretending to endlessly brush his teeth while singing Prison Six songs.

\* \* \*

(The roaches were yarning away, taking advantage of the afternoon siesta which Babelech-und-Farfel were taking in the Jerusalem garbage dump. One, a venerable bug who had come over from the Old Country with the Second Aliyah (1906 precisely), told the following story:

'Once, a meeting of the very first Bolshevik government – eve of 1918 – began to over-run a little. Trotsky (Lev Davidovitch Bronstein), looking at his watch, leaned over and said to Zinoviev (Grigory Evgenovitch Radomylsky): 'Listen, I have to go soon, I have to make up a minyan* for a yahrzeit.'** Zinoviev shrugged and, nodding towards Lenin, said: 'No problem. Wait till the goy*** goes and we can have it here.')


... Eventually, accumulating clues led Inspector Tarablus, still hunting the killer of Klander under the deepest cover, to arrange a meeting with the notorious clochard Bin-Zabl, King of the Old City beggars, touts, professional perverts and hashasheen. This had to take place in the Swedish Tea Shoppe, as Bin-Zabl had not set foot outside it in living memory. Like an engorged Sidney Greenstreet he sat in his darkened niche, under the portrait of Stockholm in autumn, dispensing a summary justice by means of gestures, snorts, grunts, chirrups, wheezes, tummy rumbles and farts, indicating, to the initiated, such instructions as 'Buy', 'Sell', 'Hold', 'Kill', 'Mutilate', 'Cash Money', 'Call Zurich pronto'. Tarablus, in his guise as Splendida, the She-Hog of Manahat, dragging his elephantine leg behind him and pushing Shpilkes the Infant, a streetwise urchin of eighteen months

---

* Minyan: a quorum of ten male Jews needed for prayer.
** Yahrzeit: annual prayer for the dead at anniversary of the deceased.
*** Goy: a gentile.

who hired himself out at thirty lire the hour, in a rusty pram before him, made his slow painful way through the Jaffa Gate, down the narrows of the Jerusalem bazaar. Tourists, decked in midsummer greed, scattered, their deodorants, face creams, aftershaves, colognes, totally over-powered. Porters, carrying toppling towers of crates on their backs by means of bands secured round their fore-heads, kicked him with knobbled, sandalled feet as he befouled their path. A dog, host to a nation of fleas, leapt at Shpilkes the Infant but retired, with an ear bitten off, howling, towards Casa Nova. An American tripper, one Casper J. Engel, of Sentinel Butte, North Dakota, took a Kodak of this gross phenomenon, which was to become smudged, torn and faded as it passed from hand to thrilled hand in the Sentinel Butte Baptist Centre. 'The absolute, genuine article!' Mrs Engel enthused, snapping open a Doctor Pepper with her teeth. 'One could just imagine Our Lord's hand on the wretch, lifting his dreadful afflictions . . .'

Unclean! Unclean! Jingling, metaphorically, the bell of his putrefaction, his fetor, his abysmal pong, Tarablus crawled past the wrought-iron gates into Muristan. Past the luggage vendors, who placed handkerchiefs sodden with tapwater over their offended faces, up the side alley to the Tea Shoppe. Farouk the waiter came out with a broom and a flick knife to chase him away, but a deep double belch from within bade the supplicant enter the sanctum.

While Farouk opened every door, window and ventilation shaft, plugged in fans in each corner of the room and stood by with an army blanket, flap-ping it to move the air, Tarablus lay, breathing stertorously, on the red lino, looking up into the giant doughball of Bin-Zabl's face far in the dis-tance like a balloon poised to cross the Atlantic upon which, as on a funfair figurine, a red fez wobbled.

'Speak,' said Bin-Zabl. Or rather, he farted, in the mode known as a short 'Brahim. He fiddled with quick fingers that belied their grossness with a Golden Khedive snuffbox.

'Is it safe?' Tarablus murmured, inclining his head towards Farouk.

The monarch shot a second brief fart out, while stuffing a cavernous nostril.

Tarablus, looking far into those azure, almost pupil-less eyes, which reminded him of something, buried deep in the collective unconscious, that he could not for the life of him pin down, paused, gathered his thoughts, stuck his calloused palm over Shpilkes the Infant's mouth, and commenced to tell his long tale . . .

XII

LE PENDU

New York!
Manhattan!
The Big Time!

Blok floats, at the foot of glass towers, in the back seat of a yellow cab. Mama mia, the crowds! The sounds! Human waves, breaking upon fifty-storey battlements ... Times Square! Forty-second Street! The colours, asargelusha! The neon lights on the eyeballs! What? All this has been going on here, day in, night out, while I moped in the styx, in Takhkemoni Street? Eek! For shame the blind inertia of the provincial soul!

Here is Yissachar Pri-On's address, clasped in Blok's sweating paw, the letter forwarded him to the Old World from 'Juancito' ensconced in the New: 'I have made it, you shirker! Come West, Young Man! Are not the streets paved with gold? Remember the mission? Report to base, soonest, in full combat gear, with kitbag!' And the sudden turn of fortune, compensation for lost, forgotten Uncle Itsik, whom everyone thought had done a bunk to Australia in 1938 after ransacking his employers' bank branch in Graz but had, it turned out thirty years later, gone to ground locally and been swept up as oven fodder; the new German bureaucracy,

259

as efficient in a good cause as in a bad, winkling out every last burnt ember, carefully weighing every spoonful of ash . . . (Papa said: 'I shall offer Avram an allowance from this sum to do as he wishes. I shan't blackmail him to come home if he's not yet ready.' 'As you wish,' said Mama, 'scourge me with scorpions . . . one more knife in the back makes no difference.')

Forty-fourth Street, then, between Eighth and Ninth Avenues. Blok enters through swing doors into a dim, cave-like lobby, carrying his old red tartan suitcase with all his earthly belongings in it: three frayed shirts, five pairs of socks (darned and redarned by Mama and Nili), six crumbling, virtually shredded underpants, a paperback copy of Alexander Solzhenitsyn's *The First Circle*, telling tales of woe, not upon us, to dwarf our quotidian fears; a notepad filled with indecisive scribbles: Memoirs of a Stranger, Down and Out in Stamford Hill, night agonies of abysmal, censored verse . . . drafts of letters unsent to Nili, even to Papa, old photographs hidden in a tatty envelope, a seldom-used toothbrush and a cake of soap packed by Mama for his May '68 trip and, squashed in a corner, asargelusha! – a pair of Eisav's heavy winter socks, with a צ stamped upon each one of them . . . On the broken-down board at the end of the lobby Blok soon finds Yissachar's firm, as per instructions – Dementia Praecox Films, there it is, punkt below Gums of Novocaine Inc. upon the eighth floor. He ascends in a lift filled with loud Puerto Rican messenger boys. Out, threading empty grey corridors, soon finding himself in a maze of little rooms looking uneasily familiar, lost among film cans, bust editing tables, discarded amplifiers, cardboard boxes, outbins flowing over with rejected scenes from epics unknown, endeavours he could only guess at . . . Eventually signs of life, young men and women, behind acres of chaos, hunched over flickering prisms . . . ahoy! the sweatshops of the media age, dreams retailed feverishly on the assembly line . . . it is his destination: they direct him to a further room where Yissachar himself, the man triumphant, attends the altar of a large, three-screen machine. On its central glass a naked lady is straddling a hairy, muscular man who, wearing nothing but bright purple socks, reclines on a ver-milion sofa, stretching thus the tolerance of Eastman Kodak's colour process to its breaking point. Upon the right-hand screen, the lady turns her eyes to heaven, contemplating – could it be? – ersatz nirvanas, or mere dollar signs . . . Upon the left screen, a clapper board, its clapper raised, frozen, poised for action, partly conceals the bulbous con-tours of a hairy scrotum.

Welcome to the goldeneh medineh! Yissachar and Blok enclasp formally, exchanging masculine endearments: 'Hey, man!' 'Fuck your mother!' 'You piece of dried shit!'

Blok, still pie-eyed with acute culture shock, jetlag and mental concussion. 'Well well well,' he babbles, 'so you've made it at last . . .'

Indeed. The cramped room, the flowing outbins, cigarette ash on the floor. The celluloid valhalla. On the right screen now a feminine tongue licks out, to catch a frozen spurt of white jism.

'Yes,' said Yissachar, 'indeedy. You have come at the right time, commander. What you see here is just a flanking manoeuvre. But we'll be ready soon to mount our offensive. Deposit your worries in the left-luggage department, because here everything is under control. I have plans, my friend . . . but we'll leave that for later, after all, you're fresh from the plane . . . give me half an hour here, I'll take you to my apartment, a temporary base, but don't worry . . . here nothing's permanent, all is in flux, you are always either rising or falling . . . and sometimes both, at the same time, ya baba! – never a dull moment . . . New York, my friend, the United States of America! Who would have ever believed it?'

He took Blok into the bowels of the earth, at the Forty-second Street station. Aboard the E train he pushed him, punkt in the rush hour, crushed among the human flotsam. ('Fix bayonets,' he cried, as they crunched through the turnstile, 'steel helmets on! Follow me!') Then change at Fourteenth Street, dots in the mêlée, on to the Canarsie Line . . .

The apartment was in Avenue A, a byword for urban decay. By day, the poorest Jews, Puerto Ricans, blacks, plied the schmutter and pischifkes trade. By night, the grimy tenements with their snakes-and-ladders fire escapes stood sentinel over empty streets, down which residents en route for their homes dashed for safety from the subway station. Safe within, they treble-locked their doors, and checked that the rusty iron grilles over their windows were impenetrably secured. Only then could they relax, switching on the TV, drowning the mayhem outside: police sirens, breaking glass, pistol shots, screams of the wounded, maimed, dispatched, or just night people driven beyond their tether. In fact, Yissachar cheerfully averred, Avenue A was exceeded as the roughest, toughest, orneriest street in town – outside the ethnic ghettos – only by Avenue D, where, it was said, one's chances of survival matched those in the Gulag Archipelago. 'We are far from the worst,' he told Blok breezily. 'I am so glad to hear that,' said Blok.

The apartment itself was a shambles, too: the owner, an editor at Dementia Praecox Films who was absent for some weeks visiting her mother in Maine, was not the tidiest of persons. Books were piled on the beds, records under the sofa, blankets filled the toilet, sheets the kitchen sink, socks were hung on walls, prints of paintings hidden in chests of drawers, and various toiletries covered the bookshelves. Tins of cat food were everywhere, so that the provenance of her two animals, whom she had left behind, should not be out of mind for an instant. It was to provide for these creatures, named Alfredo and Zunz, that Yissachar had been loaned the apartment in the first place. ('I had a great pad up on Broadway and 70th,' he mourned, 'but it became full of Israelis . . .') Alfredo was lean and whitish and jumped about everywhere. Zunz was black and obese and rarely left his own padded armchair. 'My main moral problem,' Yissachar explained to Blok, 'is whether to fulfil my instructions to the letter and stuff these foul beasts with yum-yum, or whether I should starve them for a couple of days and force them to have a go at the roaches.' For the roaches of Avenue A were numerous, though pragmatic, keeping generally to the kitchen, where they busied themselves, day and night, with ingenious schemes to enter the fridge. In keeping with the American Ideal, they were ingenious, industrious and diligent. Several succeeded somehow in making their way into the freezer and were found in the morning, little blocks of black ice with beatific grins on their faces. They were distant relatives, needless to say, of the roaches that lived in Babelech-und-Farfel's accoutrements, being a sub genus of *Blatta orientalis,* the migrating Russian schmootz. They even sent gift parcels to their landsmen in the Holyland at Passover and High Holidays, and contributed handsomely to the' JNRF, the Jewish National Roach Fund.

Yes, it is America, without a doubt, this cannot be mere imagination. Blok and Yissachar, in the Lower Depths, dreaming their dreams of glory:

after a hard day's night with the fuck flick – in the maw of the Times Square subway. Cavernous corridors. Footfalls of terror. Stairs etched with green slime. The IRT underpass, stretching ahead like the reversed view from a telescope. A booby-trapped ante-chamber to the lost mineshafts of Gagool . . . An old man wags his weenie at them as they timorously sidle by. 'They're watching!' he cries. 'You won't get away with it! they won't fuck it up next time!' 'Excuse me,' said Blok, skirting round him, tip-tapping down the tunnel. Move, man, move, from carriage to carriage, avoiding the young black man with foam on his lips, the tramp fastened in a pool of his urine. The invisible driver, locked in his cabin, calls the stations in a squawk-box tremolo. 'Fourteenth Street next!'

Exit here, night heroes. Better to walk, taking risks in the open, not trapped in the Canarsie Line . . . Wisps of steam curling up from iron gratings, from Mephistophelean underpasses. A night bus swishing by with its silent cargo of early-morning shift workers. A lone taxi, rolling over the buckled asphalt like an intent yellow dolphin. On the pavement a figure lies sprawled by an overflowing dustbin. Perhaps he is dead, perhaps he is drunk, or is he lying in wait for the gullible? Blok and Yissachar, imbued with New York, give him a wide berth. Surely he must have been born, wet his nappies, played hopscotch in the sun, feared, hoped, desired, dreamed dreams . . . Now he is flotsam of the road. Infected, our heroes turn their back on compassion, thinking glumly of Avenue A . . .

'This cannot go on much longer!' said Yissachar, handing Blok a cocksucking scene. 'Time to map out one's routes of advance, to strike camp and move one's forces!'

'Indubitably,' said Blok, impaling on a bin hook his friend's celluloid circumcision.

'You think I'm having you on,' said Yissachar, 'but I can tell you, it's only a matter of time. I have a contact, the producer who got me this job, an old friend of Shpilkman and Brodie. The High Command, my friend! This is only a sideline, a favour the man owes some people ... this is America, man, not Liam O'Habashland – amateurs skulking in corners ... the hard core is Mafia business, commander, Cosa Nostra, il syndicato ... but my producer is a man of substance, a fallen giant who will rise again. I'm just waiting for the word, ya ibni, then it's off to the West Coast, brother ! Los Angeles! Hollywood, California! The happy hunting grounds!'

One night they returned to Avenue A to face an unexpected disaster. On leaving the flat that morning Blok had neglected to close all the windows as instructed. Consequently, Alfredo and Zunz, for reasons known only to their own feeble feline brains, had squeezed through the window grilles to the fire escape and vanished from human ken. Blok and Yissachar sallied forth into the night, flashing pocket torches in corners and rummaging in alleys and yards. What could the street's nocturnal denizens, rapists, muggers, mass murderers and policemen, have thought of this foolhardy odd couple as they poked their heads into dustbins crying: 'Freddo!' 'Zuntzie!' 'Moots moots moots!' and even 'Here pussel pussel pussel!' History does not record, but one assumes, by their survival, that in Avenue A, as in other savage societies, the true fruitcake is unmolested.

'It's no use,' said Yissachar, 'they've probably been eaten by now.'

When his friend, Debbie, returned from Maine two days later, she ordered them out of the flat. 'I'm sorry,' she said, 'but after a month with my mother, to come back and find the only two human beings,

265

so to speak, that I can relate to, gone – that is just more than I can bear.'

Hit the road, Jack! She allowed them one night's notice. They shared a joint from the stuff she had brought down from Maine and watched the Korean war on TV. Then Debbie and Yissachar retired to make love in the bedroom, while Blok, on the sofa, considered the recurrence of exile. In the morning she helped them pack their bags and, giving each a chaste peck on the cheek, cast them elegantly to the winds.

'Don't worry,' said Yissachar, 'a temporary setback. Normal service will be resumed shortly.'

They took to bedding down in the D.P. cutting rooms. A sleeping bag and some blankets amid the ripening porn. By this time Blok was in advanced culture shock and had experienced one attack of the Fear, rampaging through the cutting rooms, on the stroke of high noon, screaming abuse at the cosmos. Later he was ashamed and hid in the toilet, but had to emerge to face the world after the Puerto-Rican messenger boy had pestered him with perverse enticements, inquiring: 'Do you want a big toffee apple all covered with honey?' Yissachar told him he was dumb to reproach himself for his outburst. No one, he revealed, had noticed anything out of the ordinary: such behaviour, in the bowels of Manhattan, was really extremely common.

Eventually Yissachar unearthed a jewel of an apartment which belonged to an old Polish lady who had known his parents in Buenos Aires, and who was about to leave for Israel for four months. He met her at a Yiddish Language Preservation Meeting at the geriatric ward of Mount Sinai Hospital. ('What the fuck were you doing there?' Blok hissed in frustration, but Yissachar kept his secret.) It was a large apartment, three rooms and a hall, on West 77th, imagine! 'I told you not to worry,' said Yissachar smugly, 'if you lie in ambush long enough your destiny comes by, to be grabbed firmly by the balls.'

He could now put in action his long-cherished plan to climb out of the hard core sewer. ('What our mothers told us is the absolute truth,' he told Blok, 'this stuff really rots the brain!') He purchased a number of Greyhound Bus schedules, and lay in bed rolling exotic stations off his tongue, savouring their mythic resonance: Greensboro, Winston-Salem, Blacksburg, Tuskegee, Montgomery, Pensacola, Biloxi, New Orleans, Yazoo City, Las Vegas, Lompoc. For he wished to cross the continent on his arse, and feel its vastness in the bones of his body. But Blok was beginning to enjoy the city, having found a place of rest and discovered the Park, the Hunam Taste and the H&H Bagel Shop. Came October, and leaves fell from the trees, squirrels gambolled, joggers jogged, 'loose joint' vendors multiplied, and dreamy dog-owners followed their pooches, wielding small brushes and pans. The imp of the perverse beckoned him again, as the threat of achievement loomed. 'I don't like the beach,' he said, 'I can't stand the sun. And I don't believe in your mythical producer anyway, the fallen giant who owes the Mafia favours . . .'

Battle stations! A thrown gauntlet, cholera! Yissachar immediately bristles. 'Suit yourself,' he says tartly, 'who asked for volunteers? I shall embark on a solo mission.'

He left, then, in the maw of a Greyhound Bus, with a rucksack and a gleam in both eyes. Technicolor glories glowed on his retinas, John Wayne, in the Merkaz Cinema . . . the guttural rasp, horses' hooves, the chewing of sunflower seeds, the scrunch of feet over the bed of husks . . . the potato drawl of Jimmie Stewart pursuing Justice in Vista Vision . . . Blok, remaining in the apartment of the old Polish lady, with the squirrels, and colour TV. Washing out the detritus of previous years. Trying to Put His Life in Order . . .

But Yissachar's movie mogul fallen from grace did exist, and was none other than **Irving Klotskashes**, king of the Fifties Z-features. Did not his credits include *SLIME! (Invasion of the Giant Snails), Beast of Bataan, The Thing From Beyond the Stars, GRIME! (Invasion of the Monster Worms), The Giant Rat of Sumatra, The Martian Bolsheviks, Blood! Blood! Blood!, The Slashers From Beyond Time, AAARGH!, Jackboots From Beyond the Stars* and *The Murderers Lurk Within Us?* The defence rests.

His parents, Chayim and Sadie, pioneered the now lost silent Yiddish cinema (with titles in both Yiddish and English) with productions such as *Chayim in Wonderland, A Yiddischer Beach Boy, The Ballad of Redwood Berl.* Their first son, Irving, born 1911: first taste of the industry in animation, assistant inker on Farmer Al Falfas . . . Initiated Pepito the Wonder Dog, who was a complete failure. Switched to live action with the coming of sound, as an actor – his first job: in the crowd scene at the climax of *Frankenstein*, the mob with torches, slavering for vengeance . . . Later formed the Metronome Company with 'Limpy' Cohen, né Wolfgang Amadeus Kohn, a Fritz Lang alumni who had begun his career as a dwarf juggler in Tod Browning's *Freaks.* Their first feature, alas totally lost to posterity, was *Werewomen of Zlataplan* (1939) which was reputed to be so bad that the distributors, Universal, threatened to destroy the negative . . . Then, in the early Fifties, they hit their stride, with the famous series of low-grade, ultra-cheap quickies which bored drive-in audiences throughout the land and burned the brains of an entire generation, the Klotskashes alumni . . .

Alas, since fallen from grace, estranged from partner, studios and public. His failed foray into Beach movies: *Bebopaloola From Beyond the Stars*. His mounting Shove-Ha'penny gambling debts contracted in Pismo Beach. His retreat to Ek Therapy in the wilds of Big Sur, within sight of migrating whales. His forced return to film helming, at the insistence of Don Cic ('Il Garrotto'). And his dreams, his hopes of a return to the days of glory of old . . . nurtured by Yissachar, ignored by Blok in his blissful Manhattan ignorance . . .

Yes, Blok, alone in the City, trying to Put His Life in Order. Grooving on a White Christmas, cholera. Flakes cascading past the apartment window as if poured from a colossal carton of washing powder. Puerto-Rican Father Christmases. Noel! Noel! Walking about in the snow and sludge, among people all wrapped up in gauze and goggles like Claude Rains in *The Invisible Man*. His spirits are high. He throws snowballs at strangers. He tweaks the tails of strange dogs. In the Park, people are walking on water on the lakes and the ponds. He does not attempt this. But for the first time aloneness glimmers as a possible boon, not a curse. He can sit and goggle at TV inanities any hour of the day or night. He can rummage about in second-hand bookstores (what an overload for the Magpie!), or just walk the streets, the open-air museum, New York, the Human Zoo. Garlic bagels from Chinese bakeries. Jewish dictums from fortune cookies. The Hundred Per Cent Charcoal Broiled Burger Joint: any fries? An onion rings? Never mind the siren telephone calls of frère Yissachar from Never Never Land: progress is certain . . . contact is imminent . . . I am closing in on the objective . . . (He had got into the habit, on his cross-country detour, of calling at odd hours from the oddest locations, such as Van Horn,

Texas, at four in the morning, or Chatahoochie, at midnight, using fake credit card numbers: the local Greyhound station, Avram, you wouldn't believe it! It's in the fucking laundromat! Indeed, said Blok, indeed, his eyes glued to Channel Twelve's Hispanic wrestling show. *'El Gran Massa del Havana Cuba contra Los Indio del Connecticut.'* Bliss indeed.)

But can this last? Once people were doomed by Destiny; today by the contractions of modern society that some call the global village. One very cold day the postman delivered a thickish envelope to Blok addressed from the British Isles. Blok recognized instantly the handwriting of Victoria Happenstance. *Gevaldt!* His heart sank and rose at the same time, a singular sensation . . . He cursed and blessed the day he'd sent off, in a moment of weakness, a picture postcard with a return address to Stamford Hill. He fortified himself with a can of beer and some peanuts and tore open the envelope. It included two items: a long seven-page letter from Victoria with stapled newspaper cuttings, and a much readdressed envelope from the Holy Land which seemed to have traversed the globe several times. Within was Nili's wedding invitation, for an event he had heard of by rumour. (Papa: 'Avremel, did you know that . . .') Merde, alors! Sapristi! Lord save us! Mas'at-Nefesh, Eisav Ben-Gever. Many waters cannot quench love . . . No, surely such madness could not exist . . . he hid the card under a cushion. Turning to Vicky's letter he perused the cuttings: 'Bantu and Whites Should Dwell Separately: Like Impala and Kudu, Says Fouche.' 'Tons of Dagga Hidden in Hills.' 'Practical Ranch Management: A good intelligent African who can work with animals is worth two or more weak ones who have no animal sense and no hope of acquiring it in the future.' Very sensible advice,

Blok thought, what does the woman want with me? He closed his eyes firmly, counted to forty, then opened them and read her letter:

Dear Blokkie [she wrote],
So much to tell, so little space, so difficult to try to convey clearly what I really want to say. I still can't believe I'm back in logical grey London. I almost kissed the tarmac at Heathrow! South Africa! My God! Maybe I just dreamed it . . . whatever you imagine or read in books, it's nothing like the real thing . . .
I know, Blokkie, you felt lousy at not coming with us because you thought you were letting me down, but believe me I don't feel that way. If you'd come there you'd just have been sucked into something I know you wouldn't want to take on, and shouldn't be expected to. I know what you have to contend with on your own account, and I wish you luck wherever you are, you crazy Yiddischer clown! (New York, eh? the bright lights! the streets paved with gold! Poor old Blokkie, and his holy grail . . .)

Eek! Eek! Eek! he skipped three paragraphs, and moved to page three:

. . . to see the gleaming streets, the tall buildings of the white cities, shops crammed with all the goodies you don't need – remote-control toasters, electric toenail clippers, bracelets for dogs . . . and the armies of black men and women in overalls, keeping it all spick and span . . . those ever-present signs . . . 'Europeans Only' . . . 'Best Steaks – R.3.00; Servants' & Dogs' Meat – R.2.50' . . . and ten minutes away the black townships, the endless rows of drab houses, you wouldn't believe it, Blokkie . . . Almost no one about during the day except for children who run

271

to and fro in the dust of the unpaved roads . . . and nothing changed, nothing really changed, in the last thirty years . . . I remember J.D. once told me a story of his childhood: of the children who used to go off to school without breakfast because their parents could only afford one meal a day. On their way they would stop by the fish and chip shop and press their noses up against the window netting. They would take a deep sniff at the flavour from inside, then grab an imaginary mouthful and move on, and that was their morning 'meal' . . .

Asargelusha! Blok thought. Why is she telling me all this? He gazed guiltily at his peanuts. He skipped two more pages dealing with the horrors of 'homeland' life, peasant poverty in the rural areas where deportees from the cities were dumped to starve, her travels with Davina in a battered Deux Chevaux across Natal, the Transkei . . .

. . . But I mustn't rabbit on, boring you to death, I'm sure you have your own obsessions . . . I am trying to put it down on paper now, but how to capture the essence of it . . .? The overwhelming oppressiveness, amid a landscape of such beauty . . . I suppose it's one thing to be bone poor, but another to commute every day between your own poverty and your masters' affluence . . . to be dazzled by that city gleaming because you have scrubbed its floors, washed its windows, painted its 'slegs vir blankes' benches . . .jostling with the boss on his pavements but required to be forever separate . . . spoken to like a child of five even when you're a white-haired seventy . . . and the daily fear and uncertainty, knowing you can be picked up any moment for a pass law offence, slung in the back of one of these wire netting vans that zoom by crammed with the day's intake

. . .Wherever one goes, Blokkie, wherever you open your eyes, so much evidence of man's utter vileness to man and yet – finding the victims so resilient, so ready to talk to you and open up to anyone white who just approaches them as a human being . . . the sheer power and sharpness of emotions felt when a situation is so clear, so unmuddied, so obvious a contrast between what's wrong and what's right . . .

All right, Blokkie, I'll get off the soap box, I've drivelled enough, I think. Back to the drawing board, to try and make sense of it all, to put together our shriek. (We are writing a book together, J.D. and I, but who will ever read it, I wonder?) Luck, honour and love, from all and sundry, J.D. sends his greetings. He says not to worry, the main thing in life is to be true to yourself! Keep well, Blokkie, don't go under!

Venceremos! x x x x x x
Your one and only
Victoria (Mama Ngina)

Aargh! Aaargh! Aaargh! the delicate balance of Blok's fragile peace was shattered. He left the apartment and went out on to the icy pavement upon which people slithered and slid, past the barking man who appeared in fine fettle, yapping at the passers-by. Striding east, past the Natural History Museum, above which Yissachar, one October evening, had claimed to see a flying saucer. Into the Park, where only one lunatic in a sweatshirt passed him, steaming, determined to live for ever . . . A freezing tramp at the gate was about to accost him for 'gimme a quarter, man' but desisted, repelled by his vacant stare. Past honking, frustrated cars, spitting grey sludge on either side, across Central Park South, down Eighth Avenue. The wind howls, the sky's virtually black, excellently matching his mood. Who wants sunny

California? Open your floodgates, Blok, to the sudden tidal wave of despair, dejection, the utter sense of uselessness . . . time to change gear, from blithe joviality to the perverse, terrifying joy of sinking deep into the slough, the lower depths, Babelech-und-Farfel-land . . . To his right, a sign, flashing bravely at the icy noon: 'Cum Inside. Fantasy. Romance. Exitement [sic]. Make Up For Lost Time. No Matter What Combination You Want, We Have a Winner For YOU.'

Not so. He pondered whether to turn left, at Forty-second Street, but remembered that only a few days before he had seen the Habad Hassidim's Mobile Mitzvah Waggon lying in ambush at the Times Square junction. Come fair weather or foul, bearded zealots, flushed with spiritual enthusiasm, accosted anyone who looked even vaguely Jewish and harangued them, with tears in their eyes, to come and lay tfillin within. He walked on, mingling with the crowd round the Port Authority Bus Terminal. Should I follow Yissachar, nevertheless, in his march towards the Hollywood Grail? Or drop off on the way, at some remote hidey hole where Reality could not possibly reach – Ogunquit, or Pascagoula, or even Perdido Junction? Or just get on the subway, fling myself downtown, to the horrors of Avenue A . . . Or the Bowery, join the oppressed on the bottom floor, and work my way up the hierarchy . . . Find my private Klander in the urban gutter, disappear, consumed by the Moloch Manhattan. Drop out of human ken, become a cipher in the register of missing persons. Blok? N'existe pas! Never heard of him, my friend. The immigrant ship, *Irma Klein*, torpedoed in 1946 by the Royal Navy, sunk like a stone with all hands, not a smidge of a rag of a page of a forged passport floating to mark her exit. Not Baruch or Rosa Blok to give birth to a bouncing Avram. I refuse to think, therefore I am

274

not – put that in your pipe and smoke it, Maître Descartes.

As he stood in the eddy of crowds, a portly tramp with a good-natured face accosted him, asking him for the time.

'I'm sorry, I left my watch behind,' said Blok.

'A wise move indeed!' said the tramp. 'I perceive you are a non-American,' he continued, in a rich upper-class English accent, 'like myself, a stranger in town. I knew it as soon as I saw you hesitate at this corner, this nexus of the city's vice. I can see in your face that you are a person of discernment and sensitivity. People like us are wasted in a place such as this. Eat, drink, fuck, kill and be killed, anything for a fast buck. Mind you, I do not want to put down America, my long-adopted land. People here do not hide their angst under a bushel. No, they flourish it, wave it about, belabour you with it. The city positively shrieks in your eardrums, it brings out the kinks in your brain. I have been through a great deal, my friend, I am sure you would never believe it. I was once a Professor, emeritus, at a highly distinguished academy. I was married three times, each time to a lady more ravishing than the one before. I had homosexual affairs with several peers of the realm. A Judge of the Court of Appeals committed suicide after I jilted him. I owned a number of businesses, speculating in the commodity markets. My downfall came over cocoa, in which I had invested the very highest hopes. The West African weevil was my nemesis, devastating the crops of three nations. Can you imagine, an insect not the size of your thumb, laying waste half a continent. From then on my decline was swift. I spent seven years in prison where my bum was, so to speak, at the service of my fellow man. Several times I escaped death narrowly, by the jealous lovers of my paramours. Once I was at death's door for three

275

weeks, with twenty-three separate knife wounds. When I was released I had fifteen shillings and ninepence, and not a single friend in the world. But never once, during those grisly ordeals, did I give up and consider suicide. Do you know why, my worthy friend? Curiosity, that's the fellow's name. Damned curiosity, man. I just *had* to hang on, I just *had* to know what pot of piss they'd think to serve up next. What new calamity life's twisted skeins could conjure, what cataclysms, tribulations, holocausts could turn up next to top the ones before.

'The one thing I have learned from my life,' said the gentle tramp, 'is not to worry, because *nothing* is under control.'

If Blok had been able, at that precise moment, to sit down and encapsulate, with pen and ink or a typewriter, the state of his brain, his fragmented essence, his jangling ganglions, his Manhattan blues in the wake of the day's postal harvest, he might, or might not, have set down the story buzzing around in his head since the winter of '69, amalgam of the cries of Eisavian pain echoing from the Suez Canal and the shrill squeaks emanating at zero celsius from his own embattled genes; i.e. the story entitled:

# The Man Who Counted the Gold Teeth and Spectacles at Auschwitz

XIII

LA MORT

He was due for a five-day leave, to commence at seventeen hundred hours. The little brown pass lay before him, stamped and signed. He folded it carefully, down the middle, pressing the crease with his thumbs. Then he tucked it in his left shirt-pocket, together with his identity papers and the white clean handkerchief he used only for wiping his spectacles. He daydreamed at his desk: at home spring should be breaking out, in daffodils and bluebells. There would still be snow on the peaks of the Brocken but elsewhere the thaw, swelling the streams flowing in to the lakes of the spas, presently dormant. In the village they would somehow produce, despite the 'hard' winter of '43, puddings, and apple dumplings and make-believe Easter Eggs. People would gather on the village green, casting bowls as if there were no war, sitting on the benches smoking their pipes, yarning about old times. He would sit with them, silently watching the children play hopscotch on the old paved square. He would try to avoid the glances of women, asking mutely of the Eastern Front. He had become quite proficient at avoiding the desolation that sprang from people's eyes.

He glanced at his wristwatch. Three forty-five.

One hour and a quarter to go. To his left there was still a small sheaf of papers to be filed from the In to the Out tray. At four he had to join Feldwebel Schultz on the daily warehouse inspection. He would keep precisely to schedule and not steal one moment from the period of his allotted duties. For where there is precision there is salvation from the vice of primordial chaos. And where else was the threat of chaos greater than here: 'the world's arsehole', as the men all called it, railing against the bad luck that had posted them, rather than someone else, to this vile and filthy detail. And this despite the compensations: the brothels of Jewish, gypsy or Slav women (and men, though this crossed the firm line of legality); the cinema, on alternate Sundays, with Karl Martell and Zarah Leander in the latest Ufa comedies. Not to speak of the weekly pay bonus, for onerous and fatiguing duties, decreed by the Reichsführer Himmler himself, who had explained the true worth of their service.

'Often one bends, one fears one is breaking under the intense pressure: the crowding, the stench, the long arduous hours, the endless crushing vigilance. Even the natural repulsion of our soldiers to press on with this thankless task. But we must remember it is a task God Himself entrusted to the German people in general and to the German soldier in particular. As the Führer himself has stated: "The battle in which we are engaged today is the same battle waged, during the last century, by Pasteur and Koch." You are Mankind's pest controllers, and future generations will remember and honour this, your valiant sacrifice.'

No man is an island. No man can opt out, without entering a realm of dire peril, from the orderly running of things. This much he had learned in civilian life, at the sorting desk of Halberstadt Post Office. Letters arrived from the four corners of the earth, bills and invoices to fuel the wheels of commerce, postal orders for services required or rendered. One could not just throw the day's mail into the garbage. The world is not a madhouse.

One by one, he smoothed out the papers that remained to be dealt with. They were mostly order forms, forwarded by Division, from metropolitan firms. The Hadamar Geselschaft wanted seventy hundredweight of high-grade hair for pillows for clinics and hospitals. The Hamburg Optical Company wanted ten thousand spectacle frames already authorized by the Department of Health. Dortmund & Sonnen Gmbh filed for recycled dentures to be used in the manufacture of toothbrushes. And a paperclipped sheaf of routine slips from the Reichsbank concerning precious metal residuum. All these had already crossed Feldwebel Schultz's desk and been stamped by his hand in red. It was his turn now to extract from its rack on the right-hand drawer the appropriate rubber seal and the pad, which he had re-inked at fifteen hundred hours, punctually on schedule. It was a mark of his application that he always made sure of the maximum legibility. A smudged date, or obscured departmental number, could so easily cause a document to be wrongly filed, a consignment to be wrongly directed, even lost in the tangled labyrinth of the general government. His fingers were at their steadiest at this moment of responsibility, as, with adroit timing, he breathed on the rubber and placed it firmly in the right position, before filing them. These files, specifying the various items available for shipment, were neatly arranged on the shelves behind him, under printed labels such as Headgear, Footwear, Underclothing (Men or Women), Overcoats, Tunics, Eyeglasses, Rings & Jewellery (Ersatz or Genuine), Residue (Fat, Ashes, hair classified into Dark, Light, Miscellaneous).

Herein lay his satisfaction. It rested with him, with his precision, care, honesty and diligence, to ensure that nothing went to waste, that everything the gas chamber details assigned to him went out for the common good. At night, when he lay racked and riven by the yells of the roistering guards coming back from the brothels or the boozing dens of the Polish town, he could reflect on this and find solace, reaffirming his modest worth. These regular SS were mere ruffians, scoundrels, the scum of modern social decay. If it weren't for the few honest functionaries in the camp everything would be stolen, the future enterprise corrupted and defiled. The Reich would see nothing but leavings and spoilage from all these vast labours, the dregs of the debauches of looters. Had they not, just last year, arrested Graebner, Gestapo Political Officer, for pilfering the residual gold? Primordial chaos, ever-looming, menacing both the high and the low . . .

4.05. Feldwebel Schultz was late. Today of all days! The truck into town would leave at five fifteen. The train south-west would depart Oswiecim station at seven o'clock, and was usually on time. Missing it would mean waiting till morning, a loss of seventeen hours. As it was he would not reach Halberstadt before the following evening, given three change-overs . . . And then – bliss! Two full days of repose, an oasis of familiarity in a world full of lurking surprises. The truth was, he found the village more congenial now that the young men were gone. They had been mostly loud, foul-mouthed and unpredictable, wearing their uniform as the badge of their new dominion, their licence for Schweinerei. Now their remains littered the Ukraine, scattered like chaff. (It was said the soldiers had died horrible deaths in the snow, their anuses congealing with ice when they tried to relieve themselves, causing internal ruptures . . .) When the war was over there would be less of them around, and they ought to be quieter, perhaps wiser, certainly more subdued. God always found a way to balance the books, to keep order among the profane.

Yes, he would be able to wander the village streets unmolested by the cries of beer-sodden louts. He would join his brother Conrad, Conrad's wife Greta and their two children on a bicycle ride to the mountains, to Elbingerode, or Tanne, and they would sit and unfold their picnic baskets and breathe in the pure air, looking over the panorama of undefiled Mother Nature. Little Helga would 'pick flowers', presenting Conrad with a bouquet of weeds. Greta would fuss about brambles tearing her stockings. The boy Rainer would follow Wolfgang, the flop-eared mutt, 'rabbit hunting' in the bushes. Conrad would just lie there puffing on his corncob pipe, sending smoke signals of contentment into the bright blue sky. The joys of an ordered family life, savoured at second-hand, not having to risk the fleshly disorder that would accompany first-hand experience. Thinking of them, one must not forget to take, for little Rainer, the wooden dancing acrobat that Tischler, his ex-clerk, had carved the previous Christmas. He opened the left-hand desk drawer, where it reposed, waiting, wrapped in crisp brown paper. (4.11! where the devil was that ponce, Schultz?) Tischler. He had been a good clerk, diligent, cautious, anxious to please. But he had contracted TB and the camp doctor, Mengele, had him sent off to the showers. He had had two gold teeth, now one came to think of it, so his service to the Reich did not end, after all, with his inevitable demise.

4.15. A decision was now called for. He could no

longer wait for Schultz. One could not allow a colleague who played loose with procedure to disrupt the entire programme. In cases of emergency, illness or incapacity, a solo inspection was possible. He called his present clerk, Hertz, who poked his shaven head round the office door. A healthy-looking specimen, he might last the course, decent servants are hard to find. 'I am going ahead with the inspection,' he told the Jew, 'Tell the Feldwebel that I shall be at the Block.'

He crossed from the admin section to the warehouses across the guards' drill field. The sky was dull and grey, the air pinching cold with the wind slashing from the marshes. He saluted a captain who bicycled by him, splattering his trouser leg with mud. By Block D he could see a line of inmates, trailing back from a shift in the quarries. They shuffled their feet leadenly, their picks and shovels slung sloppily across their shoulders. They had no pride and no discipline, merely their utter desolation which he had learned to shun. Even at this distance, though, he caught a whiff of their terrible stench. It pervaded everything – walls, clothes, hair – one feared one would carry it everywhere, to the grave. Beyond them, the crematoria chimneys loomed, Number Three curling light smoke. Anus mundi, the arsehole of the world indeed. Shaking his head sadly at the thought of the merciless necessities of God's will, he walked through the great barn doors.

Here he was back in his element. The warehouses were curved corrugated iron hangars, used before for the storage of machine tools, stripped vehicles and spare parts. Then, for a long time, Primordial Chaos reigned, with the 'Canada' and Sonderkommandos dumping stuff all over the place, matériel vanishing by the hundredweight between the bath-houses, the cremos and here.

That culminated in Graebner's organized crime ring, which was broken in November by the new camp Commandant, Obersturmbannführer Leibenhenschel, the new broom to sweep the bawdyhouse clean. He was an efficient and humane man. Even conditions for the prisoners selected for labour improved under his supervision. The warehouses were rationalized. Since gassings took place, under normal conditions, once a day at ten thirty a.m., sorting could take place in an orderly fashion between eleven and two p.m. The sorters would stand at three rows of tables separating the various items, and these items would then proceed, category by category, to the appropriate fourth and fifth rows where they would be counted and weighed. They were then stored in numbered lofts, secure under lock and key. All this under armed supervision of guards watched in their turn by either himself or Schultz or both together. Thus serious abuses came to an end and honest accounting could become the watchword of the day.

This then was his routine in the sorting period: he would walk up and down the lines, surveying the work, making sure items did not fall to the ground or into the folds of the sorters' clothing. He also made comments, politely but firmly, to the guards, about the need for vigilance. He did not care that they mocked him after hours, called him Weasel-Puss, Arse-Face and That Little Prat in the Warehouse. It was water off a duck's back, for he knew that Oberst. Tannheuser, the Section Head, and above him the Chief himself, viewed him with crucial favour. Now the sorting tables were empty, swabbed down, ready for the work of the morrow. He began the last part of the daily ritual, mounting the stairs to the lofts, unlocking the loftrooms with his immense batch of keys, checking their contents in general terms against the lists he carried with him. He always found this the most soothing part of the schedule. Gone the bustle and mess and smell of the earlier period. Apart from the armed ensign at the stairway, there were usually only himself and Feldwebel Schultz, alone with the goods they kept and dispensed for the wheels of the Reich's economy: the hair, for example, piled on different shelves for different shades of colour. (And what good did it do on top of people's heads anyway, Schultz once said frivolously, what a wasted weight on one's brain! Here I am, shorn like a sheep, and I feel as light as a baby!) . . . The spectacles, however, were his favourite. He would stand for long minutes, fingering the ebony shapes, the piebald tortoiseshell rims, the odd bits of bone or safety pins people had used to shore up broken hinges. Schultz shared with him this esoteric interest, saying one could tell a person's whole personality from the shape of his or her eye-glasses. But Schultz was a rather sensitive soul, in secret; some said he even wrote poetry, though no one had seen an example. Unlike Schultz, what he liked about the spectacle frames was the sheer texture of the material. He did not, like Schultz, receive any vision or image of a person, living or dead, behind them. They existed independently, strange artifacts sprung from a void. The only items that stimulated him into speculations, fantasies, oddly enough, were keyrings. He would turn the keys over and over, dreaming of the doors they would have opened, the rooms into which they gave egress; even, at night, unbidden, the figures that might lie there in beds, at the mercy of the keyholder. There was a disturbing magic about keys. Now wallets, love letters, photographs, amulets, these left him completely cold. He always had a revulsion, a reluctance to examine them closely. Oberst. Tannheuser, on the other hand, collected them. He had albums, locked in his office safe, of family portraits, men, women, children, grandfathers, uncles, aunts, family pets, vanished worlds, preserved for posterity in a secure anonymity. There were other, more perverse collections. The Commandant's wife in Buchenwald, it was rumoured, had lampshades made of the skins of executed prisoners. Hazards of the job that could make one callous beyond Christian moderation . . .

4.50, and still no sign of Schultz. Procedure could not be maintained. The final stage had to be forgone: the upper strongrooms where the precious metals, gold teeth, rings, ornaments, were specially stored under permanent armed guard. There it was mandatory for both inspectors to be present. Damn Schultz! Despite Herculean efforts, the schedule came to nought in the end.

Tension overtook him, throbbing in the veins of his neck. He returned, crossing the yard without a thought for the freezing rain that now poured from the dour sky. Hertz was waiting for him in the office. 'The Feldwebel phoned,' said the Jew impassively, 'he has been in special conference with the Herr Oberst. He is on his way back and says for you to wait till he comes.'

Dismissing Hertz with a glance, he sat down at his desk, neatly cleared for his departure. He took off his glasses. Even the shortest walk in the open air smudged them with the camp pollution. Unfolding his glasses-wiping handkerchief, he carefully cleaned away the detritus of crematoria ash. Five o'clock had passed. He unfolded his permit of leave in front of him, as if, by examination, it might be invested with magic powers.

At 5.15 the Feldwebel's heavy step sounded outside. Schultz strode into the office, flopping down by his own desk and tossing his cap off his balding sweating head on to the table top.

'Well,' Schultz said, breathing heavily, 'they've done it to us again, haven't they?'

He said: 'Begging your pardon, Feldwebel, you are over an hour late. Inspection has not been done properly and my leave has been valid since seventeen hundred hours.'

'You know what you can do with that piece of paper,' said Schultz, showing no sign of his poetic nature, 'you can stuff it straight up your arse, that's what. You can dip it in the Jews' latrine and eat it with cayenne peppers. All leave has been cancelled, comrade, until further notice. And that means till your arse freezes over.'

It was crystal clear what this meant. 'More transports?'

'So many more transports we'll all be drowning in our own and their piss and shit. The war's going so badly so the powers that be are hurrying to clean up Hungary. And as usual, comrade, it's us who have to bear the full brunt of this shit-detail. Suddenly they've woken up to the fact that there are four hundred thousand live kikes down there that somebody's overlooked. Not only that –' Schultz leaned forward, 'Liebenhenschel is for the chop. Some new troubleshooter, Bar, Baer, whatever, is taking over next month. The watchword is double double. All four cremos to be in working order. They want twelve thousand – do you hear me, twelve thousand bodies to go every day! Shit! They're all running around like chickens with their heads cut off, no more lolling about, poor darlings! As for us, our little empire's expanding, doesn't that make you proud? We're getting double the number of Canada and Sonderkommando. The railway line is going to be extended right up to the bathhouses proper. No more ten-thirty detail, sort and store once a day. No, it's non-stop, my pussycat, right up to our pearly white ears! Midnight tonight, punkt, the first trainload arrives. So you'll have to forget your sauerkraut and beer by the hearth and join us poor devils down here, stoking the boilers! How do you like that now, Mister Signed-and-Sealed-Five-Day-Pass?'

No man is an island. No man can opt out, without entering a realm of dire peril, from the orderly running of things. His disappointment lasted one, perhaps two or three minutes. An image of blue open skies, air clear of cremo stench, a bright church steeple, a giggling gambolling child, a dog rooting for rabbits in the bracken of a mountainside, glowed for an instant and then vanished, like twinkling angel dust. He thought with regret of the wrapped package in his desk drawer, the wooden puppet for brother Conrad's boy. It would remain where it was. One day, perhaps, it would reach its destination, the eager little hands of innocence. Meanwhile a man had to do his duty. Kindness and laughter would have to wait. One had to fulfil one's obligations to society to the best of one's poor abilities. After all, the world is not a madhouse.

'DON'T THINK THAT JUST BECAUSE YOU'RE
PARANOID WE WON'T GET YOU!'
– Graffito upon English lavatory wall, 197–

Nevertheless, the tale Tarablus told the King of the
clochards, Bin-Zabl, in the Swedish Tea Shoppe:

## THE BEGGARS' SOAP OPERA
(*Three Agorot Opera* or *Brother Can You Spare a
Herzl?*)

*Dramatis personae:*

Father Andronicus (Oswald Hittlemacher-
   Probst), a priest
Wilma Bankie, a pious old nun
Major Uscuglu, a sadistic Turk
Reb Zev Kook Zweischaften, a Cabbalist of world
   repute
Pipiklech-mit-Milch, a yeshiva student, formerly
   a Communist, formerly a yeshiva student
Babelech-und-Farfel
Groise Metsiyes
Yosske Zichmich          beggars, agents of
Scheiss-mit-Reiss        foreign powers
Old Maclachlan, a Scots lunatic

Aaron Himmeltraub, a Hebrew newspaper editor
XBZ Three, a secret agent
Asa'el Mahatz (Zetz), a patriot
Sigmund Freud
Carl Jung          }rival psychoanalysts
Moses Klander, a disciple of Freud
Yokohama Sal, a prostitute with a heart of gold
Abe Cabiddle, a fishmonger from Czechoslovakia
Yin and Yang, Chinese illusionists

Hooded figures, a reformed Nazi, and a chorus of itinerants, schizophrenics, phenomenologists, roaches and other assorted shmootz.

*Act l, Scene l: June 1916 (Pre-Dawn of a new epoch). The Khan or Inn at Sha'ar Hagai, gateway to the Jerusalem hills. After sunset. Weary travellers snore under mounds of blankets. A donkey, in the courtyard, defecates. Plop.*
Father Andronicus (*enter*): What fateful times! What critical concatenation of events! But yesterday, the telegraphic wires hummed with news of Ishmaelite revolt in the Hijaz. At Medina the Turks have been assaulted by the warriors of the Sharif Hussein, at whose tight saddlebags the English pederast Lawrence runs, emitting his masters' voice. In far off Manchester, ba gum, the Jew Chaim Weizmann, toiling in his laboratory, prepares from orange peels and husks of corn ingredients for high explosives earning thus the gratitude of HMG which will pay ambiguous dividends in days to come ... The British, 'trenched in Egypt, planning their campaign to chase the Ottoman curs back to Constantinople. Messrs Sykes & Picot, in their marble halls, have meanwhiie carved the New Imperial Middle East

between them, laying deep mines for the future hopes of Arab liberation. But who am I to know these mind-boggling facts of statesmanship, skulduggery and worldly foile shtik? I, a modest servant of Our Lord, a poor priest with naught but an allowance of nine kreuzers per quarter to keep my soul from leaving its frail, harmless and utterly insignificant abode . . .

Offstage: Halt, miscreant! Who art thou, who walkest thus abroad when everyone else is shnorkeling away within? A spy, I'll wager, sending thy foul masters secret messages nocturnal . . .!

Andronicus: I am innocent! I merely sought the toilet and, caught short, did squat in this here ederberry bush. A wandering sacerdote I, a thing of shreds and patches . . . a German national, withal, devoted heart and soul to Kaiser, Volk and Reich! (sings) Deutschland, Deutschland . . .

Turkish Soldier (entering with colleagues): Seize him! To Jerusalem with him, for questioning, to prise from him the names of his seditious henchmen! (twirls moustachios grandly)

Andronicus (carried offstage): Long live the Emperor Franz Joseph the First! Long live the Sultan! Long live Enver Pasha, Saviour of the Eastern Hemisphere! (his voice fades in the distance)

Scene II, the kishla, or jail, in Jerusalem.
Enter Major Uscuglu and Warders. Andronicus, trembling, held by swarthy yobbos stage right. The forces of law and order sing – KISHLA SONG:

Uscuglu:        I'm a Turkish jailor,
                    Not a Swedish sailor,
                    I jail criminals by the score –
                    Bandits, pandits and lots more!

```
                        I have burning pincers,
                        Racks and chains and mincers,
                        And I have the latest fad-o
                        The electric bastinado!

Warders:                He's a Turkish jailor,
                        Not a Swedish sailor,
                        He jails criminals by the score –
                        Bandits, pandits and lots more!

Uscuglu:    I extract confessions
            In the shortest sessions,
            And if he's a tight-mouthed fucker,
            I apply the Greek falaka!

Warders:                He's a Turkish jailor . . . etc.

Uscuglu:    No one remains silent,
            I'm a man so violent,
            Dishing out torments of hell
            Is for me a bagatelle!

Warders:                No one remains silent,
                        He's a man so violent,
                        Dishing out torments of hell
                        Is for him a bagatelle!

Uscuglu:    Dunking in the snake pit,
            Snipping off the right tit,
            Crushing genitals to mush,
            Ripping open of the tush!
```

(*With a horrid clang, rusty iron cell doors slam shut*)

*Act II, Scene I: Interior of kishla cell, sixteen months later.*
*Andronicus, with roaches, seated on straw bed writing, oblivious of his awful surroundings, with a nail dipped in filth upon the margins of an old shit-encrusted book, held on his knees. To aid his concentration, the roaches sing 'Sweet Adeline' (sotto*

*voce). There is a commotion offstage. Bugles blast, shots are fired. Screams. Hammering at the cell door.*

Voice from without: Knock knock.

Andronicus: Who's there?

Lancashire voice: Allenby.

Andronicus: Allenby who?

Lancashire voice: Allenby damned if ah'll fuck about with ye, padre! Coom on oot. War's over for tha', old cock. Abdul Turk has lit oot lahk burnt sultana.

*More bugles, cheers, snatches of song: 'We'll hang our washing on the Sultan's prick'* . . . *A sign in four languages, English, Hebrew, Arabic and Serbo-Croat, descends from the flies:*

LONG LIVE GENERAL ALLENBY,
LIBERATOR OF JERUSALEM!

*From the barracks, a chink of teacups. Church bells begin to peal.*


*Scene II, a bare cell in the Chapel of Our Lady of The Spasm, next door to the Armenian Church of that name on the via Dolorosa.*

*A single shaft of sunlight, shooting through a high tiny arched window, illuminates Father Andronicus. Now white-haired and wrinkled he hunches over a desk, his white beard gently trailing on its dusty top, poring over his manuscripts while, through the walls, come the faint echoes of Armenian folderol.*

Wilma Bankie (*entering with glass of tea on a tray*): Oh, my lumbago!

Andronicus (*looking up kindly*): Come in, dear sister. The Lord be with you in your affliction. (*She puts down the glass of tea and turns to go, but he raises a frail hand*) Stay, dearest sister. I would have words with you. (*Pause, filled with Armenian flimflam*) For thirteen years I have sat, not stirring from this room, fulfilling the labour assigned me by God. And each day you have faithfully, silently brought me my cup of thin gruel and my glass of tchai, not to speak of my inks and parchments ... Now, when my fearsome work draws to a close and my time comes to shake up these old bones and set forth ...

Sister Wilma (*soaking his hand with tears*): Nay! Nay! thou canst not leave me ...

Andronicus: Nay I must, to seek the key among the bones of Judas of Karioth. I take with me but a few leaves, in case the Scottish Hospice sisters show that Presbyterian scepticism that enshrines their heresy. With you I leave this, the Book that Private Pusht, in lieu of Scheiss-papier, threw into my dank cell. There is no other copy in the world. Dear sister, harken: if the Lord requires that I return not from the culmination that His grace has granted my grey hairs, but rather render up to Him the soul that, in His Divine Wisdom, He hath loaned to me for my brief sojourn in this vale of tears, then takest thou in thy fair, sweet if bewrinkled hand, this Book to the address which I, with this last quill, upon this pallid page of parchment set. Courage, mother! If I fail, I know not all is lost, for I have left the fate of Mankind in good hands. Farewell!

*Exit Andronicus. Sister Wilma, clasping the old battered Book to her bosom, stands facing the high arched window, the light past the lattice forming on her glowing face the shadow of a crux ansata. The roaches all fall on their knees and turn their black little faces towards Golgotha (a hundred yards down Dolorosa, left at Barakat's Antiques, past the money-changer, into El-Attarin, right to Aftimos, to the picture postcard stand, you can't miss it, check your bags with Security, Shalom, Pax, E-Salaam Aleikum, Selah.)*

*Interval: Sigmund Freud and Carl Jung, in the back rows of the audience: Freud, smoking a self-rolled Turkish; Jung, sucking thoughtfully on briar pipe.*

Jung: Well, what do you think of it so far?

Freud: As far as religious mania goes, I fear it is all too clear. The bones of Judas obsession, denoting fear of the elder brother who caused the death of the primal father ... the revenge of the father, i.e. the castration complex. Not to speak of the ascetic ideal in general: self-denial, the repression of libido, thirteen years in one room and not even a shower to boot; the excreta-encrusted holy Book, referring perhaps to a baby born of the anal cavity ... a common childhood fantasy, to anyone who has given my work even the most fleeting of glances. An obvious case of anal eroticism leading to extreme narcissism. To demonstrate this, gebst a kik at this following diagram – (*he holds it up*):

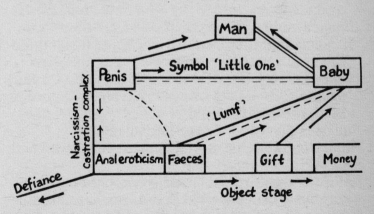

Jung: Lieber Herr Professor! Once again you are gumming up the wrong shoetree. Certainly things are clear: this holy man has embarked on an enterprise of incredible moment, a journey of discovery into the primeval depths of his psyche, there to find the mother lode, the spiritual truth which is the lapis philosophorum, the alchemists' philosopher's stone, the heiros gamos, the paraclete, the holy grail of legend. And you have the bare-faced gall to tell me it's all a childhood obsession with his kakky?! Kiss my ass!

Freud: Precisely.

Jung: Oh, I give up! (*snaps briar pipe over his knee*)


*Act III, Scene I, Sixteen years later. November 1947, Jerusalem. Zion Square. Café Vienna. Present round a white tablecloth: Reb Zev Kook Zweischaften, father of the Monk, a mature sage of 75. His sidekick, Pipiklech-mit-Milch. Aaron Himmeltraub, at that time still a journalist with the* Palestine Post. *Across the way the Zion Cinema is showing* Duel in the Sun *starring Joseph Cotten and Lillian Gish. A newsboy rushes by flourishing his wares:*

Newsboy: UN Committee recommends Jewish State! General Assembly vote imminent! Many dead and wounded!

Himmeltraub: A momentous occasion.

Pipiklech-mit-Milch: A disaster. This is where the Zionismus comes a cropper.

Himmeltraub: It is sad to see a Jew set against his own people. Did not the Lord say to Abraham: Unto they seed will I give this land?

Pipiklech-mit-Milch: Not to the Socialisten.

Himmeltraub: Give us 'Nationalists time, we shall inherit what's ours.

Reb Zev: Boys, boys, let us not argue politics over this excellent kaffee-kirsch. Reb Aaron has asked us here to discuss a troubling dream. I suggest, to borrow a phrase from a great goy, we should lend him our ears for a while. (*Reflecting softly to himself*) I wonder if they have creme-bavaria today . . .

Himmeltraub: It happened one day last week at the office . . .

*Scene II: Newsroom at the Palestine Post. Compositors, copyists, columnists, hacks rush about in great hustle and bustle. Music up.* SONG OF THE MODERN JEWISH JOURNALIST:

Hacks: I am the very model of a modern Jewish
   journalist,
      No ineffectual intellectual self-effacing
      humanist,
      The times are hard, our souls are scarred,
      Our dreams of beauty have been marred,
      We've all had sadly to discard the role of
      sentimentalist.
      We put into our paper all that makes our
      people resolute,
      All deeds of valour, heroism and auda-
      ciousness to boot,
      And anything that's dissolute,
      Or leads our citizens to doot,
      Will probably wend its true way towards
      the waste disposal chute.

      I am the latest scream of a humane and
      gentle Zionist,
      No stern, uncouth, bitter and ruthless
      militarist chauvinist,
      A patriotic socialist,
      A liberal conservatist,
      I am the very model of a modern Jewish
      journalist!

*At this point in Tarablus's tale the vast bulk of Bin-Zabl stirred and, with an infinitesimal twirl of a pudgy finger, he conveyed to the disguised Homicide detective the following message: Get on with it, portion of a camel's dung, or I shall kvetch you with my foot. Tarablus therefore hurried on to Aaron Himmeltraub's dream, he, Himmeltraub, seated behind a vast desk marked 'Editor-in-Chief', Andronicus, standing before him, having just paid*

299

*ninety-five piastres for the insertion of the following advertisement:*

> 'URGENT. To the Betrayer, Judah Man of Karioth. Time is running out. I know you are still down there. Come on out and face your medicine. Signed, Oswald Hittelmacher-Probst.'

Himmeltraub: Will you include an address, or a postal box number?

Andronicus: He knows where to find me. I am grateful for your help. I have tried notice boards, leaflets, even flyposting cars and pillboxes. But to no avail.

Himmeltraub: The *Palestine Post* will not fail you.

Andronicus: It had better not (*vanishes cackling, in a puff of rancid smoke, with the distinct after-whiff of bitter herbs*).

Pipiklech-mit-Milch: What treife dreams! On all our enemies . . .

Reb Zev: Sha, Pupik! there is more to come.

*And Himmeltraub proceeded to relate how the next day, Old Maclachlan, the noted Scots lunatic who used to stand at the Jaffa Gate every Easter and Christmas, screaming abuse at the pilgrims, burst into the newsroom of the* Post, *demanded to see him, Himmeltraub, and warned him, in his glottal falsetto, that he had been sent personally by Judas Iscariot to warn him, Himmeltraub, to keep off his, Judas' back, or else. 'Keep the Papist creep off me!' he screamed as the cops clamped their mitts upon his knobbly elbows, 'I have ma ee on ye! I am underneath ye! I am using the Judas Shuttle!' It was the finish for the old nut, who, like Blok twenty years later, was taken to Klander's institute from whence, sadly, he had to be sent to T–t, to be locked in the disturbed ward.*

Reb Zev: The Judas Shuttle! That is very interesting
. . .

Pipiklech-mit-Milch: Heretic bibble-bobble.

Himmeltraub: I came to you, honoured Reb, because I know you alone among the sages have made a study of the so-called Christian Cabbalists, Reuchlin, Pico della Mirandola, Boehme, von Rosenroth, and you keep an eye on their schemes. Who knows what millennial, pogromist flapdoodle they may be planning on the eve of our historic destiny . . .

Reb Zev: Leave it to me. But Mum's the word, old son, just keep it all under your tsitsis.

Bin-Zabl's nostril flared. His big toe stirred. Tarablus proceeded therefore to –

*Act IV, Scene I, a guarded bunker beneath Jerusalem, August '48, mid-war. Some say it lies under the blitzed Taunus building; others, the municipal sch'chita board. On the walls are maps, some ancient, some modern, and a notice board hastily nailed on the back flats of ersatz brick, with the following drawn upon it:*

*Present, on wooden folding chairs: Moses Klander, Reb Zev Zweischaften, Agent XBZThree as a young man, Asa'el Mahatz – a young Lieutenant, contemporarily teaboy to the great but destined for higher things – and three figures dressed in grey sacks with black pointed hoods over their heads, in which rough eyepieces are cut. Also present: roaches, whose indistinguishability masks secrets too fearful to contemplate. (Missing segments in the*

*following due to censorship, memory loss, dementia praecox and Tarablusian obfuscation.)*

Hooded Figure I: Let us not beat around the bush. (Lieutenant, will you bring us a pot of tchai?) The dream of Himmeltraub, the outburst of the Scotsman, denote a possible breach of security concerning the . . . that we will have to tackle. Meanwhile, though the war is turning in our favour, we cannot fail to plan for the long-term. We need to have our hidden talons, teeth and claws to make our enemies fear us. That is why, comrade Klander, Reb Zev, we must ask you to keep these revelations of the . . . as an absolute secret.

Klander: I accept, within reason . . .

Reb Zev: I too see the point. But spiritually, I fear that . . .

Hooded Figure II: We are concerned with these aspects. But we cannot avoid our priorities. The Nation has determined that Holocausts should not recur.

H.F.I: Not without the gentile world paying a heavy price.

H.F.II: This we have vowed.

H.F.I: Without question.

H.F.II: Without scruples or doubts.

H.F.I.: So determined that we have accepted the expert services of our, uh, colleague here, even though he is our mortal enemy. Perhaps in expiation, honoured Reb, of his sins . . .

H.F.III *(who has been stum so far)*: Ja-ja, natürlich!

H.F.I: For we know the hard path is the only possible one for us.


*Music up. SONG OF THE UTILITY OF SECRET ENDEAVOUR.*

H.F.I:      For Man's a ravenous beast,
            That no one can deny,

From furthest west to furthest east
He's ripe with Schweinerei –

For our State's security,
There's no one whom we can trust,
Innocence and purity,
Will soon go to rust.

H.F.II:    So gather, hevre, round,
And don your thinking caps,
For centuries we have been
hounded,
now *we'll* build the traps!

For our State's security,
Nothing can be left to chance,
No one will stand surety
But our own recognizance.

Both:    For Man's a ravenous beast,
That no one can deny,
From furthest west to furthest east
He's ripe with Schweinerei –

For our State's security
It's our mission to enhance,
No more victims of impurity –
NOW WE'LL BE THE SCHVANTZ!

*(Maps are unrolled, plans unfolded, but a fog of
official secrecy, creeping through the ventilation
ducts, obscures the entire scene from view.
Coughing roaches flee in panic, bearing Jung on
their backs. Screams, yowls, howls, moans of
those bereft of the light of day . . .)*

'That's enough.'

Bin-Zabl, departing from hallowed tradition,
broke his silence. His voice, like the croak of a frog
hibernating since the Palaeozoic. 'Farouk, close
down for the day.' The waiter, rolling his eyes at
the thought of enclosing Tarablus-Splendida's

stench, nevertheless obeyed, snapping shutters shuts, wooshing curtains, padlocking the front door. Tarablus protested:

'But there's still Act Five! The clochards! The truth of Klander's assassination! The meaning of the Book! It's all been advertised – the cast list posted, patrons have paid their cash!'

'Buki-sriki!' said Bin-Zabl, and Tarablus stopped short, for he suddenly noticed the fat man's voice came not from his mouth, which had not moved, but from a point in his massive stomach between the second and third waistcoat button. Bin-Zabl, in fact, had become utterly still, not a toe or a nostril quivering, frozen, Golden Khedive snuffbox in hand.

Like the machine that he indeed was, Bin-Zabl had been switched off.

As Farouk closed the last chink of daylight out, the entire Swedish Tea Shoppe, with its fake wood panelling, its itsy flower vases, its smörgåsbord, its portrait of Stockholm in winter, began to descend with a low electric hum. It was somewhat like the Haunted Mansion at Disneyland, where the walls appear to distort and elongate, the ceiling recedes and the whole shtik, which is in fact a giant lift, sinks deep into the bowels of the earth.

It came to rest a mere ninety seconds later, though Tarablus, and Shpilkes the Infant, who had been miraculously struck dumb by metaphysical panic, lost all sense of time. Bin-Zabl remained nailed in half light in his niche, an immense, malignant doll. Farouk, in grim solemnity, stood by the bar, his arms folded. And in the ersatz panelling, softly and silently, a real panel opened, through which Agent XBZThree entered jauntily, waving a cheerful greeting.

'Ahlan wa sahlan!' he called to Tarablus, 'I knew, come rain or shine, through thick and thin, you would break through to us at last, stubborn dick that you are. Welcome then, Inspector Tarablus, to the Judas Shuttle Control!'

Points of clarification:

*1. Pipiklech-mit-Milch*
In his youth, in the Polish town of Bialystok, the man who earned this curious nickname was a precocious talmudic scholar, for whom great achievements in midrashic exegesis were forecast. But he became seduced by the great wave of millennarian Bolshevism that swept across Eastern Europe in the wake of the Great War. Agonizing how to break the news of his conversion to his devout parents, he remembered that his mother had told him: 'The essence of Yiddischkeit is not to eat milk and meat together – to avoid pipiklech mit milch.' So, after several weeks of hiding in the woods he finally gathered his wits and went home, saying, as he crossed the threshold of the house, to his mother: 'Mother, I have just eaten pipiklech mit milch.'

*2. Old Maclachlan:*
Old Maclachlan, who came to Palestine sometime in the 1920s, had the following basic obsession: he believed the levantine city of Jerusalem was in fact Edinburgh, and vice versa, i.e.: Edinburgh Castle was the Biblical Mount Zion, Arthur's Seat the Mount of Olives and Joppa, sitting upon the Firth of Forth, proof positive of the whole matter. He therefore considered the thousands of pilgrims who came to worship in the Levant at Easter and Yuletide all deluded dupes committing acts of idolatry, and his mission in life to apprise them vigorously of their gross error. He was apprehended several times on the Temple Mount, looking for the crown jewels of King James in the Mosque of Omar, and he would

climb the stairs of the YMCA, which he took to be
the Walter Scott Monument, to look out over 'Holy-
rood Palace', i.e. the Tower of David, in case George
the Fifth, that vile sassenach, arrived to try and
pass the summer there. He died in T–t, in 1953, with
his beliefs, and his secrets, intact.

### 3. Aaron Himmeltraub:

True to Reb Zev's prognosis, he did rise in the world,
becoming editor of the Hebrew daily *Yediot
Rishonot* – First News – in 1951. His original
interest in the Judas Pig and all things occult blos-
somed into a belief that the spirits of dead biblical
heroes were talking to him in his sleep, and often
they wrote his editorials, which he claimed to see in
letters of gold on the ceiling above his bed. Readers
in the know could attempt to decipher, by the tone
of the polemic, whether today's piece was the work
of Elijah, Ezekiel, King Uzziahu the Great or the
minor Prophet Malachi. His columns became full of
code words only the initiated could translate: Belial
for Bolshevism, Babylon for Russia, Beelzebub for
Stalin, Amalek for the Arabs, Nebuchadnezzar for
Gamal Abd-el Nasser, Ophir for Washington DC,
Daniel for Menachem Begin, Ahab for David Ben
Gurion, Jezebel for Golda Meir, and the Wor-
shippers of Stars and Constellations for the Mapai
Socialist Party.

'It's a funny old world, man's
lucky if he gets out of it alive . . .'
                            – W.C. Fields, *You're Telling Me*

Blok in New York, mourning the reopening of Victorian and Nilian wounds. Consoling himself with pornographic magazines and the small ads of *Fuck Bi-Weekly*: 'SENSUOUS SHERRY: I am gorgeous, young and willing to be your sex-toy, your lover and your friend. Let me use my body to give you pleasure and that includes my perfectly rounded ass for those of you who want to try something different and exciting.' But he does not lift a finger to dial her number, choosing in his solitude to use his right hand for other purposes. He recalls Patricia, big-breasted receptionist of Dementia Praecox Films, another Blok failure, for all she wanted from him was information about the kibbutzim. She planned to emigrate to one marrying a soldier named Dudik she had met and been smit with over there.

'I know it's very old fashioned,' she said, 'but I want to keep myself for my husband.'

Alas, Blok, reduced to spilling his seed in a Polish old lady's apartment. While all around him swirl Plots and Conspiracies, Contrivances, Intrigues,

Cabals . . . Agents of the Sûreté, who have been on his trail since May '68, carrying in their pockets the dog-eared photofits of Blok as Abu Jilda . . . Mossad operatives who had snapped him with O'Habash, years ago, from Bin-Zabl's belly . . . US Immigration Agents with tight fedoras, who knew he had not entered his spell at Klander upon his visa application . . . spies for Hersh Leib Kalisher, set on him by Reb Friedman, après his Original Sin – both being, it appears, members of a hassidic group influential in the world tsatske trade, they had been financing Jewish zealots settling illegally on land expropriated from Arab peasants on the West Bank of the Jordan (a strange end of the line, not so, for the fruits of poor Zulu miners, themselves dispossessed over a century ago by British Imperialism, and now digging those precious stones out of a big hole in the ground for pitifully inadequate wages, in a country ruled by Nazi sympathizers). Friedman and Kalisher thought Blok might be an agent of the Zionist Labour Government, but their CIA contacts said No, he was not on those books, perhaps a new Soviet mole? Aye, sapristi, who knows how many of the residents of the house on Seventy-seventh Street were actually Blok-watchers? Listening from cubbyholes to his conversations with Yissachar phoning from Der Goldener Stadt – transforming the boiler and laundryrooms in the cellar into a nest of advanced surveillance . . . Indeed, to this end they would have had to have signed a pact with the roaches, who had set up their own HQ there and were plotting to take over first Broadway and Amsterdam Avenue, then the world . . . This might be tied in, too, with the flying saucer Yissachar had claimed to have seen over the Natural History museum: It was oval in shape and ringed with what appeared to be yellowy Mazda lightbulbs. Hovering in total silence for about ten seconds it then moved off at an incredible speed without even the trace of a whisper. Yissachar said the sighting had been reported by others, in the *Aetherian News,* a journal of UFOlogists, but when pressed to produce the magazine he claimed to have wrapped in it the remains of a Zaybars meal, which had already been carted off, in the dead of night, by the New York refuse collectors.

Oh! the joys and hazards of nocturnal emissions! and Yissachar's midnight calls: 'I am laying deep mines, along strategic paths, like rabbit traps in the forest . . . what are you doing there, Avram? Our future lies here, with the renaissance of Irving Klotskashes . . . The man is eager, he wants back in the game . . . the fruit's ripening on the tree . . . we just need a concept to develop into an idea, to pitch at the right moment at him . . . you must meet this guy, you would love him, Avram, a dinosaur from the Lost Age . . .' 'I don't care if he's the Loch Ness monster,' said Blok, 'I'll stay right where I am . . .'

And in this way a year passes.

1972! Momentous events: Maurice Chevalier died, Quang Tri was captured by the North Vietnamese, George Wallace shot in Alabama, Angela Davis acquitted of murder, kidnapping and conspiracy, five burglars caught bugging the Democratic Party headquarters in the Watergate Hotel, Dr Henry Kissinger travelled to China, Idi Amin Dada expelled thousands of Asians from Uganda, Arab guerrillas trumped the Munich Olympic Games, Richard Nixon was re-elected President. But Blok, zut! asargelusha! played no part in world affairs. It is in fact an opaque era, a cataract descending between ourselves and our hero, our hero and the rest of mankind. Yissachar telecommunicates, to no avail: the Polish lady has repossessed the apartment. 'Vot? Abram? Zhere iss no Abram heah!' she grates, cutting him off, running to check the silver. Yissachar, worried, considering travelling east, until, in May, a postcard arrives, saying 'See You Some Time. Abu Jilda.'

Later, rumours arrive on the exile Hebrew grapevine – do you know what that nutcase is up to? He has been glimpsed, as an actor, in a hard-core production, the notorious *Hassidic Bike Boys From Williamsburg*. He was not one of the seven burly yeshiva students who roar across the bridge on Hondas, but appeared to be one of the Arab guerrillas who, in reel four, kidnap the Scarsdale girls' hockey team. Behind the chequered kefiya of Abu Juha, who had forsworn all earthly pleasures until the Unsurped Land was freed, were the mournful Magyar Blok eyes, claimed the rumour-mongers. If so, even in the realm of art, Blok did not get to fuck in New York, merely to be stomped on as the chain-wielding Bike Boys, beards and sidelocks flying, burst in on the rape of the Jewish maidens in the nick of time – for the soft-core version – and too late, for the hard. But where could anyone have glimpsed this apocryphal epic which, repudiated and banned even by the Mafia, vanished after its preview, its negative burned, its director, Hy Buchenwald, reduced to ghost writing the memoirs of blind German emigrés in Paraguay? More enigma. Perhaps, after all, Blok merely spent his lost year in nondescript digs, stuffing envelopes for petty cash or waiting on tables, mumbling 'Oil and vinegar, thousand islands or roquefort?' into the hairy ears of punters?

Be that as it may, in December Papa Blok, in Jerusalem, received a letter. Blok's money had run out. Any more Uncle Itsiks? A forlorn hope, if ever there was one. In answer Papa sent an open-dated one-way airline ticket to a Brooklyn Post Office number. Thus endeth another era, with the whimpering sigh of a deflated whoopie cushion.

And the threads, cholera?? The web of his terrors? The network of his global guilt???

In February '73 Blok arrived back in Israel. It was a blustery day at Lod Airport. Flak-jacketed soldiers stood by the gangway, nervously training their guns on the passengers. They had been jittery since the previous year's massacre, in the arrival lounge, of twenty-three Puerto-Rican pilgrims by three Japanese terrorists doing a favour for the Palestinian Cause. Perhaps, Blok thought, the soldiers aim to get us before the Enemy has a chance. Nevertheless, he survived. Papa, looking drawn and about five years older than he had seemed two years earlier, met him outside the gate. 'Mama's not well,' he told Blok in the taxi, 'she has passed beyond Psalms and Proverbs and is reading the Book of Daniel. Some idiot who the Rebetsen Syphilis-Face put her on to has been teaching her Aramaic.'

'That's sad,' Blok agreed, 'but I'm sure she will pull through.'

'But will I?' said Papa, casting an eye over his son. 'You look all right. A little thinner. You vanished for a long time. Couldn't you have brought us a million or two from the treasures of the goldeneh medineh?'

'It's not lying about in the streets, Papa,' said Blok, 'waiting for a man with a shovel. It's always just around the corner, just past the next disaster.'

'Home is best,' said Papa, 'not because it's any good. In fact it's a load of crap. But at least it's your crap, not another's.'

Blok said nothing, but gazed out of the taxi window at the landscape of slush and grey brightness that flip-flopped past the windscreen wipers. He could see Papa was in a bad way. Half an hour had passed since they'd met and Papa had made not one

crack about stamps. Was he losing the neurotic
boyishness which alone kept him from despair?
Papa said: 'Yes, things have been bad here ...
you've heard about Lod Airport, Munich ... They
want to kill us all, to leave not one soul alive.' A
skull-capped co-passenger with sad eyes nodded
sagely: 'We are too few in this country. What we
need is the Atomic Bomb.'

I am truly home, Blok reflected, as the taxi
climbed, swishing softly, into the Jerusalem hills.

In two years, Jerusalem had changed little. Yes, the
government had put up a number of ugly apartment
blocks for Jews only, so the Arabs of the City might
know quite clearly who was boss around town. But
the old whore had bared her toothless gums so often
at the folie de grandeur of her conquerors that she
could afford to wait. Ashes to ashes. This too shall
be ploughed under, salt strewn on ruins, another
thousand-year Reich bite the dust. Its brash newspaper headlines studied, perhaps, by bemused
scholars of the future:

DAYAN: WE ARE AT THE THRESHOLD OF THE
CLIMACTIC PERIOD OF THE RETURN TO ZION!

GENERAL TAL: IN 1973 THE DANGER OF A
GENERAL ARAB WAR AGAINST ISRAEL HAS
DIMINISHED

SABOTAGE CELL REVEALED IN SH'CHEM:
MANY ARRESTS

ANOTHER RESERVE SOLDIER SENTENCED FOR
'CONSCIENTIOUS OBJECTION'

A WAR HERO SMUGGLED FROM EGYPT KEPT
HIS OATH: FOR FIFTEEN YEARS HE SWEPT
STREETS IN BNEI BRAK

A WOMAN WHOSE THREE HUSBANDS DIED

CATEGORIZED AS 'LETHAL'. THE RABBINATE
FORBIDS HER A FOURTH MARRIAGE

CHIEF RABBI YOSEF: THE COMING OF THE
MESSIAH IS CERTAIN BUT NOT IMMINENT

Ah, so. And he retraced old walks, rediscovering his Jerusalem: the view panoramique from the Mount of Olives. The lost hill of his childhood with its abandoned house and *Sturmer* bunker, buried under a new housing estate, the scene of his wait for the rare Halperin bird, now a cat's cradle of washing lines. (He avoided unchanged Cordovero Street where Patrolman Abutbul might still be waiting for a second Blok indiscretion.) Across the City, to Nietzsche's Harav Salant Street, the shutters firmly drawn and bolted over the madman's windows. Down, into the Old City, under fast-scudding grey clouds. February approaching March, spring shimmering round the corner ... Passing under the arch of the Damascus Gate, past the money changer and the Arabic magazine stand, garish covers depicting Umm Kulcum, Marlon Brando, Yasir Arafat and Christiaan Barnard holding a pulsating heart. Into the crowd. A pitta vendor almost crushed his foot with a cart armed with iron wheels. Revenge of the conquered, orthopaedic terror. Corner shops leered at him, offering ikons, boiled sweets, halva, portraits of the deposed King Constantine of Greece. Escaping into the quiet of Muristan, strange carpets with designs of dogs playing billiards or cheating each other at poker. Two Armenian priests ambling down the paving, happily chomping cashew nuts. A peek, dare one? into the Swedish Tea Shoppe, business as normal, but no Farouk. The new waiter, a tall black man in US Marine combat jacket, serving beers to a group of sullen foreign youths, probably waiting for the local pusher. The niche in the far corner empty, the fat man completely absent. Romance, where art thou?

Quotidian vibes. And the ancestral home, at Yehezkel Hacohen Street, greeting the return of the prodigal son: Gaga the Bloodhound bringing a bouquet of flowers which Papa later threw in the trashcan. 'Another plot,' he mumbled, 'to try and kill us with carbon dioxide.' Aunt Pashtida phoning from Kfar Pippin, her shrill blessings vibrating the walls. Then Elchanan Adir, Papa's only surviving blood relative, turned up in person to pay his respects. A gaunt, ramrod-backed man with short, cropped white hair and sad sunken eyes, he had fought, in his day, with the Red Army and the Irgun Zvai Leumi. He and Papa always clashed over Holocaust Remembrance, which Papa tended to shun, although all his family, except Elchanan, had perished in the Nazi camps. 'I just take the money and run,' he would say, bringing Elchanan's blood to the boil. Elchanan refused to take even a single pfennig from hands red with Jewish blood. This debate somehow turned into a futile discussion about Insurance and the Holocaust. Elchanan was now a partner in a Swiss firm called Reassurance Universelle. He had checked with his Calvinist colleagues, who agreed one could not insure against genocide, which they classified together with Acts of God. Papa mischievously said he didn't see why God should be saddled with the vileness of Man, nor, if He chose to challenge the matter, say in the International Court of the Hague, He might not have a watertight case. Mama, stomping off to her room, given her migraine cue.

No sooner had Elchanan been shuffled off to the State Archives, to search for a long-lost relation who might have survived the Red Hell of Stalin, than the doorbell rang to announce Brigadier N. (ret.), Mama's relative, ex-co-editor of *BABASIS*.

He now ran a publishing company translating government propaganda into obscure tongues, such as Pushtu, Swahili, Albanian, Tamil and seven Nigerian dialects. In the Biafran War Israeli pilots had leafleted the combatants with oodles of such material, three tons of which had been eaten, it was reported, by starving Ibo children. He bent Blok's ear unsuccessfully, trying to persuade him his future lay along these lines. Or why not rejoin *BABASIS* as a civilian, a job of true national import. But Blok said, No, I am opposed to present policies of the State and the Occupation of Arab Lands. N. shook his head sadly and withdrew prematurely, prompting Papa to say to Blok: 'My son, if those subversive sentiments can clear the house so quickly, I advise you to pursue them further.' But Blok said: 'Well, Papa, politics aren't really my line . . .'

But in the Jaffa Road one day he met Fat Avi, who took him to the Ta'amon Cafe, legendary abode of left and right extremism occupying separate tables. Fat Avi, who was actually now rather lean and hungry, had become politicized since the Six Days' War and had joined the 'Israeli New Left' – 'SIAH'. The Levant, it appeared, had caught up with the vigour of the late Sixties in Europe. The war had ushered in a period of prosperity. Chauvinists dreamed dreams of Empire. Building contractors made millions constructing the fortifications along the Suez Canal, the invincible Bar-Lev Line. But moralists, breastfed on 'Jewish Justice', had terrible pangs of conscience. Students, 'bohemians', intellectual youth, heard echoes of Paris, London, Vietnam. (Some had even heard of the burning Bourse, though none, of course, knew the shattering truth of it.) Bob Dylan had told them the times were a-changing. John Lennon said, Give peace a chance. A working-class hero is something to be.

315

Hi-fidelity, slowly wafting across the Mediterranean Sea.

So there they sat, Trot and Commie, Social-Democrat and Anarcho-what have you. Some had been there, squabbling within four square metres, since the 1956 War. The veterans, around whom acolytes clustered, moths round receding angsts. Adam, the Dorian Gray of Jerusalem, who had not aged in twenty years. Dzhigan, who was the only known surviving member of the Uzbekistan Bundist Party. Zlik, who had erased Proust, line by line, with a succession of chinagraph pencils. 'If Marcel could write it, I can erase it,' he said. He also made totally opaque lampshades, and teacups with the handles inside. Burko, who had met Stalin in the Kremlin toilet, and Old Jabra, the first Arab Trotskyite.

The talk turned to a current issue: the shooting down by the air force two days before of a Libyan airliner with a hundred and seven passengers which had strayed over the Sinai desert. The army had feared it was a terrorist kamikaze headed for an Israeli city. Several points of view were aired: one regular said it was sheer lust for murder on the part of the air force pilots. Another said he had it on good authority that the Chief of Staff was drunk at the time and incapable of a rational decision. Burko said the plane had flown over a secret base where weapons were stockpiled that could, in time of crisis, be deployed to wipe out the Enemy's population centres. A little grey-haired man who sat drinking a Russian tea and obviously had no idea of the den of iniquity he had entered, protested, crying: 'According to you it's Nazis we have running the country!' 'You got it, daddy!' said Wild Buber, of the faction which had split with the Fourth International over the interpretation of Trotsky's *Message to the Byelorussian Working Class* (1925). Gurgling incoherently, the old man bared his arm, flourishing his death-camp tattoo. Dzhigan, standing, pulled up his sleeve and showed the angry stranger his own. 'Snap!' cried Wild Buber. 'It's a photo finish, comrades!' The man, spluttering, paid and exited, mumbling about police action.

Too much, the whirlwinds of raw emotion. Blok hurriedly leaves the bearpit. Resuming his walks, criss-crossing the City, site of his internal exile. Unable here to hold little dialogues with Karl Marx in the sky – out of so many faces, thicketed with beards, the Marxian eyes peek from under fur streimels . . . Has he become like Mama, blanking out his frustrations with the aid of spiritual migraines? Unable to respond, unable to act, even upon his own beliefs? Reported to sick bay; the disease – Indifference, Abstention, Solipsism. 'I think, therefore I am,' that, too, may be illusion, leading to absolute zero. The danger of vanishing, like the worm oroubouros, into the arsehole of one's own doubts. 'God thinks, therefore I am?' Do us a favour, brothers. In a world of such pestilence and destruction, a broken crutch to bear down on? And Free Will, that loaded lottery, God watching Man flounder in ignorance . . . if there were such a deity, ought one not to oppose Him? Maybe that would be worth a commitment: Diabolism, Blok? conjuring demons, praying backwards, dancing naked in moonlight, daubed in woad, in the Hammersmith Cemetery? All things, mon Blok, in the fullness of time, are reduced to the absurd. Whether one reads the Book of Daniel with one's mother, or runs about in the dead of night with a pot of red paint, scrawling 'MENE MENE TEKEL UPHARSIN' on the walls of the sinning City . . . A blast of cold air sweeps orange peel, soggy newspapers, squashed cigarette packs to clamp round his trouser legs. Head down, hands deep in his pockets, he proceeds down Ben Yehuda Street, leaning against the swirl, battling, aimlessly, perhaps merely by instinct, towards a future he cannot fathom.

But there are cycles yet to follow! Millwheels yet to tread! Buzzing rotors, busy castors, gyroscopes and windmills. Kismet decrees further turns of the screw, nothing will avail, ya dzalameh! On an early spring day when the poppies were blooming and the gardens dotted with Jerusalem cats frozen in transcendental meditation, he took a walk down one of the cypress-lined streets of his childhood and met Hava, Nili's ex-flatmate, wheeling an immense pram. She had married Elkayam, Klander's strong man, and herein was the fruit of their union. 'How's life?' murmured Blok to the large thingie in there buried in woollen blankets, but the phenomenon merely drooled.

Some enlightenments are unavoidable. 'Have you seen Nili around?' he asked, with polite nonchalance. A mere side issue. 'How is she making out with the Unknown Soldier?'

With equal sang froid, she dropped her bomb on him, its fins boring it into his skull: 'Oh, Nili and Eisav are divorced now. I thought you already knew.'

One thinks one has safely sealed a chapter. Suddenly the can of beans is reopened.

'Really?' he said. 'What a shame.'

'You should phone her,' said Hava, 'she's still at the apartment. Eisav moved out to barracks. He was cited for bravery,' she pointlessly added, 'for killing four Fatah single-handed in a clash in the Jordan Valley.'

Don't give me too much incentive, he thought, leaving her to wheel on her burden. Walking on against the waves of the sudden typhoon, salt lashing in his wounds.

318

But he phoned her. 'Avram!' she cried, at the first moan of his voice. 'Where the fuck have you been? Where the fuck are you? Put your tootsies on and come right over!'

Fresh water, dashing the salt away. He put his tootsies on and came right over. He found her dressed in a fluffy blue dressing gown, demolishing a bag of mixed nuts.

'I'm on night shift,' she said, 'but I can't sleep in the day. I am not, despite what you may think, an owl.'

'I never thought you were,' he said.

Out of the ashes. He let his eyes feast on her. Nili-Honey, the constant, unchanged. Plus, minus a husband, what the hell, still the elemental force. It was as if he had gone out of her door only yesterday, or just five minutes ago, to get the afternoon paper, instead of two years before, to chase after a different life. Was it not Sigmund Freud who said: in the unconscious time does not exist? Stronger than Death is Life, et cetera? A therapy, despite all, for Blok?

'Are you still working at Klander?' he asked, making conversation. 'How's everybody down there?' It was another confrontation he had managed to avoid for the past forty days.

'Business as usual,' she said, 'some are up. Some are down. Nietzsche is back, regressing. Catatonic fits, I'm afraid. I think he thinks he is travelling back in time. You know Nietzsche, he plays things close to his chest. Davidov, of course, is back again. Sometimes I envy them, you know, despite their fears and troubles. The petty problems that trip us up are so much buki-sriki to a man who thinks he's the Messiah's brother or a woman who sees everyone without heads. But don't dodge the issue, now that you're here. Tell me what the fuck you've been up to. I want the full story, Avram, not the censored-schools-board version.'

He found himself telling her the whole shtik, more or less, although he did not really want to. Vicky Happenstance and the South African chicken run and Yissachar and his chase of Klotskashes, though he left out the *Hassidic Bike Boys* and the full extent of fear and loathing and roach scuttling in the dead of the night. But the dreams, the longings, the false hopes came cascading out of him without warning like a suddenly flushed drain.

As he zigzagged back and forth along the lines of his narrative, recapitulating the search for Alfredo and Zunz in the garbage cans of mugging alley, she began to giggle infectiously, and soon they were both out on the bed, drumming their feet on the covers and hooting like deranged owls. Eventually they surfaced, snorting like steamers after a boiler explosion. She got up and leaned on a chair. 'Breakfast,' she said, although it was three in the afternoon. 'One egg, two, or three?'

He sat in the kitchen, watching her crack the eggs into the pan, marvelling at his sudden catharsis. 'Nili, Nili,' he said, sighing ethnically, 'I pour out my soul to you and all you can do is laugh at me.'

'Laugh and the world laughs with you,' she said, 'cry and they stone you to death.' She began to cut bread, wielding the knife firmly. 'What about you?' he asked. 'Eisav and all that jazz? I thought you were spliced for life.'

'A person can only take so much,' she said. 'Let him live his life. I can't participate endlessly in his Götterdämmerung fantasies. We quarrelled every day. He was always babbling about Death. One row over the placing of the ashtrays and plumpf, off he went, threatening to die on the border. And it was no fun and games at Klander either, I can tell you. Flusser was ill, crap-head Veltsch trying to impose his own version of *Ivan Denisovich*. Order, discipline and obedience. Sieg heil. All it meant was more tension, relapses, crises, don't ask. Eisav had a solution for all this: the pitter-patter of tiny feet.'

'So?' said Blok. 'I thought you were all for children?'

'In principle,' she said, opening a can of pickled cucumbers, 'but not then, not in that era. Not with Klander vibrations giving me visions of a kid who might turn out loopy . . . anyway, it wasn't the time to throw a rope into the future. So we fought some more. From volcanoes we passed on into the Ice Age. Then one day he left, at the crack of dawn, with kitbag. And still, as Galileo said, she revolves . . .'

They sat down opposite each other across the kitchen table, tucking in to their late brunch. After their burst of mutual information they were silent, humming in unison Homeland ditties while they washed up the dishes. They then adjourned to the bedroom, where she kicked off her slippers. 'Now I'm properly drowsy,' she said. 'It's a good sign. It means seeing you is good for me. Who would have ever believed it? Stick around, honeybunch, make yourself at home while I catch a short nap.'

She discarded her dressing gown, giving him a flash of her magnificence as she manoeuvred herself between the bedclothes. He sat in a wicker chair, watching her, catlike, settling. She turned over, showing her sleek auburn hair. After about ten seconds she turned back to face him.

'Avram, why don't us two get married? We can have fifteen kiddiwinks if you want to. And if you don't want any, that would also suit me fine.'

'But Nilikins,' he protested, using Nietzsche's pet phrase inadvertently, 'I've only just got here! And anyway you don't really love me and though I'm crazy about you, I don't think I love you either.'

'Love!' she scoffed. 'It's an old wives' tale.' And

she turned over again, re-exhibiting the shock of her plumage.

He sat on, reading her well-thumbed copy of *Crime and Punishment,* as she shnorkeled away quietly.

Ten days later, he moved in with her. Following her divorce, which had been stamped and sealed, properly disapproved by the Rabbinate, she should have vacated the army-leased apartment, but Eisav insisted on moving out himself, just to show her how noble he was and what a stinker she had been to him. While in the diaspora Blok had blithely kept warm in Eisav's army winter socks, he was more than a little apprehensive about moving into the man's home and bed. What, he said, if the award-winning commando burst in on them one night, spitting them both, with an ear-shattering cry, on his bayonet. 'You don't know him,' Nili said, 'that would be out of character. His aggressions are neatly pigeon-holed.' 'You mean,' said Blok, 'he only kills Arabs.' 'Exactly,' she said, breezily. 'That,' said Blok, 'is the most reassuring thing I have heard so far this year.'

He moved in, though he still did not love her. And pretty soon they were quarrelling, and moved into separate rooms. In fact they saw eye to eye on almost nothing. He had not a smidge of patriotism left and she virtually blubbered if she so much as saw the picture of the national flag in a magazine. He accused her of 'that Polish sentimentality which has fucked up this country so much'. She said his nihilism could only lead to him eventually becoming her patient. Sexually, however, she still excited him and, for some reason, she kept up the pretence that he excited her . . . moaning and mewing in their intercourse, raking his shoulders with her finger-nails and promising, in goo-gooing baby talk, to be his slave and chattel for ever. Could Blok afford to pass up such delights, after two years of drought? No. And she? Perhaps she preferred the unexciting familiarity of Blok to ditto that of a dozen other hard cases – Moroccan footballers, famous eye surgeons, manic tattooed seamen . . . gevaldt, who can summon up the energy? They did have moments of calm: discussing Dostoyevsky and Freud, walking the hills, going to movies, which seemed to affect Nili as they had the first audiences of Lumière – so great her wonder and involvement with the celluloid illusion that she constantly pummelled him, pinched him, squeezed his arm to a pulp and poked him vigorously in the ribs. Sometimes even in the advertisements.

And every weekday, morning, afternoon or evening, depending on the shifts, she ventured off on the bus ride to Klander, there to continue her ministering to the lost, the despairing, the abandoned, the fallen, some – possibly – the malingerous . . . Paradjanov, now convinced the football tote moguls had robbed him of his rightful millions . . . Schechtella, combating hysterical blindness . . . Margarita Conforti, still nimbly escaping the Bulgarian Cheka who were cutting through the walls to get her . . . the Magpie, stealing the screws off all the air-conditioners . . . And the dangerous duo of Nietzsche and Davidov – Davidov, committed by his wife again, as ebullient as ever; Nietzsche, reasonably hale between his seizures. These occurred at irregular intervals, lasted between ten and fifty minutes and could possess him anywhere without warning: in the toilets, in the corridors, in the session rooms, in the garden. Waking from each trance he was exhausted and secretive, and would discuss his experience with no one, hinting only at past eras rediscovered and voyages no one could fathom. Neither Flusser nor

Veltsch could dent his reticence, and even Nili was shut out, though she said to him: 'All right, I'll believe you're crazy; we'll promote you to the National League.' But Davidov told her: 'You don't understand. The Philosopher's beyond your control now. He is soaring out there, like an eagle, far above us mere rabble. Our friend is embarked on important business on which the future of the world depends.'

But this air of normality on all fronts could not last. Turn, wheel of chance, cholera! Whatever Nietzsche's self-imposed stewardships, Nili's hopes for a non-Eisavian stability, Blok's tentative truce with the reality principle (he had even made a step towards Papa and Mama, applying half-heartedly for the university entrance exams – History and Psychology would you believe??! – no matter it would come to naught . . .), whatever Fat Avi's new commitment to the oppressed, and the Ta'amon Café dwellers' vision of Injustice being swept by rhetoric down the gutters of the Jaffa Road – all, all, in the present financial year at least, were doomed. For on 6th October, the Day of Atonement, the yearly apotheosis of the Jewish guilt complex, WAR, like the bubonic plague, broke out once again between Israel and the Arab states.

October 6, 1973 . . .

Topics . . .!\*\*?    Death . . .
      war –    mutilation . . .

        stupidity of governments,

  perfidiousness of States.

      The Meaning of 'patriotism' –/

Sanity/Insanity/Sanitation/sanatorium/crematorium/ . . .

    Holocaust In The Desert
      \*\*\*\*\*\*\*\*\*\*\*\*\*\*\*\*    (T.E. Lawrence in striped pyjamas,
     $$$$$$$£££££££££    buggered by paperback Nazi)???????\*!

(Rorschach Card No 3: next door neighbour
  blown to bits by phosphor grenade    POW!SHAZZAM!KAPLOOM!

(it is better to light one footcandle than to nurse the darkness . . .)

    Nixon on nuclear button: aw gee, let's try (deleted)
                      WOT?
                   NO HUMANITY?

    Escape into the occult
alchemicalastrologicalcabbalistic
cartomanticcaephalomanticcrystalo-
graphouseromanticgeomanticgimatric    Exclusion
notaricpyromanticscarpomantic    (deliberate?)

JUDASPIG!MESSENGER  SAMAEL!THE  SCAPEGOATSRETURN!(the
corpse of God?)

   Exculsion———(it's all in the mind)(run rabbit run rabbit run run run)

(a monograph:
'MASTURBATION &    (but after all, everyone means well . . .)
THE HOLOCAUST'    (elucidate)
by Dingam Zich)

       reason for living on: curiosity???(new york
          tramp. fear as a material commodity –
('WHY not    'gebstsumir swei kilo fun terror, bitte . . .')
BESTIALITY?'    (note:take yiddish lessons)
by Konrad Shumacher)    holocaust remembrance
          the world as a    as necrophilia
Freud uber alles:    holocaust with int-    (develop at length)
castration by the father    ervals for popcorn
(i.e. castration by God?    and fudge . . .    scrap ↑
basis of Nietzsche hang up?)

       stoptheworldiwanttogetoff(cliché)
on going bald as O)

    ?ARE WE SANE AND DOES IT MATTER?

---

XVI

LA MAISON DE DIEU

(The Tower Struck by Lightning)

Attempts to commence a chapter on the 'earth-quake' of the October War:

I.

'We will show the Jews whose boots will litter the desert dunes now!'

The words of Mahmud Abu-Ali, Commandant of the Northern (Kantara) Sector, as he gave his tank and infantry commanders their last-minute battle orders. For six months, the ~~pot~~ top brass had been engaged in secret ~~cacu~~ calculations concerning moonlight ~~sonata~~, canal currents et cetera, while the lower ranks consumed great numbers of porno-graphic novels supplied by Liam O'Habash about Israeli girl soldiers which primed them into an erotic frenzy. Now the great day had come, in which twenty-five years of Arab humiliation were about to be drowned in rivers of ~~Jewish Hebrew Israel~~ enemy blood ~~gore~~. At ~~precisely two p.m.~~ on

II

When he first heard the news of the surprise Yom Kippur attack, General Zetz went white as a sheet. Just two days before he had said categorically at GHQ: 'I believe the probability ~~if~~ of either ~~Egypt~~ Egyptian or Syrian, or co-ordinated attack is

327

extremely low. We all know about Arab sabre rattling. And even if some commandos get across the Canal, they'd be instantly blown to smithereens.' Others agreed. 'The Bar Lev Line,' said General (Retired) Bar Lev, 'is impregnable.' 'Three cheers for the Bar Lev Line!' called General Palanka, who thought they had all gone loopy.

*III.*
Noon, sixth October . . .

Blue Canal, conceived by de Lesseps . . . born in the graves of 50,000 Egyptian workers, opened by Empress Eugenie of France and Franz Josef of eugenius Austria in a mighty November beanfeast (Ah! the splendour of the Orient, bismillah!) . . . lost by the French, taken by the British, grabbed in '56, by Gamal Abd-el Nasser and closed by him, eleven years later, during the Six Days' War . . . several ships and tankers lay, suckled scuttled by Suez and Ismailia, a quiet and undisturbed home for small tropical fish and octopi gambolling between soggy bales of cotton and the charts of abandoned voyages . . .

*IV.*
After the glorious victory of June '67, the glossy victory albums, the chink of copper coins, the rustling of paper notes . . . Songs of confidence over the state radio – 'Nasser says he waits for Rabin . . .' 'O Sharm-a-Sheikh, we have returned to you once again . . .'

*V.*
Several months after it was all over, the following item appeared in one of the Hebrew newspapers:

'THERE IS NO INDEPENDENT JEWISH EXIST-
ENCE IN THE STATE – WITHOUT WAR,'
said the candidate for Prime Minister, Yitshak Rabin, yesterday at a memorial for the fallen . . .

the writer Y.M., who lost his son in the War, delivered a passionate obituary:

'We have been living in this land for decades, always on the brink of the end, for there is no house which has no dead in it,' he declared. 'However, our fallen were not led as sheep to the slaughter in the Nazi crematoria and were not hanged on the scaffolds of Arabia, because they fought for their existence. This is the first time, for hundreds of years, that this privilege, to fight for our existence, has been given to the Jewish people.'

(Yediot Aharonot 24.4.74)

... I can't possibly believe this, thought Blok, as he found himself once again belting down the Bir Lahfan road in the *BABASIS* magazine jeep. It is a nightmare from a bygone age. A time warp, caused by a shift of the earth's axis, by a profound rent in the universal, cosmic fabric.

But no. It was merely the stupidity of Man, in general, and of a small number of political leaders, in particular, that was propelling him west towards the war zone.

Once again, by the miracle of Reserves' Conscription, Sa'id T – the driver, flashing the undulled gold tooth of Yehoshua behind the wheel. A muddle characteristic of the whole business had sent them off alone in the jeep, but around Ashkelon they had collected two soldiers in civilian clothes who were joining their brigade at Bir Gafgafa. They had flown all the way from Miami Beach to defend the nation and were all agog for the action. However, the closer they approached the battle lines the less reassuring the lies of the Israel State Radio appeared and the clearer became the true dreadful state of affairs on the ground. They grew quieter and quieter and by Abu Agheila signs of doubt at exchanging pina coladas in Florida for posthumous glory in the sands of Sinai were etched in their fallen faces.

Circumstances had trapped Blok in a vice which left him no escape. Once the sirens had gone, one could not rush to Lod Airport and buy a ticket for the earliest flight to Honolulu. One's secret mobilization reserve code (inserted like a malign fortune cookie message behind the photograph in one's reserve card; Blok's was 'Fried Fish') was broadcast, over and over again. One need not await the fearful Call Up Form Eight to rally to die for one's country. One was summoned, in great gobs, in masses, in veritable multitudes . . . Had he not been living with Nili he might, despite it all, have stayed put, hiding out somewhere in Jerusalem (in the Judas Pig tunnel, perhaps?) till the hurricane had blown over and then emerged, pleading deafness, insanity, sudden paralysis, or a combination of all three. But there she was, beside him, phoning the hospitals and arranging her own conscription within two and a half minutes of the first horrid wah-wah, wah-wah, wah-wah of the genuine air-raid alert.

Remembering it from Tel Aviv of June, '67, but then there had been three weeks of warning . . . black-out time – tottering, as if blind, about streets of switched-off lamps, blanketed windows and car headlights dimmed by thick dollops of blue paint, an eery landscape of total pitch, in which little blue glow worms shuffled . . .)

World change. Just one week before Avi inveigled him into wandering down to the park by the arcade of Yemin Moshe, where flower children and peace freaks were gathering in response to a call from the Peace Ship. This was a pirate radio station anchored off territorial waters broadcasting the most up-to-date rock music in the entire Fertile Crescent. It was run by Abie Natan, an ex-pilot and restaurateur, who had twice flown solo missions to Egypt to talk peace with Arab leaders. Each time he was returned to sender, putt putting along over Sinai. Now he talked peace from the brine, interspersed with the Top Ten. The fans reported for duty, several hundred strong, colourfully dressed in the late September sun. Youths with long hair and beards, girls with roses in their hair, dogs, guitars, an oud or two. Tanned hope, yes. All we are saying, is give peace a chance. Where are they now, thought Blok, in their austere anonymous khaki, off to the front, clutching their weapons of death, some ploughed under already?

For Yom Kippur, the Atonement Day itself, he had made the traditional plans, setting up, by phone, the link of homes in walking distance where apostate food was available. For on the day the Jewish city grinds to a total halt, the place is dry as dust for twenty-four hours, unless one treks what might be quite a way in the sun, to the Arab sector, where business is as usual . . . (an odd consequence of conquest that Jerusalem, the most devout town in Israel, was the only place in the country where one could escape the drought).

Nili, of course, was fasting. 'A,' she said, 'it's good for the waistline. B, it's good for the soul. And C, if you don't like living in a Jewish State then get the fuck out of here, shmendrick!' 'Why did I leave the Blok household,' Blok moaned, 'if I get the same twaddle here?' He went out, toiling a mile up the road to destination A (breakfast, elevenses), returning, just after one o'clock, with some cookies, to try and subvert her will. But she was busy on the phone. Army friends of Eisav had called her discreetly, with a veiled warning of impending disaster. And at two minutes past two all doubts were dispelled, as the air-raid sirens blasted . . .

No, no escape for Blok. An hour later Papa

phoned him, saying *BABASIS* Magazine had called curtly, demanding his immediate presence. 'I said I might not be able to find you,' said Papa, 'I didn't give them your number.' 'You can give them my number,' Blok replied, knowing the trap was closed. Nevertheless, a peace message from Papa he did not fail to appreciate. Yes, even the reserve journalists were being drafted, all hacks called to the flag . . . Still, it took three days of panic, confusion, and bureaucratic entanglement before the time-warped Blok–Sa'id reunion was kitted out and sent on its way . . .

At Jebel Libni they all had a nasty turn. By the junction a battered open-backed army truck had drawn up by a fresh khaki van. Soldiers with beards and skullcaps were nervously milling about. They began rolling back the tarpaulin which covered the rear of the battered truck. Underneath it was a pile of bodies, slung, one on top of the other, like carcasses in a slaughterhouse dump. There must have been thirty or forty of them, and they were all in the distinctive fatigues of the Israel Defence Forces; one could see the צ-s, or the 'Property of Tsahal's, stamped on dust-caked, torn and blotched trousers. They were stiff, and legs ending in big brown paratroop boots, stuck out like semaphore poles. It was not possible to look at the faces once you had caught a glimpse of glazed eyeballs, glaring fishily out of the mound. The Burial Unit heaved them out of the truck to the van like blocks of mutton. At one point an arm fell off, which an officer picked up immediately. One of the religious soldiers sank down on the sand at the edge of the road and wept, while a colleague stood by holding him gently by his racked shoulders. The two volunteers with Blok, so recently watching the azure Caribbean through the haze of a mint julep, went into a mutual spasm. One just sat and shook, the other ran behind the jeep and vomited. Blok and Sa'id sat and looked forward, like two rabbits hypnotized by a cobra.

Finally the last corpse was stashed in the van and the back doors were secured. The weeping soldier and his companions squeezed into its cabin and on to an adjoining jeep. The truck, which had in fact broken down, remained at the roadside. Its two drivers hitched a crowded ride with the *BABASIS* jeep into the Jebel Libni base. They were clearly very tired, and did not say much. But they shook their heads a lot, and sighed, and one mumbled: 'Wallah, I can tell you, this is not my idea of a war . . .'

THIS IS NOT HAPPENING TO ME. THIS IS NOT HAPPENING TO ME. THIS IS NOT HAPPENING TO ME. THIS IS NOT HAPPENING TO ME. THIS IS NOT HAPPENING TO ME. THIS IS NOT HAPPENING TO ME. THIS IS NOT HAPPENING TO ME. THIS IS NOT HAPPENING TO ME. THIS IS NOT HAPPENING TO ME. THIS IS NOT HAPPENING TO ME. THIS IS NOT HAPPENING TO ME. THIS IS NOT HAPPENING TO ME. THIS IS NOT HAPPENING TO ME. THIS IS NOT HAPPENING TO ME. THIS IS NOT HAPPENING TO ME. THIS IS NOT HAPPENING TO ME. THIS IS NOT HAPPENING TO ME. THIS IS NOT HAPPENING TO ME. THIS IS NOT HAPPENING TO ME. THIS IS NOT HAPPENING TO ME. THIS IS NOT HAPPENING TO ME. THIS IS NOT HAPPENING TO ME. THIS IS NOT HAPPENING TO ME. THIS IS NOT HAPPENING TO ME.

(An author's problem: how to write adequately about war . . . by what means can the full impact of

333

having your life on a hair's breadth of someone else's decision be brought home to those sitting at home in their armchairs, nibbling a garibaldi . . . Does one describe in great detail the multiple maimings and mutilations of bodies torn to pieces and mangled by shrapnel and high explosive, burned, like an overdone meatloaf, by napalm and phosphorous bombs; the screams of the wounded and crippled: people blinded, emasculated, paralysed, people with both legs cut off like Ronald Reagan in *King's Row* . . . descriptions that distance the sensitive and merely titillate the sadistic shadow person that lives within us all (wanna see some filthy pictures, mistah? porn of war?) . . . Or, alternatively, does one try to involve one's audience in the fears and hopes of particular characters and then, like God in His more Hitlerian aspect, kill 'em off, to the reader's momentary chagrin . . .? Perhaps the solution might be the insertion of small, flat but lethal mines, somewhere within the pages of one's book, with sufficient power to blow the reader's hands off, or the eyes out of his (or her) head. The random inclusion of such devices in, say, one volume out of a thousand might bring into play the element of Russian roulette: the spice of gambling with one's life and limbs at the shelf of one's local bookstore might lead to a sharp rise in sales, even bestsellerdom; thus the horrors of war would be brought home to the reader with unparalleled authenticity, and the financial interests of the writer advanced at the same time. Caveat emptor . . .)

Meanwhile, around the world, millions of people were watching the whole thing on television. Commentators, dressed in snazzy suits, explained everything in air-conditioned studios. Some had maps, others, topographical models of the battlefield upon which they moved little Dinky-toy tanks with long pointers, like frustrated generals. What they were most worried about was whether the Arab states were about to embargo their oil supplies, as they had been threatening to do for some time. This would make life in the West less cushy for those whose life had been cushy, and even less cushy, for those whose lives weren't cushy in the first place. A great deal of dislocation and potential unrest for powers that cherished their status quo, and thus could not remain idle for long. President Nixon of the United States was having a hard time anyway due to lies he was telling about the Watergate burglary, and there was no guarantee that, if pressed too far, he would not blow the world up in a fit of pique. People all over the globe did not know why *they* should have so much trouble from two ornery peoples, the Arabs and the Jews, who wanted to kill each other. But then most people were hopelessly confused anyway, by the floods, avalanches of media data that was sweeping them off their feet. 'Aiuto! Au secours! Hilfe!!' they cried as they bobbed on the waves. Meanwhile, back in the Sinai desert . . .

As they continued west towards Bir el-Hamma, Sa'id, sensing their need to escape, somehow, from the horrors of the moment, told them the story of the Rubber Woman From Beersheba, but he had not come to the end of the tale when an impassable obstacle loomed on the road ahead. As they slowed to a crawl they saw it was the tail end of a massive convoy of reinforcements – tanks, armoured cars, half-tracks, water carriers, mobile artillery, bound for the beleaguered front. It stretched ahead as far as the eye could see, an endless metallic centipede stalled in a wasteland of dunes.

They mingled with the soldiers, swapping rumours and secrets about the fate of their predecessors. It appeared that the counter-attack of 9th

October had failed. The 190th Armoured Brigade had been virtually wiped out, and the commanding officer taken prisoner. The Egyptians were using new portable Soviet missiles with which one man could destroy a tank. The Bar Lev Line was a write-off. The reservists of 6th October, secure in their leaders' complacency, had been roasted alive in their air-conditioned bunkers by Egyptian commando flame-throwers. Some outposts were still holding out but, the wags commented gravely, their plots had already been booked at the Mount Herzl Military Cemetery. 'It's Auschwitz in the desert,' said one soldier. 'We might as well have stayed in Poland.' 'Not to speak of Morocco,' said another, logically, 'where we didn't even have our own Nazis.'

The news was all bad. There was not even a smidgin of comfort. Information about the battle with the Syrian army on the Golan Heights was unbelievably sketchy. Judging by the facts in the south, one could not trust Israel Radio's assurances that we were well on our way to fulfilling Chief-of-Staff Dado's pledge to 'break all the enemy's bones'. For all anyone knew, the Syrians had advanced into Galilee up to the outskirts of Afula. People's home towns might be ashes and rubble by now, their babies' heads spattered against the walls, their womenfolk ravaged and taken off to Saudi Arabian harems. There was a strong rumour that Dayan himself had broken down in tears and been shuffled off to the funny farm. Official communiqués were as reliable as Egyptian ones had been during the Six Days' War. (The general comment was: 'They learned from us how to fight, we learned from them how to lie.') A North African soldier reflected that living under Arab occupation might end the encroachment of ashkenazi European food into the national cuisine. Another said that given the shitty situation in life, Death might not be as bad as the propaganda would have one believe. An officer said: 'Death will be nothing to the ass-fucking you'll get from me if you don't get that carrier moving . . .'

The two civilian soldiers left the *BABASIS* jeep, taking a ride with a command car which left the main road and took a short cut, bucking up and over the sand dunes, into the great Sinai emptiness. (Far, far from the Holiday Inn . . .) Sa'id offered to follow with the jeep but Blok ordered him, on pain of castration, to stay put. 'I'm not going to be one of those lost skeletons,' he said, 'photographed by American tourists on their Instamatics, the last time, to show their Bnai Brith chapter back home.' He might have added, 'Not to speak of those who took loose bones and skulls, even, to adorn a mantelpiece in Fresno . . .' Eventually, though, they both tired of waiting for the column to move, sitting duck that it was for Egyptian sneak air attacks, and began edging past it, on the margins of the ragged asphalt, little by frustrating little.

Night fell before they had passed Bir Salim. Between convoys, they thundered on an empty road. An almost full moon bathed the flat desert plain with a pallid and ghostly glow. Sand, everlasting, drifted across the road. The idea that a few hours further on, men were locked in the bloody chaos of combat was strictly a hallucination. Or were the moon, the ghost dunes, the rattling jeep and its occupants, merely chimeras, to be blown away with the grains, the everlasting grains . . .? Sa'id told no more stories of alien events ten million years ago which made up their civilian past. His eyes fixed on the ruler-straight road, he seemed in a trance, the bucking jeep carrying them on by its own volition, a modern Nosferatu's carriage. Blok, fatigued and shattered, could not have cared less.

337

Life and Death were mere feathers, held in the
hand of who-knows-what dice-playing deity, first
cause, nature, or his own disembodied psyche . . .


**And in the hiatus:**
**Sa'id's Story: The Rubber Woman From Beersheba**
'Yes, friends and comrades, after years of chasing
the boumboulinas up and down valleys, fucking on
the beach and in the back seat of the Wyllis, I was
finally caught by the forces of destiny in the matri-
monial net.' He passed round in the jeep a colour
snapshot of a young lady with black sparkling eyes
holding an infant with a puzzled expression. 'It was
a conspiracy, cooked up by her mother and mine.
Before I knew what was happening I was under the
canopy with the Rabbi mumbling under his beard. It
was a situation even Yehoshua couldn't get out of.
Well, we have to earn our bread, don't we, and
become a useful part of society . . . A friend took me
into partnership, in the travelling housepainter
racket. Yes, Yehoshua seemed set to be a husband
and provider, and a contributor, as you can see, to
the next generation . . .

'But as you know, folks, the flesh is weak, and the
call of ''manousch'' – fuck – doesn't die . . . A travelling housepainter's much like a driver, no? You
call, the housewife lets you in, brews some coffee,
invites you to sit down. You chat about this and
that. One thing leads to another . . .

'One time, we had a rush job in Petah Tikva that
took us up to Independence Day Eve. Shabtai, that's
my partner, had friends in the town, so we arranged
to stay over. I phoned Hedva, that's my wife, and
she said OK, as long as you don't fool around. I
promised. Not a chance, I said, I'll use it only for
pissing . . .

'Well, we finished the job right on sunset, washed

up and went out on the town, looking for the festivities. I don't know if you know Petah Tikva, but it is the last hell hole on the face of the planet. Life is so boring people sit in the cafés and the spiders spin webs around them. The town centre is "Desperation Square" – the only way to describe it is like a TV programme I saw once called "The Dance of Death". The hevreh move around and around, hoping for the messiah, or, please God, a little manousch to turn up. One hour is usually enough to make you think seriously about suicide. But this was Independence Eve: the Entertainment Stages were set up in the square and hundreds were gathering, wistfully hoping that this night would be different from all other nights . . .

'When Shabtai and I got there, a terrible band was playing, trying to wake up the populace. Here and there people were thinking of forming circles, wondering whether to limber up a little. It was a bit like the funeral of a secretary of the local council whose guts everybody hated . . . Then the acts began: you know, the man doing the hit parade on the xylophone, the comedy skit by two old fogies just about to cash in their chips, the usual routine. But suddenly, just as we were about to fall asleep on our feet, the compère announced, 'Ladies and gentlemen! What you have all been waiting for! From the wilderness of the Negev – Shulamit, the Rubber Woman From Beersheba!'

'Ah! She was really something! Even Yehoshua was impressed. About five foot tall, in form-fitting tights, and the form – ya eini! a midsummer night's dream! A little, tubby, bald man accompanied her with a concertina while she went through her act: doing the splits, a bridge with her back narrower than the Jordan in August, touching her toes with her nose from behind, arched backwards in a ball, rolling about the platform . . . man, you wouldn't

339

believe it! Rubber, comrades? She was pure caout-
chouc, I can tell you!

'Every male in the square was smit. What do you
expect, after years on the millwheel of Desperation
Square, every one of them could have taken out a
Certificate of Miserableness. It was not surprising
that they dribbled and drooled at the mouth.
Myself, I thought, get yourself together – Yehoshua
has a job tonight!

'But how to do it, among a thousand open-jawed
wolves, with old baldie, probably her Pa, keeping
her on the leash of his eyes? Trust Yehoshua.
Shabtai and me, we did the old Charlie Chaplin
routine. You know that movie, when Charlie's kid
breaks the windows, and he comes along with the
glass? Right? Back of the stage we found their van,
couldn't mistake it, it had posters for the Rubber
Woman plastered all over its flanks. And while
everybody's gooey-eyed following the spotlights, we
flick the bonnet open and yank out the spark plugs.
Twenty minutes later, when they finish their act,
the girl and old baldie, huffing and puffing, wander
up to find who else but Yehoshua, flashing his gold
tooth, beaming at the starry sky . . .

'Well, it all goes as expected: mother's cunt,
Shula, the car doesn't start! Open the bonnet,
honey. 'Scuse me, says Yehoshua, having a spot of
bother? Allow me, I was a mechanic for years . . .
Oh, it's nothing, spark plugs disconnected, we can
have that fixed in a jiffy. Bloody kids, no pity even
on Independence Day, what sort of country is this?
See, everything's back to normal . . . Going far
tonight, sir? Beersheba? Why, that's amazing,
that's where I live! Missed the last bus, thought I'd
be stuck here all night . . . A lift? Why, that's very
kind of you, madam. No, I don't have to collect anything, a man travels light these days . . .

'Right, we're in the vehicle, first stage of mission

340

accomplished. Second stage, too, works out . . . I sit in the back with their props, she's in front by baldie's side as he drives, keeping his eyes, as the good book says, on the road. The only snag is, we find out as we chat he's her husband, not her old dadda. That's a problem, but on the other hand – think of the implications! I mean, look at her, pretty as a picture, slim, maybe not much over seventeen; and him: gross, middle-aged, hairless, a walking piece of absolute nothing. As the journey progresses southwards, things begin to really look up. In the dark of the long night road, glances fly between her and me . . . her hand touches mine, 'accidentally', as she drapes it over the back of her seat. Man, the air was becoming so electric between us you could have run the car battery off it!'

Sa'id paused for a moment, closing his eyes at the wheel. 'Hoch ya baba . . .' he sighed, as the wide open spaces of Sinai sped by. His listeners, alarmed, thumped his head and shoulders, and Blok shouted: 'Wake up, shmendrik! I don't want to die, in the midst of the War of Apocalypse, for the Rubber Woman of Beersheba!'

He reopened his eyes. 'Some way before Kiryat Gat,' he resumed the story, 'the van began to judder and shake, and soon it came to a complete stop. "Out of gas!" said baldie, punching the dashboard. "Mother's cunt, that petrol marker's stuck again!"

' "We passed an army gas station a kilo and a half back," says I, "they'd serve us tonight, someone could fetch a jerrycan."

'We looked at each other, realizing the dawning problem. I knew if I wanted to safeguard the future I would have to take risks in the present, like the Israel Defence Forces. "I'll go," I said, "the sooner it's done the better."

' "No," he said, really surprising me then, "I'll do

341

it. We pass here often and I know the fellow in charge. If it's me he'll drive me back with the petrol.''

'Off he went. I could hardly believe my luck! Someone up there must have said: ''We've been giving Yehoshua plenty of shit lately, let's do him a real favour.'' Ya habibi!

'OK – a kilo and a half on foot, then the same distance back, driving, that didn't leave us, if you get my drift, that much time . . . But I can tell you – that girl was no chicken! In no time our hands were touching again and in no time and a half she is clambering over the front seat and settling with me in the back. And then those tights are off and hopplah! we're doing what comes naturally . . .

'Don't worry, I am keeping my eyes on the road . . . oh, but zelda . . . the positions . . .! Arabian nights! the *Kama Sutra*'s not in it! Not even in Swedish movies . . . ya weili! The legs, where you expected the arms to be! The mouth, coming at you from ambush . . . Ah, ina'al rabac! Yes, friends, Yehoshua was truly lost in paradise, nibbling from the tree of life . . . but just as we were coming round to take a second bite, as it were, the serpent, as the good book says, broke in on us. Blam! A torch is shone in my face and, hribaitak, there's baldie, shouting, spitting, and, dear God, waving a fucking pistol!

' ''Get out of there!'' he howls, breathing heavily like he's going to have a seizure on the spot. I don't have a choice. I climb out, minus trousers and underpants, my small one, I can tell you, in a particularly vulnerable state.

' ''It's all right,'' I tried to soothe the maniac, ''it's all a misunderstanding. Everything can be explained.''

' ''In your arse!'' he cries, ''I set a trap for you and you fucking well fell right in it! You're not the

342

first time, I can tell you. You can join the fucking queue! In Jerusalem, a kashrut inspector, in Dimona a Georgian, in Ashkelon a policeman, in Ramat Gan a stinking actor and in Haifa, God help us, an Arab!''

' ''It's not true!'' she shouts from inside the van, ''it's not true about the Arab!''

' ''It's going to end right here,'' he says wildly, ''a man can only take so much. I'm going to kill both of you and then put the last bullet into my own brain.''

' ''You can't do that,'' I said, sweating like a pig, ''they'll bury you outside the cemetery.''

' ''I don't care!'' he cried, ''they can burn me, if they like, like Eichmann!'' '

It was at this point that Sa'id had to stop, as the *BABASIS* jeep had come within view of the massive stalled convoy. So disorienting was the entire scene that followed that the two 'civilians', shellshocked even before the first intimations of cannonfire, left without hearing the ending. (And for all we know they died, out there, with the predicament still unresolved.) It was not until several days later that Blok remembered to question Sa'id about the dénouement of his Boccaccian tale, and that was when they were both under severe bombardment, in a second defence line bunker:

'What happened in your story?' he yelled, shouting above the din of the shelling. 'How did you escape from the maddened husband who wanted to be burned like Eichmann?'

'It was all a bluff!' Sa'id shouted back, his nose screwed into the gravel floor. 'He just left me standing bare-assed in the small hours, on the outskirts of Kiryat Malachi! The ''empty'' gas tank was a ruse, he just jumped in the van and took off. I was picked up eventually by a large friendly moshavnik, who loaned me a pair of his own pants in which I looked like the Sheikh Fadi Abu-Hatem reviewing the Tunis camel races.'

'And the girl?' bellowed Blok, as the thwack of the shells literally threw them around like ninepins, 'What happened to the girl?'

'I caught their act again, a year later, in the Municipal Hall of Safad . . . There she was, on the platform, tying herself in knots, with old baldie, down at the side, twiddling his concertina . . .'

'What did you learn from it?' shrieked Blok, anticipating imminent death. 'What's the metaphysical pay off?'

'Never monkey,' Sa'id screamed back, 'with Rubber Women From Beersheba!!'

Life's coda, as the guns of the Egyptian Army hammered on their battened hatches . . .?

. . . At 9.45 on that Yom Kippur morning Zetz alerted Eisav by telephone to stand by in his quarters and be ready at any moment for a Special Assignment. Eisav retreated to the neatly made bed in the annexe behind his office, packed his toothbrush, canteen and personal bandage in his emergency belt and sat waiting calmly, reading, as he often did in moments of crisis, the poems of Heinrich Heine. The book fell open, naturally, at the ode *Clarissa*, which expressed so well his feelings towards Nili:

'Every hour, everywhere,
You may wander, I'll be there,
And the greater wrongs you do,
Greater grows my bond to you.'

At twelve noon came an order from Zetz to report at the old Schnellerbunker, defunct since its use by the High Command in the 1948 War. Tucking Heine in his pouch he made his way there, descending in a battered old lift to what appeared to be a rag-and-bone warehouse. To his surprise, Zetz was waiting for him there alone, and led him on a winding path through mounds of old tarpaulins, cast-off boots, broken crates and chairs, a blackboard with a faded chalkmark of 'WOT? NO ARABS?', bits of truck and car chassis, to an old iron door with rusty locks looking as unused as Jonah. But it slid smoothly open to the touch of a remote-control device fastened at Zetz's trouser belt. 'After you, 007,' Zetz said, with uncharacteristic levity, as they stepped into a shining aluminium elevator which, at a further touch of the device, shut, descended, plummeted into depths that stirred Eisav's DNA (or could it have been, mayhap, perchance, merely the revenge of breakfast?).

Zetz spoke, as they fell, in electric silence: 'The war is about to begin. Certain processes have failed us by our human error, and we may be facing our ultimate challenge. But we still have our trump cards, in our concealed pockets ... You, my boy, are going to be one of them. I have been grooming you for a long time, for this, your true ordination. When you stepped into this lift with me your whole life changed, and will never be the same again. You will soon be a confidant of the Inner Circle, with all the privileges and obligations that carries. Though the privileges, mostly, are just the opportunity to take even greater risks for the Cause.'

'I would not want it any other way,' said Eisav.

'I knew you would not,' said Zetz. 'Soon you will be privy to the Highest State Secrets. But even these revelations, for all we know, are merely the tip of the iceberg. Who knows what lies below the threshold of even our most esoteric and lethal constructions? What truths might flame in the heart of the creative-destructive furnace of Belshazzar, of Meshach, Shadrach and Abednego? Will we be consumed? Or will it be us, rather, who will, in our consummate, desperate wrath, in one great hammer blow of vengeance, swallow up the world?'

Zetz's eyes glowed, with what might have been a strange inner power, or perhaps just the reflection of the lift's neon lights. His question did not demand an answer, and Eisav did not give one. But a verse of Heine, unbidden, clicked into his mind:

'Mortal, do not mock the devil,
Soon the road of life is run,
And perdition's no mere story
That an idle brain has spun.'

The lift slowed, and stopped. The door slid open. They stepped out into a grey tubular aura, the low electronic hum of . . .

When the war broke out, Liam O'Habash was having a slow coffee at Abu-Saleh's, a hole in the wall in El-Wad Street, just round the corner from the Chapel of Our Lady of the Spasm. He had just delivered to the proprietor, a Greek named Petros Papadopoulos, a consignment of specialist bondage magazines ordered by a senior official in the Ministry of Religion. This transaction was a sideline for Abu-Saleh, whose main business was supplying the Minister of Defence with ersatz ancient coins, fake Dead Sea Scrolls and counterfeit Hasmonean potsherds, which the Minister then sold for high prices in Suckerland USA. (Some say teams of gnarled gnomish experts toiled, deep beneath the floors of the shop, to hammer the numismatic goods into shape and laboriously inscribe old papyrii . . . they had not seen the light of day since 1906; wanted by the Turks for bestiality with Ottoman Army Property, they had been kept in total ignorance of the turnover of regimes . . .) They were in the midst of their third après-kahva sigh over the vicissitudes of the universe when the sirens from the New Town sounded. 'What's this?' exclaimed Liam. 'Isn't this the Jews' Yom Kippur?' 'That's not a test,' said Abu-Saleh, 'it's an attack by the Syrians in the Golan and the Egyptians in Sinai. My wife heard it was due from the fishmonger down the road this morning.'

'Do you think it's the end of them?' asked Liam, meaning the Israeli occupiers, as he craned his neck at the wailing.

'Quite possibly,' said Abu-Saleh, 'but what's the difference? Whoever comes, business is business.'

'How right you are,' said Liam.

'More kahva?' offered his host.

They sipped it calmly as, several hundred kilometres away, the first soldiers began to die in the agony of modern technology.

'Now that you don't mention it,' Abu-Saleh said, raising a finger, 'I have a message for you, to be read at the outbreak of hostilities. Yusuf the Midget brought it earlier in the day. It is private and confidential. Naturally I tried to decode it but it is beyond my limited powers.'

'Oh dear,' said Liam, because there was only one person who might send him an uncrackable message. He perused the little crumpled sardine-can label, inscribed with Sumerian hieroglyphs. His face became set in a dead-pan mask, the scuttling mice of his eyes frozen, as if zapped in a vivisectionist's surgery by a massive dose of curare.

'Bad news?' Abu-Saleh, hovering solicitously with the coffee pot.

'Oh, nothing,' said Liam, 'just an overcautious customer . . .' He tucked the soggy scrap in his pocket, absently. 'God forbid, you know, if the wife finds *Sadie's Dungeon Frolics* tucked in their dirty underwear . . . ha ha ha.' 'Heh heh heh,' Abu-Saleh concurred. 'I must go now,' said Liam vaguely, 'les affaires, toujours les affaires.' He wandered off, but not before the crafty Greek had picked the note from his pocket with a pair of lazytongs, a trick he had learned from a Marx Brothers film. Later that day he passed it to his CIA contact, who cabled it to Langley, Virginia. En route the Mossad copied it and knew instantly it was from Beirut KGB desk chief Zorza. But the content of the message remained totally baffling in its sinister simplicity, to wit:

'Blizzards at Bcharre! Glaciers on el Knisse! How can you do this to me? The Nachtnebel Annexe, toute suite, spalpeen! Get on with it, tchorta mati! Or shore an' it'll be your poor old mama crying her eyes out over the deep blue briny!'

Liam knew, when he missed the note later, that the vile Abu-Saleh had gypped him. But, following his instructions, he proceeded south, to Klander, retracing the Mad Monk's journey, while all about him the streets emptied rapidly, the Arabs sliding indoors in anticipation of trouble and the Jews hurrying into their underground shelters, waiting, like Chicken Little, for the very sky to fall in.

Davidov, with impeccable timing, chose this moment of crisis to reveal the identities of the current members of the Elders of Zion, by means of a handwritten bulletin posted on the asylum notice board. They were:

Yankel Tillimzoyger, of Brooklyn Heights.
Zev 'Meshuggener' Weitz, of Greensboro, South Carolina.
Eliezer Conforti (no relation), of 40 Drukman St, Bnei Brak.
Nathan 'Jacque' Hadayah, of Rehovoth, né of Baghdad.

Zunz, the Ba'al Shem of Vienna.

Azaniah, of Azaniah Carpets & Tapestries, Weizman St, Petah Tikva.

Reb Zvi Kook Zweischaften (the Monk), of Hevrat Shas St, Jerusalem.

Berl Eibeschutz, descendant of the eighteenth-century prodigy Jonathan of that name.

Heimie Goldschlaeger Son of Mottel.

Irving Klotskashes, of Hollywood, California.

Blok, arriving in the asylum in the wake of traumas yet to be related, challenged Davidov on the last named.

'Bullshit,' he commented, 'it's only from me you ever heard of the man.'

'Proof positive,' said Davidov, 'of the whole schmeerkez. You are Destiny's messenger boy. I've known for years you are the nexus of great events. It is written all over your kisser. The third eye in the forehead, the buddha-lump on the head. No, don't bother to deny it.'

Blok wished to explain he had received the lump in the service of the Nation in Sinai. But Davidov was already off down the corridor, throwing open doors and tossing in sweeties, eau de colognes and slim panatellas. 'Banzai! Banzai! Banzai!' he cried, vanishing into the distance.

And Nietzsche said: 'What care we certified loonies if the straight world chooses mutual suicide? The self-destruction of the underprivileged, the nebesches in our midst, is something I wrote about in great depth ninety-five years ago. It is the mark of the Overman that he can stand aloof, trimming his fingernails, while nihilism reaps its harvest. Give me a lyre, anybody, and I'll fiddle over the flames. Who knows, this might even be the spark of the final showdown, the great nuclear scourging that will burn off the brushwood and leave the ground clean for a new, less crowded beginning. The Overman, sensing this, perfects his means of escape. Not to be caught like a rat in a trap, or like a cinema audience rushing en masse in a fire to a tiny loo window . . .'

So saying he went immediately into a trance, and transported himself to the Fleulen Hotel in Switzerland, in 1872, to resume a conversation he had had there, in his previous life, with Giuseppe Mazzini, exiled head of the abortive Italian Republic of 1849. For Nietzsche's catatonic fugues, though they might have begun involuntarily, had become increasingly self-induced. They were the culmination, he had decided, of two lifetimes of rumination on the enigmas of time, life and 'reality', manifest in the ninety-two notebooks of code which made up the Revaluation, carefully crafted over the last fifteen years both at Klander and Harav Salant Street. The breakthrough had occurred about fourteen months previously, mid-August. Thursday, two-thirty. Klander siesta time – all about him patients reading the newspapers, playing sheshbesh or just shnorkeling in their chairs. Outside it was parched, parched, parched, and the trees were as limp as dry dish rags. Inside the air-conditioning emitted a constant, unbearable hum. Nietzsche was staring at himself in the reading room mirror, wondering whether, in trimming his moustache earlier, he had not given the left side just a smidge of a snoop too much. His mind had, uniquely that instant, rid itself of any profounder thoughts. And suddenly – SHAZZAM! – he was gone. The entire asylum vanished around him, swept away in the twink of an eye. He was standing with his slippered feet sinking in crunchy snow, on a mountain outcrop overlooking a landscape of breathtaking beauty and haunting familiarity. As far as the eye could see, tall majestic peaks, carrying snow-capped pines, climbed into a steel-blue sky. By his feet rushed a spring of limpid water, leaping between dark rocks. It was bitterly cold, but his heart was aflame. Suddenly he knew precisely where he was. There could be no doubt, it was genetic certainty, inscribed on each cell in gold. North-west, two kilometres, from his old haunt of Sils Maria in the Swiss Alps. And the date, too, was abundantly clear, 15th June, 1887. He did not even need to trek the distance down to the house, as he did on a later occasion, once the 'travelling' was under control, to see the man, his primo ego, Nietzsche Number One, hunched in pain over the table with the porcelain pitcher and the piles of bottles, an apothecary's dream, quack's potions to drive out the stomach cramps, the spasms, the migraines, scribbling, scribbling with no reward in sight, his latest opus: *Genealogy of Morals* ... ('Under what conditions did man construct the value judgments *good* and *evil*? Have they thus far benefited or retarded mankind?') Ach! Ecce Homo! ('The will to truth itself needs to be justified.') In the coming months he spied on himself often, tempted more than once to rap on the windowpane and climb in and embrace the wretch, crying: 'Right on, brother! Keep it up! There's a pay off! What you prophesied will be, your name used to endow chairs at universities and to scare children and pregnant women!' But he would always withdraw in time and return to the frustration of Klander. (The journey itself was akin to the infinite stretching of a mental rubber band; learning to control the point at which one was jerked, flung as by a catapult, back to one's starting line . . .)

But this time he was pulled back from a very satisfying harangue in the lobby of the Fleulen Hotel by a sound which penetrated even the matrix of alternate time and space, the piercing, terrible screams of a shell-shocked soldier wheeled in only the other day: 'Medic! Medic! Stretcher-bearer! Oh God! It burns! It burns!' Not a background conducive to cerebral precision or reflection on the winds of time. God, spare me, he raged, these petty battle-fields, these distracting local squabbles. Elkayam put him to bed and gave him his Largactil pills, which he secreted in his cheeks and spat in the toilet as soon as the male nurse left. He lay back on his bed, still raging inwardly at the oafishness of mankind. I used to see virtue, he remembered, in wars, but now they are such a fucking bore . . .

Meanwhile, back on the battlefield: 16th October, while the forces of General Arik Sharon were sneaking across the Canal north of the Great Bitter Lake (by what was known as the 'Chinese farm'), Blok and Sa'id were pinned down by Egyptian artillery ten kilometres east of Suez. Another counter-attack had bitten the dust and a large number of Israeli soldiers were stuck on a makeshift Bar Lev line not far from the Mitleh Pass. If the enemy could capture the Pass all Sinai would open up to them and they could roll on, presumably, towards the heartland of Israel. The measly piece of dry beach that the two armies were deadlocked on was therefore of vital importance, although the only people who could bear to linger there in normal times were the bedouins who lived off the kif trade, and even they were just passers-by, blowing their minds on their merchandise and leaving behind nothing but exhausted roaches mingled with camels' turds.

In the bunker, with Blok and Sa'id, were about two dozen soldiers from an Ordnance Corps rearguard who had somehow found themselves at the front. They were bone weary and shell-shattered and loudly bemoaning their fate. The war had lasted a full ten days now and there appeared little chance of anyone here attending the victory parade. If indeed it did not end up being cancelled, one wag suggested, due to a lack of wheelchairs.

In a rare lull, a discussion developed over the best way to cash in one's chips. Each person took it in turn to soliloquize upon their preference. One man said: 'A direct hit, in the torso, by a 105 shell. You don't feel a thing, and since you're blown to atoms, your family's spared the expense of a funeral.' Another man countered him with morose logic: 'The army buries you free anyway, so where's the saving in that? The best way,' he said, 'is to have your head sheared off by shrapnel, since your brain is separated from your heart you can't possibly feel any pain.' A recruit with an eccentrically religious bent said: 'The best thing would be for my penis to be shot off, because then I could devote my life to meditation and study, without the fear of temptation.' They all leaped on him furiously. 'What d'you mean by that? How could you say that? How did they let someone like you in the army?' So incensed were they, they nearly tore him limb from limb on the spot. 'The best way is to be killed in your sleep,' muttered a fourth man. 'You just wake up and presto! you're no longer there.' 'How d'you wake up if you're dead?' everyone asked him. They had entered a frenzy of pedantry. 'Poison gas,' one fool said. 'LSD,' said another. 'You laugh your way into the grave.' And yet another said: 'Nuclear Holocaust, then you won't be alone in the Next World.' An atheist scoffed, 'Listen, brother,' he said, 'when you're dead you're dead, that's the end of the whole shtik.' The devout protested. 'Why don't you go back to Russia?' they demanded, though the man was from Uruguay. 'I'll go anywhere,' he responded reasonably, 'if you postpone this bloody bordello.'

Blok was taking all this down on his Nagra tape recorder. With grim relish he was committing every blasphemy, every obscenity, to a magnetic posterity. Sa'id contributed a number of condoms as containers in case the tapes had to be left on the spot due to death or similar misfortune. ('Is that what you brought to the war, daddy?' Blok asked him. 'A man should never be caught short,' Sa'id answered, with supreme sang froid.) He had also recorded a selection of rigorous, harsh, unremitting commentaries, for a dream issue of *BABASIS*. They went something like this:

'Dawn, over the Suez Front. The flies settle once again for their breakfast on the eyes of a dead infantryman. Desert ants carry off to their lair the intestines of a youth from Afula. Over a spared transistor radio come the sweet grand-motherly tones of Golda Meir, telling us every-thing is under control. The hevreh spit in the sand at the sound of her hated drivel. The old bat, whose corrupt and greedy policies led to this dis-aster, will not escape the wrath of the soldiers who, if they survive, can think of nothing more satisfying than fitting their hands round the rump of her scraggy neck . . .'

Or:

'Why are we killing each other, the soldiers, in their waking delirium, ask. What have I got against some poor Ahmed who's been torn from the bosom of his sheep somewhere in Upper Egypt and marched down to this hell hole and told to shoot down the Jews? I know he would much rather be fucking his girlfriend or wife, just as I would, or play shesh-besh on the banks of the river until the cows come home. I mean, if we have to shoot somebody, just to satisfy the bloodlust They tell us is the Lot of Mankind, why

don't we shoot the people who got us into this
mess? If we have to commit brutalities, and
obscene atrocities, why don't we find a way to do
it which would, somehow, benefit our fellow
oppressed? For example: roasting the war criminal Dayan on a spit, till his stomach splits open
and his other eye pops out, squelching into the
fire? Why don't we put a grenade up the arse of
Sadat and scatter his foul carcase, not ours, over
the desert sands? Why don't we napalm the
Presidential Palace in Cairo, or the Knesset in
Jerusalem, instead of Stronghold Number Forty-
five? Why can't the politicians, in their immaculate suits and ties, their shampoo, manicure,
pedicure, become blazing, shrieking torches,
rather than the men of Ordnance Company
Eighty? Why shouldn't They get a phosphorous
bomb in the eyes for the sake of the Security
Effort? There is no doubt, Company Eighty deter-
mine, that a parachute drop of parliamentarians
into the battle zone would do no end of good for
morale.'

And so on.
After a time, as is their wont, the tapes finally ran
out. There were no more reels to record on and Blok
was loath to wipe previous matetrial to make way
for new revelations. Outside, the shells were still
keeping up their fearful barrage. Some said the
bombardment seemed to be slackening, but the
sceptics said No, we are merely all going slowly but
steadily deaf. Once this latter idea gained credence
it became, inevitably, imbued with a certain mad
attraction. One could see, from people's faces, that
they were giving serious thought to the proposition
of poking out their own eardrums in order to end
the incessant clamour. A bizarre telepathy spread:
if anyone produced so much as a toothpick he would

355

be instantly pounced upon, wrestled to the ground and divested of the dread weapon of potential self-mutilation. A man who merely wanted to sew his socks up during a brief lull was beaten almost black and blue when he took out his needle. It was a madhouse without a doubt. The elements of mutual protection and bare aggression had become completely confused. And the whole thing might go on for days. The food might run out, and people might eye each other with sinister new desires . . .

But a miracle happened. Suddenly it was over. What had occurred was this: the forces of Arik Sharon, having bridged the Canal above the Great Bitter Lake, had begun pouring across in strength. The Egyptians, waking up to their oversight in downgrading the Canal crossing, hastily diverted their forces to deal with this unforeseen body blow. The tanks and artillery, earmarked to blow Blok and his colleagues apart so as to proceed to the Mitleh, were now rushing north to kill some other poor bastards. Thus Sharon, whom Blok and many others regarded as the most dangerous right-wing fanatic in the entire Fertile Crescent, had actually saved Blok's life, at the expense of others' . . . Blok and Co. emerged, brains mushed and ears ringing, into a moonscape of smoking craters. But at the rim of the bunker he and Sa'id stopped short, stunned by a further miracle: the *BABASIS* jeep, from which they had scrambled pell mell into the hole thirty-six hours before, was standing there serene and untouched except for a few shrapnel scratches. A centurion tank, thrown by a blast on its side, had shielded the jeep in its shadow throughout the entire bombardment.

'If it'd been us out there,' Blok scoffed, kicking the vehicle, 'and not this dumb asshole machine, you can be sure we'd have bought it proper.'

They loaded the tapes, secure in their condoms,

on to the jeep's back seat. Sa'id brought from the bunker the dusty but undamaged Nagra. 'Where should I put this?' he innocently inquired.

'Give me that thing!' cried Blok, wresting it from him savagely. It had 'Property of *BABASIS* Magazine' taped over its battery hatch. 'I'll show 'em *BABASIS* magazine!' he said. 'Fuck 'em all! I'm not going to carry this deadweight with no tapes to record on.' He turned to the soldiers, who were hesitantly taking the air, 'Hey, hevreh – has anyone got a grenade?'

He was handed one and, with a surge of confidence such as he had never felt before in his life, taped it round the recorder with the last of the sellotape spool. Then, while Sa'id wagged his head, scratched his chin and mumbled incoherently behind him, he strode forward, ten, twenty, thirty metres out into the open desert and, facing northeast – Tel Avivwards – he set the thing down in a crater and, pulling the pin out, ran hell-in-his-pants back to cover.

'Grenade!!' he bellowed, throwing himself on his face. Sa'id, and everyone else in earshot, dived, hugging the ground, thinking the whole shtik was resuming.

CRASH-BANG!!!!****!!! – One Nagra tape recorder, State Property, left this sad vale of tears. Cogs, screwlets and levers, cams, pinwheels and sockets, leads, wires, transistors, all assembled with loving care in Switzerland, land of the Alp and yodel, the slalom and Toblerone, sprayed, twisted, burnt, splintered all over the Sinai dunes.

Blok, in mock ceremony, made the sign of the cross over the smoking remains. 'Pax vobiscum,' he intoned, dredging, from his addled memory, the words of an old school howler.

(But after all, doesn't everyone mean well, in their

357

own funny way? Take Napoleon, for example: he wanted to unite Europe. Or take Hitler: he wanted to unite the Germans. He wanted them to walk proud, and the hang with anyone else. Was he so different from you and me, in some of our darkest hours? Genghis Khan, Tamerlane, Attila – they just couldn't stop moving, sweeping stick-in-the-muds out of the way. Yes, they meant well. And Jesus, the most well meaning of all, they say, but look at the consequences. Look at Buddha, and at the Samurai. Mohammed – and the sweeping sickle . . . Karl Marx, for example, wanted to free the whole world. Bakunin, Lenin, Trotsky-Bronstein (steeped in the blood of Kronstadt). Stalin-Djugashvili was more modest, he wanted Socialism in One Country. No doubt he meant well. As did the good parliamentarians of Europe, circa 1914, who sent their young men to die in the trenches. And ditto those of today . . . and the sellers of arms, to blacks, browns and yellows, to balance white national budgets. And Nobel, of gunpowder and the Peace Prize? Einstein, with $e = mc^2$ . . .? Or the social utopians, Owenists, Fourierists, et al. . . . Zionists, who wanted their people to walk proud and ended up grinding another people's face in the dust for the sake of the highest ideals . . .? They were no different from anyone else. They just wanted to do their own version of Good, but ain't we the ones who get done, meine kinder?)

At the moment of blowing up the *BABASIS* Nagra between the Mitleh and Port Tewfiq, Blok declared his own private, unilateral cease-fire. He took to the road with Sa'id, proclaiming absolute neutrality. They became the Phantom Scribblers' Command Car, and were able to vanish for five days between the gaps in the jurisdiction of different brigades and battalions. Technically, was this desertion in time of war, carrying, according to GHQ law, a possible sentence of life imprisonment? Certainly there were still serious opportunities for sudden and heroic death in the Land of Goshen, which was what army mapmakers were already calling the cross-Canal territories conquered by Arik Sharon's venture. Journalists and photographers were streaming over with the troops, all agog to set foot on Africa. But Blok said: 'I do not wish to go there. Our forefathers kicked up such a shry about being let out I don't see what's the rush to get back.' 'Let my people go home, to Safad,' said Sa'id, being in complete agreement.

'The two of us,' pronounced Blok, 'shall be the reverse of Don Quixote and his Sancho Panza. Don Quiblok and Sa'adiah, an unbeatable combination! We shall do everything the other way round: when we see giants and ogres we shall say – pschtt! these are just innocent windmills, and get the hell out of harm's way. When we see damsels in distress, apparently threatened by Brigands, we shall know they are merely the secretaries of Brigade Thirty-five pursued by lecherous Field Security Officers. When we appear to see prisoners, led in shackles to the gallows, we shall know it is nought but the Nation, en route for the front, clutching their call-up papers. Wherever and whenever we see an opportunity to do something noble, courageous and chivalrous, we shall turn it down and, taking to our heels, nip to the nearest shelter. Where the sound of battle be, there shall we not. We know with absolute certainty now that nobility, magnanimity and heroism are trash, that there is no princely castle in the mist at the end of the road, and that our Dulcinea Del Toboso, Golda Meir, is truly a whore and a witch.'

'Anything you say,' said Sa'id, 'as long as we can get at the munchies.'

They had left the main routes, of which there were only a handful, and were following classified concealed army trails marked on a map they had found in the bunker. They had traded it from an Ordnance Corps Sergeant for their last bar of Lieber chocolate. Sa'id had a compass, which they thought was in order, though of course they could not be sure: heading, apparently, into the depths of the peninsula in the direction of Mount Sinai, they might crest a dune and find themselves on the Gulf, facing the Egyptian Fourth Army. This reverse Don Quixote gambit was not without its metaphysical pitfalls . . .

The sky was blue, the ground was red, ochre and grey, wrinkled and scuffed by the pitiless hammer of Time. It might well have been here, along these labyrinthine secret IDF paths, that the Tribes of Israel under Moses got hopelessly lost and wandered for forty years. No wonder they turned out such a cantankerous lot, and their God such a crusty old bugger. They had both mislaid their steel helmets and army berets. Sa'id was wearing a triangular blue and white tembel hat with 'Club Méditerranée' upon it, and Blok a knotted handkerchief, faded and tattered, a left-over Bar Mitzvah present.

As they drove, Blok repeated derivatives and anagrams of the name Don Quixote, first under his breath, then loudly, rolling them against the bare hills:

'DONKEY SHOT!' he cried, conjuring a nine type headline. 'Darn key's short . . . dankish sort . . . dun key sought . . . dun quiche sought . . . dank ee, sot . . . dunk Ishot!' et cetera. Or: 'Ned Toxique! Quotid Oxen! Quex Doonit! Quoted Onix! Untide Xooq! Oot Denquix!' And so on. The hills did not answer, but they approached, perhaps to hear what the fuss was about. Pretty soon the shadows were lengthening, the landscape reddening, and an appalling loneliness could no longer be bellowed away. It was nearly teatime and they had not eaten since elevenses, when they had met a 105 battery whose commanding officer, shell-shocked gaga, had been carted off to the rear. ('Are we on the right way to Suez?' they asked, after opening their K-rations. 'No,' Blok told them. 'Very good,' they said, continuing upon their course.) They had not even reached, at this stage, the Jebel Musa range. 'Damn it!' said Blok, breaking off his literary musings. 'The map says there's an Ordnance supply camp, right punkt at the foot of that mesa.'

'Maybe they pulled up and went west,' said Sa'id, ever ready with the mallet of logic.

'Why on earth should they do that?' Blok fumed. 'Don't they know there's a war on there?'

They drove on, low in spirits, food and, naturally enough, petrol. But eventually they were succoured by roving bedouin, who, appearing like Apache Indians on jagged crags above, offered them a kip for the night. They ate freshly baked pittas with goats'-butter, Sa'id regaling the nomads with the tale of the Rubber Woman From Beersheba, and, in lieu of pudding, they smoked a brand of hashish which almost took the top of Blok's head off. ('A head without kif, strike it off with a knife,' say the bedou.) They also discussed the movies of Joan Crawford, on which their sheikh was a devout authority. ('Have you seen *A Woman's Face*?' asked the old fox. 'I could hardly keep from wetting my seat.') In the night Blok imagined he could hear, in the distance, the sounds of the unceasing battle. But it was merely the pounding of the cells in his totally roasted brains. In the morning they thanked their hosts profusely and continued south, upon their Quiblokian destiny.

*IV*

'One must forgive one's enemies,
but only after they have been hanged.'
                                   – Heinrich Heine

**Zarathustra Rides Again (Nietzsche's narrative):**
I warned them, but of course they wouldn't listen.
I knew they wouldn't. Since when does the mass,
bred in resentment, ever lift up its head, except to
proclaim to a fakeful heaven the allegiance of their
eternal slavery? And don't speak to me of the 'leaders', the 'élites', the 'thinkers', the 'intelligentsia'
. . . Don't make me laugh, I have a throat infection.
No. There was never anything there but a desert,
with a few old baobabs perhaps, pretending to be
great oaks. Rubbish, the whole lot.
   The biggest laugh was the way they always tried
to blame *me* for the whole damn schmeer! Down
with Nietzsche! they cried. A bas, Zarathustra!
Down with the Overman! Long live the Common
Man! They did not realize until it was too late that it
was the Common Man made king, chairman, chancellor, duce, who was to bring about their
destruction. Today it is a very common man, a small
number of abnormally common men, and even
women, who can, with the flick of a switch, bring

the whole shtik to an end. But although I await the atomic Armageddon with a measure of wry amusement, I cannot view the approaching prospect with total equanimity, as my work, despite the great leaps forward of the last decade, is still far from complete. Not only are the shell-shocked soldiers still disturbing my concentration, throwing themselves down flights of stairs, hiding under beds or sticking their heads in the toilet and shrieking at all hours of the day or night, but there are also signs of a rebellion from within: my tenure of this second body creeping to an end. How weak, this piddling shell of flaking flesh! The bowels, as usual, sounding the first warnings: your lease is up, schmendrick, they burble, impelling me in unseemly panic towards the WC. And no guarantee at all that another body, convenient as this, is waiting in the wings. In fact if that fart Schopenhauer and his Hindu mystics have it right I might end up trapped in a cockroach, chaffing my way through life munching ticks and other garbage while my notes rot or are stolen by the Magpie from their hiding places . . . Down there, Arthur boy! Stop snapping at my heels . . .

Perhaps the man-made Armageddon then would be a boon . . . Salvation from the fate of Nietzsche Number One, the trailblazer in Sils Maria, driving his brain ruthlessly while the body decayed around him: the liver, the pancreas, the intestines downing tools . . . Not to speak of the eyes, cones and stems signing off one by one . . . After a while I stopped peeping in on him on my travels, I could not bear that agony *again*, cholera! once was quite enough: the slow descent into inclarity, paralysis, the mind contracting into the dark womb of chaos whence it came, the true pity of the eternal recurrence which I had only *begun* to fathom . . .! Then death (24th August, 1900, pedants!), going down without a squeak, with the grandeur of a plucked kohlrabi . . .

And the passing of forty-five years, mon dieu!! Nada! nada! nada!

But I remember the Awakening –

The exact moment: 1st May, 1945. Farkash-Fenschechter, in whose carcase I found myself, typing some dreadful Hungarian mish-mash on behalf of the Jewish Agency. Regulations for hygiene, would you believe it, for refugees in the displaced camps. Boil your water, herds of cattle, fill in lice forms in triplicate . . . the words 'instant amelioration', I don't know why, swam like whales before my eyes. An immense cacophony all about me, people shouting in a dozen languages. Babel, Babel, Babel. A man rushed into the room, yodelling about something he had just heard over the radio. (Radio? what was that, I thought.) Leaping towards me he clapped me on the shoulder. 'He's dead,' he cried, tears almost running down his cheek, 'the bastard's dead at last!'

'Who? Who?' I cried, my mind a ship on a storm-tossed sea.

'Hitler!' the man shouted joyously. 'Adolf Hitler, may his name be erased!'

'Who is Adolf Hitler?' I asked, innocently.

Very soon I grasped the need for dissimulation. I confided in one man, Aaron Himmeltraub, *Palestine Post* reporter and a patron of sorts of Farkash-Fenschechter from his arrival in the country back, if I remember rightly, in 1939 . . . It was my first and last mistake. Not that he betrayed me, but he was a complete crank. He embraced the Hindu-Schopenhauerian fallacy that transmigration of 'souls' and reincarnation are universally valid, whereas I knew then, as I know now, that they apply only to the few. He wanted me to appear on public platforms, like Bridie Murphy, proclaiming the great discovery. Luckily for me – for I was weak and groggy in those first few weeks and hungry for reassurance and, putrid thought, pity! – no one showed half a groat of interest. With the Second Great War at an end, the demon Hitler (how could I have failed to recognize this avatar of my fears?) charred to a crisp in Berlin, who wanted to hear of the rebirth of Nietzsche, tarred as one was, in those days, with the brush of Nazi co-option . . . Luckily, for if they'd believed me I might have been burnt at the stake there and then, or carried off in chains to Nuremberg, to stand trial as an instigator . . . I can just hear the brave prosecutors – Russian Socialist, English Liberal, utilitarian Yankee: 'Here he stands, ladies and gentlemen, the man who set fire to the world!' Always hang the bearer of bad news. Ah, what commedia dell'arte!

Yes, Himmeltraub failed to convince anyone that Nietzsche had come back to life. So he went on to other fads: Judas Pigs, lost mythologies, Biblical kings and prophets who scribbled banalities on his ceiling fresh for the next day's editorial . . . And I simply scaled down the Hungarian hygiene instructions, faded out to the flat in Salant Street and began the long haul back, then beyond, towards the Revaluation . . .

Why Palestine? Why Farkash-Fenschechter? I often pondered these conundrums. There was the physical resemblance, no doubt; the body, waiting for the mind to drop in from wherever it was constrained to wander. I must confess I do not have the final answer to this, yet. Perhaps it is this: Jewish Palestine, more than anything, represents that rebellion of the resentful, of the victims, of the 'oppressed', that Nietzsche Number One identified as the mark of nihilism . . . the dead bones of the gas chamber rise and demand their day: they too shall have guns, aircraft, the means to a nuclear genocide. The eternal recurrence, I have found, functions often in the parameters of a certain grisly irony. The world may be chaos, but there is an impish joy of a sort in the terrible pranks of eternity. Is it malicious? . . . In Palestine, the Jews have finally abandoned their selves to ape the Christians, whose own wretched hypocritical strictures were vulgarly aping the original Judaic Creed. A cycle appears to have closed here. The Zionists apply their own final solution: cease to be different! Be like everyone else! A sure recipe for destruction. Nietzsche One veered between the Germans, whom he loathed, and the Jews, whom he admired for their stubborn arrogance and pride, the virtues which made the gentiles hate them. Now the Germans, having embraced nihilism and pushed their own self-destruct button, have faded away, becoming nothing but a fat greasy audience for Scandinavian erotica, while the Jews in Palestine have become Germanic: consider Meir, Sharon, Dayan, the junkers of reactive militarism. And to think these atavistic tribalists spring from the same soil as Heinrich Heine, say, or Baruch de Spinoza! The prosecution rests. Furthermore, that they may yet, due to global politics, be the wretched spark that sets off Götterdämmerung . . . Ah! to say the least, that has some fearful piquancy: in at the beginning, in at the end, one might say, of the whole damn schmeer . . .

What is the goal? The revaluation of all morality and values. What are the means? The uncovering of the true driving forces. What are these forces? The eternal recurrence. What is their consequence? The end of all history. What is history? The search for a 'meaning'. What is the 'meaning'? A fata morgana (God). What follows God's death? The deluge of freedom. What is freedom? The greatest fear of the gullible. What follows this fear? The creation of new Gods. What are these new Gods? Fata morgana. What are their consequences? The cycle continues. How can it be broken? By the Overman's triumph. What is his triumph? The eternal recurrence abolished. (This, Nietzsche Number One failed to recognize.) What follows thereafter? The Overman's freedom. What is his freedom? The power of creation. What shall he create?

Ah! There's the enigma!

No mass rejoicing, this time round. No populace, deliriously happy, throwing sweeties at returning heroes. No songs. One or two Victory Albums, unsold on kiosk shelves. But glory still, yes, glory, among the leader writers. Himmeltraub:

'LET THE TYRANTS OF ARABIA AND THEIR BOLSHEVIK MASTERS TAKE HEED AT THE FAILURE OF THIS, THEIR FOURTH BRUTAL ATTEMPT TO LIQUIDATE THE STATE OF THE JEWS. NEVER SHALL WE FORGET OUR GALLANT HEROES WHO WITH THEIR VERY BODIES HALTED THE STEAMROLLER OF DESTRUCTION. AS THAT GREAT WARRIOR, ALUF (GENERAL) ASA'EL MAHATZ – OUR VERY OWN ZETZ – DECLARED: "THEY FOUGHT LIKE A LIONESS DEFENDING HER CUBS . . . THEY ADVANCED AS A COLUMN OF FIRE UNTIL THEY WERE BURNT AWAY . . ."'

But the soldiers said of their dead friends: 'He finally stopped smoking.' Or: 'He's gone to sniff the flowers from below.' Or of their maimed and crippled selves: 'I gave a hand to the security effort.' 'I took my cue from the yellow pages; I let my fingers walk before me.' 'Now at last I can learn the whole Torah on one leg.'

Nili returned, after the third and final cease-fire of Saturday, 27th October, to a numb, grief-stricken

Jerusalem, to an empty apartment, which was welcome, to a solitude that she craved. Though within it echoed the wraiths of its two former male inhabitants: Blok, disgraced in the wake of his Sinai hiatus, Eisav, on the list of the missing. Zetz himself had phoned her. (He did not believe in divorce and knew She, the Woman of Valour, still had her role to play . . .) He hinted darkly at a lengthy special mission somewhere whose outcome could not yet be clarified. You must not give up hope, he reiterated, we do not abandon our own. Is he a prisoner? she asked. But he could not confirm that, adding merely: Time will tell.

She roamed about the flat, gazing at the empty space on the shelf where the Heine collection had stood. She was trying to decide whether she missed either of them, the Patriot or the Shirker. Her mother appeared, taking charge, as mothers do, straightening, tidying, dusting. What could Nili say? 'I need absolutely to be totally, completely alone . . .' Could she tell her about those twenty-five days in the emergency wards? The repeat performance of '67, with the devil's jester's cap and bells . . . boys whose mamas only yesterday allowed them out after midnight, now turned into worse than pumpkins. Brothers with no arms to embrace with, fathers who would father no more. Husbands who would lie there the rest of their lives, of no more use than a cabbage. And the fear, that the next flayed face that will appear as the field bandages are unwound will be one that is all too familiar . . . But Marta Grunbaum did not need to be told all this, as she busied herself wiping these visions that she too knew well, off the tables, the shelves, the chairs, the cupboards, with the flick of a dampened schmutter.

'Stop it, mama,' Nili finally said, 'before I have to check in as an outpatient at my own fucking

371

workplace.' 'Fine, let it all out,' said Marta, 'scream, yell, break furniture, tear the whitewash off the wall. Don't just stand there. Kick something.' She indicated a blotched cream cabinet Eisav had got for a song and which she had always hated. What else could she say? Was this the time to talk past horrors. Janek Grunbaum, Granit, in the snows of Poland, starvation in the ruins of Poznan and the grey misery of reconstruction, the world, like a phoenix, rising from its own ashes only to prepare itself for a new even more brutal immolation? No, Instead she began cooking a strudel. They could not, in the end, avoid discussing the war, but they confined their talk to snips of gossip: so and so who got off with three chopped-off toes, so and so who got stuck on the besieged Hermon outpost and could only extricate himself by becoming a raving hero. Thus, over coffee and eats, atrocities were reduced to the manageable, personal disasters like traffic accidents striking the helpless at random. For in the end they were two battered cynics, trying desperately to conceal from each other the true terror of recurring cycles. But Marta finally broke the conspiracy and said: 'I have survived, my honey. You might have to be content with the same.'

And the days passed and the gloom in the streets deepened as people realized the full extent of the casualty list. More than two thousand three hundred dead, several thousand wounded, of whom who knows how many condemned to be living wrecks, exhibits at annual memorials . . . To add grisly irony, it was election time and the posters, extolling the virtues of two dozen political parties, were appearing, like potato blight, all over the city's billboards. The voting code letters, like cabbalistic graffiti: לע. גחל. כך. ו. יש. נס.זה. פ. ב. ג״ד a mosaic of false messiahs. Worst of all, the ruling Labour Party's code letters אמת – making up the word

372

'EMET' – 'TRUTH', a ton of salt rubbed in the wound . . . The nation's leaders, drivelling on television, using the bones of the dead to grind their political axes . . . the Religious Coalition, hypocritical swine, spewing out fire and brimstone: 'SURPRISE ATTACK AT THE HEIGHT OF A PICNIC! IF THE ARAB LEADERS HAD LAUNCHED THEIR ATTACK ON ROSH HASHANA (THE NEW YEAR) THEY WOULD HAVE FOUND A MILLION PEOPLE AT MASS PICNICS IN THE FORESTS OF GALILEE, AND WHO KNOWS WHAT THE PRICE IN HUMAN LIVES WOULD HAVE BEEN AS A DIRECT RESULT OF THE SECULAR CULTURE THE STATE HAS ADOPTED AND THE DESECRATING OF OUR HOLY SHABBAT, STRAYING FROM OUR ETERNAL VALUES – VOTE TORAH RELIGIOUS FRONT!' And the Nationalists, waiting in the wings to impose their own brave new world . . . Ah! cry the beloved country, vultures and wolves afflict thee, false prophets carve up the living flesh, self-cannibalism thrives . . .

She went north, to the kibbutz, taking the early morning train. It is an archaic, quaint form of transportation, winding slowly upon Ottoman gauge tracks past gorges and crags one did not know existed among the rolling Judaean hills. Past broken-down quarries, abandoned mine workings, forgotten railway sidings overgrown with weeds, waving wild corn and shoulder-high great blue thorns . . . one might expect bearded old men in Mexican hats to be sitting in rocking chairs, chewing corncob pipes, ghosts of an eastern western; but at the few lazy stations there was usually only a bored railway employee with a thermos of coffee and a Mickey Spillane novel, or sometimes a few kids from a nearby moshav, or a Habbad Hassid boarding to proselytize the passengers, persuading them to don phylacteries . . . perhaps even an Arab goatherd, leaving his flocks behind in the hands of a little boy. For Nili, it was a journey that never failed to restore a sense of balance. The other Israel, the Israel of dreams, unsullied by corrupt politics and the brashness of growing cities . . .

When she saw Sasha, bearlike and sloppy as ever, waiting for her on the porch, something snapped in her and she wept. Her first tears since the sirens had sounded, two months and an aeon ago. They nestled together like two lost grizzlies soaked by a sudden storm, making snuffling noises and pawing each other in a positively indecent way. 'What's this, adultery?' said Marta, poking her head round the door. 'Away, woman!' purred Sasha. 'Can't you see we're in conference here?'

So she stayed for a while, traversing old walks with Sasha, guzzling Marta's chocolate cakes. Familiotherapy, a favourite of Flusser's and of the powers that be. Making her ready for the day when she must, as fate, inertia or the bank account dictate, return, to Klander, resuming the quotidian war with her feared, loved, but unavoidable familiars – Nietzsche, Davidov, the Magpie and, returned once more upon a three-month 'voluntary' detention order – Blok.

Blok!

Ach. Himmel! After five days of truancy, and adventures too mind-numbing to be related (ah, the heat, the heat . . .) Blok and Sa'id, on 22nd October, entered a barren Sinai canyon to find a platoon of Golani Infantry nesting there, whose Communications Sergeant said to them:

'Are you the blokes from *BABASIS* magazine? There's a call out for you guys. Someone spotted you near Umm Shaumar. You have been on the missing list.'

The jig was up. They had to make contact, if only to set parents, wives, friends, rubber women, at rest. The joke, in fact, had been on them. For, as the Golani sergeant explained, far from distancing themselves from the battle, they had driven, in their wild innocence, into the operational zone of a force of Egyptian commandos, who had been landed near Sharm-a-Sheikh several days previous and were still playing ring-a-ring-a-roses with the Israeli counter-commando. 'They must have thought you were not worth killing,' said the sergeant blithely, 'thereby giving away their position.'

Not worth killing! With this final, thunderous rebuff, Blok and Sa'id headed north, Tel Avivwards. ('NOT WORTH KILLING!' raved Blok, as they tore up the asphalt along the moonscape Red Sea shore. 'Why, even the lowest house-fly, cockroach or enlisted buck-private rates this democratic privilege! It's an outrage! How could they do this to us?' 'It's the fate of Yehoshua,' said Sa'id, 'kismet. The dung of God.')

In Tel Aviv they were really hopping mad. Threats of summary court-martial flew through the air like so many wet dishrags. 'Do you know,' screeched the current editor, a runtish Lieutenant-Colonel Kugel, 'that desertion in time of war is subject to the death penalty?' Someone, some-where, had snitched on Blok's execution of the magazine's tape recorder. Some low-ranking offi-cer had, as is such people's wont, betrayed the con-fidences of the bunker. (Nor had it been ensigns or bedouin who had broadcast the BABASIS jeep's presence but a Regular Major, high above, in his lousy Sikorski chopper.) Blok, Kugel reiterated, you are in mighty hot water, the day of judgment is nigh. Sa'id, it was decided, had fallen under his evil influ-ence, though he could not hope to escape some stick. Two reporters had to be diverted from the

Syrian Front to cover the Canal Crossing that had been squarely in Blok's domain. Wilful damage to army property, to the tune of fifteen thousand lire! And the tarnishing of the name of a great unit whose journalists had always inscribed on their masthead: I March With the Nation's Vanguard . . .

But while subjected to this tirade Blok continued to turn over in his mind further Quixotian anagrams. For example: Dooq Uxtine . . . Extique Nood . . . Xen Dut-Qooi . . . Odin Xuqote . . . Id Extoquo . . . Dine Ox-Quot . . . Quitnode Ox . . .

'Luckily for you we won the war,' raved the geek, 'or there'd be firing squads at the back of this barracks . . . rotten apples should be rooted out . . . never in all my experience . . . our brave soldiers who are still ready to die for our country . . .'

Nix Quo-Toed? Doq Oxitune? Tuq de Nooxi? Exoquoid Nut?

Blok had not, as yet, put up a defence of his actions, merely replying to all queries, threats and inquisitions that their compass had led them astray. 'FOR FIVE DAYS?' Kugel bellowed, his eyes ricocheting off the wall. Blok was confined to barracks pending further inquiries, Sa'id sent off to Africa to eke out his penance in the gunsights of Egyptian snipers. But they had worked out in advance the only coherent defence, on their way north from their débâcle. 'Time to activate the Klander gambit,' said Blok, 'aggravated by shellshock and delirium. As my subordinate you can say, cher Yehoshua: I was only following orders,' as their watches, the compass, the maps of secret trails, went gloo, gloo, gloo into the Red Sea. And if there was any doubt there were the tapes wrapped in condoms, the real sockeroo, the clincher. (Though Sa'id convinced him to hold them back, in case of dire emergency: 'Golda Meir a murderess, Dayan to be roasted,' he said, 'doesn't it prove that you're sane?') Sans tapes then, Blok made himself ready to face the Sanity Commission:

'What is your name?'
'Avram Blok.'
'Where were you born?'
'Here and there.'
'Your father's name?'
'Baruch. As in "Baruch ata adonai ..." – "Blessed art thou O Lord, Our God, King of the World." '
'Do you believe in God?'
'What?'
'Do you believe in God?'
'What?'
'What do you think of the war?'
'I thought it was great.'
'Why is that?'
'War keeps the population down and saves us from falling asleep.'
'Do you love your country?'
'What?'
'Do you love your country?'
'What?'
'Do you have problems with hearing?'
'Not at all. I can hear you sound as a bell.'
'How would you define yourself?'
'With difficulty.'
'Do you hate the Arabs?'
'I don't know them well enough for that.'
'Do you hate your father?'
'I don't know him well enough for that.'
'What is your favourite colour?'
'Red.'
'What is your favourite flavour?'
'Vanilla-chocolate.'
'What about pistachio?'
'I don't like the little bits.'
'Have you thought about death?'

'Fairly often.'

'What do you think about it?'

'It's great, isn't it?'

'Why do you say that?'

'Well, everyone around seems to think so.'

'Who, for instance?'

'I am a-political.'

'You are having us on, Avram Blok, are you not?'

'Not at all. I am a genuine lunatic.'

'Which would you prefer: to live in our country or abroad?'

In lieu of an answer Blok stood on his chair and gave forth a loud ku-ku-ri-ku.


**The Plot Thickens:**

'There are more things in heaven and under the earth, Tarablus,' said Agent XBZThree, as he accompanied the undercover inspector through the ersatz wood panels of the counterfeit Swedish Tea Shoppe, 'than are recorded in the *Police Journal*. Gebst a kik, for example, at these fascinating underground tunnels, the existence of which I am sure you did not contemplate in your wildest dreams.'

Indeed, Tarablus was scunnered with awe. Everyone knew the Old City was as riddled with old excavations and workings as a colossal slab of ementhaler. But these were no soggy, dank pitshafts of crumbling bricks, dripping peewater and gushing odiferous sludge. In front of the inspector stretched a wide tubular corridor about twelve feet in diameter, made of a grey seamless metal alloy and illuminated by fluorescent light, from which, at regular intervals, similar tubes spewed to left and right like the boltholes of giant moles. Even Shpilkes the Infant was struck dumb, miraculously, and sat drooling heavily into the filth and rising ordure of his pram.

'Is this not truly something?' purred the secret

agent. 'I wish to have your unfettered opinion.'

'It is truly something,' said Inspector Tarablus. 'How long has it all been here?'

'This is it then,' said Zetz, as the technicians strapped Eisav into the capsule's cockpit, snapping shut the tempered plastic cupola through which everything was distorted funfairwise. His voice continued to echo through the cockpit radio: 'You are now fully primed for action.'

Big deal. Eisav adjusted his arse in the seat, facing a control panel he could not control and steering gear he could not steer. ('All NASA,' Zetz had enthused when briefing him on the capsule, 'all Apollo-approved, field-tested on the dark side of the moon.') 'All our thoughts are with you,' Zetz's drone reverberated, though he did not clarify whether he meant Tunnel Unit 90, the Israel Defence Forces, the Nation or the entire world. Eisav waved, the unmistakable gesture of 'Save the sauce, cholera. Get on with it.' Zetz gave him the thumbs up and, turning to the board, pressed the master control button, propelling the capsule along its monorail – kapow! – like a bolt from a cross-bow, into an inky blackness . . .

At about the same time Blok was admitted to the asylum, on a diagnosis of chronic malingering, Liam O'Habash, too, infiltrated the Institute, in the guise of Matilda Algehzi ('Yama Ama'), a Moroccan charlady with a floor-scrubbing compulsion. He had undergone plastic surgery by a dentist named Visher, who was firmly in his debt for two decades' supply of infibulation postcards. The good doctor, whose best work was carried out on the nights of the new moon, had even designed folds of flesh to conceal Liam's groin, covered with dead virgin's fur. But for good measure he urged him to simulate an additional obsessive unclothing phobia. Such a subterfuge was de rigueur as Nietzsche, Davidov and Blok, who knew him, were all wintering en maison.

During December, and well into January, he scrubbed his way, inch by inch, through the main building, out to the Annexe pathway. Scuffing his knees on the rough stones, wielding with both hands a thick brush wrapped in a sopping schmutter he progressed, hour by hour, day by day, towards Dr Nachtnebel's laboratory. Before his eyes the message received at Abu Saleh's, spurring him on to his long-delayed KGB task of penetrating the Annexe's secret. Moving in upon its closed and shuttered bulk, with its apparent air of abandonment, his days were nights and his nights were days as on torn knees he slowly closed the gap. Staff and patients began taking bets as to when he would actually touch the door, and what terrible, ethereal threat might materialize to punish his transgression. And meanwhile, as his obsessive search dragged on, the whole trade in erotica in the Fertile Crescent began to judder and come to a halt. Clients were left empty-handed with nothing to fuel their sybaritic fantasies. A tide of frustration and repressed libido began spreading over Western Asia. Winds howled, will-o'-the-wisps gibbered, djinns rattled about in bottles. Clear harbingers, if any were needed, of the new Retrogressive age . . .


**From the summarized minutes of the Elders of Zion: (at Mottel's Delicatessen, 20th December, 1973)**
There being a quorum at 09.20 hours, Zev 'Meshuggener' Weitz, of South Carolina, accepted the chair and called the meeting to order. The first item on the agenda was the screening of an 8 mm

movie of the wedding of Natan 'Jacques' Hadayah's daughter, which had taken place three weeks earlier at the Berl Katznelson Centre in Jerusalem and had been attended by five hundred guests. Irving Klotskashes commented favourably on the lighting and camerawork but criticized the mise-en-scène. When old Grandma Hadayah slips on a stuffed pepper and falls into the humus, he said, the camera should have simply allowed the event to happen, rather than zoom in to a close up. In comedy, he averred, it is the reaction that counts. Zunz, the Ba'al Shem of Vienna, begged leave, with respect, to disagree. Being hurled with the motion of the zoom into the occasion was, in his humble opinion, an extremely effective technique, a cinematic equivalent, might one venture, of Sartre's concept of 'engagement'? A lively discussion followed, which the chairman cut short, reminding the meeting that several items of acute cosmic importance awaited their regard. He expressed the entire board's feelings in congratulating Jacques Hadayah, his family, daughter and the groom and wishing the couple many years of happiness and procreation until a hundred and twenty. He then called for coffee, tea, bialys and orders of omelettes and fries.

'Our second item,' the chairman declared, 'concerns the collapse of Western civilization, which, I am reliably informed, is, give or take twenty years, imminent.'

'Just millennial blues,' said Azaniah of Azaniah Carpets and Tapestries, 'as the Christian year two thousand approaches. We might as well take note of 1984, the novelist Orwell's dystopia . . .'

'In our numbering.' said the Ba'al Shem, 'you are aware that 1984 is 5744, the word תשמד – Tashmad: "she will be destroyed." Or one might add the ה , the 5 of the thousands, to make התשמד , i.e. the query: "will she be destroyed?" '

Zunz: 'You may also note the year 2010 is 5770 – תשע – "she will be redeemed." Or, again, with the thousands, התשע , or the question: "will she be redeemed?" '

Eibeschutz: 'This is all schoolboy stuff. Why don't we get down to basics?' With a karate cry, he stabbed with his fork at the eggs over easy Bella the Waitress had just clunked before him. One yolk broke, oozing yellowly into the white. The entire group crowded round to perceive the consequent pattern.

'Well, I'll be . . .' said Weitz.

'Hoch ya eini . . .!' said Azaniah.

'. . . azoi . . .' murmured the Ba'al Shem.

'Hot diggety dog!' exclaimed Klotskashes, momentarily transferred to his early animation days with Pepito the Wonder Dog.

Silently, reverently, they all stood watching the soft yolk flow, inexorably as lava rivulets, into the matrix, which clearly revealed, without the shadow of a doubt, the true ultimate fate of mankind . . . Klotskashes, returning to Malibu on the midnight clipper from Kennedy, finding a seventeenth letter from Yissachar waiting in the mail for him, calling for his resurrection . . .

'Pig-Time!' said Davidov, Christmas Eve approaching, 'and this year it is a dead certainty. A time for reflection upon the ontology of the omniscient porker (Do you not see him, Elders, chaffing at daylight, pawing the secret passageways?): PIG – the most ancient symbol, the proliferous but devouring Earth Mother, the sow who eats her own farrow. At the centre, with the snake and the cock, of the Buddhist Wheel of Becoming. Its attributes are Greed and Ignorance. In the Egyptian myths – an aspect of Seth, in his Typhonic form, though no images appear to have survived on the ancient tablets. Is this not the first instance of the Pig as censor, the Pig as distorter of history? Sigmund Freud says the Egyptian fear of the Pig is the source of the Hebraic revulsion. Elsewhere in the East the Pig appears to be sacred, an aspect of the Mother Astarte. Some keynote here, of homosexual panic? Freud has left us bereft on this issue. In ancient days there was often a confusion between the sacred and the profane. One cannot be sure whether something was worshipped or spat upon and reviled. (Now isn't that the Middle East for you, comrades?) Even the Christians, who cook and eat the ferfluchte hayeh, have mixed feelings about the critter: in their symbolism he represents greed, gluttony, unbridled lust and passion. For the Jews he has always been an A-one pest: Eater of the Holy Vine. (An element of the feminine part of the God-head, without which the repair of the broken vessels which contained the light of the sephiroth before the Fall cannot take place.) And also: Retarder of the Messiah. Thus his centrality in the Quest of the Elders, who cannot ignore his presence. They are sure to turn up here, at the tomb of Iscariot, if they wish to achieve their goal . . .' So saying he checked his kit for the annual Pig-vigil, and saw that it was good: three sweaters, big booties, four pairs of socks, one torch and thirty-five spare batteries. Prepare thyself, High Priest of Enlightenment, he cried as he plunged below ground. And the evening and the morning were subsumed in the gloaming of the umpteenth, umpteenth day . . .

. . . Tattered election posters, fluttering on bill-boards the length and breadth of the nation . . . the voting code letters of the failed false messiahs fading away forlornly. Some already obscured by the smirk of Clint Eastwood or the breasts of Sophia Loren. Vandals have slashed the ubiquitous and

mocking. אמת – 'EMET' – 'TRUTH' of the victorious
Labour Party. For, although the Pig had failed to
appear again on Christmas Eve midnight, the government of Golda Meir was re-elected, on the 31st,
with a reduced majority. But this triumph did not
last long. In the spring of '74, Blok's friend Fat Avi
brought the government down single-handed . . .
This was how it happened: exhausted by the rhe-
torical exertions of the Ta'amon Café, he was
idling out his yearly reserve duty in the quiet of the
Suez Canal, as luck would have it, punkt upon that
fatal Yom Kippur when the shit hit the fan. Avi and
three comrades held out in their bunker for twelve
days, till they managed to sneak out, bleeding and
wounded, in the dead of night, in a lull. They were
acclaimed as heroes, beribboned, bemedalled, but
Fat Avi burned white with fury. He became thin as
a rake, his hair turned grey and his eyes took cover
behind his cheekbones. (Where art thou, young
Fattie, the planks in the puddle, salad days, buried
treasure?) The government published the casualty
list, a paperback of two hundred pages. The army
issued forms to be filled in by relatives, for a Memorial Book of the Dead. It looked something like this:

Born at . . . . . . . . . . . at . . . . . . . . . . . ;
Father's name . . . . . . . . . . . . . . . . . . . . . ;
Mother's name . . . . . . . . . . . . . . . . . . . ;
Studied at . . . . . . . . . . . . . . . . . . . . . . . . ;
Was Outstanding/Diligent/Attentive
    Pupil (delete if inapplicable);
Excelled at . . . . . . . . . . . . . . . . . . . . . . . ;
His Aim in Life Was . . . . . . . . . . . . . . . . ;
His Ardent National/Religious/Social
    Beliefs were a cornerstone of his
    character (elaborate) . . . . . . . . . . . . .
    . . . . . . . . . . . . . . . . . . . . . . . . . . . . . ;
He will be greatly missed by . . . . . . . . . .
    . . . . . . . . . . . . . . . . . . . . . . . . . . . . ;

And so on. But this only made Avi burn all the whiter. So he sat down at the gates of the Prime Minister's office and proclaimed a hunger strike until the PM and other ministers responsible for the 'Blunder' of the October War resigned. And lo! Hundreds, then thousands, then tens of thousands joined him, besieging the seat of power. Day after day they ringed the building, grim-faced, consuming nothing but orange juice. And finally the walls of Jericho fell: the blunderers all resigned. Golda Meir, Dayan, Eban, Sapir were swept from office and ex-Chief-of-Staff Rabin, untainted by the débâcle as he had been Ambassador to Washington at the time, became the new Labour Prime Minister. And the Nation, sated by loss, grief, continuing terrorism and incipient revolution, sighed grate-fully, turning the other bum cheek upwards, and fell into a deep coma . . .

Meanwhile, inside Blok's brain:

Blok: 80% water. 10% spirt. 3% Ama.
2% gall. 5% blather. 4% spleen.
0.1% gut, 100% nut. 100% rut.

Beepbeepbeepbeepbeepbeepbeepbeepbeepbeepbeepbeepbeepbeepbeep-
beepbeepbee
Mayday Mayday SOS Save Our Sabbath Sin on Sodom Sod off Sinners Sick
Oaf
Simmers Suck off Sodomites Sadists?Odd Sods – – – – – – – – – – – – – – –

Papa Mama Aunt Pashtida Uncle Elchanan Brigadier Nahman(Ret) General Zetz Adolf Hitler Neville Chamberlain Ernest Bevin Joseph Stalin Yoshka Rosencrantz Golda Meir Moshe Dayan Pinhas Sapir Abba Eban the Rebetsen Twilliger Syphilis-Face Gaga the Bulgarian Bloodhound Dr Emmanuel Veltsch Harold Wilson Richard Nixon Leonid Brezhnev Charles de Gaulle Clemenceau Woodrow Wilson Kaiser Willhelm Malka Halperin Victoria Happenstance Nili Grunbaum-Yakir Eisav Ben-Gever Diane Bloomstein David Ben-Gurion Menahem Begin Davidov Nietzsche Schopenhauer Kant Spinoza Berkeley Hobbes Locke Hume Thomas Aquinas Rabbi Goren Rabbi Akiva Hillel Shamai Mohamad Jesus Moses Isaiah Ezekiel David Koheleth Noah Adolf Eichmann

J'accuse!

# Vanity of vanities, all is
## all the rivers flow into the sea yet the sea is not full; unto
for in much wisdom is much grief and he that increaseth knowledge increaseth sorrow ~~~

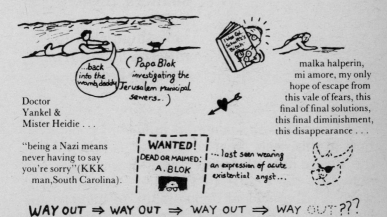

...back into the womb daddy

( Papa Blok investigating the Jerusalem municipal sewers.. )

I Was Col. Schultz's "Bitch"

malka halperin, mi amore, my only hope of escape from this vale of fears, this final of final solutions, this final diminishment, this disappearance . . .

Doctor
Yankel &
Mister Heidie . . .

"being a Nazi means never having to say you're sorry"(KKK man,South Carolina).

WANTED!
DEAD OR MAIMED:
A. BLOK

.. last seen wearing an expression of acute existential angst...

WAY OUT ⇒ WAY OUT ⇒ WAY OUT ⇒ WAY OUT ???

**I wish there could be a sea in which my vision could stretch into every shore and fjord, lapping at craggy eternal mountains, the rocks upon which truth shatters, flowing back, indistinguishable, into the ocean from whence it came.**

'For example – the potential failure of compensation, in this case, must be counted as devastating: the desire for superiority here encompasses, in actuality, the entire cosmos, the "ocean", as it were ... the evident impossibility of this striving must lead, inevitably, to a retreat into illness, since only neurosis can provide the conviction that such an outcome as total control, total superiority, can, in any form, be achieved.'

(Adler)

'A very clear and, in fact, unmistakable rendering of the death-wish into poetic, or pseudo-poetic terms: the subject yearns for a return to the womb, within which, he surmises, he will be rocked so to speak in the cradle of the amniotic fluid, sheltered from the "craggy mountains" and "rocks" of ego-fulfilment; a very primal dream dreamed by the id, freed, for perhaps a fleeting moment, from the stern strictures of the superego, which would, like those very "craggy mountains", shatter these impossible wishes of harmony and return to an instinctual, pre-civilization state, in fact a retreat from the conflicts inherent in life to the inorganic, pre-life condition – i.e.: the eternal peace of Death.'

(Freud)

'And what more clearly proves, conclusively, the existence of a collective unconscious than this passage? Words fail me to describe the inanity, the ineptitude and sheer dilettantism of those who seek to deny that which every child knows to be irrefutable. Truth, the mind grasps here instinctively, is not a concept that can be extracted, split off, analysed, polished and set in a glass case in the museum of dogmas, but is but a drop in an ocean of knowledge that can have no end, and scarcely, therefore, a beginning, save in the mind of God. The mind of Blok here perceives, as a fleeting vision, that absolute harmony from which life stemmed and to which it exerts itself, the archetype mani-fested in the rituals of Christianity, in the researches of the gnos-tics and the alchemists, in the disciplines of the Tibetan Book of the Dead, the fundamental Way of the Tao, nirvana, the imago dei, the heiros gamos, the philosopher's stone, blah blah blah blah blah.'

(Jung)

'The science of behav-iour can only conclude

that this mode of thinking is destructive of the fabric of a culture in which we depend, more and more, on the participation of the individual in useful, pro-social activities. The culture of advanced technology, which alone can assure our development out of the states of barbarism, is illserved by such namby pamby, uncontrolled and socially undesirable thinking.'

(Skinner)

'*A simple cry for love from a person abandoned and shat on by a lousy and cruel world.*'

(Laing)

'A clear victim of capitalism seeking an alternative social modality."

(Cooper)

'What does he want of me? Why is he never satisfied? What's wrong with the boy? Why doesn't he settle down with a nice, warm Jewish girl and start thinking about his future? It's all this running about among the goyim that's addled his brains ... Dreamers, revolutionaries who want to change the world – they can afford such mishigayes. A Jew just needs a quiet place somewhere, where he can be a human being, and look after his own for a change.'

(Mama)

Released from Klander, he took a cheap apartment in an old stone Arab house at Abu Tor. The house was in Ein Rogel Street, on the hill adjacent to the nuthouse, overlooking the Old City walls at Mount Zion and the sweep of the Jericho hills. It was part of a row of abandoned dwellings, which had stood punkt on the old border. They were earmarked for progress, to become health food shops, art galleries, tourist panoramas. But so far they were empty, bare, available for transients and bohemians. Up above, on the hill, a new Jewish housing estate was growing by leaps and bounds. Below, on the terraces, the Arab villagers watched it all in stony silence. The whole street, a bare third of a kilometre, was a microcosm of the entire dilemma.

Here, in No Man's Land, in splendid isolation (the other flats in the house were unoccupied) Blok locked himself in, with provisions piled high in the fridge, with a kitbagful of old files and guff and an ancient seventh-hand Hebrew typewriter which sounded, when operated, like a battery of Gatling guns. This, then, was his retreat: the room, four metres by five, the walls of faded Jerusalem white-wash, the chipped floor tiles of a somewhat beige colour, with a design in faded red of the curling leaves of a vine. Hung on the walls: one old brass coffee plate with a big dent in its centre. One bed-ouin saddle bag (contributed by Blok) to be stuffed with discarded paper. One very faded framed sepia photograph, en face, of a man with absolutely extreme crew cut and a large moustache waxed to points, officer's collar buttoned tight under the chin, in the voluntary garrotte mode. Blok is certain he is Kemal Ataturk, saviour of Turkey, but there is no evidence to support this theory. One gaily col-oured Jewish National Fund calendar, circa 1953, bought for a song in a rummage sale in the Mea Shearim Market, with loud pictures of sheep shearing, sheave cutting, hay mowing and other masterpieces of Zionist Socialist Heroism. A man with large, clean, tanned muscles stands over an anvil. A stout woman bends over the soil. Slogans of each month proclaim: 'Work Is Our Life, Our Salva-tion From All Ills.' 'Our Hope Has Not Yet Been Lost.' 'It Is Good to Die For Our Country.' At the north-eastern end of the room, a makeshift kitchen-ette, with one-ring electric cooker, battered refrig-erator. At the south-eastern, WC and shower. By the eastern wall, single bed, sheets crumpled but reasonably clean, set below the window from which Blok looks out over the dappled hills. In the centre of the room, a wheeled writing table with folding flaps. Upon it, Blok's jalopy of a typewriter, scattered mounds of paper, coloured pens, card-board files, papers crammed with Hebrew letters in neo-cabbalistic designs, a kvetcher, prised caps of fizz bottles, sticky labels, scissors, maps of Jerusalem, Mandate Palestine, Europe, Asia, the World. On the typewriter keys, Blok's fingers, steadily pumping away. Attached to Blok's fingers, his hands, now somewhat pudgy, attached to arms leading to hunched shoulders, above which the head, upon which receding hair tickles over the ears, while old army spectacles perch on broken Jewish nose, as if balanced on the pit of perdition. Behind them, brown eyes gaze with fierce hostility upon the recalcitrant page . . .

He was compiling a scrapbook of items gathered from his wandering years. For example: the lady from the Weathermen underground who hid from the FBI in redundant New York subway shafts for twelve years, living off rats, roaches and the stolen pack lunches of inadvertent tourists. Or the French Professor of Philosophy who strangled his wife and jumped out of the sixth-floor window. Or the care-fully preserved treasures of the *American National Enquirer*:

'Topless Waitress Wishes to Start at Bottom.'
'Government Shells Out Your Taxes to Study Sex Life of Snails.'
'Tragedy of Three Deaf Sisters Who Are Going Blind.'
'The Boy Who Can See With His Ears.'

In between the paste-ups he jotted down random thoughts and excogitations:

Irrational Fears:
—that while I meditate on the profundities of Life and Death, small flying creatures will come

through the holes in the window netting, mate and reproduce indefinitely.

— that the fabric of existence will totally crumble. A Ta'amon Café-dweller's theory: Life is a conspiracy of the original DNA to reach its fellow DNA in another galaxy. Once this goal is achieved via space flight, there will be no need for the carrier and Life will be cancelled forthwith.

— (apropos small flying creatures: Troubled by a persistent blue-bottle, I once went to the grocer Zachariah in Takhkemoni Street and asked for a fly exterminator. How many flies are troubling you? he asked. One, I replied. You should learn to live with him, he said, like with the Palestinians.)

Rational Fears:

— that I might miss the nuclear war in my sleep.
— ditto in slumber: that Arab terrorists might blow me up before I have a chance to explain to them I am on their side.
— that religious mania might engulf me; I might end up totally bald, except for a topknot, a saffron robe and cymbals, chanting: hare krishna, hare rama, hare krishna, hurry hurry . . . (etc.)

Inconsequentia:

On the remote Scottish island of M—, the islanders fed their farm animals a strange weed that had been washed ashore off a smuggler's dinghy. The animals became very quiet and thoughtful and the crops grown with their manure had a curious effect on the populace. They took to spending their evenings gathered en masse on the island's main crag, Beinne a Chreekie, looking out over the Atlantic Ocean and silently observing the sunset. But it was not till their consumption of whisky plummeted that the police began to investigate, finally identifying the strange weed as

Other animal items:
Heard over the radio: a Turkish scientist has determined that loud noise, such as that in discothèques, can drive mice and pigs homosexual. But what were the mice and pigs doing in the discothèque in the first place? Mysterium. (Terrifying data can be imbibed over the wireless, especially in the small hours: a woman in Los Angeles is allergic to fluorescent light, leather, the moon and daylight. Another woman, in England, can eat nothing but peas and cabbage. The BBC in London once announced: 'The price of gold took another tumble this morning because of the lack of bad news.' Also: 'The plane crashed, but the pilot ejaculated safely.')

More animal lore (via the IDF broadcasts):
Apparently the more stress caused to animals before slaughter, the lower the quality of the meat. Scientists advise soothing music in abattoirs. I have news for you, comrade agronomists, this is all old hat. What about the prisoners' ensemble at Auschwitz? QED. In the electronic age, all gas chambers will emit muzak. The poison crystals will fall to the beat of the Top Ten. Or, if you prefer, Mantovani.

From America:
Adolph's Meat Tenderizer. Was there not a jingle which went: 'Tam-ta-ra-ram, sprinkle some Adolph, ta-tam'?
    Is there a guiding intelligence?

On Paranoia & Conspiracies:
(from the local press)

FEAR OF BOOBY TRAPS IN POTATOES BOUGHT
AT AUCTION:

The Israel Police spokesman announced that between the 3rd and the 8th of this month [Feb. '74] potatoes were sold by auction at the Kfar Saba 'Tnuva' branch. It is possible that among these potatoes there are sensitive and round explosive devices, the size of grapefruits, fallout from the Yom Kippur War. Anyone who bought potatoes in auction is requested to act carefully while handling them. If a suspicious object is found it must not be touched and the nearest police station must be immediately informed.

One is biting into one's din-dins and suddenly – POW! – there are your brains on the ceiling. My reaction is: They are performing a service. Without evasion They are at last telling us the truth: Watch Out, Nothing is Safe.

Some years back They tried another tack: They informed us the Arabs were scattering minute Chinese 'button mines' all over the streets of our cities. People walked about in tennis shoes for months. Cola tins, cigarette packs, went unsquashed on the ground. The usual Jerusalem soft-shoe shuffle was abandoned for the skip-and-jump format. Pictures of these lethal gew-gaws were in all the newspapers. They looked like miniature flying saucers, flown by microscopic homunculi, thus:

I must clarify my position (wrote Blok): I am not really concerned with Davidov-style conspiracies: Elders of Zion, Illuminati, Rosicrucians, Unsolved Mysteries such as the Great Stone Balls of Costa Rica, the Talking Frogs of Bali, the Levitating Rabbits of Saragossa or the case of Fred Bassit of Cherryvale Pennsylvania who was killed by a shower of

Paracetemols which fell suddenly out of a clear blue sky. (I rashly told Davidov of Yissachar's New York UFO, and he pestered me for his address till I gave it to him. So now an umbilical cord of bilge-water stretches between the Klander asylum and the heart of Hollywood. What might be the consequences? The mind boggles, with the Klotskashes wraith in the wings . . .) No. The Conspiracy I am concerned with is a strictly personal one, aimed directly at my liquidation.

The thing is easily proven, beyond the shade of doubt. It began literally at my birth. No – before that. Let us eschew genealogy, to avoid ethnic chauvinism. Begin then at conception, the place: Hungary, 1944. While Papa and Mama are huffing and puffing, trying to get me started, both the Russian and German armies are lobbing high explosives precisely in their direction. I will draw here a map of the relevant sector of Budapest, with the location of the opposing forces:

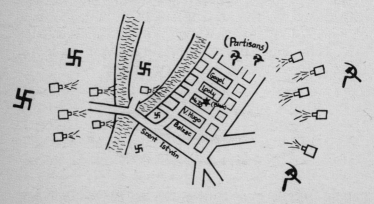

Observe: the Germans and Arrow Cross on their final fling, are on the Buda bank of the river. The Red Army already in Pest, pouring fire towards the enemy. In the ruins and rubble the partisans are everywhere, with Ipoly Street in particular between them and the retreating Nazis. In the cellar of No. 23,

down a flight of stairs already zapped to smithereens, Pa and Ma Blok, inexplicably, are embarked
on the Creation of Life. (Did they mean to? Perhaps
after eleven months in separate hiding places they
found they just couldn't wait. Even one's parents
are human.) It was only due to the bad aim, due to
battle fatigue, of both the Reds and the Blacks, that
all three of us were not snuffed out there and then
and scattered all over the City. First try.

Second try: The *Irma Klein*, en route for
Palestine, Blok pushing his way out of the womb.
The time it was the British, tfu cholera, who tried to
do me in. Two destroyers set out, from Athens and
Limassol, but a fog bank descended and they got
lost, shouting at each other over loudhailers in the
thick pea-souper: 'Surrender, yidlah! You won't
make Haifa!' 'Halt! in the name of the British
Empire!' RAF planes, loaded with the bombs used
to bust the giant Ruhr dams, performed Immelman
loops far above.

All right, They let me grow up, become infected
with the seditious germs of hope, expectation,
desires. Biding Their time. Till – ZAP – in the Six
Days' War, They let fly. The bullets that flew in the
Mitleh Pass. It was only a blunder on Their part
that saved me. My name *was* on one of the bullets
that zipped past my ear, but they had made a slight
error in the address: They put 45 Yehezkel
Hacohen Street instead of 43. There's bureaucracy
for you. Six years later, in '73, They tried to rectify
their mistake by bombarding my bunker with as
much ordnance as had been dumped on Berlin in
the last month of the Second World War.

What made Them fail so far? God, watching over
me? The old man with the dirty white beard? I
always envisaged him farting from on high at the
very mention of Mankind. As little Rosenzweig
shouted at the Twenty-Fifth General Congress of

397

the Soviet Union, after the Chairman's speech: 'If everything's so good, why is everything so bad?' Didn't Nietzsche Number One write somewhere: If there is a God, how could I bear not to be God? Therefore there is no God. Now there's proper solipsism for you. I only say: If there were a God, I would be bound to oppose Him, It is right to rebel against reactionaries – Mao Tse Tung. Selah.

No. I accept Nietzsche's position: it is a random factor. Dice, loaded by Happenstance . . . (a pun, maestro! Gesundheit!) . . . Also They have time. They are not in a hurry. Perhaps They enjoy watching me twitch, squirm, shudder and bite my nails (the bones, elongating, becoming putty . . . muscles, brain, turning to blancmange . . .) . . . Nietzsche says: They do not exist, it's all buk-sriki, comrade. Unless you can abandon your thirst for religion, we are not going to get anywhere! It is an empirical issue, I tell him, pointing to the weaving threads of the intrigue: the temptations of Vicky, the spies of Friedman, Abu Jilda, the Manhattan roaches – don't think I have noticed nothing, I wasn't made with a finger! Not to speak of the symbols, the event stigmata – the death of Klander, the quest of O'Habash – trying to draw me into the matrix of Their terminal reality . . .

And still They warn me! With infinite malice, They make it clear there is no escape – after my second ejection from Klander, Nili and Veltsch collaborating to oust me (cast out, like Adam and Eve: 'Out, ya h'ribaitak!' snarls the Lord, grounding an applecore in the dust. Double-locking the gate, strewing powdered glass over the fence . . . 'Fascist pig!' cries Adam, in futile defiance, giving Him the Middle Eastern three fingers . . .), I went to the travel agent, thinking again to give the furies the slip, abroad. But, with the flight data, I was given a small booklet, warning of International Terror.

This bears quoting at some length, as it is Final Proof of the plot. Thus:

HOW TO BE CAREFUL IN THE AIR:
—You will not fly, of course, in aircraft of Arab airlines.
—You will not fly in aircraft which might land in an Arab country.
—If your plane is about to land in an Arab country, ask the Captain to land in a non-Arab country, or to take you under his jurisdiction.

HOW TO BE CAREFUL OUTDOORS AND IN THE CITY:
—In a train, travel only in occupied carriages. The presence of passengers should foil attempted attacks.
—Never enter a taxi which stops by you at the driver's own initiative.

In the Hotel or Rented Apartment:
—Do not open the door to a visitor without first making sure of his identity. (Mon dieu! think of the implications! – B.)
– Prefer living close by other Israelis. (!!!! – B.)
– Fit a chain to your door as well as a lock, and an observation eyepiece.

When Touring, Walking:
—To foil terrorist attacks, avoid routine. Refrain from a fixed timetable of leaving and returning home.
—Avoid using regular transport routes.
—When travelling, be in the company of 2, 3 persons or more.
—Keep a regular contact with relatives.
—Do not visit places which are frequented by Arabs.

\* \* \*

To this there was no answer but to cancel all plans and stockpile one's K-rations. Also I appended to the booklet a cutting which appeared to have surfaced in a crack of my suitcase: 'Terror at Burger King: Man Has Beef With Restaurant.'

What conclusions can one draw?

(Freud, on Paranoia as a surefire sign of homosexuality . . . Flusser questioned me on this once. I told him about the man who used to creep up on unsuspecting youths in the Saturday evening crowd by the King of Falafel stall and, grabbing their balls from behind, would squeeze lightly, say 'Maksh! Maksh!' and vanish. Also, I perused a couple of gay magazines in New York. I think I am immune, I said. Flusser laughed, the bastard, scribbling in his notebook.)


On the other hand, Moral Dilemmas:

– The Problem of a code of conduct culled from the experience of history and one's own life. Interpreting same. Truth and Falsehood. The old hacksaws, cholera.

– Politics and political action (Fat Avi, anti-Zetz, etc.): Whether 'tis nobler to suffer . . . or risk doing bad to do good: War for Peace. Lies for Truth. Cholera . . .

– Democracy (Asargelusha!) – the people's right to make moronic choices. And my right to opt out of same? Impasse again, comrades.

– Holocaust and revenge against the innocent: gotta kill *somebody*, daddy . . . On the decent people who wouldn't hurt a fly but support statesmen who lie, steal, murder and befoul the earth (clip this in: 'OPPOSITION LEADERS JAILED AS GRENADA GETS FREEDOM') – all evil, or just psycho, like me? persecution delusions en masse, or our collective gay libido decloseted, prefiguring the complete dying out of Mankind in about sixty-five years – the

Big Bang, or just seed plopping on sterile ground? Yes . . . after the '73 War, I jotted down the following doggerel:

## SONG OF THE LITTLE MAN
I don't want to hear about
red hot pokers and the knout,
of high-voltage electrodes,
iron tongs and cattle goads,
prison cells awash with dung,
men castrated, shot and hung,
burnt to cinders in the sands,
separated from their hands,
cries of pain and yells of rage,
stink of gaseous sewerage,
All that I would like to see is Mary Poppins on TV.

Maksh! Maksh! When will it all end?


**Blok's narration, continued:**
Then one day Nili visited me, bearing her own cross (I am not the only one, it appears, with a personal mark of Cain. Perhaps she was making up for the embarrassing time she gave me in the loony bin, passing me the morning Largactil pills as if they were strychnine, rattling keys, as she saw me pass in the corridor, like a jailor at the Lyublyanka.): Eisav, the Disappeared, fallout of the October War. (Would he qualify as a big round object? might we locate him at potato auctions?) Despite divorce and dead embryos she ended up pining for the big lug. She looked thinner, tougher and more worried than I ever saw her, as she stepped gingerly over my threshold surveying the mess of my life.

'Oh Avram,' she said, 'you look absolutely dreadful.'

'Thank you,' I said. 'You look a bit hard yourself. Like a twenty-minute egg.'

We exchanged more pleasantries. As usual she was sizing me up from a professional point of view. But she said:

'I need to talk to you, Avram. You're the only person I know crazy enough to understand my problem.'

'What about Nietzsche?' I said.

'Nietzsche is too crazy,' she replied.

'I am the median line,' I inferred, 'the golden rule.'

She told me her problem. Have I mentioned before Nili's telepathy? This was something about which I had my doubts. It was one of the cornerstones, so to speak, of her relationship with Eisav, that they remained in tune, in some sort of communication, even when they were apart. Not that they could pass precise messages to each other, or bend forks, like Uri Geller, but there was a kind of mental itch, a 'my-love-is-thinking-of-me-now' syndrome that she claimed was going down. She used this to drive me out of my mind in Onkelos Street, nights when Eisav failed to phone from the Canal. She would toss and turn, mumble and wake up and go into the kitchen to boil an egg. For some reason a boiled egg was a damper on all forms of thought transference. 'He was talking to me,' she would say, as I groaned my way, bleary eyed, to the toilet. 'Doesn't he have a telephone token tonight?' I would growl, fed up with all this flimflam. Myself, I received not so much as a noodge from her when we were apart, in all my born days.

So this was her problem now: lately, in the last few weeks, she had been receiving dispatches from the missing hero over the mind telegraph. A whole shlong of general emotions: love, longings, frustration, hunger, cold, coming from a vast distance. 'At least a thousand miles,' she said, 'north, almost punkt. Don't ask me how I know. I know.'

Three centuries ago she could have been burnt for that. Today, merely certified. But that of course left little choice, for Zetz had told her, after much humming and hawing, that Eisav was a prisoner of war somewhere in a non-front-line country.

'So, your ex is in a camp in darkest Russia,' I said. 'Well, well, what do you know . . . I hope you have told no one else about this?'

'Of course not,' she said, 'how can I?'

'Very wise,' I said. 'We each have our own personal concentration camp guard. Our own killer alsatian, snapping at our heels. If we take a false step, we're doomed.'

'Are you feeling all right, Avram?' she was anxious. 'Are you sure everything's in order?'

'You are receiving telepathic messages from the Gulag Archipelago,' I told her, 'and you're asking if *I'm* in order?'

The Prosecution rests.

She began visiting me regularly, appointing herself, as usual, mother. Clearing the flat of debris, dusting the coffee plate, wiping fly gunge off Kemal Ataturk. Was I becoming a substitute Eisav? I bared my teeth at myself in the mirror, checking for increased aggression. But I saw nothing but my receding hairline, giving me that not unwelcome Greenwich Village appearance.

'Am I going genuinely mad this time?' I asked her.

'Probably,' she answered, breaking a cup and shovelling it into the wastebin.

I quizzed her about strange and outlandish psychoses she might have come across in her time. I had a second-hand psychiatric dictionary I had purchased at Gertwagen's, near the Habirah Cinema. Amnesic fugue, folie de doute and the Smiling Depression were, she said, fairly common. But she had not come across 'koro', the terrified conviction that one's penis is shrinking. It is found, apparently, only among persons of the Chinese persuasion. Perhaps it shall remain a mystery.

There was no sexual contact between us. This was at her insistence. I am always ready for a poke, but she bent my ear about the beauties of platonic relationships, which, she sincerely thought, were possible even where sexual attraction was present. She had, she said, spent a night once in bed with her religious politician, and no physical endearments took place apart from a gentle stroking of her hair by means of his pudgy fingers. She said it was one of the calmest, most relaxing nights of her life. I said I had spent a night like that once in Manhattan with Patricia of Dementia Praecox Films. But I became so tense I had to go masturbate in the bathroom where, having consumed half a bottle of malt whisky earlier in the evening, I puked in the toilet bowl, fell asleep and woke to find her gone the next day.

'What can I do with you, Avram,' she said, 'except knock your head against the wall?'

What indeed? Once, when I was alone in the house, thinking blank thoughts of the future, seeing nothing but whorls of ultramarine with red stars dancing a slow-motion kazatski, an extremely odd event happened: an alter ego of mine, clearly a figure of substance, materialized in front of me, seated in a black leather armchair. He had a neatly clipped goatee, was dressed in a white roll-top sweater under a brown jacket and had a Havana stuck arrogantly in his puss.

'You are quite right,' he said to me, 'I am Avram Blok, the Success: film producer, raconteur, wit and best-selling auteur de luxe. What a schmuck you are, country cousin, moping in the styx when you might have persevered in the Big Apple and ended up showering in shekels. The world is divided into those who make the system work for them and those who let it work them over. There are hundreds of thousands of goyim out there, itching to be Pontius Pilate. Just rub their noses a little in the old ethnic guilt, and they'll cross your palm with silver. Gebst a kik at this, you incorrigible nebesch, the foundation stone of my triumphs.' He slapped into my mitt the July '73 issue of *Playboy Magazine*, held open at page 95, 'Fiction: The Man Who Counted the Gold Teeth and Spectacles at Auschwitz, by Abraham S.L.S. Blok.'

'What does S.L.S. stand for ?' I asked.

'So Long Suckers,' he said, blowing smoke screens. 'Read it.'

I read it in three minutes, utilizing the Strabismus Technique of treble-speed reading, then turned my attention to Playmate of the Month, Andy of Tuscaloosa, the Southern Belle Everyone Wants to Ring. 'Well?' he said, impatiently. For some reason I was reminded of one of the Eshkol jokes: Prime Minister Eshkol, on his African tour, is told the popular thing to do when meeting the populace is to bathe naked in the river. Every time he does this the crowds roar 'Zumba! Zumba!' After the dozenth occurrence Eshkol asks the local chef de protocol: 'Sugstsumir – what is this Zumba, Zumba!' 'Oh, it's nothing,' the man says, 'they've just never before seen a Prime Minister with such a small Zumba.'

There was no point in relating this tale to my doppelgänger because, being me, he would know it. Instead I just commented: 'Not enough laughs,' and handed him back the magazine.

'I wash my hands of you, Avram Blok,' he said huffily, 'you will never amount to anything.' And he vanished in a puff of rancid smoke taking with him, alas, Andy of Tuscaloosa.

But he was only the first. For a whole week they badgered me, my alter egos, taking over the flat, occupying the toilet, the bed, the chair, the floors. Scribbling graffiti all over the walls: BLOK SUCKS, FREE SCHARANSKY, HONKY SHIT GO HOME, A LONG LIFE TO CHAIRMAN MAO. Bloks who married Malka Halperin, Georgina, Nili, flaunting their wedding rings, their dinner pots, hideous Kodaks of their squalling offspring. Bloks who went to South Africa with Victoria Happenstance, gabbling in fluent Sotho. Even worse, Bloks Mentioned in Despatches in the Wars of '67, '73 '82, parading their campaign ribbons! Is there no limit to baseness? If I could, I would have shown them the door. A Blok who became a star in the New York hard-core racket, dubbing verbal abuse in twelve languages, stayed for a whole morning, bending my ear, till I had to stuff both lugs with cotton wool. Marxist-Leninist Bloks lambasted me endlessly, calling for blood and action. Humanist Bloks wooed me with saccharine Reason. Homosexual Bloks, in black leather jackets, blew me kisses, grabbing at my jumblies. (Maksh! maksh! merde, alors! No, this is not tolerable!) I strung garlic all over the windows and doors, and, when it ran out, spring onions. But still they gathered, slithering in the bath, squatting on the fridge, the writing table. They were taking it in turns to type out their memoirs, I could not get a moment's rest. Thuggish Bloks, in commando uniforms, with necklaces of Palestinian fingers. Religious Bloks, in kapotas and streimels, wielding placards – 'Save Our Holy Shabat!' Gormless mongoloid Bloks, zapped in child-birth. Blok Prime Ministers, with immense Zumbas. Elderly Bloks laying about with their canes, whacking shins, shoulders, bald pates, cackling. Blok idiot savants. Neurotic artist Bloks throwing severed ears like frisbees. An Ascetic Blok (tiens! not hare hare!) handing out stencilled leaflets: 'THE ETHERIAN UNIVERSITY: Postal and

Residential Courses, taught by forces OUTSIDE THIS UNIVERSE. Peace of Mind and COSMIC UNDERSTANDING are inevitable to all who study the ETHERIAN WAY. $3.80 + s.a.e. to –'

It could not last. By lunchtime on the seventh day there was no room to move, we were all standing on each other. By five o'clock tea we had reached the ceiling, there was not a whiff of air. I blacked out. When I came to, at seven thirty p.m., the whole phalange, thank whoever, had departed. It took me two hours to clean up the mess, the shit, the vomit, the blood, the dribble. To shovel the severed ears into the wastebin, to file the etherian leaflet. Then I boiled up an Osem soup from a cube, gazing at the soiled plate after. It was one of the sole remaining mementoes of my first sojourn outside home, in the flatlet at Takhkemoni. Halcyon days. The market, the warthogs, the long walk to Nili, the peels of love thrown out the window . . . I composed: Ode to a Plate:

O Plate,
Off you I ate,
At a quarter past eight,
With no date,
For whom to be late,
O Plate.

Ein Rogel Street seems very quiet now, at night. Even the Fatah guerrillas, operating from the Valley, creep discreetly by in their tennis shoes. Upstairs, in the uninhabited flat above mine, there are stealthy, regular footsteps. In the bathroom, a tap is dripping. Plonka, plonka, kaplonk. Straining my mind, I can actually catch the fleeting spark of an Eisav SOS message: Hut Three, Bunk One Hundred and something, it goes. 'Send woolly underwear, haminados, tshoolent. Co-ordinates' – then it gets lost in static and water drips. But nearer home, shit, there are others listening, and I can begin to pick them up now, the spies who are on my trail: street beggars in the pay of the KGB. French police, tracking Abu Jilda. Lubavitchers working on the Friedman dossier. Robot sensors of the Mossad. US Immigration agents. Roaches from Seventy-seventh Street, who have travelled across the oceans packed in tubes of suntan lotion. Everything is converging (mon dieu! are THEY returning??) – I feel static again, from across the hill. Is it from the sinister Klander Annexe, or just Davidov sending messages to Yissachar on a home-made morse-code transmitter? Beasts from Irving Klotskashes movies, threshing about in celluloid vaults? (Beware electricity, Nili once warned me, a sure sign of schizophrenia. And a convention of one's alters? Send for the ambulance, señors.) I cannot tell if I am closer to solving my riddles or further away than ever. A biblical verse that Fat Avi, Square Gideon and I used to giggle about, around the time of the *Sturmer* volumes, edges its way into my brain: There shall not remain, it affirms, one who pisseth against the wall. That, at least, is clear. Even three thousand years ago They were on to me. Already warning, wagging their finger at the victim to come. Watch it, Blok! He that pisseth against the wall can expect not a smidgin of mercy! Doom beckons. Doom nears. Nietzsche, where are you now? Into the escape hatch, merde, alors! squeeze in, close the airlock! Diving stations, cholera! mayday! mayday! maksh! maksh! Is anyone out there, over?

... The fried egg threatening to congeal, Berl Eibeschutz sprinkled a little Adolf upon the drying yolk and smashed a bottle of tabasco on it. 'Oi! Oi! Oi!' lamented Heimie, Son of Mottel, seeing his tablecloth ruined. 'That's the ticket!' enthused Yankel Tillimzoyger. 'Let's get a little more pep into this.' The Elders moved even closer together, their heads meeting in a ten-rayed mandala. An electric charge passed through the circle, causing the hairs of the less depleted members to become entangled. 'Oof!' 'Ouch!' 'Scheiss-mit-reiss!' They disengaged to a safer distance. 'Shush, hevreh,' said 'Meshug-gener' Weitz, 'a little more concentration here, please.' They fell silent, examining the blotch that moved pitilessly across Heimie Goldschlaeger's table – fading embers of sunspot desires, hopes gurgling down tabasco roads, the glimmering fates of those trapped in the coils of their ambitions and duties ... Eisav, propelled by Zetz into myth, Tarablus, still stalking his prey? Yama Ama/ O'Habash, still scrubbing away, leaving the mashraq's lusts unrequited ... and, oh yes, the usual fates of nations, the volcanoes of their collective fears ...

Beware! Beware!

DREADFUL TALE OF A GOAT THAT PRO-
PHESIED, IN THE NEGEV, THE MESSIAH'S
COMING, AND DIED:

(from the Israeli press, September '74)

Many of the population of the Negev villages
swear to the truth of the following occurrence:
the tale of a woman who used to milk her loyal
nanny goat every morning, while greeting her
with a cheery 'sabah el hir' ('good morning', in
Arabic). One blazing hamsin morning a week
ago, when she began as was her custom to milk
the teats of the goat, she heard to her amazement
a loud voice addressing her in fluent and Biblical
Hebrew: 'What ails thee, woman, that thou
speakest in the tongue of Ishmael? Are we not in
the Land of Israel? Speak Hebrew!'

Stunned and choked with emotion the woman
let the jug of milk fall and pulled away from the
goat, which continued with the following speech:
'Know thee that these days of parched autumn
are but the heralds of the Coming Salvation, and
Messiah Son of David will appear, three months
from this very day . . .'

The terrified woman ran for her life to the
nearest moshav house and alerted the local
Rabbi and many neighbours, who came running
to see the miracle. But, lo and behold, when they
reached the spot, they found the goat lying dead
upon the baking hot ground.

This story has spread across the entire Negev
and is even being discussed as far afield as
Beersheba and Kiryat Gat. When the learned
Rabbi Almoshnino, of moshav Shuva, was asked
to comment, he said: 'Whether the tale is true or
just sucked out of a finger, there is no difference.
For one thing is clear – the footsteps of the Messiah can already be heard in Our Land.'

Indeed –

Elders to Klotskashes: Time for action!

Klotskashes to Elders: Roger.

Klotskashes to Yissachar: Now about your proposal . . .

Yissachar to Klotskashes: Aye aye, sir!

Yissachar to Davidov: The man is biting! Send syn-
opsis, treatment!

Davidov to Yissachar: Full script in the mail,
brother.

Klotskashes to Elders: The threads are connecting . . .

Yissachar to Davidov: Er, the man wants a rewrite
. . .

Davidov to Yissachar: What?! Up yours! Art is
sacred!

Klotskashes to Yissachar: When I hear the word
art – I give orders to burn the negative. Have no
fear, my ace script lady, Zelda Haemoglobin, will
be on the job in no time. Shooting is imminent. The
crew is ready. Now about the location arrange-
ments.

Yissachar to Davidov: The green light is on, comrade! This is what is about to happen . . .

**The Story So Far:**
Avram Blok is a brothel guide in fifteenth-century
Izmir. He falls in love with the beautiful Princess
Begin, who infects him with gonorrhoea. Only the
famous Dr Mark O'Polo, in far off Samarkand, can
cure this dreaded ailment. He sets off into the
Anatolian mountains. Meanwhile, invaders from
Mars, laboriously surveying the earth, have landed
on Mount Ararat. They capture Blok and, turning
him into a frog, let him loose in the Jerusalem suburb of Kiryat Moshe, with TV cameras for eyes, in
the late twentieth century. Gradually hopping his

411

way across the brown terraced hills, he reaches the Prime Minister's office. In her bedroom, Golda Meir kisses him and he turns into a ravening Golem, rampaging all over the City, raping virgins and eating the Old City walls. To save the world from this menace, planners meet in the Pentagon to decide whether to nuke the City. Meanwhile, in Bokhara, the great Rabbi Akiva Lokshenshvili has invented a magic yarmulka. His daughter, Fat Sara, puts it on and is transformed into Princess Meng, an heiress of the T'ang dynasty. Meanwhile, in Jerusalem, the National Convention of Religious Ball Bearings Manufacturers is about to open. But as the chairman, Nachman Kimche, bangs his gavel for the first session, an immense cloud of dust rises and the doors at the back are flung open, revealing . . .

(now read on)


### Nietzsche's narrative:

Finally, in the autumn of '74, Blok approached me, asking to join in my travels. There he was, leaning against the doorbell of my apartment, desperate to become my disciple (I was on a short home leave at the time). I told him, firstly: our launching pad had to be the Klander, I was never able to travel from any place else. Secundo: Madness was not a commitment to be undertaken lightly. A slight slip and one might end up completely gaga, a case beyond Klander's brief. One could find oneself in the state loony bin of T – t, plugged into the ECT machine, or even on the operating table, having bits scooped out of one's brain. But he waved all that off, with a glint in his eye that I found not at all unpleasing. I have reached the stage, he said, where drastic action is called for.

There are questions for which I need direct answers. For example:

Who am I?

Where did I come from?

What's going on and how did it get that way? Did it all go wrong somewhere along the way or was it all ferkakt from the start?

I told him I couldn't oblige him right now, I was on my way out to Zisselmacher's Laundry, that he should enrol in the University as his mother wanted him to, or buy a diploma on the black market. But he put his foot in the door and said: don't give me that guff, I want to know things as they are.

I saw there was a shimmer of a glimmer of a spark somewhere behind that thinning forehead. We walked together down Salant Street in the bright sunshine, each carrying a navy blue laundry bag. 'Before I play Mephisto to your Faust,' I said to him, 'I have to be clear on one point. You are not, I hope, wandering down the mystic cul-de-sac? Cabbalism, tarot, Gurdjieff, Ouspensky, ouija boards and other ou-la-la?' He swore blind that was not his drift. 'I have boned up more on your works,' he assured me, '*Beyond Good and Evil, Twilight of the Idols, Zarathustra, The Antichrist.*'

'Adolescent stuff,' said I, 'nothing to what's coming.' We entered the laundry, battling through tides of doss-schvitz and boiled soap, fidgeting customers gnawing their tsitsis. Old Zisselmacher, a cross between a wizened Chinese coolie and a nanny goat, tottered forward to receive my soiled togs. 'The world will shake,' I continued to enlighten Blok, 'the mountains will skip like rams, the hills as sons of sheep. No starch on the shirts,' I told the Ancient of Days, 'you know I can't abide stiff collars.' 'You will get what the Lord Blessed Be He provides,' croaked the mummy. 'If you are He,' I riposted, 'you certainly look as He must feel.' He turned away muttering, and the claque spewed the ends of frayed tsitsis. I shall probably never see my laundry again.

413

I felt the old anger rising as I walked with Blok back up the road, gesturing behind me at the roof-tops stretching to the Old City. 'Look at it,' I said, 'everything that is wrong with our Judaeo-Christian culture has its origins in this wretched bivouac. The dome of the Temple Mount, where Blok's name-sake Avram played chicken with the Lord . . . "Oh what a sweet world this might have been if the old gods had kept their power!" ' Dionysus against the Crucified – I had put it so well in a nutshell. But as I toiled up the slope, past the true believers in their black shrouds and sombre faces, I felt, for the first time in years, in decades, almost a century in fact, the need for a new disciple, a new Gast to ease my lonely burden. Blok? This equally lonely ship-wrecked drifter, lost in mid-ocean with his last tin of mouldy old captain's biscuits rapidly running out?

'I am due back in Klander soon,' I told him, 'but you will need a ruse to get in there, a pretext, seeing Veltsch is against you. But not too strong, mind, as I advised, lest you miscalculate . . .'

'Don't worry,' he said, with a sang froid that was encouraging, 'did not Our Founder, Theodore Herzl, say: if you will it, it is no fairy tale?'

'No fairy tale? I'll show 'em!' cried Irving Klotskashes, rising from the depths of his sitzbath. Cigar glowing red in the moonscape of his face like a spacevessel poised for take off. 'Smee!' An Algerian gnome slapped a bathtowel around his pot. 'Prokofieff!' His legless Japanese valet wheeled forward bearing the day's apparel. They were both refugees from the golden age of the Z-movie mogul's triumphs. The first, from *Beast Men of Bataan*, the second from *Mango Swamp Terror*. Slapping on the costume, the blue dashiqi with the green zodiac roundels, he strode out on the porch, below the San Simeonesque belfry in which an audio-animatronic of Lon Chaney Senior swung upon a cracked ninety-pounder. 'Ze bells! ze bells!' it croaked horribly, punkt upon the quarter hour. To the lawn, past the garden gargoyles of Lon Junior, Boris, Bela, Basil and Ernest. His zouave pilot, Goritsas, held open the door of his private Sikorski chopper, World War II vintage, khaki camouflaged, with the imp Samnaglof painted on its tail. In no time at all they were clattering over Mount Baldy en route for Los Angeles Airport. Yissachar's Davidov script, reworked by Zelda Haemoglobin nestling in his briefcase, along with an exchange of letters, proposals, agreements, with a certain asylum director. Yes, everything converges, as Blok, in Ein Rogel Street, prepares a real cock and bull pretext to enter the asylum for the third – and last? – time. Irving K., the Great Has Been, hovers over Beverly Hills, on the first lap of his journey east to Jerusalem, to the hill of Klander, to fulfil his filmic come-back and the threads of his destiny, the consequences of fried egg visions, viz: to shoot, upon the authentic location (where the whole schmeer happened!), with staff and patients for actors and a crew unrevealed, the Z-movie par excellence, the apotheosis of schluck – the true legend of the Judas Pig . . .

AND THE FEAR, CHOLERA! THE CREEPING TERROR! MAKSH! MAKSH! WILL IT NEVER END?

# V

ON THE UNIVERSAL TENDENCY TO
DEBASEMENT IN THE SPHERE OF LOVE.
                    (contributions to the psychology
            of love, II – Sigmund Freud, 1912)

'He who travels in one direction only, without inter-
ruption, enters the void.'
                              –Franz Fuhman

            '. . . ugh, kek, ptah!'
                              – James Joyce

LE MAT

Dawn over the asylum. Tendrils of grey creeping steadily up from the Jericho hills. Within, the soft lights of the early morning round click on. The nurses soft-shoe through the corridors pushing before them upon squeaking wheels the trolleys with the magic pilules: Thorazine, Stelazine, Trilafon, Haldol, Vesprin, Moban, Loxitane, Compazine, Pheergan, Dartal and Tindal, Taractan and Repoise. To chase away gremlins, open a cream-coloured door on a bright, chemical future. Most patients fake it, flushing the stuff down the toilet as soon as staff's back is turned. The rats and roaches, in the sewers below, are the most tranquil in all Jerusalem. Softly they dream their dreams of glory, lulled in warm technicolor. Flusser's wet liberalism still holds in check Veltsch's demands for tighter security. 'What's better,' says the old man, 'patients doped to the eyeballs or just quietened by the pretence of being so?' But the Director is ageing fast. Gnarled as his cane now, he sits in group and staff sessions, plastered down by his great thatch of white hair, wheezing like a beached whale. Veltsch, sinking his behaviourist harpoons into the dying hulk. Just wait, the guard will soon change around here, anarchy will not prevail. 'Need we state the obvious?' he cries, flicking schmeck from his ear. 'Why are we acting like ostriches? Resistance, disobedience and bloody-mindedness are rife throughout the entire Institute. Secret meetings, occult rituals, political subversion. We are on the verge, I think, of the Laingian fallacy of allowing patients to proceed, as it were, on the "journey" of their psychosis. And I fear the director's assent to the Metronome film project is just making matters worse. Patients are becoming excited, weaving fantasies and hopes that cannot be fulfilled. Not to speak of the Nietzsche and Blok disaster, a signal warning to us all. I fear,' he ends darkly, 'we are sowing a harvest that will reap bitter tears.'

He could mention other seeds, lying around, waiting perhaps for the radio-active burst that would bring forth their full malignancy: the Atomic Bomb in the belly of Bertha Bloom, Conforti's Bulgarian Cheka, the Magpie, still searching for the one item that might set his fingers at rest. Yama Ama/ O'Habash, still scrubbing away at the floors and crazy paving ... the commencement of his/her forty years' wandering round and round the Promised Land of the Annexe? And Nili, walking the wards at night, as we shall see, sunk in her own woes. Reverting to Nili, Professional Nurse, as morning scuds up the Valley, pale winter sun illuminating the Nietzschean graffiti scrawled sometime when her back was turned:

'LIVE DANGEROUSLY!'

'MORE HORROR! MORE DANGER! MORE EARTHQUAKING!'

'THE EARTH HAS A SKIN, AND THE SKIN HAS DISEASES, ONE OF WHICH IS CALLED: MAN.'

'GOD DIED OF HIS PITY FOR MAN!'

'TRUTH IS CROOKED, TIME IS A CIRCLE.'

## 'EVERYTHING CACKLES, BUT WHO WANTS TO SIT QUIETLY AND HATCH EGGS?'

Who indeed? Seven years to the day after his contretemps with Justice Ben Horin, one year after his débâcle in the October War, Blok re-entered the Klander asylum. He claimed to have discovered the historical matrix in which he found himself living was shared with him by nobody else. To wit: I have been told, he said, that I am inhabiting an alternative historical epoch. Blok's version was this: Germany has been a Communist state since 1923, Leon Trotsky ruled Russia for forty-four years till his death in 1967, Adolf Hitler and his colleagues escaped to the United States, where Adolf eventually became Senator for the State of Illinois and his son ran for President on a third-party ticket, in an alliance with Southern Democrats. An uneasy peace has prevailed thus in a divided Europe for over five decades, with the large Jewish populations of Eastern Europe and Russia supporting the small Jewish yishuv in Palestine, which remained under British rule until 1973, when the State of Israel was finally proclaimed after a long war with the Arabs, who had formed their own separate independent cantons in the West Bank and Gaza.

'A likely story!' scoffed Veltsch. 'Call for the military police!' 'We must help the lad,' said Flusser, 'to face his Munchausen complex, to break out of his own web. We must try and comprehend the issues which led to this unique amnesic fresco.'

'An intriguing scenario,' said Nietzsche, approvingly, 'let us see if we can place it in situ.' So saying he flew off to Alexanderplatz, Berlin, September 1926. Returning, fairly swiftly, having seen the first run of Pabst's *Geheimnisse Einer Seele* at the Metropole (with Werner Krauss, Ilka Gruning, Ruth

Weyher, Pawel Pawlow and Hertha von Walther). 'No,' he said, 'it's business as usual. You have got it wrong somewhere. Still, we should not stop trying . . .'

He immediately instituted a course of intensive training to prepare Blok for temporal travel. The Great Leap, he described it, into the eternal recurrence, the primal chaos of existence. ('Will I need sunglasses?' asked Blok, pushing innocence too far. With kitbag, Sergeant-Major? With kitbag.) The training included eye exercises in the Jerry Lewis mould, trick memory drills at random ('where were you at eight p.m. on 12th January, 1954, asargelusha?') and readings from The Book, which Nietzsche had adopted as a catalyst for short-cut mind clearance. The Book, which he had received from O'Habash five years earlier in the Swedish Tea Shoppe, with Nili and Blok looking on and the Mossad agents snapping the scene from inside Bin-Zabl's belly. The same volume, of course, that Private Pusht had thrown through the bars of Father Andronicus's cell in the Jerusalem kishla, circa 1916, in lieu of Scheiss-papier, and had been handed by him to the pious Sister Bankie, fourteen years later, to pass on to person or persons unknown: *The Cabalogus Sephiroticum* of the Gnostic martyr Iphictitus, though it had also been known by a variety of other titles: *The Handbook of Dromedary Care* by Don Jose y Pepe, the *Awali Family Planning Guide*, the *Mens Insana* by Corporal Sano, the *Cookbook of Haroun al-Rashid*. It was rumoured, in fact, to be the lost *Book of Krates*, the ur-Alchemical source work. Davidov had fingered it for Nietzsche, years before, as an impenetrable matrix cypher, but it was not till '68 that O'Habash tracked it down to a tiny second-hand bookstore in Bokhara, Uzbekistan, where it was masquerading under the title *Some Appendices to the New*

*Program of the Uzbek Communist Party, Volume XXIII: On the Uprooting of Bourgeois Ideology in the Ball Bearings Industry*, a cast iron guarantee, one might have thought, of its remaining upon the shelf. But no, purchased, for nine kopecks, by O'Habash, delivered, through rack and ruin, to the Philosopher's eagle eye, now put to good use to befuddle Blok's brain and sharpen his alienation . . . 'I can't make head nor tail of this!' he cries, facing the impenetrable gothic script, the graphic basilisks and unicorns, giant worms winding round umlauts. 'Excellent!' riposts Nietzsche. 'But you are still comprehending! Abandon becoming. Be!'

The film crew arrived, upstaging the drama of Blok and Nietzsche's outgrabings. Pouring out of a Volkswagen van one morning direct from the Kings Hotel: Irving Klotskashes, in maroon knicker-bockers, camouflage jacket and a red beret; cigar glowing in puss and Yissachar, bowing and scraping, before him: Yes, sir, no sir, this way, Massa K, baas, effendi, tuan, bwana mkuba, Herr Oberst . . . The unknown crew, rather smaller in number than might have been expected for a feature film, shambling after, oddly out of place with their profes-sional uniforms: tattered jeans, tennis shoes, roll-top sweaters. Everyone remarked on their unusually high average age, and the way they contrived to wear hats in or out, tam o'shanters, furs, tembels, kepis. How they kept scratching uneasily shaven chins as if mourning vanished shrubbery . . . Not to speak of their incredible clumsiness in handling the movie equipment: the cameraman caught trying to screw the lens in the viewfinder, the grip connecting live wires with bare hands (said Scriabina), their general stumbling over cables, boxes, dolly tracks, tripods, lights. Crash, Bang! another 1K bulb shatters, almost tripping the air-raid sirens. Staff expressed concern, but Yissachar calmed them, saying: 'They are just a bit rusty, they have not worked for a while, they are a team from the good old days.' But Davidov, counting them, ending on his tenth finger, came to the unavoidable conclusion: 'You are the Elders of Zion,' he told the sound recordist, 'I claim my ringside seat.' But the man merely sighed, continuing to press his microphone to the asylum's floors, ceilings, walls . . .

'Avram!' cried Yissachar, spotting him in a corridor, 'are you all right, old friend?' Blok looked at him blankly. 'Don't you remember me, Avram? It's Peron, your old pal! Remember Holyland Films, Shpilkman, Wilkman and Brodie? The lost pussycats of Avenue A?' But Blok brushed by him, saying: 'I do not think we have met. Pray get out of my way, rapscallion.'

Thin Avi came to visit him, trying to entice him back to life with passes, spells and incantations. Words like 'bourgeoisie', 'oppression', 'poverty', 'dispossession', 'police' and 'exile'. But Blok's face just became sadder and sadder, and a clump of his hair fell out. Avi, Yissachar and Nili adjourned to a café, down on the Hebron Road. Overlooking winter mist and shabby warehouses, heavy trucks rumbling south to Bethlehem. How can we save our friend, they mused, having ordered three 'upside down' coffees. But the rain, dropping out of a leaden sky, washed away their conversation, leaving each a silent island wrapped in his or her contemplation . . .

And the days passed, the asylum transforming into interlocking film sets. Arab labourers, working to the K.'s instructions, stripping the Institute free of all the manifestations of comfort that made the place liveable: wallhangings, cupboards, bookshelves, paintings, pin-ups, bric-à-brac, carpets.

The script called for a strict pre-war institution, a bare prison of fear and misery. The patients, in a vast, unprecedented meeting, had enforced this spartan proposal. 'We don't want to show the world an image of happiness,' said Bertha Bloom, 'let's tell the Truth for once.' The Truth! Veltsch cried silently. The fucking Truth!? Almost keeling over on the spot. Apart from him, only the Magpie dissented, fearful that his secret stashes would be uncovered. He laboured deep into the night, moving his pischifkes into emergency burrows. Nik! Nik! Nik! one heard his little chisel picking far into the small hours. And Yama Ama, scrubbing away, wondering at the shadow that flitted from bush to bush. Wearily turning his/her nose back to the grindstone of the maze of crazy paving. The Annexe, above, looming silently, as it had for the past year. He/she gazed wistfully at the ten feet of lawn between the paving and the Annexe door. If only the path actually reached there . . . the whole quest might soon be over. But no use dreaming when hard facts prevail. On she scrubbed, slapping the schmutter. Deep inside the ersatz charwoman, the pornographer stirred, squirming and squeaking tinnily. Let me out! Let me out! there are clients to serve, perversions to placate, KGB bosses to appease . . . nachtiger tug. Stay there, Liameleh, this is your new home . . . your drive, your quest, that Schmuck in Beirut must come to terms with this. Nose, fake warts, plastic moles and wig bent tragically towards the Klander ground . . .

While, inside, Nili wandered, through the stripped wards, open to night shift static. Groans and moans, incontinent farts, long yusufs, abrupt brahims. Eyeless cameras watching her, headless tripods stum while she strives to commune with her lover: Come in, Eisav, your honey awaits you, Come

425

in, pascudniak. Over. Dot-dot-dot, dash-dash-dash, dot-dot-dot, over. Where the hell are you, little lost boy, which void have you fallen into? – Recollecting her efforts to screw enlightenment out of Eisav's scourge, Zetz: trying to track down the Iron General, chasing secret telephone numbers Eisav had entrusted to her in the good old days before. Till finally the Man himself phoned her, out of the blue, inviting her round for Sabbath afternoon tea, to be held on the verandah of his new home in the Old City's rebuilt Jewish quarter. There they sat, then, with Zetz's wife, a pantheresque kibbutz lady, serving cookies, veiled in corporate silence. Zetz looking very odd out of uniform, the leopard with his spots in a cupboard. For he had gone on the reserve list after the war and had launched a new, political career. Stomping up and down the country, doling out warnings against the Decline of the Nation. Against Moral Laxity, International Communism, Self Hate and Assimilation. Zetz spoke here, Zetz spoke there, invoking God on Mount Sinai, Moses, Jabotinsky, Clausewitz. Zetz denouncing Richard Nixon for betraying himself in the wake of wet liberal pressure. Zetz praising the Shah as a bulwark of Freedom, on a semi-clandestine world tour. Other heroes Zetz lauded: Pinochet of Chile, Nicaragua's Somoza, Romero of El Salvador. In South Africa he embraced Balthazar John Vorster, and laid a wreath at the Voortrekker monument. In Vermont USA, passing through, he had breakfast with Solzhenitsyn. He addressed the Kansas City Bnai Brith, and called Yasir Arafat 'the Heinrich Himmler of the Modern Age'. But with Nili he was all olive oil and butter on the verandah overlooking the City. In front of them, giant construction cranes towered over the Western Wailing Wall and the great Islamic domes beyond of silver and of gold. From below they could hear the devout loudly keening their objections to ancient injustices. Zetz, keeping a proprietorial eye on the hub of the whole damned schmeer. He confirmed her 'feminine instinct' that Eisav was alive, a prisoner of war 'somewhere'. More than that I cannot say, of course, Nili, you understand, you are one of us. And he repeated the catechism: We do not abandon a prisoner or a casualty in captivity or in the field. Adding: Is not Eisav my younger brother, raised and moulded on the Mahatz farm? A Holocaust chip, off the felled tree of Europe, replanted in ancestral soil. And what soil! He regaled Nili with tales of old Mahatz, his father, who had just turned eighty-five. How he had chiselled the first furrows in the rock-hard ground, in '08, by tying his feet to a wild swamp buffalo and using his head for a plough. In those days the men were the tanks. Zetz sighed, today you need General Dynamics . . . But a buzzer in his ear informing him of a phone call cut short his reminiscences. He took the call in a padded communications room, secured against eavesdropping and surveillance by powerful electronic scramblers. Leaving Nili to make her own polite exit and walk home through the Arab bazaars. Dot-dot-dot, dash-dash-dash, dot-dot-dot, over . . . I lift up mine eyes unto the hills, from whence cometh my help, over? But the hills are mute, and the fear of discovery jams the anguished cries of longing . . .

December arriving, replacing dappled November with a chilly monochrome grey. Shooting commenced despite Yissachar's misgivings about the smallness of the crew. 'Anyone can do it!' declared Klotskashes, grandly, appointing Elkayam and Marciano as grips, Nurse Nitsa (El Bzaz) as script girl. Nathan Hadayah was gaffer, E. Conforti, art director, Meshuggener Weitz and Tillimzoyger on the BNC camera, Berl Eibeschutz and Zunz on sound. Heimi Goldschlaeger, as caterer, fought with Mrs Patchouli, Azaniah carefully guarded the props. Irving K. functioning as director-producer, executive producer and Lord High Everything Else. (This leaves the Tenth a mysterious absence, which will be dealt with in time.) First slates then, on the lawn, with Mrs Conforti cast as the Scottish Sister MacTavish. A defrocked Rabbi named Katz, who had eaten lobsters on Sabbath, played the cracked Father Andronicus, the resurrected mogul having screen-tested everyone who was even vaguely compos mentis. He was frustrated only by the Magpie, who cursed him in Spanish, and Nietzsche, his first choice for Andronicus. 'That kisser! that bush! I must have it!' the K. cried, but Nietzsche brusquely waved him away. 'My image is not for sale,' he said, rejoining Blok for their evening training session. Hanging upside down by the feet from a hook illegally hammered into the ceiling, reciting together the most obscure Book section, the recipes of Haroun al-Rashid: Body of Christ Sauté with Green Peppers . . . Unicorn Roast on the Horn . . . Whale Jonah (cooked from within) . . . Djinn Tarts, Virgin's Farts in Yoghurt, Poached Cyclops Eye Bayildi . . . 'This cannot be done!' Blok cried in annoyance. 'True,' said Nietzsche, 'we have not the ingredients. But battle on, my little Blokhead, enlightenment may strike like lightning . . .' Nili, chancing on them at the start of her shift, wearily cutting them down. Warning Blok: 'Cut it out, lunatic, before it is really too late.' 'Why should I take your advice?' he said huffily, having landed on his head. 'Because I love you, you idiot,' she said, ramming his instep with the sole of her foot and withdrawing.

LOVE??

Surely not! That fleshly struggle, the slap of skin

upon skin. Or not, as the case might have been, with the Friedmans, and their wee hole in the sheet . . . LOVE??? The peels scattered thereof, in Onkelos Street, vigorous wrist action for Victoria in Stamford Hill . . . or for Malka Halperin, all over Jerusalem, spilling one's ample seed . . . where falls a drop of Blokonan moisture, will flowers or weeds spring forth? 'Sexual Love,' said Square Gideon, 'is a tremendous force which motivates and guides man's actions . . .' Avaunt! spare us, Professor, your erudition, we have more important matters at stake . . . Elisha Haggis (minched Youths in Bear Stomachs), Braised Scheherezade (after failure of 1002nd tale), Garden of Eden Fruit Salad (taken at diner's risk) . . .

Beware! Beware! Beware!

And the clans continuing to gather outside the asylum; transferred from Ein Rogel Street. Name them: Detective Hercule Picherot, winner of the 1966 Charles de Gaulle Medal for placing his head, in which a steel plate had been inserted after Dien Bien Phu, between the President and an assassin's bullet, squatting in the rhododendrons, nursing in his pocket the faded portrait of Blok/Abu Jilda. Ignatius 'Droopy' Muldoon, ex-FBI, ex-CIA, et cetera and part-time writer, under the pseudonym of Prunella Squeegee, of such tender pieces for British ladies' journals as 'Teatime for Gran', 'Mum's Sweetie Jar', 'A Kiss Before Teatime' and 'My Dog Gave Me a Hickey', lying on the roof drilling silently through the walls to place minute 'tear-drop' video cameras punkt above Blok's whereabouts (serving both US Immigration and the Friedman/Kalisher axis; in London he had spied on Blok in the guise of an ice cream van man, in New York – from inside the Lubavitchers' Mobile Mitzvah Waggon). Babelech-und-Farfel, each schmootz in their putrescent clothing sending coded messages to Moscow, crouching mumbling just behind the stone perimeter fence. Further down the hillside, Mossad agents kibitzing from inside ersatz molehills.

As if this were not enough, the bent figure of an extremely old and wizened Arab man makes its slow way up the hill on a cane. He is none other than Nagib Abd-el-Khalik, Abu Shawareb of legend. Now eighty-eight years old, he had never left home as he had dreamed to fight for the Cause, but remained, under the thumb of Fatima, the Jackal of Silwan (God rest her soul now), in his house not a stone's throw from the site of his pre-war contretemps with Father Andronicus. While decades passed, sons, grandsons, great-grandsons grew up and vanished, many swallowed by the National Cataclysm, scattered to exile or prison cells or planted in early graves, the old shepherd, flying stubbornly in the face of gathering gloom, diligently re-grew his shawara, so burnt and devastated that cruel night in the Judas Tunnel. For days and nights now he had been mooning about the Klotskashes production, hoping to be offered a small supporting role, like the ones he had had in *Exodus* and *Jesus Christ Superstar*. (In *Blazing Sands,* a local production, he had set a mine under a Jewish bus, killing fifty men, women and children, his only contribution, ersatz alas, to the National Cause.) His present dream is of spending his final days at a poolside in Beverly Hills, flat on his back, salved with suntan lotion and sipping a rum daiquiri. But this is unlikely to be achieved, as the K., after much deliberation, had decided that Yissachar should, wrapped in fake hair and burnoose, play the legendary Arab's role. So the old peasant, bereft of glory, kibitzes, as the film rolls into the can, and Blok and Nietzsche, in the toilets, their room, the corridors, struggle on for temporal fugue, and the clouds scud and

December riffles by, creeping up upon Christmas Eve . . .

And Davidov, tagging after the sound man, Berl Eibeschutz, in the breaks between shooting, a pair of binoculars glued to his eyes like a character from *La Jetée*. 'It's the Pig you're after, is it not, ya Rebbe? It's clear, Davidov can't be fooled.' 'Shush!' Eibeschutz touching finger to lips, straining for headphone data. 'Next Thursday, the twenty-fourth, in the morgue tunnel,' said Davidov, 'I'll bring the thermos flask.' 'If you're following me around you might at least make yourself useful,' Eibeschutz handed him his accessory bag. Peeking therein, Davidov found an assortment of measuring devices – a geiger counter, a diagometer, an ergometer, an embryoscope . . . 'I salute you,' said Davidov with passion, 'you are a man after my own heart.' Adding his binoculars to the hold-all he noticed an implement he had not remarked before. 'What's this?' he asked, lifting the leather strap, the strange metal clasp and chain. 'It is a Sowescu Pig Harness,' said Eibeschutz, 'a discount offer from the *Farmers' Weekly*.' Without hesitation, Davidov dropped to the ground and kissed his redeemer's feet.

Yes! 24th December dawns, a braw, bricht, brillig, gusty, cloud-scudding day. The Old City filled with sectarian hubbub, parades well on their way to Bethlehem. Bearded guests, in flowing robes, yodelling and swinging censers. Lo, a child will be born, in a stable, the Son of God, man, no shit. He will grow up to preach loving kindness and all manner of positive vibes. But his best friend, so the story goes, will betray him to the relevant authorities, who will nail him up, in the holy sepulchre (some say in the Armenian chapel, others in the Latin or Greek). Perhaps driven frantic by the gnashing and

431

wailing that is rife in the enclosed grottos he will rise from the dead three days later and, after an impromptu press conference, will depart for heavenly spheres. The bulk of the Jews, who will reject his divinity, will be blamed later on for his death, with dreadful consequences, despite claims by theologians that the death was both inevitable and necessary . . . ah, what a stubborn and headstrong people, insisting on their own narrow path . . . diverging, along the way, down all manner of weird trails – Shabetai Zvi, Frank, Herzl, Zetz . . .

Evening falls, and the time is ripe for the apotheotic moment: all cast and crew descending after supper (chicken à la Mrs Patchouli, Danish pastries by Heimi Goldschlaeger) into the morgue tunnel. The Big Scene – reconstruction of the seminal Pig-exorcism of 1963. Only this time it was to be done in style: flickering torches of black rags and tar were set along the short passageway. The bathroom tiles were covered by papier-mâché rock walls, and plastic bats hung upside down from the ceiling. Clockwork roaches scurried along the floor. Water dripped from hidden pipes in the network. Fake bones lay about in small piles. From a trunk marked Twentieth Century Box the crew of nine extracted the props – the candelabra, the black candles, incense sticks, purification board. With elaborate ceremony they unveiled a singular scroll of the Torah which was so old it threatened to crumble even in the tender grip of their hands. Everyone immediately donned headgear, skullcaps, handkerchiefs, socks. For the entire asylum, in effect, was present, welcomed to kibitz on the final slates. Nili, Renata and Pitsi standing by with an ample supply of syringes, pilules. The entire asylum, that is, except three: Yama Ama, scrubbing, scrubbing above, and Blok and Nietzsche, who had declared their lack of interest, pursuing their rituals in Ward

Three. Nili, biting her nails and wondering whether she should have left them there, but already, a faint static crackling nags at her inner ear . . .

Meanwhile, deep underground . . .

Meanwhile, far far away . . .

Meanwhile, deep in one's genes . . .

(Davidov, with a plastic bat on his head, fastened with a rubber band round his chin, sidles up behind Eibeschutz, whispering:

'Canst thou draw out leviathan with an hook? or his tongue with a cord which thou lettest down? Canst thou put an hook into his nose? or bore his jaw through with a thorn? Will he make supplications unto thee? Will he speak soft words unto thee? Will he make a covenant with thee? wilt thou take him for a servant forever? . . . Shall the companions make a banquet of him? Shall they part him among the merchants? Canst thou fill his skin with barbed irons? or his head with fish spears?'

'I don't really know,' said Eibeschutz, checking his Nagra recorder, 'but at least we can give her a whirl.')

'On your marks!' shouts Klotskashes, 'no time to lose now! Camera! Sound! Slate, goddamn it!'

'Excuse me, sir . . .' Yissachar, timorously gathering courage to ask the K. the sixty-four-thousand-dollar question that had been bothering him since the building of the morgue tunnel set: 'I know it's stupid of me and I'm obviously overlooking something self-evident, but – are we doing the exorcism scene?'

'Yes?' The K. passed him a look which made the plastic bats squeak tinnily.

'Who,' said Yissachar, still dressed in his burnoose, 'are the actors who will play the exorcist Rabbis?'

'Actors?' cried Klotskashes, 'ACTORS, you bastard??! When I shoot a film – it's for real!'

\*     \*     \*

'These ethical ideas [of the Jews] cannot, however, disavow their origin from the sense of guilt felt on account of a suppressed hostility to God. They possess the characteristic ... of obsessional neurotic reaction-formations: we can guess, too, that they serve the secret purposes of punishment.'

– Sigmund Freud:
'Moses and Monotheism' (1937)

### Instantly a December Storm Leapt Up

Instantly a December storm leapt up, lashing the Jerusalem hills. Not the gentleness of April showers but the real thing, scattering the parades, sending everyone running for cover, hijacking dustbin lids, pulling sweaters over their heads. Lightning shears the night, yakkety-yakketing like the laughing policeman gone mad. Clouds empty their guts, turning alleyways into rivers, clogging sewers, gushing away through cracks in the ground far into depths unknown. And after the celestial flush the City releases into the streets a sortie of a different kind: bearded hassidim, aboard an old Wyllis pick-up, rattling up the Mea Shearim road. Clattering between time-warped stetl houses leaning in at crazy angles, every brick plastered with dire warnings in Hebrew, Yiddish and English:

'KEEP OUT!'
'DO NOT ENTER!'
'PISS OFF – THIS MEANS YOU!'

They carry a banner, flicking past shuttered windows: 'BEWARE, SONS OF THE WISE! HERESIES

434

UPON THEE, O ISRAEL!' Après deluge lamplight glistens off their plastic waterproof streimel hats like a constellation of halos. In the cabin of the vehicle – the Monk, the missing Tenth of the cabal, delegated to whip up metaphysical support for the Elders in their hour of need. (He has to wear a false beard and wig to disguise his cinematographic disguise.) The devotees, happy to oblige, particularly tonight, to counter the idol worship of the gentiles in the Old City. Vigorously chanting God's name, they proceed to Geula, their beards oscillating in fugue.

The Monk, having egged them on, left them at Schneller retracing his steps towards the south. He now had a difficult duty to carry out, which he had postponed till the last moment. It was this: to break in on the hermetic seclusion of his father, Reb Zev, alias the Revered. Now one-hundred-and-four years of age, the old man had lived locked in his room since 1948, his isolation relieved only by the voice of his housekeeper, the Widow Eisenstein, now eighty-seven. She passed his meals of bread, milk and royal jelly through a hinged flap in his door, retrieving his empties and slops. For twenty-six years he had set eyes on no one, not even his own son. But now time was running short, the exigencies demanding a unique breach of fidelity. The Monk quickened his pace, along Mea Shearim road, passing under the great sign slung across the thoroughfare:

| | | |
|---|---|---|
| JEWISH DAUGHTER! | בת ישראל! | אידישע טאכטער! |
| THE TORAH OBLIGATES | התורה מחייבת אותך | דיא תורה |
| YOU TO DRESS MODESTLY. | ללבוש תלבשת צנועה. | פערפליכטעט דיר |
| WE DO NOT TOLERATE | אין אנו סובלים | צי געהן |
| PEOPLE PASSING | שברחובותינו תעבורנה | צניעותדיג געקלידעט. |
| THROUGH OUR STREETS | בתלבשת | מיר פארטראגן נישט |
| IMMODESTLY DRESSED! | בלתי צנועה! | דאס מזאל דורך געהן |
| COMMITTEE | | אונזערע גאסין אינאאום |
| FOR GUARDING MODESTY | ועד משמרת הצניעות. | צניעותדיגע קלידונג. |

And the scrawl, upon a bare stone wall:

✡ = 卐 = ☭

DEATH TO AUTOPSIES!

HANDS OFF OUR MESSIAH!

But the storm, having raged, had also released from bondage a projection of a different kind – mystic lettering, in a dim alley behind the Independence Park אמת – EMET – TRUTH – the very word inscribed by the medieval Rabbi Judah Lev Ben Bezalel on the forehead of his clay creation, the Golem ... But this is a talisman of another lost magic, being merely an election poster for the Labour Party, which has survived the wrath of the young Nationalist visigoths of Menahem Begin's Freedom Party for an entire year, but has finally succumbed to the weather, time and pissing dogs. So that the storm, slashing by, tore it loose from its moorings and sent it scuttling over the pavements ... Au secours! it cries, as the rains pummel it, the wind wraps it round a lamp-post, where it remains, until the storm dies, and the City's cineasts, dumping dustbin lids, file up for action. Paul Newman at the Orgil, Greek lesbians at the Ron, who can resist this, comrades? But a frustrated Nationalist, passing by the lamp-post, tore the poster off and sent it rolling. The wind, gusting now, riffled it past Abu Shaul's, into Yoel Moshe Salomon. Picking up a little more, lifting it, sog and all, into the sky above Zion Square, and from there it banks, it soars, like an eagle over the Celestial City ...

\*　　\*　　\*

Blok and Nietzsche, alone in Ward Three, enjoying a moment of quiet. 'Is this not a moment of quiet?' said Blok, munching a peanut butter sandwich. 'Ah, indeed,' agreed Nietzsche, combing his shawara, 'if only 'twere ever thus.' A break in training, forsooth, Blok gazing at a particularly calming page of his scrapbook, incorporating some of his best clippings: 'RABBI YOSEF: AGAINST KISSINGER WE NEED THE HELP OF THE LORD', 'MAN WITH TWO HEADS LOOKS FOR LOVE', 'WORLD'S FIRST LASER CIRCUMCISION' and 'IF A MAN WEARS A TOUPEE, NEED HE ALSO WEAR A YARMULKA?' Also a photograph of a woman, in Wisconsin, giving mouth-to-mouth resuscitation to her cat. And the greatest prize of all: 'MOST RABBITS DROWN: ONLY THREE TYPES CAN SWIM', a notion so melancholy it never failed to bring tears to his eyes.

He was fondly remembering old daydreams: he was not who he was, of course. He was actually the secret agent of a galactic empire, biding his time until the invasion. His fiancée, the blonde bomb-shell Princess Vishniak, was in constant telepathic contact from their home base on the planet Shree Marmalada XVI. Soon, as the earth's total incapacity for self-government became clear, Blok would spring into action, co-ordinating the landing of ten thousand Shreean space vessels from his makeshift headquarters in Flusser's office. After the take-over his role as Commissar for Terra would be revealed. He could not quite remember the details but in the past it had all been worked out. A harmless paralysing weapon would disarm the world's armies. World leaders would be paraded, nude, on television. There would be equal rights for all. Naturally he would soon be assassinated, but the Princess would continue his life's work. Black-bordered stamps, bearing his profile, would appear in over one hundred nations. Papa Blok would receive a secretly minted flawed block, which he would sell for ten million dollars.

(In this connection he recalled from the hazy past the old joke about ex-Finance Minister Sapir: they issued a stamp with Sapir's face on, but it would never stick to the envelopes, because people spat on the wrong side.)

Ah, but all our hopes and dreams are dashed upon the rocks of our nightmares. As the spies close in, and Abu Shawareb wonders whether all the Jews have gone bonkers, below, in the morgue tunnel, the night shoot at last begins: Yissachar's klotskasheh – fool's-question – answered by a reversal of roles – crew as cast, cast as crew – the Nine of Lodz, Klotskashes included, in shot, hands linked in a mandalic circle. Beardless, like shorn Samsons, in their sweaters and dungarees. Higher staff roped in: Flusser, holding the Torah, Veltsch, under protest, the candelabra, Elkayam and Marciano the cup of embers, the incense and the purifying board. Yissachar operating, Davidov as his assistant, Margarita Conforti on sound. The Magpie on lights, although he had stolen all of the spare bulbs. Nili and Co. on guard, although everyone seemed to be on their best behaviour. All rashly awaiting the manifestation of Irving Klotskashes's motto: 'In real life, as in the movies, anything can happen. The main thing is to grab your audience, by fair means or foul. Take 'em by the scruff of the neck and shake 'em. Dip 'em in shit if you have to. My father, Reb Chayim, said: Go for the pupik! Don't let 'em fall asleep, goddamit! Whenever you might think Nah! this is too much – double and triple the stakes man!'

Quiet, and the Elders' lips a-tremble, mumbling at quintuple speed. The torchflames flickered, the plastic bats held their breath, the clockwork roaches paused. For the Elders had embarked on a marathon recital of the Five Books of Moses. 'In the beginning,' they mumbled, before anyone could notice, 'God created the heaven and the earth . . . and the earth was without form, and void, the darkness was on the face of the deep . . . and God created great whales, and every living creature . . . and God blessed them, saying, Be fruitful . . . and God said, Let us make man in our image . . . male and female created he them . . . and they were both naked, the man and his wife, and were not ashamed . . .'

As they reached Chapter Four, Blok, up above, began to feel a slight cramp in his toes. At Chapter Seven the hairs on his left shin suddenly grew extremely ticklish. At Chapter Eleven he twitched irritatedly, scratching his right thigh. At Chapter Twelve, verse one, the irritation had definitely reached his groin. 'I get that too,' Nietzsche said sympathetically, 'it's the local-made knickers, you know.' But the itching did not diminish, rising unto Chapter Seventeen: '. . . and the Lord appeared to Abram, and said unto him, I am the Almighty God: walk before me, and be thou perfect.'

Indeed? Por favor – don't give me that old-time religion . . . I am too young for love . . . per amore, nomolesta . . . but the itch has reached his belly button, his sides, the very swatch of his oxters . . . He is dancing up and down, leaping like a dervish, video pictures of his silhouette leaping through the ether from the spy cameras outside. Yama Ama, looking up from her scrubbing. The Elders, aware something is amiss. The film, juddering in the gate. Nietzsche, calling admiringly: 'Hey, that's all right, my boy! I can see you're getting there! Don't stop, carry on, cholera!' Clamping his hand on the dancing Blok's shoulder, bellowing in his ear: 'Don't stop! feel those rhythms, schmendrick! Dig that neocosmic flow! Seize the time! Go, man, go, for the eternal recurrence! Jump, asargelusha, JUMP!'

'CUT!' cried Klotskashes, 'someone peeked in the camera. Take Two – let's go through it again!'

'JUMP! JUMP!'
Into darkness, vacuum über Alles ... objects around them, floating free, like astronauts cut loose from their vessels: ancient gourds, pierced with bullet holes, emitting bagpipe wails ... water wings used by the children of Israel to cross over the Red Sea ... dybbuks, perusing the classified pages of the *Jerusalem Post* ... blown-up condoms marked with exhortations on behalf of impossible causes: 'Vote Quixote for Law and Order', 'Sigmund Freud for Pope', 'Ronald Reagan for President' ...

'What do you actually do then, Philosopher,' Blok, in vacuum, 'on your magical mystery tours?'

'This and that,' Nietzsche, nonchalant, 'a few diversions here and there ... I drop in sometimes on Berlin University, 1820, to hear Schopenhauer. He schedules his lectures at the same hour as Hegel, and so speaks to an empty classroom. I drive him spare with a press of questions the poor klutz just cannot answer. Or I drift off to Koenigsberg, 1790, to lie in ambush for Kant, in the park. As he walks his poor mutt I bombard him with vegetables, crying: 'What is the thing-in-itself of these tomatoes, ya ibn kalb?' '

'That does not seem much fun,' said Blok, somewhat peeved, 'but cannot we for instance try ...'

Cut! Au Secours – what is this? It's the Purim pageant, at Blok's old school, '58 – There is Blok himself, dressed in a white sheet, and Fat Avi, round as a barrel, with a tierchel upon his head ... it cannot be! But it is, their own schoolboy version of *Julius Caesar*, updated ... boxing gloves on their

440

hands, a crude Kiryat Moshe in the background . . . and who's this? Zounds, sapristi! Entering stage right? No. Yes. Malka Halperin, blonde, pig-tailed, twelve-years-old and her bosoms latent . . . as per script she spits at Blok's feet three times – 'tfu! tfu! tfu!' and exits. 'FILTH!' cries Blok-in-the-audience, 'DEGRADING OBSCENITY! WHERE IS THE SCHOOLS' INSPECTORATE?' But Nietzsche hauls him, fuming, to the aisle, towards the exit, scrunching parental toes with his booties . . . 'GO! GO! GO!' cries Nietzsche. Blok, closing eyes, pinching nose –

Paris, May, '68, amid the snaking throng. Demon red in sunset glow upon the Pont Neuf. Revolutionaries jostle them, digging their ribs with the pole ends of banners: 'TOUT EST POSSIBLE A LA CLASSE OUVRIERE EN ACTION!' 'What inanity!' Nietzsche protests. But he changes his tune as youths press all around him, proffering autograph books. 'C'est Nietzsche!' 'Merde, alors!' 'Formidable!' echoes on every side. He is handed a placard inscribed with his own adage: 'NI DIEU, NI MAÎTRE!' 'Dieu est mort? Dieu est mort!' cry the besotted louts, chairing him, carrying him in triumph past the Palace of Culture. 'KILL! BURN! DESTROY!' cries Nietzsche, entering into the spirit. But a CRS helicopter swoops, black upon the crimson sky. '**&&*!!&&*!!*! It is Avram Blok, the petrolleur of the Bourse!' Armoured cops, beetle-black, shin down thin ropes with cattle prods. 'AIUTO!' cries Blok, mixing latin tongues, pulling at Nietzsche's pyjama tail. The twilit idol responding reluctantly, grabbing Blok by the collar . . .

Proceeding along Take Two, the Elders had passed Leviticus, and were well into Numbers, rushing through Chapter Thirty-three, for 'these are the journeys of the children of Israel, which went forth out of the land of Egypt . . . and they removed from Rameses, and pitched in Succoth, and they departed from Succoth, and pitched in Etham . . . and they removed from Marah, and came unto Elim . . . and they departed from Hazeroth, and pitched in Rithmah . . . and they removed from Libnah, and pitched at Rissah . . . and they removed from Jotbatah, and embarked at Ebronah . . . and they removed from Ezion-Gaber, and pitched in the Wilderness of Zin . . .' Never a dull moment . . . Meanwhile the Monk had safely traversed Mea Shearim, and had arrived at his father's house. Rapping the iron door knocker, in the shape of a lion of Judah, upon the old iron door. Pretty soon the wizened features of the Widow Eisenstein peeked through a rusty grating.

'Vot you vant?' she said.

'I must see my father,' he said, 'it is a matter of Ultimate Destiny.'

'Is it a case of saving both This World *and* the Next?' croaked the old bat. 'My instructions are strict: saving This World alone is not a Sufficient Cause.'

'It is the vessels,' he said, for he knew she was no ordinary servant, the only woman in the city who had herself performed exorcisms, including one upon the high seas. 'There is an imminent danger of a further breakage, perhaps a total collapse of the zimzum.'

'Always trouble,' she said, 'why don't men leave well alone?' She opened the door, leading him through a dank hall up a crumbling stone flight of stairs. 'He's been very quiet the last seven years,' she warned, 'he might have lost the power of speech. He did say one word, in 1969, and another, last shmini atseret.'

442

'What words were those?' The Monk, making polite conversation.

'The first was "reech",' she said. 'The second, if I'm not mistaken, was "rach". It is all a complete mystery.'

Not at all, thought the Monk. A reech-rach, in colloquial Hebrew, was a zipper. The old man was commenting clearly that Creation's fly was undone. He was obviously not as cut off from events as one might be led to believe. The Widow left Reb Zvi at a grey battered door with a hinged flap at its base, having removed a tin plate with a crust of Kümmel and stumbled back downstairs, kvetching. The Monk waited a few seconds, then knocked on the door lightly. Then waited again, and knocked more heavily.

'Father!' he called. 'It's me, Zvika! I'm sorry to bother you, but a Moment of Truth is imminent!'

There was a long silence not unlike that of an abandoned tomb. Then at last there was a faint sound from within, like a very old chicken scratching with its claw its last will and testament on an antique parchment. There was a tinkle and scrape and the Monk sensed the door had been unlatched. He waited a further thirty seconds and then pushed the door open and stepped inside.

The room was small, almost a cell, with a tiny window high in the back wall. On an iron cot, with neatly folded sheets on it, and almost hidden by a mountain of Tversky issue school copybooks, sat the sage. He was dressed in a dark gabardine jacket over a faded brown waistcoat, his frail head capped by a black velvet fez-like yarmulka. His beard was pure white, reaching down to his thighs, and his hair flowed down to his shoulders like a snowdrift upon a shadow. He was so thin and wispy his clothes seemed to enclose nothing but a ghost that had refused to depart this world. But his gaze, as he looked up into his son's eyes, was as clear as that of a youth. Instantly telepathic union was established, as each transferred to the other information gained in the past twenty-six years. The sage's shoulders sagged a little under the pressure, but the impact on the Monk was considerably more severe: his wig and false beard withered, leaving him completely defenceless, and a wisdom tooth, which had been plaguing him for several decades, flew out of his mouth and chipped the enamel washbasin. His left leg, which had a bone defect, suddenly became four centimetres shorter than his right, giving him a pronounced limp throughout the rest of his life, even if that were only to amount to a little under half an hour . . . or not, as the case might be . . . and to cap it all the sage spoke, in a firm baritone, as if he had not been totally stumm since the Mandate, giving forth his word, pronouncing his pronouncement, enunciating his ultimate message –

. . . 'I can feel something coming . . .' Davidov announces, his hands plunged in a black changing bag. Is it the EMET poster he senses, tacking sadly over the City? mourning, as it drifts with the wind, the fading of the Good Old Days . . . Work is Our Salvation, A.D. Gordon, pioneers tilling the soil . . . blue and white collection boxes of the Jewish National Fund, kiddies' pocket money, pensioners' pfennigs . . . as it passes over the street of Blok's childhood, where Avremel spat into the matsohs . . . the Russian Compound police cells, where he had languished after his night of shame . . . but what cares our Labour poster, did it not represent once – A Destiny? tugged, by the wind, over vanished No-Man's-Land, south towards the hill of Klander . . .

. . . 'I can feel something coming . . .' Elkayam to Marciano, embers to incense, over. As across the hill from the heathen temples the bells of mass begin to toll ... pilgrims in Bethlehem cram the Nativity grotto, nearer home, the crannies of the sepulchre ... spearsmen of Herod, nervous and ratty, nose about maternity wards ... the Pope is about to speak on global television ... anyone for outside broadcasts?

... 'I can feel it coming ...' Nili too is subject to extra special perceptions. Is it Eisav, breaking through the fog of non-communication? Or the buzz, from below, in Zetzian tunnels, of a thousandfold surveillance? Or is it just Blok and Nietzsche, roving incessantly somewhere in the psychic void? The plaintive bicker of Blok: 'I don't understand it: how could the flics have been on to me before I'd even done the deed?' Nietzsche: 'Ah! it is typical of the eternal recurrence that it plays hell with both sense and sequence. Sheer criminal murder, I can assure you, with both essence and substance ... Forget this small diversion of your own worthless time strain – let us merge with the mainstream!' The Elders – do they hear something coming? – not pausing in their litany: '... and they removed from Kadesh and pitched in Mount Hor ... and they departed from Mount Hor, and pitched in Zalmonah ... and they departed from Zalmonah, and pitched in Punon ...' into the mainstream, schmendricks! Blok and Nietzsche, swanning off, entire lifetimes in twenty minutes – to Voltaire, at Ferney, discussing the existence of God over a decanter of burgundy (the sage was specially keen about Einstein's relativity, which they totally failed to elucidate) ... to Karl Marx, in Soho, catching him haggling over a brace of mackerel; Blok showed him photographs of gaunt prisoners in Novaya Zemlya, but the old prophet turned to the vendor and said, 'See that, Alfie? These Prussian agents follow me everywhere, they don't give me a

445

moment's rest.' 'It's an 'ard life,' agreed the fish-monger, 'bein' an old 'Egelian.' . . . To Bollingen, to frighten the daylights out of a slumbering Jung . . . to Vienna, 19 Berggasse, abode de Freud, who said to Blok: 'Show me your underpants.' Blok: 'We are not achieving anything!' Nietzsche: 'What is there to achieve?' Blok, absently tearing out the little that remained of his hair . . .

And they departed from I-im, and pitched in Dibon-Gad, and even there they had no sitz-fleish . . . Blok, hitting upon a desperate plan to put a mark on history . . . the two of them arriving at Braunau-am-Inn, July 1888, with a clutch of noise-making devices: a klaxon motor horn, a Purim rattle and a plastic Independence Day hammer. Hiding as night fell by the window of Alois and Klara Hitler, Schillerstrasse 23. Intent, by use of implements thereof, to interrupt the attempts of the good bur-gher and his spouse to conceive their baby boy, Adolf. Rattling on the windowpane at the first signs of nookie, raising Cain to cause instant shrivel . . . 'Can we not save a full fifty million lives,' Blok hisses, 'by non-violent positive action?' 'No,' says Nietzsche. 'That implies cause and effect, which the eternal recurrence denies! Read my notes on determinism and teleology. It's all as plain as soup.' 'Bouillabaisse?' says Blok. 'Consommé,' says Nietzsche. Nevertheless – rattle-rattle, honk-honk . . . Alois, maddened, rushes forth in his nightshirt, letting fly with his shotgun, both barrels. 'Hilfe! Räuber!' Exeunt Blok and Nietzsche, pursued by Bavarian posse. Police whistles blowing. Fire bri-gade bells. Glockenspiels going wild. 'JUMP! JUMP!' yodels Nietzsche. Blok, feeling the Itch rise into the skin of his scalp . . .

As the EMET poster arrives in the sky above Klander – no one visible in the grounds below but

Yama Ama, tracing her exile in Kleen (though, behind every bush and tree, the gathered clans converge). The camera rolling on below decks, the Elders having reached Deuteronomy: 'GO IN AND POSSESS THE LAND WHICH THE LORD SWORE UNTO YOUR FATHERS . . .' Nili, suddenly hearing the voice of her lost lover battling through waves of static:

'Nili! Nili!'

'Eisav, my honey! Big Schmuck, is that really you?'

'It is I! It is I, my love! Safe, for the moment! I've escaped – but not a word to anyone!' 'How? Where? What? Why?' Her mind, sending out random shafts. He named a place: Karaganda, a Soviet prison camp in Central Kazakhstan. He had just broken out together with two ageing Trotskyists and a man who had copped life for Esperanto. Taking advantage of midwinter they had fashioned an ersatz Uzzi and two Kalashnikovs out of their frozen stool. Breaching the fence, burrowing through thirty-foot snow they had now reached the outskirts of the town of Uspensky. Only another two thousand kilometres to go, ya manayeg! – across the Betpakdala, the Iaxartes river, the Turkmen SSR, the Kyzylum, the Karakum, up to the barbed wire dividing the USSR from Iran, Brezhnev from Shahinshah, Slavery from Freedom, the House of Jacob from bondage . . . 'Beware the Tunnels!' he calls to her, across the steppes, Granit to Nili, over . . . 'Beware the Tunnels! Don't speak to Zetz – never again volunteer!'

'Aye, the Tunnels!' Reb Zev, the Revered, shouted, and the whole of Jerusalem trembled. 'The Secular Heresy! Self Determination! What an absurd delusion! National Independence! Statehood! I knew it would end in tears! Have we not been around the tables for some time? Do we not know a dud pack when we see it? Defence! Security! Ultimate weapons! I warned them, by G-d didn't I? In my secret meeting, with the Zionisten, in 1948, in the bunker. Woe betide you, said I, if you tamper with the passageways under Our Holy City. For they are solely for the use of the Resurrected to make their way through on the Day of Judgement. Even the Christians steer clear of them, calling them "Judas Shuttle", in the name of their demon, whom the wise know escaped down there and is still alive to this day. For it is the essence of Jerusalem that her mysteries are infinite and can drive men to despair! Eternal City of Dualities: Good and Evil, Divine-Profane, War-Peace, Creation-Destruction, Love-Hate, Magnanimity-Greed, I could go on for ever . . . she is the seed – Adam and Eve to the Nations, it is her rise and her fall that they recapitulate . . . Hands off! Hands off! I gave them fair warning, but they would not listen: A great Enemy of our people, an engineer, a Nazi, had come to trade his life for a Secret – an awesome, complex, weapons system, an ultimate strategic defence! A bargain with the devil! Even they hesitated! But some of them knew no shame. A brash young soldier there, Mahatz, said to me: "We'll give your dead a hand, grandpa, wide air-conditioned corridors with plenty of legroom and hi-speed transport." Their leader, the old lady, rebuked him, but said to me: "We must do what we must to survive in this world. What the next has in store for us I'm sure we'll all find out in good time." So off they went, disturbing men's bones . . . digging away under the City . . . Oh, the shame of it! I can take it no longer! I hereby lay my curse upon them!'

'Oh don't do that . . .' said the Monk, hurriedly, 'they are not all that bad really –

'THEY MEAN WELL . . .'

'Eek! Eek!' screamed the Revered, putting his hands over his ears.

'Eeeeeeeeeeeeeeeeeeeeeeeeeeeeeeeeeeeeeeeek!'

The Scream reverberated, shooting forth from Mea Shearim. Houses cracked, eardrums shattered, slates fell from roofs. In the Old City the tongues of midnight fell upon fractured bells. The Pope's broadcast was cut off instantly, and the whole City plunged into darkness. In the morgue tunnel, the film-set torches flickered and went out. The camera cranked to a halt. Even the Elders fell silent, although they had in fact reached the end of their recital: Deuteronomy, 34, 12 – 'and in all that mighty hand, and in all the great terror which Moses shewed in the sight of all Israel . . .'

And The Scream reverberated, far below decks, in the tunnel master control room . . . and in the private bunk, where Engineer Heinz Kammler had spent the last twenty-nine years – part of his bargain, to be buried alive in the womb of the brainchild of his genius – true, no Führer, no Eva Braun – but does not the spirit live on in steel, concrete, gunpowder, uranium 235? . . . And The Scream reverberated, tripping alarms, panicking the Tunnel Corps guards . . . Inspector Tarablus, creeping out in the tumult, closing in on his prey – three years trapped underground, as Shekem Canteen Officer, but a policeman's job never ends – in the red light, of Tunnel Alert A, he sees the murderer of Moses Klander . . .

And The Scream reverberated, jangling ganglions, causing hair to stand on end. Braces snapped throughout the City, pantaloons fell, shirtfronts burst open. The papier-mâché exorcism tunnel collapsed, staff, lunatics and film crew were routed. But as they broke out on to the asylum grounds, they were all in time for the coup de théâtre: the EMET poster, drawn down by The Scream towards Yama Ama, in the shadow of the Nachtnebel Annexe: plummeting, wrapping itself round the forehead of

the ersatz charlady. And she/he, shrieking, letting
go of her schmutter, trying to tear off the Word:
אמת    – EMET – TRUTH, bonded tight upon that
kisser. The face, the body, the limbs changing as
everyone watched, passing comments. Rump, shin-
bone, flank, trotters, the drooling snout, and the
tufted ears . . . Nili, braver than all the rest, leaping
forward, jabbing it with 10 cc of Thorazine. An
error, for the beast went completely wild, breathing fire, eating the sundial. Berl Eibeschutz and
Davidov danced around it, lunging with the Sowescu
Pig Harness. Zunz and Goldschlaeger trying to get
near enough to tear the Aleph off its forehead –
thus leaving the legend  מת – MET – DEAD, stop-
ping the creature cold. But Klotskashes, cee-gar
lighting his face like a red-filtered inky-dinky, bellowed: 'Take it alive, you suckers! It's the biggest
catch since King Kong! Eye-zakkar, you fucking
bastard, where are you? Slate! Mark it! Speed! Roll
'em! Action!'
   But the monster took off, flying over the City, an
inky blot on the sky. All masses and parades halted,
all eyes upturned in the darkness: Is it a bird? Is it a
Zeppelin? A friend? An Enemy, launching another
Yom Kippur? as it soars, banks, wheels, hovers,
dropping pats of dung and shrieking. While, in the
asylum grounds, flames swallow the trees, the
bushes, the rhododendrons . . . spies, secret agents,
beggars, burning like torches, little roach wraiths
floating up to heaven . . . Everyone else scattering,
down the terraces, Abu Shawareb with his moustaches ablaze again – always, in this accursed
land, destruction, followed by a careful renurture
(or can it truly be the finish, is this the end of Ricco?)
. . . Nili, trying to push Eisav aside in her mind,
crawling towards the Uzbek Republic, performs
her heroic hippocratic role, dragging bemused
patients to safety, remembering, suddenly, Blok

and Nietzsche, left behind in Ward Three ...
Summoning Elkayam and Marciano, dashing in to
drag them out, over the fence, into the open, setting
them down, like pillars of salt on the hillside, facing
the eternal ham, their bodies, slowly, beginning to
soften, as The Scream draws them home ...

While beside them, Bertha Bloom, kicking and
threshing on a thorn bush, hollering fit to bust, gave
birth at last, in pain and sorrow, to her Atomic
Bomb.

# VI

The Two Pedestrians of
The Apocalypse, or
The Last Journeys of Nietzsche and Blok
(incorporating Act V of
The Beggars' Soap Opera
and a Reunion with The Man Who Counted).

'Where the fuck are we?

'Is it past or future?'

Whatever it is – the Pit: crater gouged, fire belching from volcanic rifts in the midst of sludge, mud and ash, littered with innumerable pieces of paper, leaves of the nuclear fall: income tax forms, television licences, army call-up orders, matriculation certificates, rejected manuscripts, grocery lists, diaries, love letters, shredded classified dossiers and a zillion items from zapped stamp collections, still falling, falling, falling from fog acidtrip-coloured dew.

'Well,' said Blok, 'they do say, don't they – there's no place like home.'

Indeed – Jerusalem, having apparently received her final come-uppance and been consigned to the dustbin of history. Screwing their eyes in the mist they could just discern the remains of one or two of her landmarks: the tip of the Tower of David, the conical dome, like an upside-down dreidle, of the Dormition Abbey, the stone skullcap of the YMCA. But they could not make out the traditional contours of the City, for she had been seized and whirled as in a celestial cocktail-shaker and rescattered in a complete jumble, with Arab and

Jewish Jerusalem, too late alas, totally integrated: Sheikh Jarrah had been blown into Rehavia, the Great Synagogue was punched into Gethsemane, Ze'ev Jabotinsky and Salah-e-Din streets lay entwined in the embrace of death, and the Orion Cinema had been blasted into the mosque of Omar, leaving four hundred matchstick-charred Hebrew cinefans gaping vacantly at the footprint left by Mohammed as he leapt into heaven.

'Not a pretty sight,' said Blok.

'No,' said Nietzsche, 'but that's how the cookie crumbles.'

Not even the Swedish Tea Shoppe nor the Ta'amon Café had survived, though somewhere, from the rubble, came the stifled muttering of Marxist-Leninist factions, still trying to fix the blame for the Fall. Upon the far horizon, however, loomed the unmistakable shape of the Nachtnebel Annexe, puffing terse black smoke from its chimney like a misplaced Apache message.

'Let's go,' said Blok. They began to descend the cliff-face, staggering in the muck and mudge. Here gas masks were de rigueur, not only for social reasons, but because of the poison fumes, mustard gas, mace, Tabun, phosgene, DC, DM, to name but a few. Halfway down they found an enamel bathtub and climbed in it, propelling themselves, with discarded broomsticks, through the ash and molten ooze. Blok, trying to lift their spirits by means of the old Palmah sing-song:

'We're a platoon on patrol . . .
♫ Along the hills and wadis we shall stroll . . .' ♩

But he stopped there, for it echoed in the hollow of his mask like a dromedary with tonsilitis.

As they paddled on silently, along sluggish lava, a figure loomed in the vapours ahead of them. It was Aaron Himmeltraub, balanced upon the top of a

456

Volkswagen Beetle. 'Fenschechter!' he called, catching sight of Nietzsche. 'Have you seen A.P. or Reuters?' 'Not recently,' said Nietzsche. 'Excellent!' cried Himmeltraub. 'Then it's a world exclusive!' But a trick in the flow carried him away from them before he could elucidate further. Pretty soon, however, they found out the cause of the editor-in-chief's excitement. For as the mist lifted there they were, on a lake of tepid tapwater, adrift on a flotilla of loose doors, dustbin lids, billboards, naval dinghies: The Dead, as predicated by The Revered, a costume show of the ages – from Poland, Galicia, Renaissance Italy, Babylonian man about town . . . entire families carrying trunks and suitcases filled on the say-so of Shabetai Zvi, Passover Eve, 1666, coming ashore, unpacking towels, bathing caps, suntan lotion, Egged Tour brochures . . . many old people clutched the twigs thrust in their hands at death to dig their way through to the Holy Land, unaware of Zetz's modernizations . . . a group from the Auschwitz-Birkenau Survivors' Association, in tuxedos and bow ties, rushed about vainly, looking for the Hilton Hotel . . . and still others were climbing, drawn, chalked and limestained, out of a funnel still gushing water at the lake's bottomless navel.

The lake widened into a landlocked sea. The body of Bin-Zabl rocked upon its surface like a colossal buoy. Floating on its back, its face was of Klander, with fruit machine symbols for eyes. Harpoons were embedded in its abdomen, toes, forearms, nostrils and ears. Frayed tablecloths, plastic vases, soggy danish pastries, clustered round like a marauding shoal. The red fez bobbed behind the corpse, covered with roaches who had hoisted the skull and crossbones. They drifted to starboard, emitting a low buzz akin to speedily fermenting cheese. ( ♩ 'Fifteen men on a dead man's fez/yo ho ho and a rotten old bum . . .'♪♪ )

But the sea soon vanished, giving way to a vast expanse of pitted cracked baked earth. The plains, after a million years of drought. Alors, Blok and Nietzsche abandoned their bathtub and trudged on afoot, with knotted handkerchiefs over their heads, heading for the Annexe visible. At one point, they glimpsed the contours of the *BABASIS* jeep, with Sa'id and an earlier Blok in it, meandering upon the horizon. But it swiftly vanished into a gully, and they never saw it again.

Following is the authorized map of Nietzsche and Blok's peregrinations:

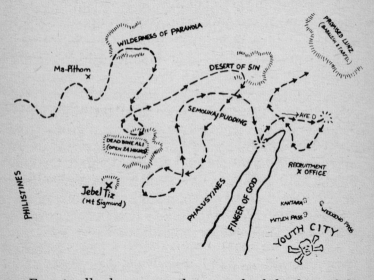

Eventually, however, they reached the foot of the Annexe, to find Liam O'Habash sitting there. The skin of Yama Ama, dry and crumbling, lay by him like a discarded chrysalis. 'I wouldn't go in there if I were you,' he said, 'I have had an order for full-colour glossies for ten months, but not a murmur. You remember that book I got you?' he looked up at Nietzsche. 'I wrote it myself, you know. An idle century, in the Dark Ages. One had to keep one's head down then.'

'You are Judas Iscariot, aren't you?' said Blok. 'I thought I recognized your face.' He had seen it on postage stamps of minor dictators, on sergeant-majors and clerks of the court. Also he recognized in it the beginnings of the contours of the face of the Man Who Counted. The pornographer sighed, the running mice of his eyes looking down on the hard ground. It's a hard life, that familiar sigh said, being an eternal wanderer. Blamed for everything that happens when one is merely trying to make a living. We can't all run after the latest prophet, devour the latest avant-garde journals . . . 'No wonder the mad priest couldn't find your grave,' said Blok. 'You cunning fox, you weren't in it.' This left, of course, the Pig at large, the dybbuk vanished in the crowd. And Dr Nachtnebel, the Klander bogey, laughing behind this very door?

'I wouldn't,' repeated O'Habash. 'There is Knowledge and Knowledge. What's wrong with a quiet life?'

In answer Blok walked up to the big wooden door and rapped with his fist three times. Nietzsche, dropping a coin in O'Habash's palm, followed him, smoothing his walrus.

'I am tired of being fucked around,' said Blok, 'Open, asargelusha!'

Slowly, the door creaked three-quarters open, revealing a dim corridor at the end of which a small balding man sat hunched over a table in a triangle of anglepoise lamp light.

'Hello, Papa,' said Blok.

'Hey Avremel,' said Papa, acknowledging him quietly. 'Do you remember the King Haakon obituary issue? I seem to have mislaid the ten ore . . .'

'Papa,' said Blok, 'this is Friedrich Nietzsche, the world-famous philosopher.'

'Servus,' said Nietzsche, bowing and kissing his hand.

459

'I read your books once,' said Papa mildly. 'You are so keen to be different you end up all alone in a receding universe. No wonder you died mad,' He raised his hand to forestall argument. 'Please. Keep it tranquil. Mama is not well. She is napping in there.'

Nevertheless, Blok peeped into the adjacent room. It was not a pretty sight. She was lying, an immense whalelike shape, upon a wooden bulkhead, an ice-pack on her forehead, cold sweat running off her into a ring of plastic shisels. Her stomach was split open, a gaping cavern, pulsing with a dim orange glow. Drawing closer and peering in, Blok found the glow to be that of art deco lamps, illuminating a slow escalator which clanked wearily into darkness. At its sides, posters dimly extolled the virtues of defunct and impossible causes: The Pomeranian Liberation Front; the Othmar Spann Association; the Zubatovist Movement; the Magyar Naval Commission; the Lusitanian Empire; the Max Stirner Collective. As they descended the moving steps Nietzsche, for the first time, appeared to be somewhat perturbed. 'I don't like this at all, comrade. I hope you know what you're doing.' 'No problem!' Blok answered, as they continued down, rocking in limbo, while ghostly pig chortles echoed ahead of them and in the distance loudspeakers rendered the anthem of Kossuth Lajos.

Scene Two:
    An empty residential street, midnight.
    Grey Central European apartment houses.
    Ice and slush in the road. Freezing cold. No one about at all.
    At road's end a moving escalator appears briefly. Nietzsche and Blok step off it. It vanishes.
Blok: Now this doesn't look like Jerusalem to me, comrade.

Nietzsche: Not even in December (*tightens jacket around him; stamps slippers in slush*). It does look familiar though. The sort of familiarity that is like a broomstick up the arse.

Blok: Let us look at the names on the door jambs. Shit! They are all Hungarian!

Nietzsche: Budapest, asargelusha! And by the feel of it, a bad time for one and all.

Blok: This seems intriguing! I have never been here. Which way is Ipoly Street?

Nietzsche: I don't like this at all. My bunions are aching. Look, a newspaper rolling towards us! (*Seizes, uncrumples same*) Aargh! Aargh! November '44! Look what you've got us into!

Blok: Isn't that something now? Do you realize, somewhere, not a stone's throw from here, Blok, Avram, will soon get started!

Nietzsche: And finished, milacek! Don't you understand? The Russians are coming, schmendrick! In a month this whole place will be muck and rubble, bits of flesh wrapped around lamp-posts! (*They freeze, for the sound of a vehicle engine stutters in their direction.*) Shit! Nowhere to hide!

Blok: Who's hiding?

Nietzsche: It's a patrol, you idiot. Run! (*He takes Blok's arm, pulling them down the road. Run rabbit run. Slap slap slap slap, their feet upon the ice and slush. Blok caught in Nietzsche's panic. Down the way they came. Round the corner, to the train terminal.*) Damn! the Vàci Road! (*Increasing sound of vehicle engine.*)

Blok: Isn't it exciting?

Nietzsche: Fuck that. I got the hell out of here in '39, my friend . . . no return trips for me, I can tell you. Let's lift off . . .

Blok: The hell . . . let's stay. Where is there to return to anyway?

Nietzsche: Shit! Shit! Shit! (*Pulls Blok on, down*

*freezing cobblestones. The train station, draped with a swastika. A second patrol car emerges suddenly from the corner of the Square. Escape is impossible. Several figures in Arrow Cross uniform, black as the night, surround them, barking Hungarian.)*

Nazis: Papers! Papers! Empty your pockets! Keep your hands up, swinefodder! *(They rummage through their captives' jackets.)*

Nietzsche *(whispering to Blok in Hebrew)*: Want to split now, comrade? Take your chances . . . Had enough of this charade? *(Blok shakes his head.)*

Nazi: What was that language? What are you whispering?

Second Nazi: Hey, looky here, Istvàn, I think we got us a couple of spies! *(Peruses puzzled the flotsam of their pockets: a ticket for the merry-go-round at the 1900 Paris exposition. A piece of string through an old Turkish coin. A crumpled tag from Zisselmacher's Laundry.)*

Educated Nazi: I recognize that lettering – that is Hebrew! Shit, we have nabbed us a couple of Yids!

Uneducated Nazi: Take down your trousers, pigswill! Ha! A certainty – no doubt about it! Into the jeep now, Jewboys! You're due for a little trip abroad, aren't you? Travel broadens the mind! *(The jeep accelerates, down Attila Avenue, the patrolmen singing lustily the Party Anthem, beating time on the torsos, stomachs, groins, limbs, faces of their supine prisoners, thus:)*

Nazis: Free of Jews! Free of Ruthenians! Free of Poles! Free of Slovenians! Free of Czechs! Free of Serbians! Free of Slovaks! Free of Ukrainians! We are true blue Carpatho-Turanians – Magyars of the March of Hungaria! Ferencz Szálási is our Leader – Magyars of the March of Hungaria!

Nietzsche (*between moans and groans*): Here's another fine mess you've got me into . . .

Nazi: Silence, Jew! (*Grinds hobnailed boot in face.*)


Scene Three:

A cattle truck en route to Auschwitz. Men, women and children crammed, wedged in. The stench of shit, piss, vomit and fear. Tears mingle with the detritus in the sawdust of the vibrating carriage floor. Clickety-clack, clickety-clack, clickety-clack.

Nietzsche: You know, this is beginning to be of interest. A true test case for my proposition that great suffering ennobles greatly. It takes me right back to Nietzsche Number One – the pain, the migraines, the struggle to define one's ego . . .

Blok: I think my arm is broken. I can hardly see out of my left eye. My shirtfront is soaked with spew and I think I have just dunged in my pants. I want to get out of here.

Nietzsche: Nonsense. Is this not the ultimate experience you have been yearning for? The apotheosis of Jewish guilt? You must have known all along, in your heart, what lay ultimately behind the Annexe door: Nacht und Nebel – Night and Fog, a real Satan, not an ersatz one . . .

Blok: I hurt all over . . . my insides are bursting . . .

Nietzsche: Good. Don't resist it. Dig deep in your pain, accept what comes, and you will dredge up the finest of pearls . . .

An Old Bald Man with a pince-nez and filthy sweater interrupts: Excuse me, sir, I could not help but overhear your statements, which are the most fearful rubbish.

Nietzsche: Indeed?

Old Bald Man: Undoubtedly. Human beings do not seek pain, unless they have contempt for themselves. Look at nature: do animals go about testing their endurance for the sake of some

463

abstract concept? No, Man's natural state is to seek pleasure, like any other living being. Is it perhaps, as Freud says, the very growth of civilization which frustrates Man in pursuit of his biological heritage? the superego taking tyrannical powers to suppress an inherent aggression? Is it original sin, separating Man from gold? Whatever it is, it cannot be in itself desirable. Fakirs, hermits, flagellants, puritans, fanatics of the false joy of self-repression in the cause of some higher, more 'sublime' or 'racially pure' notion merely lead us where we are now: puking in a putrid cattle truck, on the road to our liquidation.

Nietzsche: So what is your conclusion?

Old Bald Man: People should be nice to each other.

Clickety-clack, clickety-clack, clickety-clack.

Train rolling stealthily
Over the border,
Shunting the droppings
Of the New Order.

Cries drown in silence,
Tears turn to ice,
Death is a stranger,
No one lives twice.

Blasted the flatlands.
Stunted in birth –
Trees wither greyly,
Scorched is the earth.

Here are the gates,
The last dawn is nigh,
Hope is abandoned,
Arbeit Macht Frei.

By the selection ground
The Man Who Counts,

464

Cleanly examines,
Weighs up his ounce.

Avram Blok's spectacles,
Nietzsche's moustache,
Will they too moulder
On Birkenau marsh?


Scene Four: In the Gas Chamber.


Blok: I don't want to die.
Nietzsche: O spoilsport Blok! where is your affirmation
of the world beyond good or evil?
the self-transforming fire bounded by nothingness –
the only true will to power!
Look at you, Blok, trapped as always
in your own measly body.
Observe it yourself – does it look worth preserving?
knobbly knees, flabby muscles and that paunch
which would eventually protrude, drowning your belly-button.
In six, seven years you would be totally bald,
children would piss on you from first-floor balconies
and pretend to you that it is raining.
If I were you I would be glad that all choices are over,
and hope for a better deal, if luck has it,
in another space–time continuum . . .
Look at me, I had a bag of diseases first round
and this time I was as fit as a fiddle. But do I shry?
No, I am fully prepared to say Yes, cholera,
to the random fall of the dice.
Call from above: Chow time! feed in them crystals, Fritz!

465

*(From vents in the slatted ceiling the hiss of the poison gas seethes. Men, women shout, moan, scrabble along the walls. Children cry, scream, defecate on people's legs. Some recite the prayer of imminent death. Others curse, howl, drool, climbing on top of each other, a stifling pyramid of fear. Nietzsche, moustacheless, his face upturned, sings, in a loud, ringing bellow, Zarathustra's song:)*

Nietzsche:  'O man! Attend!
What does deep midnight's sleep
contend?
I slept my sleep,
And now awake at dreaming's end:
The world is deep,
Deeper than day can comprehend.
Deep is its woe,
Joy, deeper than heart's agony:
Woe says: Fade! Go!
But all joy wants eternity,
Wants deep, deep, deep eternity!'

*(The poison swirls. Vomit and blood fleck the ceiling, the walls, the floor.)*

Blok: I'm going, Fenschechter, I'm going!

Nietzsche: You have nowhere to go. It is too late. There are fires in both your past and your future. Defeat all these fears in your joyful acceptance: say Yes, Yes and Yes again!

Blok: No!
No!
No!
No!


Scene Five:

And will the sun rise?

# VII

Selected Aftermaths – Secrets
Revealed – and a Coda in the Laundromat.
(Mottos: Victory or Death; An End
to Innocence; Play It Again, Griselda)

**Pre-resurrection blues:**
The alarm bells ringing, the sirens sounding, all over the wretched system. Zetz, underground, in the tunnel control room, suddenly facing dead screens. Where previously banks and banks of monitors revealed a range of peephole visions – the master bedroom of the President of the Egyptian Republic, the command bunker of the Iraqi kamikaze squadron, the billiards room at the Athens US embassy, the interior of the Ka'aba at Mecca – yok. Everything blank. And ze bells! ze bells! signalling the cataclysm that had occurred above, but how? Shades of 6th October, '73, when, having misread the coded warning of imminent enemy attack as a routine VD report, he had had to send Eisav, alone and primed, along the Apocalypse Tunnel . . . Not again! But can one afford to hesitate, can one afford to linger, with three dozen new Eisavs ready and waiting, jacked up to ride the whirlwind? . . . No. Zetz, burning with uncertainty, but unwilling ever to be a sucker again, stretches his finger towards the button . . .

Inspector Tarablus, as the sirens blast, seizing the time, leaps out from ambush: securing Agent XBZ Three and clapping the handcuffs on him.

'What, what, what?' yelps the astounded spooker. 'I arrest you,' intones the homicide detective, 'for ordering the murder of one Moses Klander, on 10th May, 1960. Pesach Zilberschvantz, alias Groise Metsiyes, the killer, having merely been your hapless tool. A captured and turned Bulgarian mole, you later had him fed drugs in the T – t asylum which completely destroyed his memory . . .' 'You fool!' cries the Agent. 'That was High State Security, nothing to do with you! The shrink was threatening to write his memoirs, telling all about the Tunnel Project . . . the dreams of Himmeltraub, the insights of Maclachlan, the warnings of the frum old fart . . .'

'Your confession is noted,' said Tarablus smugly, 'but mitigation is for the Judge to decide. I have just done my duty, after fifteen long years. I am only a simple copper.'

And then – KABLAM! – the whole shtik ends, with a bang, not a whimper. Zetz, having settled all scores except one, strides into Heinz Kammler's vestibule. The old oven-constructor on his knees, having rediscovered the Immaculate Conception. His life for his Secret, but with all bets off, pure vengeance could have its day. Sic, Semper, Tyrannis, with his service revolver, Zetz wastes the last anti-semite.

Consequences: Nili and Eisav, reunited in the next world, in a field of clover. He is thin and gaunt, after his demise in the snowdrifts, his red moustache has turned grey. 'Nothing,' says Nili/Marta, 'that a good chicken soup can't cure.' They enclasp. And happily ever after.

Down by the Gate, Judas/O'Habash sits, free at last of Constantine Zorza. (The arm of the KGB is long. Not all mysteries can be resolved.) Turning over in his mind hypothetical profit margins in the celestial erotic trade (objets d'art, upmarket stuff, the acme of taste, no rip-offs). Babelech-und-Farfel, who may or may not be the Messiah (or the hermaphroditic nebesch of alchemy), shamble up to squat in sympathy with the wanderer as he clicks his worry beads. Their clothing utterly free of the roaches, who have established their kingdom Below. No sign, though, of the Pig, not even a whiff of bacon ... Further downaways, on a silver-sanded beach, an immigrant ship, bearing twelve dozen selected Blok alternates, the pick of the bunch, is docking ...

So much for optimism.

On the other hand – consider an alternative outcome:

Eventually, after a thousand adventures, Eisav came back to Nili. Some said he had been caught in the snow but released, in a prisoner-of-war exchange. Boris and Lizbeta, Babelech-und-Farfel, returned to the womb of Moscow Centre. No wonder they have not been seen since in Jerusalem. Or is there another reason? Howsoever it may be, the lovers embraced and a month later they were remarried. Present at the wedding: Marta Grunbaum, Sasha, Elkayam, Hava, Flusser – retired, after the fire which had gutted the Institute. (Papier-mâché sets, with flickering torches?! the board of inquiry was livid. Veltsch, deprived of his inheritance, decamped to an experimental Skinnerite colony at Santa Cruz del Quiche, Guatemala.) Absent from the wedding ceremony: Blok, still in coma, in the T – t State Asylum. Also absent: Nietzsche, who had been buried several months before. The smoke of the fire, said the pathologists, noting the asphyxiation (but where the hell had the moustache vanished to, with not the trace of a singe?). A sad day as Nili, Davidov,

Flusser, the Magpie and a man from the Social Services, fumbling for his mislaid watch, saw the shroud lowered into the grave: by the Hevra Kadisha, the grip of the orthodoxy that he had always loathed. Was it thunder, or the Philosopher's rage, that Nili heard in the distance? Come in, Number Three, cholera, it rumbled, hip-hopping over the hills ... But for Nili and Eisav, another spring glory, as his boot  reshattered the glass. Thus art thou reconsecrated to me ... mazel tov, murmur Marta and Sasha, again. In, Out, In, Out, when will the girl make up her mind?

And ...

   ... One night in bed Eisav told her the secret of the underground tunnels (the Heine collection back on the shelf, flowers in the 105 shells, he, desk-bound, no longer out committing legal murder): 'They are the trump card, the last shtantz of the State if faced with annihilation. The Samson Gambit: I was the test pilot, lucky for all of us that ride was aborted ... There I was, in the Apocalypse Capsule, with the Bomb beneath my thighs. My mission – to place it punkt under Moscow, the ultimate checkmate threat. Other tunnels end up under Washington, London, I think there is even one under Brussels ... But my tunnel collapsed, under Rostov, and the Russkies hauled me out and nabbed me. They laughed like a drain. They knew all about the tunnels. Their own had been long operational. It appears I'd hit another passageway, criss-crossing our own. Because, my honey, everybody's at it: every pischinkeh country and its cousin are laying tunnels under every other. We are just also-rans on the global doomsday ticket ... the whole planet is riddled, like a giant Swiss cheese – it may collapse at any time, like a soufflé.' 'Don't think about it any more, big baby,' she said, 'let's just fuck.' Mounting him, sinking down, and riding ...

Or . . .

. . . He never came back. He disappeared completely, like Raul Wallenberg or thousands of others. Many waters cannot quench love, but drought – that's another matter. So she took up the threads of her life and ploughed on, visiting comatose Blok every other Friday, and picketing the Ministry of Defence bi-annually . . .

As . . .

. . . the EMET poster expires in the gutter, its Aleph torn off by porcine shenanigans, leaving it absolutely MET – dead – rotting as the months go by. Its Labour Party withering as it moulders, eaten by the worm of Power: hypocrisy, greed, hubris, disdain, vainglory and self-deception. The Minister of Housing, accused of corruption, shooting himself on the beach. The PM's wife's illegal Washington bank account. The alleged Party slush funds . . .

Through all this Blok slumbers, lying there, with the drip in his veins. Sucked by the Homeland, just as it should be, signed, sealed and delivered. Get well cards proliferating around him as the news of his withdrawal spreads globally: from Dianne of Hendon, Sa'id in Safad, Georgina in Dimona. From Dementia Praecox Films, en groupe, from Hy Buchenwald, in Paraguay. From Victoria and Wellington Frog, reunited, merde, alors, back from action in Revolutionary Portugal. But he still has no comment to make concerning world affairs. He does not even notice the fall of Vietnam, or of the EMET government. The ultra-orthodox parties having left the coalition over the importation of Phantom jets on the Sabbath. Elections looming again, with the Nationalists poised for their harvest . . . the Friedmans, hole in the sheet and all, reaching for the coat-tails of victory –

Aye, Blok, opening an eye again. Seeing Papa and

473

Mama before him. Seated on little wicker chairs, looking so worried, so solicitous, so committed . . . and a small child, from out of the blue-grey of the hallway, came forth and looked over him. 'Mummy, mummy!' it cried, running back into the gloaming, 'why is that poor man bald?'

**Coda (in the laundromat):**
'What, Griselda? I can tell you, I'm just as disgusted as you are. This is what they call art nowadays? I ask you. The end at the beginning, the point of view schmeered all over, and nothing but complete moral confusion at the end of the day . . . what's the name for it? – Post-modernism? Semenology? I tell you one could die of shame! Once writing was a respectable calling, a social contribution. Mr Agnon! There was an artist! promenading au boulevard every morning, neatly dressed, with a kind word for everyone, tipping his hat to the ladies . . . ecce homo! Today they don't even begin to qualify unless they're lying in the gutter, mouthing obscenities, shooting heroin into their veins . . .' 'Exactly, Matilda, you took the words out of my mouth. When I hear the word Art nowadays I reach for my biodetergent . . . you should read today's editorial column, in *Yediot Rishonot:* The man is a bit right wing, I'll grant you, but he hits the nail right on the head –

AH! THE JOYS OF CONSPIRACY!
by A. Himmeltraub

An outrage! that books can be written, let alone published, which not only reveal the deepest state secrets under the guise of 'fiction', but under that camouflage, that shield of cowardice, take up those issues CLOSEST to our hearts, our MEMORIES, our very BLOOD and being, only to hold them up to ridicule, to a mockery of all that we hold DEAR. Oh! the shame of that self-hatred which so hideously deforms our history in these 'enlightened' times – a LEGACY, let us not beat about the bush, of that 'socialist' Zionism which was once a prouder plant far than that sickly weed that it has now become. Swing, scythe of history! Bring on, oh very soon, upon us that crucial reckoning at the polls when we can cast our vote and choose between the PAST and FUTURE! Now, more than ever, when our enemies gather, as of always, to 'constrain' us, to pluck from us the VICTORIES won so sorely on the field of battle ... ALL OUR ENEMIES: Bolshevik Belial, Arab Amalek and our own HOME-GROWN BLEEDING HEARTS, bearers of that 'progressive' LEGACY of doubt, uncertainty, unwarranted GUILT, the masochistic wish for punishment and self-destruction ... and for what CRIME? For being OURSELVES? For standing on our own two feet, our weapons of DEFENCE in hand, and facing the NEW DAWN???

THE END

# In The Mood
## Keith Waterhouse

'Keith Waterhouse is one of the few great writers of our time'
AUBERON WAUGH

The politicians who organised the 1951 Festival of Britain thought they were demonstrating to the world how the British had regenerated themselves after the war. That was not how three northern musketeers saw it. As Raymond Watmough, the narrator of this comic, tender chronicle of their adventures puts it:
*'Six million pounds. Four million man-hours. A million bricks. Six thousand six hundred tons of cement. Fifteen thousand exhibits. Two thousand two hundred and eigthy five employees. And all so that Douglas Beckett, Terry Liversedge and Raymond Watmough could lose their virginity . . .'*

'Riotously amusing'
THE MAIL ON SUNDAY

'Funny, touching and elegantly written; it gives a lift to the spirits'
THE GUARDIAN

'Unquestionably brilliant and hilarious'
ALAN COREN

0 552 99074 4                                      £2.95

# BLACK SWAN

# Peeping Tom
## Howard Jacobson

'The funniest book about sex ever written'
VAL HENNESSY, TIME OUT

*'I'd be prepared to say it was my own fault for tampering with the secret arts, except that it confers too much dignity on all parties. This isn't a Faustian story'.*

So what kind of story is it that Barney Fugelman must overcome his own refined distaste for accuracy and candour in order to tell? Far from his native Finchley, why is such a confirmed antagonist of all things green and growing bound to the daily ritual of roaming the cliffs of his Cornish exile, his fur coat and snakeskin shoes an offence to the serious ramblers? Whence the burden of the cliffs, in whose shadow the hapless Barney seems compelled, in all his incarnations, to tread?

In this wickedly erotic, ferociously funny amalgam of the psychological thriller, the rural idyll and the literary novel of romance, Howard Jacobson displays all the exuberant wit and sharp intelligence that distinguished Coming From Behind, his first novel (also available in Black Swan).

'Brilliantly funny and inventive . . . an astonishing display of irreverent wit, marvellous situational set-pieces and biting one-liners'
ROBERT NYE, THE GUARDIAN

'Howard Jacobson comes from behind the "tropic swamps of the imagination" to drag admirers into them again, kicking and screaming and laughing our heads off'
GAY FIRTH, THE TIMES

'Brilliant and original'
PAUL BAILEY, THE STANDARD

'*Peeping Tom* is a Jewish gambol through English literature as seen from the bedroom; it throws sex at the bookish and books at the sexish'
VICTORIA GLENDINNING, SUNDAY TIMES

0 552 99141 4  £2.95

# BLACK SWAN

# Catch-22
## Joseph Heller

'Blessedly, monstrously, bloatedly, cynically funny, and
fantastically unique. No one has ever written a book like
this'
FINANCIAL TIMES

*Catch-22* has become a byword in its own time. It is a novel
of enormous richness and art. It is deeply serious, yet at
the same time, brilliantly funny. It is without question one
of the great novels of the century.

*Catch-22* is, said Philip Toynbee in *The Observer*, 'The
greatest satirical work in the English language since
"Erewhon" ' – an hilarious, tragic novel in which an
American airforce base on a small island off Italy becomes
a microcosm of the modern world as it might look to
someone dangerously sane.

'Remarkable, mind-spinning rave of a novel. Uniquely
funny'
DAILY MAIL

'Wildly original, brutally gruesome, a dazzling
performance that will outrage as many readers as it
delights. Vulgarly, bitterly, savagely funny, it will not be
forgotten by those who can take it'
NEW YORK TIMES

0 552 99195 3                                          £4.95

**BLACK SWAN**

# Noah's Ark
## Barbara Trapido

NOAH'S ARK is a wry and sparkling account of a
marriage: an apparently incompatible union between Noah
Glazer, a solid man of science, and Alison Bobrow, a palely
captivating eccentric, who Noah suspects of 'keeping a
Tarot Pack in the bureau drawer'. For both the marriage –
after a memorably sexy and precipitous courtship implies a
serious departure from type. Noah walks undaunted into
the overpopulated labyrinth of Alison's life, coolly issuing
forth the unspeakable maxim that 'Charity begins at
Home'. The result is serenity and order, until Alison is
drawn to explore certain avenues in her past. The
consequences are both hectic and illuminating.....

NOAH'S ARK, with its lively wit, its piquant insight and its
varied and outrageous characters, more than fulfils the
promise of the prize-winning BROTHER OF THE MORE
FAMOUS JACK (also available in Black Swan)

'An achingly funny novel . . . wickedly observed'
LIBBY PURVES, LIVING

'Witty and highly polished . . . never a dull moment'
ALANNAH HOPKIN, THE STANDARD

'Zesty, intelligent and highly readable'
DEBORAH MOGGACH, COSMOPOLITAN

'Reading it is rather like being bombarded by sequins'
ANTHONY THWAITE, THE OBSERVER

0 552 99130 9                                    £2.95

BLACK SWAN